I0824461

PRAISE FOR *A LONG TIME GONE*

"In the dark, icy heart of a Minnesota winter, Deputy Packard, a smart and courageous gay cop, embarks on a mission to uncover the truth about his brother's disappearance. *A Long Time Gone* is an atmospheric, gripping, and emotional mystery about the intersections of family, memory, grief, and healing. Joshua Moehling's novel dives headfirst into the raw pain of the past, the dangers of today, and the ghosts who haunt us from within."

—Margot Douaihy, bestselling author of *Scorched Grace* and *Blessed Water*

"A big thriller with an even bigger heart! Moehling deftly weaves together a riveting present-day crime with closely held family secrets and sins of decades past, proving once again that the most compelling thrillers are written about the ones we love but fear we will never truly know."

—Lisa Gardner, *New York Times* bestselling author of *Still See You Everywhere*

"On top of being everything you could want in a mystery—riveting, layered, unfolding in surprising yet inevitable ways—*A Long Time Gone* is a gorgeous story of loss and redemption that broke my heart, then put it back together. It's been a long time since I've loved a character like I love Ben Packard, with his deadpan humor and warm heart. Moehling is a literary star with a gift for observing and conveying humanity, and he's written a mystery of the highest order."

—Ashley Winstead, author of *Midnight Is the Darkest Hour*

"With *A Long Time Gone*, Joshua Moehling returns with the highly anticipated, hard-hitting third installment of his beloved Deputy Ben Packard series. Moehling has once again penned a thoroughly engrossing police procedural with all the trimmings: intrigue, suspense, memorable characters, shining prose, and an ending that is equal parts heart-stopping and heart-tugging. *A Long Time Gone* firmly secures Moehling's place as the newest tour de force in the thriller genre."

—Heather Gudenkauf, *New York Times* bestselling author of *The Overnight Guest* and *Everyone Is Watching*

"With a page-turning plot, vividly drawn characters, and a compelling, gay protagonist with a dry, deadpan wit, *A Long Time Gone* is the kind of book you don't just read but devour. Set in a *Fargo*-esque town, Ben Packard investigates a brutal crime while also unravelling the mystery of his brother's disappearance decades earlier. Sharp, complex, and emotionally powerful, I love everything about this series."

—Christina McDonald, *USA Today* and Amazon Charts bestselling author of *What Lies in Darkness*

"*A Long Time Gone*—unflinching as a Minnesota winter—is equal parts compelling mystery and riveting family drama, and I'd follow its hero, Deputy Ben Packard, anywhere. His relentless pursuit of the truth will keep you hooked from start to finish."

—Jess Lourey, Edgar Award–nominated author of *The Taken Ones*

"Ben Packard is one of the best new mystery series on the market, and each book just gets better and better. In the third installment, two cold cases intertwine to reveal a suspicious death and the devastating truth about Packard's past. At turns harrowing and laugh-out-loud funny, action-packed and deeply personal, *A Long Time Gone* hits on every level. If you're not reading Joshua Moehling yet, clear your schedule and start today!"

—Mindy Mejia, *USA Today* bestselling author of *To Catch a Storm* and *Everything You Want Me to Be*

"Joshua Moehling is a star! This book is the proof of his singular talents: a superb and gripping story with an immersive setting and unforgettable characters, all gorgeously structured and beautifully written. Only Moehling can craft such an entertaining page-turner of a mystery, an outsider's tale, with life-changing themes and surprising solutions. *A Long Time Gone* is ultimately and uniquely heartbreaking, redemptive, and rewarding. Standing ovation."

—Hank Phillippi Ryan, *USA Today* bestselling author of *One Wrong Word*

"In his third Ben Packard novel, Joshua Moehling takes us into this protagonist's tragic past, adroitly peeling back the layers of his brother's disappearance thirty years ago. With great skill, he evokes the snow-encrusted terrain and characters in his fictional Minnesota town, Sandy Lake, balancing humor with intense detective work. Above all, Packard, a gay man and member of law enforcement, defies stereotypes of police and gay men; he is a new sort of law enforcement hero, rich with complexity and fresh in his perspective. It's a thrill to follow his journey through this series!"

—John Copenhaver, award-winning author of *Hall of Mirrors*

PRAISE FOR *WHERE THE DEAD SLEEP*

"When a diabolically wealthy family pits themselves against each other, it's hard to know who to believe, unless you're Deputy Ben Packard. Josh Moehling lays out a deliciously complex plot and turns sleepy Sandy Lake into anything but."

—John McMahon, author of *The Good Detective*

"With *Where the Dead Sleep*, Joshua Moehling solidifies his place as one of the best new voices in the mystery genre. Moehling nails the spirit of small-town life in Minnesota's unique North Country. His understanding of the darkness that can haunt the human spirit twists his story in wonderfully unpredictable ways. Fans of Walt Longmire or Joe Pickett or my own Cork O'Connor have reason to celebrate and look forward to a long life for Moehling's series and its fresh, vibrant protagonist Ben Packard."

—William Kent Krueger, *New York Times* bestselling author of the Cork O'Connor series

"Small-town secrets have never been so deadly in this compelling thriller featuring my new favorite deputy, Ben Packard. The plot will grab you; the characters keep you coming back for more."

—Lisa Gardner, *New York Times* bestselling author of *One Step Too Far*

"In *Where the Dead Sleep*, Joshua Moehling continues the compelling journey of tough as nails and conflicted Deputy Ben Packard as he patrols his old stomping grounds of Sandy Lake, Minnesota. Exploding with secrets, this novel has everything you want in a riveting mystery: a brutal crime, fast-paced action, expertly drawn characters that thrust the story from the page, and a jaw-dropping ending that you won't see coming. Looking for a new favorite hero to root for? You've found him in Moehling's Ben Packard."

—Heather Gudenkauf, *New York Times* bestselling author of *The Overnight Guest*

"A well-paced whodunit that doubles as an evocation of Minnesota small-town life in all of its messy, dysfunctional glory... The real suspense emerges as Packard figures himself out, defying expectations in quiet, sometimes devastating ways."

—*New York Times*

"Evocative and charming with a deadpan wit, Joshua Moehling's *Where the Dead Sleep* is a richly satisfying mystery with fully-drawn characters—especially the winning and deeply human protagonist, Sheriff Ben Packard. Joshua Moehling's skill as a writer and storyteller is evident on every page. I can't wait to read the next installment in this excellent series!"

—Nick Petrie, bestselling author of *The Runaway*

"This title has all the elements of a good mystery: a puzzling crime, dark secrets, fast-paced writing, and deadpan humor... Riveting and a real page-turner; fans of C. J. Box's Joe Pickett novels or Craig Johnson's Longmire series will feel at home."

—*Library Journal*

"Observant and authentic (and funny, too), *Where the Dead Sleep* is a perfect mystery, the literary descendant of *Fargo* and *Mare of Easttown* and an exploration of all the nooks and shadows that make Sandy Lake, Minnesota, an ideal place to spend a summer and a chilling place to pass a winter. I'd highly recommended it to every fan of crime fiction but especially those reading in a lake house just after sunset."

—Adam White, bestselling
author of *The Midcoast*

"*Where the Dead Sleep* sticks the landing… And if you think you've got the mystery solved in the first few chapters, you're dead wrong. Moehling has some tricks up his sleeve."

—*Associated Press*

"Joshua Moehling has quickly become one of my favorite must-read authors, and *Where the Dead Sleep* shows exactly why. The characters are rich, and the small-town setting, where everyone has a secret and everyone is a potential suspect or victim, is brought vividly to life. This is a suspenseful, gut-wrenching page-turner of the highest order. Not to be missed!"

—David Bell, *New York Times* bestselling author
of *Try Not to Breathe* and *She's Gone*

"*Where the Dead Sleep* is a beautifully written mystery that had me on the edge of my seat. Joshua Moehling has created unforgettable characters in a story that kept me guessing the whole way through. *Where the Dead Sleep* is not to be missed."

—R. J. Jacobs, author of *This Is How We End Things*

PRAISE FOR *AND THERE HE KEPT HER*

"A dark and complex mystery that will consume you, starring a protagonist who is equal parts quirky Milhone and steady Gamache."

—Julie Clark, *New York Times* bestselling author of *The Last Flight*

"Joshua Moehling is a fresh, powerful new voice in crime fiction. His debut novel is a twisted ride with a detective you won't soon forget. This book isn't just unputdownable, it's the definition of the word."

—Samantha Downing, international bestselling author of *For Your Own Good*

"When Deputy Sheriff Ben Packard investigates the disappearance of two teenagers in Sandy Lake, Minnesota, he exposes the seamy underbelly of a small American town. *And There He Kept Her* is a sharp, intense thriller combining a dark plot with a relentless pace. An absorbing, impressive debut."

—A. J. Banner, #1 Amazon, *USA Today*, and *Publishers Weekly* bestselling author

"*And There He Kept Her* plays out like something on TV, resembling *Yellowstone* in its small-town setting and larger-than-life drama set against captivatingly detailed scenery... *And There He Kept Her* is a great opportunity to get into a new detective series at the ground level. Especially if you like the idea of the hard-boiled detective novel but prefer your stories set in modern times with light touches of current social issues. Moehling's is a strong debut."

—*Associated Press*

"There's a terrific new voice in crime fiction, and it belongs to Joshua Moehling. *And There He Kept Her* is a taut, beautifully written thriller reminiscent of Karin Slaughter. A novel with heart, its protagonist, acting Sheriff Ben Packard, is the kind of hero we need today, a man wrestling with his sexual identity as he searches for missing teens in a small Minnesota town guarding secrets of its own."

—Jonathan Santlofer, author
of *The Last Mona Lisa*

ALSO BY JOSHUA MOEHLING

And There He Kept Her

Where the Dead Sleep

A Long Time Gone

BENEATH A BROKEN SKY

JOSHUA MOEHLING

Cover design by Jared Oriel
Cover images © Karoliina Norontaus/Arcangel, Hayden Verry/Arcangel, Silas Manhood/Arcange
Internal design by Diane Cunningham/Sourcebooks

Published by Poisoned Pen Press, an imprint of Sourcebooks
1935 Brookdale RD, Naperville, IL 60563-2773
(630) 961-3900
sourcebooks.com

Cataloging-in-Publication Data is on file with the Library of Congress.

Printed and bound in the United States of America.
MA 10 9 8 7 6 5 4 3 2 1

For Minnesota for resisting

PROLOGUE

In Sandy Lake, Minnesota, they would remember that summer first by the storm, then the lingering devastation, and later, the murders.

Prior to the chaos, the weather had people feeling like they were living under a glass bowl, and everything inside was being heated by the sun and moistened by the damp, unmoving air. Smoke from wildfires in Canada created a gray haze that blurred things in the distance and smelled like burning plastic. A world on fire created some beautiful sunsets, so at least there was that.

The forecast said a break would arrive with a cool front, but when it came, it brought a downburst of air that screamed across the county as straight-line winds. Rain and hail fell in torrents that poured down as if from one immense spilling bucket. Wind roared and bent trees in one direction and pulled off heavy branches and sailed them away like petals from a daisy. This was not the relief everyone had prayed for. It was just another plague, another kind of torment. Creeks flooded and washed out roads. Power poles tipped and leaned across streets, held up only by their straining wires. One man was electrocuted. A giant pine crashed through a house and killed a ten-year-old boy in his bed.

In the storm's wake: no cell service, a trio of crushed grain silos, an overturned semi. Roofs lifted off houses and disassembled into flapping shingles and whole sheets of plywood. Thousands of homes without power. For weeks, bucket trucks recruited from three states roamed the county, and wherever one stopped, homeowners came out of their dark, sweltering houses and dropped to their knees in gratitude.

People came together to help one another and share whatever they had. Tractors and front loaders and meals and freezer space. They sweated in the heat while they piled debris at the end of driveways and drank from coolers on the dropped tailgates of pickup trucks. All the best parts of a small town. The benefit of community.

For many, it was the sight of so many devastated trees that caused shortness of breath and what felt like chest pains, actual heartbreak. The wind shattered tree trunks and revealed their bone-white interiors. Across the county, some of the oldest trees—mighty oaks, gnarled cedars, towering maples, all of them witnesses to the last hundred years of history—lost their grip on the soil and came crashing down, as shocking and enormous on land as a whale carcass. Bigger than anything these people had done in their short lives. Bigger than their newfound grief. They asked themselves, if the times could bring down such magnificent beings, what chance did the rest of us have?

CHAPTER ONE

WEDNESDAY

AIR QUALITY INDEX: YELLOW (MODERATE)

Deputy Ben Packard still couldn't believe the carnage left behind by the storm. It had moved west to east across the county, a swath ten miles wide. You couldn't look anywhere and not see a damaged house, cars with hail-smashed windows, or piles of moldy carpet and ruined furniture hauled to the curb. A month later, long lines of trucks still queued daily at the dump and the tree debris drop-off site.

He pulled up in front of a house with the garbage can at the end of the driveway, stuffed so full the lid wouldn't close. He saw a flattened diaper box and packaging for a baby seat that bounced and vibrated and played music via a built-in Bluetooth speaker.

He knocked on the front door, tried the handle. "Hey, it's me," he said. Not too loud.

Jill Thielen was sitting on the end of the couch with a blanket over her shoulder, covering the baby at her breast.

"Your face looks weird without the beard," Thielen said by way of a greeting.

"It's too hot for the beard. It's gone for now."

"I don't like it."

Packard shrugged. He was six foot four, broad in the shoulders, narrow in the waist. A swimmer and a weight lifter. He was wearing running shoes and cargo shorts and a black T-shirt that was tight in the arms and across the chest. It was the first day he'd been out of uniform in weeks and he wasn't used to the lightness of casual clothes. Anytime he stood up, he practically shot off the chair, still expecting the weight of his body armor and duty belt.

Thielen looked tired. She was blond, as tall as a fire hydrant, and a new mom at forty. He'd visited her in the hospital the day after the baby was born, when her hair was stuck to her head in funny shapes and the room still smelled faintly of the marathon she'd put her body through. For the last few weeks, he'd been giving her and Tim and Emelia their space.

"I'm about to move this beast from one side to the other. Look away if you don't want to see my ground-beef nipples."

Packard looked up at the ceiling. "How are you? You look good."

"Don't lie. I look and feel like a raw turkey—just gross poultry skin and a gaping hole between my legs that this cannibal chewed its way out of."

Packard made a face. "Can you put her back in the hole and keep pushing until she goes back to where she came from?"

Thielen pulled the blanket higher over her other shoulder. "I know you're not intimately familiar with a woman's anatomy, but you should know we don't have a time machine up there."

"I was picturing more of a pneumatic tube like at the bank drive-through. Return that cannibal baby like a check you want to deposit."

"You're a complete idiot."

Thielen wanted to know what was happening at work, and when he asked if she really wanted to know, she admitted she didn't. The sheriff's office had been doing a lot of heavy lifting under the county's all-hazard emergency plan since the storm, including serving as the emergency operations center. While the entire town of Sandy Lake was without power, the sheriff's office ran on a large backup diesel generator, as did the fire station and the high school, where people went to cool off and charge their phones.

One of the many hats Packard had worn under the emergency plan was public information officer. All the official communication from the incident command team went through him, whether it was to the media or responding to public inquiries. Which roads were closed. Which areas required proof of residency to enter. Where to get fresh water or shelter if you needed it.

Rumor control turned out to be a bigger part of the job than he expected. It was mind-boggling, the number of people commenting on the sheriff's office Facebook page who insisted the storm was man-made, that they had noticed an increase in chemtrails leading up to it or seen lasers coming down from space, that this was all part of a plan for the federal government to claim eminent domain over Sandy Lake County so it could mine hidden deposits of lithium under their houses.

In the county south of them, residents were worried about erosion from a swollen river taking out a dam. Packard was more worried about the erosion of common sense.

For a long stretch, he didn't leave the sheriff's office. He showered there, ate whatever food had been delivered by local restaurants cleaning out their freezers, and slept in his office. He had to leave Frank, his three-legged corgi, with the retired judge next door who took care of him when Packard couldn't get away from work.

"We're finally coming off disaster-response scheduling. It's been twelve on, twelve off, no PTO since the storm. We're slowly getting deputies back to their regular assignments. This is my first day off in five weeks, I think."

"How's Shepard?" Thielen asked.

"He's so buried in the administrative part of this disaster that he doesn't have time to bust my balls. He's delegated as much as possible and there's still plenty for him to do, which far exceeds his preference for doing nothing."

"He should have thought of that before he decided he wanted to be sheriff," Thielen said.

After losing the election for sheriff last November, Packard had gone from acting sheriff and lead investigator to head of court security, thanks to Howard Shepard, the new sheriff. Packard had spent a long winter standing behind an x-ray machine and listening to the squeak of wet shoes on marble floors as people went into courtrooms with set faces and came out again with all-new expressions: comedy or tragedy, victorious or furious.

Last winter a man brought a gun to court and started shooting, killing one before Packard returned fire and killed him. After an investigation and two months on administrative leave, Packard came back to work as a patrol deputy on the dog shift, which was Shepard making sure he knew who was boss. Thielen was the other lead detective in the department, and with her on bed rest for several weeks prior to the baby being born followed by sixteen weeks of maternity leave, Shepard finally had no choice but to put Packard back on investigations, where he'd wanted to be the whole time.

"Reynolds is doing a really good job," Packard said. "He still doesn't love investigations, but you did great work training him."

"You're welcome. Don't be afraid to abuse him."

"I would never," Packard said, looking sideways.

Thielen was doing something under the blanket. Packard saw the shape of a foot kick out and heard the wet mewl of a sleepy baby, and then Thielen grabbed a fistful of the blanket from the inside and whisked it away. Her yellow tank top was still bunched up where the baby was pressed against her, exposing a strip of white belly. Emelia was wearing a diaper and nothing else. She'd doubled in size, like bread dough, since Packard had last seen her.

"Make yourself useful," Thielen said. She handed him a towel and the baby. "Put her over your shoulder and burp her."

It had been a long time since Packard was on baby duty with any of his nieces and nephews. He held Emelia with her butt in his hand and his other hand behind her head. She was pink from the heat of her mother's body. She stared at him cross-eyed and stupid. Adorable.

Thielen went to the kitchen for a glass of water and hollered back to ask

Packard if he wanted a beer. He said no and walked in a small circle with the baby against his shoulder.

"What's going on with you and Bud Light?" Thielen asked, leaning in the doorway. "The bartender."

"Kyle owns the brewery and is the head brewmaster. He's not a bartender. He's not a light beer."

"All I know is he's dark and delicious. I'll call him Oatmeal Stout if I want. Have you guys… Mmmm." She made a fist like she was about to throw a punch.

"What does that mean?"

"Have you guys done it?"

"Not even close."

"Have you had his tongue in your mouth or anywhere on your body?"

"Nope."

"What in the gay hell is wrong with the two of you? What have you done?"

"Hung out at the brewery a couple of times. He invited me over to his place once. Kyle gives guitar lessons on the side and a couple of his students were there. A few more people showed up with more instruments. It turned into a jam session."

Thielen rolled her eyes. "I just died of boredom listening to that story. Next time, make it filthy. No one wants to hear about a jam session. What did you play?"

"I don't want to say."

"What was it?"

He closed his eyes and relented. "Tambourine."

Thielen cackled like a witch. "Oh my god. Tambourine. I'm dead." She kept laughing, squeezing her knees together and putting a hand on her belly. "Oh, it hurts. Goddamn. Don't make me laugh so hard."

Packard was desperate to change the subject. "Here's something interesting about Kyle—he's sober."

"He's a sober brewery owner and brewer?" Thielen asked, wiping her eyes with the back of her hand.

"Yep."

"That is interesting. You're not a big drinker."

"It doesn't bother me at all. But I have known a drink or two to grease the skids when trying to make something happen."

"Is 'grease the skids' a gay sex thing?" Thielen asked with all seriousness.

"It's a figure of speech, dummy."

"Sorry! I'm just trying to learn about your culture."

Packard turned his head to see if the baby was sleeping. "My culture. Now who's the idiot?" he asked Emelia. He felt sudden pressure against his palm originating from inside the diaper. "Oh no. She just farted or shit. You take her."

"You know how to change a diaper," Thielen said.

"I will walk out the door and leave this baby in the mailbox if you don't take her right now."

Thielen pushed herself away from the wall. "You're the baby," she said.

She took Emelia in another room to change her. Packard stared out the front window and listened to Thielen coo at the baby and open and close drawers. Thielen had been home from the hospital with Emelia all of three days when the storm hit. She and her husband, Tim, had evacuated to stay with family down in the Cities until they got word a week later that the power was back on in their neighborhood.

Thielen said, "God, girl. What did you eat? A chili dog?"

Packard felt himself break into a sweat.

"Hey, speaking of food, any chance you want to come back for dinner tonight?" Thielen called out. "Tim's mom has been here for almost ten days now. We could use somebody with something new to say."

"What are you making? If it's chili dogs, the answer is no."

"Tim and his mom are at the store now. Steaks was the last thing I heard."

Packard's phone buzzed in his pocket. The screen said DISPATCH. Never a good thing on his day off. Reynolds was on duty, which meant either he was already busy with something else or this was big enough that both of them were needed. Packard swiped and listened as the operator detailed the 911 call that had come in.

Thielen came out with Emelia in a tight, new diaper.

"Tell Reynolds I'll be there shortly," Packard said. He hung up and pocketed his phone.

"What is it?" Thielen asked.

"You don't want to know," he said.

"Bad?"

"Sounds like it."

"So, no dinner?"

"Rain check," he said.

CHAPTER TWO

Packard drove home from Thielen's house, parked in the driveway, and looked at the mess in his yard. Black garbage bags filled with wet drywall and moldy insulation. Splintered pieces of hardwood floor. He'd known when he bought the house four years earlier that the chimney needed tuck-pointing, but fixing it had been low on the priority list with everything else that needed to be done. The night of the storm, while Packard was at work, the wind toppled six feet of his chimney onto the roof. It didn't fall through, but it smashed the decking and ripped off the shingles and pulled down the front gutters as a huge chunk of it slid to the ground.

His neighbor, Bert, who took in Frank the entire time Packard was on emergency duty, texted him to tell him about the chimney. The neighbors cleaned off the roof and nailed a tarp over the damaged part. Packard's initial reaction when he got home five days later was that it could have been a lot worse. Then, inside, it was. The living room ceiling was sagging with water and the floorboards beneath it were cupped. He'd slowly been remodeling the house since buying it and this part was already done. New floors, new Sheetrock, recessed can lights. Now it was in worse shape than ever. He had to pull down more than half of the living room ceiling and a significant amount of the attic insulation.

A week ago, he'd finally had an inspector out to assess the damage. He was still waiting to find out how much his insurance was going to pay.

In the bedroom, Packard changed into jeans and a black polo shirt with a sheriff's office star and *Sandy Lake County* on the chest. He wore his badge and his gun on his belt. This part of the house had been spared by the storm. He and Frank spent a lot of their time back here with the door closed, like squatters under their own roof. Packard had to buy a portable air conditioner to keep the bedroom cool at night.

Coming down the hall to the front of the house, he stopped to stare at the hole in the ceiling, the ruined floor. This was supposed to be his refuge from the world, a shelter from the elements. It was anything but that in its current state.

Packard took Frank for a quick walk ("quick" being relative when dealing with a three-legged corgi) and reminded himself that everything could be put back with time and effort. It felt selfish to complain when others had lost much more than him. Yes, he was tired and the amount of work to be done felt insurmountable, but these were temporary conditions. Things wouldn't be like this forever.

The address the dispatch operator sent him to had been in the path of the storm. Canopies that should have been thick with leaves had been blown naked by the wind. Huge limbs sat on the ground like battlefield amputations. Packard never would have claimed to have taken trees for granted, but he hadn't realized how vital they were to his sense of the landscape until they were gone. Trees as shelters. Trees as windbreaks. Trees as landmarks and visual cues.

The trees. The trees. The trees.

He felt like a madman who couldn't quit shouting at the voices in his head.

The houses on Wood Lake covered the gamut: some small original cabins, no heat, no AC, built by great-grandparents seventy-five years ago, probably overrun by mice in the offseason. Some modest year-round houses with decorative mailboxes and yard art. He followed the directions to a road called Fog Trail until the flashing emergency lights guided him to the exact house. Three Sandy Lake Sheriff's patrol cars, an ambulance, and a crime scene van all crowded the narrow road ringing the lake.

The house sat behind a detached two-car garage that fronted the road with a driveway that was all rocks and weeds. No sidewalks. From inside his vehicle, Packard spotted two yellow evidence markers outside the front door.

The switch from the chilled cab of his truck to the hot, humid air made Packard sweat immediately. He made a loop around the house to get the lay of the land. The neighbors on either side were about fifty yards away. Aluminum siding showed dents and tears from the storm. The house's air-conditioning unit had been smashed and sat crooked on its concrete base. The offending tree lay nearby, sliced like a banana by a chain saw. Next to it, a big pile of its branches.

Packard looked up at the back of the house. He was too low to see inside, but he saw a ceiling fan spinning high in one window and the gooseneck of a faucet looking out from the other. The view from those windows was of a scrubby yard, a firepit surrounded by Adirondack chairs, and the lake. A speedboat lashed to a wooden dock bobbed in the small ripples rolling toward shore. Even with the storm damage, even with the oppressive humidity and the inescapable sun, the scene retained a sense of the idyllic. This was where Minnesota memories of summer came from.

Back in front, Packard nodded at the uniformed deputy standing outside the house. Through the screen door, Packard saw a camera flash go off. What he knew from dispatch was that they had a female DOA, called in by the husband.

"They want us to use the door on the deck to preserve the path to this door," the deputy said, tilting his head.

Packard climbed two steps to the deck. A box of shoe covers and another box of latex gloves sat in a chair. Packard put on both and ducked through a sliding glass door that opened into the kitchen.

The woman was down on the linoleum floor, slumped against a wall beside the refrigerator. One hand in her lap, the other flung out to the side. No shoes.

She had dried blood beneath her nose that ran down her chin. She was wearing white shorts and a tank top with thin straps, both soaked with blood. Not from her nose but from what looked like three separate stab wounds to the chest. Discoloration around the throat. An exposed nail poked out from the wall above her where a clock had fallen and lay face down beside her. A slaughterhouse smell hung heavy in the air.

He found Reynolds in the living room, where the ceiling was low and the lack of air-conditioning made it feel dark and tight. Reynolds looked like he'd been unplugged from the wall. Mouth slightly open. Pen not moving. He was the department's youngest deputy, pink-cheeked and blond, father of two small kids.

"What do you know so far?" Packard asked.

Reynolds blinked and struggled to find his voice. "She's dead. Somebody…"

Packard looked at the body again. It was tough even for him. Many of the cases he and Reynolds worked—most of them not murders—had an ugly obviousness about them. Alcohol or drugs often contributed to brutal but not fatal violence among people who seemed to know no other way of coping. When things did escalate to homicide, there was usually a sad stupidity to the scene, a feeling that the outcome had been inevitable, considering the dull-eyed players and the complete absence of reasoning.

This felt different.

He stepped close to Reynolds and lowered his voice. "You all right? You need a minute?"

"I keep thinking of walking through the door and finding Melissa like this. Who would… Why would someone…?" He glanced over Packard's shoulder, looked away. Wiped his sweaty forehead with the back of his hand.

"That's our job to find out," Packard said. He maneuvered Reynolds so his back was to the body. "Look at me. Tell me what you know so far."

"Her name is Ashley Turner. Her husband's name is Thomas. They have two boys, Jake and Noah, ages ten and seventeen. They all had lunch together in the house around twelve thirty. Tom and the boys went down to the boat around one and were wakeboarding for about an hour and a half. Ashley gets seasick on the boat so she was going to clean up from lunch and then come down and read a book on the dock. She never made it down."

"Where are the husband and sons now?"

"Two houses down at a friend's place."

"Have you interviewed them?"

"Just Tom and only briefly. He was waiting outside when we arrived and then went to be with the boys."

"All right. Good start. I'm going to take a look around. I'll meet you outside."

Reynolds nodded and beelined for the sliding door. Packard called after him. "Was the front door propped open like this when you arrived?" He pointed to a nylon sandbag slumped against the bottom of the door. Between him and the door, three folded yellow tents had been placed next to blood spots on the floor.

Reynold bit the inside of his mouth. "Yes. I haven't asked Tom if he propped it open or if his wife would have had it that way while she was home alone. I do know the AC doesn't work."

"Did Tom and the kids come through the front door or this side door when they found her?"

"I don't know," Reynolds admitted. "Tom was standing outside the front door when I got here. That's the door I first came through."

Prints off the exterior door handle were unlikely if the boys and Tom had been in and out following whoever did this to Ashley. The screen door was old with a lever that you pushed down. The lock was a tiny button that moved up and down in a slot. The illusion of security. He would ask the crime scene techs to print everything just in case.

Packard stepped clear of the body and stood in front of the kitchen sink. The basin on the right was half-full of dirty dishwater. The suds had died and in the bottom he saw a cutting board and a cleaver and a rubber spatula. In the other basin were plates and a mixing bowl and coffee cups stacked in a dish drainer.

Her phone was on the counter nearby, face up. He bent low and saw irregularities in the surface of the screen: blood splatter. He imagined someone knocking at the door while she was washing dishes. She would have looked behind her, maybe touched the screen on her phone to see what time it was, and dried her hands on the way to the door. He looked around for a towel. It wasn't near the body. Not over the handle of the fridge or the oven. He went to the sliding door and looked for it out there. Nothing.

The crime scene techs were named Becky and Erik. The department gossip was that they had started dating recently. "Either one of you see or collect a dish towel?" he asked.

"We haven't started bagging anything yet," Becky said, squinting through the viewfinder of her camera that was pointed in the direction of the front door. The flash went off. "Just photographs and DNA swabs."

Packard looked in the sink and saw the cleaver. Not the murder weapon. He saw a knife block with slots for two missing knives. The handle on the cleaver in the sink matched the set. He looked in the drying rack for the other knife. It wasn't there. He counted two cutting boards. One dirty knife.

One missing knife.

He looked at the evidence markers near the front door. Thought of the two he'd seen outside. There was a lot of blood on Ashley's body but Packard wasn't sure it was enough to soak the killer so much that he was dripping all the way back to his vehicle. More likely that the killer had been injured as well. It was his blood.

"Let's type this blood as soon as possible. I don't think the blood on the other side of the door is Ashley's. If we have two blood types, we'll know for sure. Make sure you shoot this sink and the knife block, too," Packard said to Becky.

His sour stomach rose to the back of his throat as he squatted down for one last look at Ashley Turner, who likely knew very well how dangerous it was to be a woman in this world. Could she have imagined this? Here? In her own kitchen?

He hoped not.

Packard stood up and thought of the disaster at his house and the belief he and Ashley had probably shared—that home was a safe place, that walls and a ceiling could protect you from whatever raged outside.

Now they both knew better.

CHAPTER THREE

Reynolds was standing in the front yard, still writing in his notebook. Packard came down the deck steps. "Which way to see the family?" he asked.

"This way," Reynolds said, tipping his head.

They walked while Packard mentally filed what he'd seen and started to think of questions he wanted to ask Ashley's husband. He took deep breaths of the humid air through his nose to try to get rid of the smell of death that followed them from the house.

"Did the kids see their mom like that?"

"Just the oldest, Noah. Tom said Noah had to go to the bathroom so they came back to the dock. The plan was to do more wakeboarding. Tom and his younger son stayed in the boat. Noah went up and came running out of the house screaming." There was still a shake in Reynolds's voice.

"I need you to have it together in front of the family," Packard said. "They're the ones who get to be distressed. Are you good?"

Reynolds closed his eyes. Nodded. "I'm good," he said.

They passed a small blue house with cords of firewood stacked in a long row and covered with tarps. The next house had mangy marigolds growing around the mailbox and half a dozen bird feeders spread across the yard. A red-bellied woodpecker clung to a suet feeder and pecked at the block of fat. A minivan was parked in the driveway.

The woman who answered the door had red hair and redder eyes. She introduced herself as Emily and led them to a living room with green plaid furniture and a wood coffee table and a terrible painting of a loon watching from over the couch. Tom was sitting on the brick hearth in front of the fireplace.

Packard introduced himself. "I've been to your house. I'm terribly sorry this has happened to your family. We're going to catch this guy. Whoever he is."

Tom sat with a hand on the back of his neck. His eyes were closed and he looked like he wasn't listening or wasn't believing what he was hearing. He was in his late forties, short hair that was effortlessly messy, muscled like he knew the inside of a gym. He was still wearing a swimsuit and a bright Under Armour shirt on top.

Emily was making a lot of noise in the kitchen. She reminded Packard of a bird trapped indoors, beating itself against everything as it tried to find a way out. She brought them bottled waters and kept her gaze lowered, like she was a servant in her own home. She went outside and pulled the front door shut behind her.

"Ashley… It can't be real. That can't be my wife," Tom groaned. "We just had lunch. We were on the boat. How could… I don't understand."

Packard waited him out. When Tom stopped talking and got up and moved to the couch, Packard asked, "Is this your primary address or is it a family cabin?"

"It started out as a cabin and then we moved here full-time during the pandemic. We've been here three years. We were planning to move back to the Cities before the kids start school again in the fall."

"What do you do for work?"

"I'm a client manager for a software company. I travel back and forth to Minneapolis and to client locations a lot. Ashley's an auditor who helps charter schools with their books and state reporting requirements. She's remote."

"How often are you out of town?"

"Probably a total of two weeks a month. Sometimes more, depending on what the clients need."

"Where do you stay in the Cities?"

"We kept our home in Bloomington and rented it. The renters are in the process of moving out now that we're moving back. I usually stay at the Marriott. I have Ambassador Elite status with them."

Packard didn't know about hotel statuses. Ambassador Elite probably got him more than a warm cookie at check-in. "What do we need to know to help us figure out why this happened to your wife?"

"You're asking me if I know why someone would stab my wife to death?"

Packard stayed silent. He knew there was more coming.

"Meaning we might have brought this on ourselves."

Packard shook his head. "That's not what I said. It's not being implied either. I apologize if it came across that way." He couldn't let Tom's fury damage their relationship this early on. It was a delicate dance trying to gather the information he needed while navigating the raw emotions felt by people experiencing the worst moment of their lives.

"A terrible person crossed paths with your wife today. It's my job to determine if that intersection was random or the outgrowth of some previous interaction. To do my job—not knowing you or your wife or your family—I need you to help me. I need to know if you can think of some other event that might have precipitated this."

"You think there's a logical explanation for this?"

"Doesn't have to be logical. It probably isn't logical. Could be something or someone out of the ordinary. Some minor incident Ashley may have mentioned in passing that didn't seem like a big deal but stands out now."

Tom put his hands up in frustration. His voice pitched higher, louder. "This is ridiculous. No. I can't think of anything like that."

Reynolds spoke up then. "What about the incident at school. With the car?"

The way Tom and Reynolds stared at each other made Packard realize they both knew something he didn't. A tilt of the head from one, a sigh from the other. Eyes looking away, looking back. A whole silent conversation passed between them.

"That was kids being assholes," Tom said.

"What are you guys talking about?" Packard asked.

Reynolds nodded at Tom, who closed his eyes and shook his head. "You tell him if you think it's so important."

"There was an incident at the school back in March before things let out for the year," Reynolds said to Packard. "The Turners' oldest son, Noah, had his car vandalized at a bonfire party held at another kid's house. Homophobic slurs, swastikas, crude drawings. The homeowner's security system caught the ones who did it on camera. Some kids recorded it while it happened and videos went around."

This sounded vaguely familiar. Last March Packard was either working court security or on leave from the shooting at the courthouse. Thielen and Reynolds would have handled the case.

"Prom was canceled. Two students were suspended. In the video there were fifteen or twenty kids either standing around or participating."

"Was that the end of it?" Packard asked Tom. "No prom, a couple of suspensions?"

"My wife has been murdered and you want to talk about high school pranks?"

"That's exactly what I want to talk about. What happened after the suspensions?"

"For fuck's sake," Tom said. He sounded like a man whose time was being wasted. "Ashley didn't think the school district did enough to punish those involved. She thought that bullying kids like Noah is a known issue in the school and that the administration doesn't do enough to prevent it."

"What do you think?"

"I think my son is going to be who he is. No one is asking him to change or be anything different. He's got a lot of friends. He's got a boyfriend. Most of the comments roll right off his back. I thought Ashley was making too big of a deal of things."

"How was she doing that?"

Tom paused. He looked annoyed with himself, like he wanted to take back everything he'd already said. "She's been talking to a lawyer about suing the school district."

Packard cut his eyes at Reynolds, gave him the smallest of nods. The equivalent of a pat on the head. Good job.

"Was anyone else aware of the lawsuit?"

"I wouldn't know."

"Who's the lawyer?"

"Lisa Washington. She works—"

"I know Lisa," Packard said. She was a partner at Wiley, Washington & Prentis. The Wiley in the name of the firm was her dad, Ray Wiley, who was Sheriff Howard Shepard's father-in-law and no fan of Packard. Packard and Lisa had a good relationship despite the fact that she often served as a public defender for people who had been arrested by the sheriff's office.

"Was this lawsuit still just an idea or had actual steps been taken?" Packard asked.

"I don't know. I told her if she was going to tilt at this particular windmill, she was on her own. I'm out of town all the time and I don't agree with it. Even Noah is against it."

"I'll talk to Lisa. But this is exactly the kind of thing I need to know about. I don't see an obvious connection but it gives us a place to start."

Packard quizzed Tom for another half an hour about the exact timeline. What they did last night. What time everyone got up. What time they went down to the boat. How long they were on the water without Ashley. Packard asked about Ashley's day-to-day routine, her friends, the places she went. Packard asked if they'd seen anyone strange in the neighborhood or on the lake. Tom said no.

Packard let Tom know they would need access to Ashley's phone, her text messages, social media, her bank accounts, her credit card charges.

Tom looked unhappy at the idea. "Can I look at her phone before you take it?"

"No. It's already in evidence. Sorry."

"There's...private things."

"We'll treat everything with respect."

Tom looked less than assured.

"One last thing. I'm sorry to ask about this but...the knife block in the kitchen. Is it a complete set? Do you have all the knives for it?"

"Yes. We had tuna salad for lunch. Noah and Ashley were chopping pickles and celery and a bunch of other stuff."

"What about a dish towel? Should there be one somewhere in the kitchen."

Tom was losing his patience. "I don't fucking know. Yes, I think there's usually a dish towel."

A voice from downstairs yelled up. "There is. She always wore it over her shoulder when she was in the kitchen."

Packard looked at Tom who mouthed *Noah*.

"Let's pause here," Packard said. "I want to talk to Noah."

CHAPTER FOUR

Packard went down the stairs to a carpeted basement. In one corner was an old wood-topped bar wrapped in the same carpet as on the floor. There was a pool table and a sectional sofa set up in front of a television hanging on the wall.

He came up behind a young man slumped so low on the long leg of the couch that his chin was in his chest. He had a phone in his hands, and in the space of about three seconds he sent two texts, switched over to another app, sent another message, switched apps, took a screenshot, and texted it to someone. Packard couldn't believe the speed at which it all happened.

"Are you Noah?" Packard asked.

Noah sat up on the couch and put his phone down. His eyes were red and his hair had dried in funny shapes after being in the lake. He was wearing a lime-green Brat T-shirt that nearly covered his small, square swim trunks. He had a dozen beaded and braided bracelets around his wrist and chipped blue nail polish.

Packard didn't know how to relate to teenagers. Not even gay ones. These kids seemed like they were born suspicious of your bullshit. There was no naivete. They were experienced drug users, sexually active, and probably committing fraud or running a small business with their phones. Packard thought of Thielen's baby and wondered what she would be doing seventeen years from now. Commanding a robot army, maybe.

Packard had a seat a few feet away from Noah. Before he could say anything, Noah said, "You're the queer cop, right?"

Packard sat up a bit taller. "I am both of those things, yes," he said.

"I was trying to get a LGBTQIA2S+ group started at school. We had a faculty sponsor but then these fucking tradwife Karens on the school board found out and chased her off. I was going to ask you to be a speaker."

Packard blinked and nodded. "If you get that group going, let me know and I'll be there. Glad to." What he'd say to these kids that didn't make him sound like Grandpa telling stories from the war, he had no idea. That was a tomorrow problem.

Noah's phone chimed three times in a row. He pushed a button to silence it. It vibrated a couple more times, then stopped.

"Noah, there's nothing I can say to make things better right now. I'm sorry that this happened to your family. It's my job to catch whoever did this, and I need to ask you a few questions about this afternoon."

Noah nodded. Peeked at his phone, put it back down.

"Deputy Reynolds said you guys needed a bathroom break and you were the one who came up from the boat."

"Yes."

"Are those the clothes you were wearing on the boat?"

"Yes."

"What time was it when you came up?"

"I don't know. Oh, wait." Noah picked up his phone. "I sent my boyfriend a text because we don't get any signal out on the lake. I was in Wi-Fi range when I got close to the house. It was two thirty-seven when I sent it."

Packard wrote down the time. "Did you see anyone? Any vehicles? Hear any voices as you were coming up to the house?"

"No. I was on my phone, not really paying attention."

"When you went into the house, which door did you use?"

"The front door."

"Who called 911? You or your dad?"

"I called and my dad took the phone when he came up from the boat."

"What time was that?"

Noah looked at his phone again. "Two thirty-nine."

Packard nodded. Without saying as much, he was trying to eliminate the possibility that Noah had killed his mom. Wouldn't be the first time an angry teenager lashed out at his parents. The window was too small for him to have done this between sending the text and calling 911. He also didn't have any cuts or scratches or bruises that Packard could see. No blood anywhere on his clothes.

"How did the school year end? I heard about the party where your car was vandalized."

Noah looked annoyed by the question. "School was fine."

"Did you have any trouble with any of the people from the party afterwards or over the summer?"

"No."

"Anyone blame you for prom getting canceled?"

"It wasn't my fucking fault!" Noah said, throwing a hand up.

"I know. People aren't always logical in how they respond to not getting what they want."

"If they were pissed, I didn't hear about it."

"Your mom was pretty upset about things, though."

"She was overreacting. I told her to drop it. I know she wanted to help, but she was actually making things harder for queer kids in our school. We have a small but strong community and allies, and we can stand up for ourselves. We're moving back to Minneapolis anyway so who cares about this place anymore?"

The look on his face said he cared more than he was letting on. The boyfriend likely had something to do with it. His phone buzzed. Buzzed again.

"Anyone say anything threatening to you about your mom or what she was doing?"

"No. Never."

Noah sniffled and sighed. His phone kept buzzing.

Packard let the pause in the conversation grow. He closed his notebook and put it in his pocket. Noah picked at his nail polish. In the silence Packard heard the sound of someone crying. He turned his head in the direction of a closed door.

"That's my brother, Jacob."

"How old is he?"

"Ten," Noah said, staring at the ceiling.

Packard reached over and tapped Noah on the side of the leg to get his attention. "Hey, Noah, look at me. I want to tell you something. When I was your brother's age, my older brother died."

"What happened to him?"

"That's a long story and not important right now. What I remember from that time is being really scared, and the only thing that made me feel safe was being around my other siblings. You and Jacob are going to need each other in the coming days and weeks and months. He's going to need to lean on you. Be there for your brother, okay?"

Noah nodded. Tears ran from the corners of his eyes. He looked at his phone, the screen full of notifications.

"Everyone is finding out," he said. His face trembled and collapsed. He dropped his head and sobbed. Packard sat quietly with him and listened to the boys cry before going upstairs to get their dad.

CHAPTER FIVE

After leaving Tom with his boys at the neighbor's, Packard and Reynolds stood in the middle of the road outside the Turners' house. They waited for a couple in flip-flops and shorts walking a shih-poo to go by. The sun was on the other side of its journey overhead. Everything felt like it was radiating heat. The blacktop, the vehicles, the breeze. Reynolds was dressed in his full uniform, vest and all, sweating.

Packard moved them off the road and into meager shade.

"Everyone on duty is now working this case," he said. "Send a deputy to find out what Tom and the boys need for the next few days. Keep them out of the house while the body is still inside. I want everyone on this lake interviewed. Check for security systems, video doorbells. I want the ditches searched for that knife and the towel. I want DNA from every single drop of blood away from the main scene around the body."

Reynolds nodded, took notes. He asked, "Did you think it was odd that Tom was worried about what was on her phone?"

"Did you?"

"I don't know. I mean…a little bit."

"I get it. Aren't there private things on your phone or your wife's phone you wouldn't want anyone else to see?"

Reynolds blushed. "Yeah… I mean, no. I mean, not like that."

"Like what? I didn't say anything. Why are you turning red?"

"Never mind," Reynolds said, obviously regretting that he'd started this line of questioning.

A cloud of gnats found them. Packard waved his hand as he and Reynolds moved toward his vehicle. "I'm going to the office. When I get there, I'm going to pull your report on the vandalism incident at the party. It better be good."

"It's good. Thielen made sure I got it right."

Patrol deputies worked twelve-hour shifts that started and ended at 6:00 a.m. and 6:00 p.m. Every shift began with a debrief meeting led by the shift supervisor. Packard had an hour before the evening shift started.

He called Shepard.

"You heard about the call we got today?"

"The lady that got stabbed? I got a text about it from Baker. You arrest anybody?" Shepard made a sound like he was trying to swallow a burp. His speech was slow and just a bit slurred.

"Not yet. It's still early. You don't want to make an appearance at the shift meeting, do you?"

"Hell no. I left at noon to go fishing with my brother. We're elbow deep into a case of beer. I ain't in no shape."

"No worries. This is an all-hands situation. Just wanted you to know."

"Do whatever you hafta do. I'll catch up tomorrow."

Packard hung up. He couldn't judge Shepard for what he did on his time off. The job of sheriff was demanding. Before winning the election, Shepard had been the worst deputy on the payroll, doing just enough to get by. Last on the scene, last to raise his hand or volunteer for anything. He drove around and smoked cigarettes with a vast network of contacts that fed him town gossip. There were times when Shepard's knowledge of how everyone was connected to everyone else and what secrets they were keeping came in handy, but when Packard was acting sheriff, he was never fooled into believing that what Shepard did actually constituted work.

Back at the office, Packard gave the new shift deputies a summary of the call to the Turners' house, what they knew so far, and what he wanted done by morning. A projector hanging from the ceiling showed his laptop screen on the wall. He pulled up the location of the scene on Google Maps and then zoomed out.

"The attack occurred sometime between 1:00 and 2:30 p.m. We're trying to tighten that window up as best we can. Once you get away from the lake, there's a lot of directions traffic can go. I want every house in this rectangle checked for a security camera. Any business that has a camera pointed at the road, I want their footage from the last twenty-four hours. Check the hospital in Sandy Lake and the counties around us to find out if anyone came in covered in blood or needing stitches from a knife wound. There's a kitchen knife and a towel missing from the scene. Let people you talk to know to be on the lookout."

Packard told them to watch their email for the summary of his report so far. "It's early but we need every bit of luck we can get on this case. If you see anything out of the ordinary, anything out of compliance, light 'em up. The animal who did this might have a broken taillight, for all we know. Any questions?"

One of the three deputies about to start his shift raised his hand. "My wife is friends with Ashley. Our kid is the same age as her younger one so we know the Turners from school. We gotta catch this motherfucker."

"I couldn't agree more. Have a good night. Be safe. Plan to attend the shift meeting in the morning before you go off duty. I'll see you there."

The supervisor dismissed everyone after an equipment check, and Packard went back to his office and pulled up Reynolds's report on the vandalism. He wasn't two sentences in when he felt a hollow cramp in his empty belly. His plan to have lunch with Thielen was short-circuited by the call about Ashley Turner. He hadn't eaten since breakfast.

Packard turned off his monitor and the lights to his office. He could read the report at home after he had dinner.

A strange car was parked in his driveway.

He pulled his truck next to it and got out and walked around the twenty-year-old silver Honda Accord and looked through its windows. The dash was dusty and the back seat held a box with three-ring binders in it. A bottle of Diet Coke sat in the cup holder in the console and a phone charger hung limply from the cigarette lighter. The car's tabs were expired.

Frank watched him from the front window, ears up, tongue out. Packard leaned close to the glass, made faces at his dog, then walked around to the back of his house. No sign of the car's driver.

He called dispatch. "Can you run a plate for me? There's a car parked in my driveway and no one around."

The registration came back belonging to a Rose Simmons with an address on Colfax in Minneapolis. Packard felt something light up deep in his brain. Simmons on Colfax. He couldn't think of why it sounded familiar. He knew the neighborhood. North Minneapolis was his beat back when he was a patrol cop.

He went inside and was greeted by Frank, who twisted around on his wide bottom like a towel winding up to be snapped. Packard put him on a leash and they went next door to Bert Morris's house. Bert kept an eye on all the comings and goings in the neighborhood and took care of Frank as needed.

The door opened before Packard could ring the bell. Bert stood there in long pleated shorts with a belt and a striped golf shirt. His old-man limbs were thin and hairless and knobby. "I bet you're wondering about the car in your driveway."

"I am," Packard said. "What do you know about it?"

Bert stepped aside and behind him Packard saw a Black woman with a headscarf come through the back door with a glass in her hand. He knew who she was from the first glimpse. The shape of her head, her eyes, her skin tone. He felt the breath forced out of him as she floated like a ghost through the patterns of light and shadow caught inside the house. The glass in her hand was sweating. She wiped her palm on the back of her pants.

"You must be Ben," she said.

He could only nod and stare at her and see the face of a dead man who lived in his dreams.

"Marcus…" Packard said, almost a whisper.

"Marcus was my brother. I'm Symphony."

CHAPTER SIX

Marcus had been dead for five years.

The days since then felt like they'd been measured in miles. Packard felt far away from who he was when he met Marcus, and who he was when Marcus died, far even from the man he'd been when he arrived in Sandy Lake with nothing but a truck, a few boxes, and an idea that this place and this job would sever him from what had happened. Since then, he'd learned that life doesn't fall away like a burned-out rocket booster left behind to crash into an endless ocean. The past stays inside you, layers deep, visible rings if you were sawed in half.

He and Symphony said goodbye to Bert.

"Remember, I'm on a cruise with my family the next two weeks," Bert said. "Happy to watch Frank again anytime once I'm back."

Packard thanked him, and he and Symphony walked back to his house, hugging the edge of the road while Frank sniffed and peed and barked at a dragonfly.

Packard kept looking straight ahead. The smoky skies turned the low sun an impossible orange. A warning light. Every glimpse of Symphony felt like hearing Marcus call his name. He wanted to touch her face like a blind man, to remember the contours of Marcus that had faded in his memory.

"What happened to your dog?" she asked. "How come he only has three legs?"

"He was a rescue from a puppy mill. Got his foot stuck in the wire cage. Dog in the next cage started to eat it."

"Oh Lord. Sorry I asked. I'm afraid of dogs."

"All Frank wants are back scratches and treats. But I understand. How did you end up drinking tea on Bert's back deck?"

"He invited me."

"Did he see you sitting in the driveway?"

"I don't think so. I rang your doorbell. You weren't home. I went to his house to see if he knew when you'd be back. He didn't know but invited me to stay and wait. Seemed like he wanted the company as much as I wanted to find you."

Packard ignored the second part of that statement. They still had time to get into what she wanted. "Bert's a retired judge. He spent his life on the bench listening to people tell stories."

"I'm usually more afraid of judges than dogs. He didn't seem so bad."

Packard didn't say anything. Just thought of more questions.

They went in the house and he let Frank off the leash in the garage and closed the door. When he came back, Symphony was staring at the hole in the living room ceiling. He followed her gaze and saw the roof vent spinning lazily overhead. He looked around the place with fresh eyes and realized he had been getting used to living with this disaster. All the living room furniture had been pushed into the half of the room that still had a ceiling. Air from the roof vents blew bits of insulation on the floor that he had to sweep up every time he got home. Everything was jumbled and dusty and chaotic.

"We had a storm a month ago," he tried to explain.

"I noticed all the trees down on the drive here."

"Yeah. The chimney fell on the roof, water got in while I was at work, and that's why the place looks like this."

Symphony took a handkerchief from her back pocket and wiped her forehead.

"Sorry it's so hot in here. I don't run the air conditioner because of this," he said, pointing at the ceiling.

"It's fine," Symphony said.

He offered her something to drink, and she said no thanks and asked to use his bathroom. He told her where to find it and opened a can of sparkling water, then sat at the dining room table. After a second, he got up and grabbed a dish towel to dust off the top.

When Symphony came out, she stopped to look at the things in the bookcase pushed against the wall behind the couch. He had a few books, some photos in frames, an old typewriter he found at a garage sale. On top was the orange and white helmet his grandfather wore as a pilot in the navy.

"I guess this answers my question of how well you knew my brother." Symphony held up a photo of him and Marcus leaning toward each other from separate blue beach chairs. A vendor had taken it in Puerto Vallarta after they bought the last two grilled fish and lime skewers from him. Both of them shirtless. Sunglasses. Half-empty Coronas. Sandy feet.

Packard didn't say anything. Just looked at her.

"Why do you keep staring at me like that?" Symphony asked.

"Like I've seen a ghost?"

"Exactly."

"You look so much like him." She was tall like Marcus. Not as tall but tall for a woman. She had a pitted complexion, similar to Marcus's that he spent a fortune babying with serums and lotions. She was wearing black leggings and a blue T-shirt that was stretched out at the neck and loose around her hips. A print scarf was knotted at the back of her head.

"Did he ever talk about me?" Symphony asked.

"He told me everyone in his family was dead."

Symphony stared at the photo in her hand and put it back on the shelf. He waited for some kind of reaction. She didn't say anything. She came to the table and sat across from him.

"If you didn't look so much like him, I'd question your claim of being his sister. There's no doubt in my mind you are who you say you are. Why would he tell me you were dead?"

"The last time we talked, I told him I didn't want to see him anymore."

"What happened?"

Symphony shrugged. She took the handkerchief from her back pocket again and mopped her face and wiped the moisture collecting in the crease in her neck.

"I didn't come up here to tell you my life story. I came to find out about my brother."

"How'd you get my name?" Packard asked.

"Asked some cops in Minneapolis. Other cops in Saint Paul. Found some of his friends. Your name kept coming up so I looked you up online. You been in the news. Something about an old man who kept women locked in his basement. Said you were a sheriff's deputy in Sandy Lake County. Your address is in the phone book."

Small towns and their small phone books. He didn't even have a landline and somehow he still ended up in the book. He didn't mind. The locals already knew where he lived, knew about the gay deputy who ran for sheriff and lost, who swam in the lake until the water iced over, who found the remains of his brother after he'd gone missing for thirty years.

Sandy Lake was a long way to drive from Minneapolis. The car she was driving was registered in Minneapolis, but there was a Southern touch to her voice that made him think she'd come farther than that.

"You found me," he said, smiling. He had questions but he didn't want to interrogate her. He wanted to know what her questions were. She had a reason for coming all this way when the same Google search that pointed her to Sandy Lake would easily have given her his work number.

"How did you know my brother?" she asked.

He told her that he and Marcus met at the Minneapolis police academy. They were the same height and build, same buzzed haircuts, same intense personalities. The other recruits in their class called them the Twins, even though Marcus was as black as Packard was white.

"Did you work together?"

"Not really. After the academy, he went to work in one precinct, and I was in another. We'd meet at the gym and work out sometimes."

The way Symphony looked at him made him feel like he was the one who had to convince her of the things he was saying. Her eyes moved all over him like she was watching for the lie, the slip that would give him away. It was so quiet Packard could hear the carbonation fizz in his drink.

"Where did he live?"

"He had a house in Saint Paul. In Frogtown. Wasn't the best neighborhood but he wanted to live where he worked. He wanted to be an example and a resource for the people from that area."

"He never married. Didn't have any kids that I could find out about."

Packard didn't say anything. Just shook his head.

"Did he have a girlfriend?"

"No girlfriend," Packard said.

Symphony looked like she found that hard to believe. "Are you telling me his job was his whole life? He had nothing else going on? And then he got killed?"

Before Packard could respond, she asked, "Was anyone with him when he died?"

Packard knew more details about Marcus's death than he wanted. He'd seen the autopsy report and diagrams. He could have told her everything. How a man had called 911 and reported a domestic incident after already killing his pregnant girlfriend. How he was waiting for the police when they showed up. How he shot Marcus in the head from a second-story window with an AR-15.

"Your brother died instantly. I doubt he even knew what hit him. I do know he loved being a cop more than just about anything in the world. For him, the job was about building community. He wanted to talk to people and get people to talk to each other before they resorted to pulling guns. He wanted kids to know they had options."

"And how do you know all this?"

"What do you mean?"

"I mean who are you? Why does your name keep coming up when I ask around about my brother? Why's your name come up when I ask what happened to his house and all his things after he died? Why you got his Marvin Gaye record over there?"

They both looked at his turntable where the record sleeve for *What's Going On* was propped in a stand that said Now Playing at the bottom. Marvin in a wet raincoat with a big collar looking up and to the side, almost directly at the initials "MK" Marcus had drawn in black ink in the top corner. It was the last thing Packard had listened to before the storm hit.

"I got more than that," Packard said. "I got all his records. I got his badge. I had his dog." Jarrett. A golden retriever who had kept him company those first lonely years in Sandy Lake.

"So let me ask again. Who? Are? You?" She leaned toward him and opened her eyes a bit wider.

He knew what she meant. Had known since she asked about the girlfriend. Knew that she already knew the answer to her own question.

"Marcus and I were in a relationship."

There was a long moment of silence. Packard felt the heat in the room, hot as an attic.

Symphony unfolded and folded the handkerchief in her lap. She leaned back. "You had a relationship. You mean like…like homos?"

"Just like homos."

Symphony wiped at her face and throat again. "Nah. Uh-uh. My brother had girlfriends when we were younger. Lots of them."

Packard turned his palms up. "I had a high school girlfriend, too."

Symphony hung her head and messed with the knot in her scarf. "My brother wasn't like that."

Her brother was exactly like that. If this was about winning an argument, Packard could have described in explicit detail all the ways he knew her brother to be exactly like that.

"We dated for a little over a year. Never lived together. When Marcus switched to the Saint Paul police, he made me beneficiary on all his forms. He had a simple will that asked me to take care of all his possessions in the event of his death. I knew nothing about it until he was killed."

For the sake of their careers, they had kept their relationship hidden from everyone they knew. They never talked about what they were doing or tried to put a name on it. It was hard for Packard to look back now and assess it objectively. They might have been moving toward something. Packard might have been lowering his resistance to the idea of a relationship. Or was that what he wanted to think about himself through the lens of Marcus's death? Maybe they had reached a plateau. Maybe they had been drifting apart when Marcus moved to Saint Paul. He couldn't remember. A thing without a name has no definition. Over time it loses its shape until you're not sure what you're looking at anymore.

Symphony stood up and walked to the turntable and picked up the Marvin Gaye sleeve. She stood with a hand pressed into the small of her back while she flipped the sleeve over and looked at the back.

"I've got more of his records in those bins if you want to take a look."

"I don't give a damn about records."

"Symphony, why did you drive all this way? What are you looking for? What can I tell you about Marcus?"

When she spun around to look at him her eyes were narrow, her mouth tight. "I wanted to hear something good about my brother. That he had a life and a family and was happy before he died. Not some bullshit about him being a cocksucker."

She set the record down and cut across the room, heading for the door.

"I can tell you a lot of things about Marcus that have nothing to do with… that. That's you using that language."

She stopped at the front door and threw him another angry look. She opened the door.

"Symphony, don't go," he pleaded. "Let me make us something to eat. Or we can go out. Just stay. Let's talk about Marcus."

She waved a hand by her ear and shook her head. "No. No. No. None of that."

Packard was sweating. He was seasick with the emotions she'd churned up. Since laying eyes on her, he felt like he'd been watching a quick-cut trailer of all his time with Marcus—the action, the drama, the quiet devastation. She wanted to know about her brother. He wanted to calm the waters rocking both of them.

"Symphony, why would he tell me that you were dead?"

Her voice shook with effort to control it. "Because I told him to forget about me," she said, talking to the door in front of her. "I told him to pretend I was dead and leave me be."

The door slammed behind her. Packard slowly got up from the table and went to the front window in time to see her back out of the driveway. It was dark. The car's one working headlight swept past him like a lighthouse lamp.

Packard let Frank out of the garage and they sat on the couch pushed out of its normal spot in this wrecked room. The quiet was immense, the sound of Frank panting like a metronome. A bit of attic insulation drifted down from the hole in the ceiling. Packard still hadn't eaten but the emptiness he felt wasn't from his stomach. It was all around him. It was a cavity that swelled in his chest when he took a deep breath.

He felt like something had been taken from him. Again.

CHAPTER SEVEN

THURSDAY

AIR QUALITY INDEX: YELLOW (MODERATE)

The next shift debrief meeting was at 6:00 a.m. Packard woke up at 4:30 and felt the bad air he'd breathed all night in the back of his dry throat and in the rattling snot when he blew his nose. He went down to the lake with Frank and swam in the dark in water warm enough to bathe in. The lake got more direct sun since the storm and one end was full of sodden leaves. The owl nest he'd been watching the last couple of years was gone. Of all that had been lost, he might have missed it the most.

After Symphony left, he'd grilled a couple of brats and pushed away thoughts of Marcus by reading through Reynolds's report on Noah Turner's car being vandalized at a bonfire party. It was at the home of a popular kid. Dozens of high schoolers were there. The parents were home but not exactly supervising. In the video from the home's security system Packard saw plumes from vape pens and cigarettes. He saw a lot of heavy eyelids and sideways steps that made him think most of the kids were high on one thing or another.

The vandalism started with three guys in hoodies circling Noah's car. They must have seen something on it or known it was his. One of them had a bottle of white shoe polish and wrote the word FAG in tall skinny letters the entire length of the car hood. Packard heard laughter and *dude* and *gimme that fucking polish.* He couldn't always see what they were writing when it was on the side away from the camera. He saw BITCH and HOMO.

One of the boys drew a face in profile with an open mouth and a crude penis pointed at it. Another one tried to draw a swastika but got the directions of the arms mixed up and drew something that looked like an idiot playing Tetris. A crowd grew around the car as more people gathered to see what all the laughter was about. Somewhere a voice was chanting, *Faggot!...Faggot!... Faggot!* The kids milled about beneath an ash tree and sucked on their vapes and recorded on their phones and generally appeared in need of someone with fully developed frontal cortex to tell them what to do.

When the shoe polish ran out, a face Packard knew well used a pocketknife to scratch a penis across both doors, then smashed a taillight with the heel of his boot. Packard slowed down the video. In slow motion, the cheers and the laughter sounded like the baying of animals.

A couple of kids tried to intervene. They pushed people away from the car. They got pushed back twice as hard. Packard watched another video that had been collected from someone's phone that showed Noah appearing from the backyard. When he saw his car, he covered his mouth with his hands. Same painted fingernails and stack of friendship bracelets Packard had seen yesterday. A girl hugged him. Someone said the polish would wash off. Someone else said, *They're just messing with ya.* Packard saw every emotion wash across Noah's face, depending on who or what he was looking at. He didn't know if he was being bullied or hazed or about to get his ass kicked or what.

Eventually an adult came outside and stood next to the car with his hands on his hips, shaking his head. He said, "I hope you idiots know that all this has been captured on camera." He turned and pointed back toward the house.

Reynolds's report had a list of names and ages of the people at the party. There were screenshots from the video identifying the people who vandalized the car. There was a written account of a meeting between responding deputies and the school board. Another report of a meeting with Noah's parents. Two of the vandals were older than eighteen, and Ashley Turner made it clear she wanted everyone involved charged and treated like adults.

Packard knew one of the vandals by name. Darrel Johnson was as ugly and poisonous as a snakebite. Was the threat of being charged with vandalism enough to make him kill Ashley Turner? Murder seemed like an overreaction to the mild civil and fiscal penalties he faced but Packard knew better than to assume Darrel Johnson had even an ounce of common sense.

Packard backed up the video, thought about Ashley's stab wounds, and watched as Darrel used a pocketknife to vandalize Noah's car.

Packard arrived at the sheriff's office just as both shifts crowded into the conference room for the debrief meeting. He stood in the corner in the front while the shift supervisor called everyone to order. Reynolds came in at the last minute and stood in the back. The supervisor read out the assignments for the day that had nothing to do with Ashley Turner, reminded people of upcoming training due dates, and then turned things over to Packard.

"Night shift, tell me what you got done."

Reynolds spoke up first. "We typed the blood found at the scene. There's definitely blood from two people. Ashley Turner is O positive. The blood found outside came back A positive. We've submitted the A positive for DNA testing but we can't expect results anytime soon. There's a huge backlog at the state lab."

"I stopped at the hospital. Called the other ones you wanted," said one of the deputies. "No one came in with a knife wound, a deep cut, or looking like they'd been stabbed. Closest was a lady who took the tip of her thumb off using a mandoline. Not the musical instrument. One of those slicer things."

Another deputy said she'd collected video recordings from three properties within the search area. "Not a lot of video doorbells out that way. Or I should say not a lot with cameras pointing at the road. There were maybe another four or five but they pointed at the side yard so I didn't collect them."

The owners of businesses with security systems had been contacted and left instructions for uploading their video data to the department's secure server. A lot of them were experienced with requests from the sheriff's office and were happy to share what they had.

Reynolds spoke up from the back. "I interviewed as many people as I could on either side of the Turners. A lot of empty homes. It's the middle of the week so a lot of the weekenders aren't here. The few people I talked to couldn't recall any strange vehicles or people. We took a dog through the Turners' house, then back outside. He went to the end of the driveway and lost the scent."

Packard nodded. This case felt like a rope being pulled through his hand. He needed a knot to grab on to.

"Anything else? Any stops? Any interesting interactions?"

The shift supervisor spoke up. "We booked two in the jail last night. A D&D that we picked up at Bob's Bar. Carlson, want to tell us about the other one?"

Amy Carlson had recently transitioned from dispatch operator to patrol deputy. She was in her late thirties and had been hardened by a decade in the chair. She was no-nonsense but loved working with the public. "I initiated a stop for an equipment violation. Tabs were expired."

Packard had a sudden sinking feeling in his stomach.

"The driver was antagonistic," Carlson said. "Didn't want to provide me with ID. Eventually admitted she didn't have a license. When I finally got a name and address out of her, it came back that she was on parole and far from home."

"What's her name?" Packard asked.

"Symphony Kendricks."

"Goddamnit."

The Sandy Lake Sheriff's Office had six holding cells for short-term stays, mostly used by drunks sleeping it off or inmates from the jail in the next county who had been brought back to Sandy Lake for trial.

Only two of the holding cells were occupied. From one of them came the heavy sound of someone snoring. Packard looked in at a middle-aged man in a black T-shirt, flat on his back, mouth wide open. The drunk and disorderly guy from Bob's.

Packard looked through the window of the next cell and unlocked the door.

Symphony took one look at him and rolled her eyes like he was the last person she wanted to see. She was sitting on a cement bunk with a thin green pad beneath her. They'd taken away her headscarf. Her hair was short and thin and gray.

"This your doing?" she asked.

"My doing?"

"I wasn't five miles down the road before your girl swooped in. You put her on me."

"Symphony, you couldn't be more mistaken. I know you were upset when you left last night, but I've got no ill will toward you at all. Just the opposite."

She looked like she didn't believe him or that it didn't matter. She pulled at the stretched-out collar of her T-shirt. In her hand was a wad of jail-cell toilet paper that she used to wipe the top of her chest.

"Please, come out," Packard said. "Let's get this cleared up."

She got up slowly from the bench. He led her out of the cell, out of the processing area, back to his office. "Are you hungry? I have Clif Bars here in my desk. There's yogurt in the fridge. I can get you coffee."

"Just water," she said. Then as he was walking out the door, "And a yogurt."

He came back with both and closed his door.

"I'm sorry you got arrested. Everyone is on high alert. We had a woman killed in her home in broad daylight yesterday. All eyes are wide open for anything out of the ordinary."

Symphony didn't respond. She had her attention directed toward opening and stirring her yogurt.

"First things first," Packard said. "I heard you're on parole. What are the terms?"

"Can't leave the state without permission."

"Did you get permission?"

Symphony put the spoon in her mouth upside down and pulled it out clean. "What do you think?"

"Where do you live?"

"St. Louis."

"Do you have a phone number for your PO?"

"In my phone."

Packard called the processing desk and asked for Symphony's things to be brought to his office. "Bring the sheet. I'll sign it out."

They sat in silence. He could smell the hours in the car, the long night in jail with no sleep on her. Symphony ate her yogurt down to the spoon-scraping bottom, and then a deputy knocked on the door and handed Packard a plastic bag with a phone and a ring, car keys and some folded bills and her headscarf inside. Packard signed on the clipboard. "Find out where her car is. If there's still an open tow order on it, cancel it. I'll take care of it."

Packard handed Symphony her things and asked her to look up the number for her PO. He stabbed the number into his desk phone as she read it out.

"This is Benton."

"Officer Benton, this is Deputy Ben Packard calling from Sandy Lake County, Minnesota."

"Yeah. I had a voicemail and report about one of my charges being arrested up your way."

"I've got you on speaker. I'm with Symphony right now."

He paused and looked at her, waiting for her to say something. She just blinked at him slowly.

"Symphony, the hell are you doing all the way up there? You know you're not supposed to leave the state without permission."

"You weren't supposed to find out," she said.

"Come on now. You know better than that."

"She actually came up to see me," Packard said. "I'm a family friend."

The subtle change in Symphony's expression made it clear she didn't appreciate hearing the words *family* or *friend* come out of his mouth.

Packard explained the mood in the county to Benton and the reason for Symphony's stop. "Any other night, she would have sailed right out of here with that broken headlight. We've had a nice visit. I'll get her turned around and headed back your way. I think a little grace in all directions might be called for under the circumstances."

"I'll think about it," Benton said. "Symphony, get your ass back here and come see me before I run out of grace. You hear me?"

"I hear you."

Packard hung up. He held up the garbage can from under his desk for Symphony to throw away her cup and spoon. "Let's go," he said.

"Where we going?"

"To get your car."

He drove them in a sheriff's SUV that was overdue for a trip to the car wash. The windshield outside the wiper's arc was dusty with ash from the Canadian fires and crusted with V-shaped bug splats. Another hot, hazy day was on deck. It was already 88 degrees at 8:00 a.m.

Symphony looked uncomfortable in the seat beside him, stiff like she was trying not to touch anything. She flinched when the dispatch operator suddenly called out a badge number over the radio. Packard turned the volume down.

"You want to tell me why you're on parole?"

Symphony sighed and sank into her seat. "Do I want to? No."

"Will you?"

She rolled her head against the headrest in his direction. "You don't know?"

"I don't."

"When we were sitting in your office waiting for that man to bring my things, you didn't look at my record on your computer?"

"Nope."

"Why not?"

It was a good question. Part of it was respecting her privacy. Law enforcement had access to all kinds of information about people. They were supposed to use restraint when accessing that information. Only as needed in relation to an incident. He wasn't the arresting officer who pulled Symphony over. Their shared connection to Marcus didn't give him the right to plumb the depths of her criminal record.

"I'd rather hear it from you. Whatever you want to tell me."

She sat silently and watched the road pass beneath them. After a mile or so he said, "You mentioned earlier you'd seen plenty of judges in your time. I didn't know what that meant at the time. Was it when you went to jail that you told Marcus to stop contacting you?"

"He said he didn't know how he could ever forgive me for what I did. I said I don't expect you to forgive me. I'm never going to forgive myself."

"What happened, Symphony?"

She stopped talking. A semitruck passed them going the other way and rocked their vehicle. Packard waited. He could see her car on the side of the road half a mile ahead of them.

"I was sick in my head," she said finally. "I heard voices. After I was arrested, they eventually diagnosed me with postpartum depression and schizophrenia."

"Arrested for what?"

A pause while she worked up the words. "I drowned my baby in the bathtub."

Packard believed that life was meant to be an interrogation—a deep questioning of everything you see or believe, are taught or told. Curiosity could be a blade or a shovel. In his job, he questioned people all the time and he knew when to push, how to layer question on top of question to get the answers he needed. He also knew when an answer was the truth distilled, when no amount of whys or what-fors would add to his understanding.

He pulled over behind the silver Honda Accord on the shoulder of the two-lane road. Deputy Carlson had written the date and time of the traffic stop in bright orange letters on the car's rear windshield. It reminded him of the vandalism to Noah Turner's car.

He had nothing to say in response to Symphony's revelation. It didn't matter that he was sorry. It didn't matter that it hurt his heart to hear such a thing. She didn't need his pity or his condolences. He thought of Thielen and all her aches and pains from being a new mother and what a very long trip it would be to a planet where she would decide to hurt her baby. He looked at Symphony and saw a woman who had gone there and come back and everything the journey had cost her.

"Do me a favor," Packard said. "Follow me back to my place."

"Why would I do that?"

"I'm guessing you didn't get any sleep, thanks to the guy snoring in the next cell. You're going to have an accident if you try to make the three-plus hour drive back to Minneapolis on no sleep. Come back to the house. You can shower if you want. You can get some sleep. I have work to do today but I want to drive you back to Minneapolis later this afternoon."

"What? You're crazy. Why you acting like I'm helpless?"

"I know you're not helpless. All I'm doing is offering the help I have to give."

"Why?"

"Because you're Marcus's sister."

"That don't make us nothing. You and me."

"I know it doesn't. Listen, you came all this way looking for answers about your brother. You don't have to believe me; you don't have to like what I have to say. I'm not going to stand on my head to try to convince you of what Marcus meant to me. I want to know about you. I want to know about Marcus through you. Let me help you with whatever it is you're looking for. We can do some of that on the drive back to Minneapolis."

Symphony still didn't look convinced. She looked exhausted. She shook the keys in her palm like they were dice.

"You want to drive off in that car, I'm not going to stop you. There's a lot of small towns between here and Minneapolis. You're a Black woman without a license driving a car with expired tabs and police markings on the windshield."

"And who are you supposed to be? My white savior?"

"I'm the cop who dated your brother and got you out of jail and wants to see you get home safely."

Symphony didn't say anything.

"I'm pretty sure there aren't any other cops who dated your brother in any of those small towns between here and Minneapolis."

Symphony cut her eyes at him, then looked away. He hoped for a smile. He didn't get one.

Packard reached for his wallet. "Come on. I'm going to do a U-turn. You do the same if you want to follow me. If you decide to drive off the other way, Godspeed. Here's my card. You can call me anytime."

Symphony took his card. She got out of his vehicle and walked to the Honda and got into it carefully like she was climbing into a sleeping bag. When her brake lights came on, he pulled out and turned around and drove slowly, watching what she would do in his rearview mirror.

"Come on, Symphony. Follow me."

The silver Honda idled. The gap between them grew.

"Come on."

Symphony pulled away from the shoulder, made a U-turn, and fell in behind him.

"Excellent. Let's go."

Back at the house he went in first and put Frank in the garage. He showed Symphony the guest bedroom and rolled the portable AC from his room to hers. He put clean towels in the hall bath.

In the bare-bones kitchen, he told her to help herself to anything in the fridge, in the cupboards.

"Believe it or not, the state of the kitchen has nothing to do with the storm. It always looks like this." Plywood countertops, rust-stained sink, cabinets without doors, the old linoleum scraped down to the subfloor. "It's the last room waiting to be remodeled. I thought I'd get to it this fall, but now it looks like I'll be fixing the living room instead."

Symphony nodded through it all. He could see the urge to collapse take her over like her bones were softening.

"I know you don't like dogs. I'm going to take Frank with me, so you don't have to worry about him. I'll try to be back before 5:00 p.m. We'll jump in the car and take off for Minneapolis right away."

"How are you going to get home if we're driving my car?"

"Let me worry about that. You have my number. Call or text if you need anything."

CHAPTER EIGHT

In the truck with Frank, he called Lisa Washington, the local attorney.

"You in the office?"

"Yes," she said.

"Got time to meet with me if I stop by in half an hour?"

"Yes. Want to tell me what it's about?"

"I'll tell you when I get there."

"I swear to god, Packard. One of these days I'm going to remember to ask what you want before I agree to meet."

"But not today," he said and hung up.

Symphony was frightened of dogs and his normal dog sitter was on vacation. Thielen had a new baby and didn't need anything else on her plate. That left only one other option.

The clock on Packard's dash said it was after nine. His morning had been consumed by dealing with Symphony and now his dog. Meanwhile, whoever killed Ashley Turner was getting farther away, or closer to getting away with it.

Packard had to remind himself that he wasn't the only one working this case, that his life didn't stop when someone else's did. Even in the slowest times, he was never working on just one thing. He had a squad of deputies out collecting information.

Packard pulled up in front of a yellow house with green trim. The last time he'd been here, there'd been a wheelchair ramp. It was gone, leaving three concrete steps with flower beds on either side. A big, bearded man in dirty black jeans came out the front door with a white pit bull at his heels.

"Honey, you should've called. I'da put on a fresh pot of coffee."

"Sorry, Gary. I was making calls all the way here and pulled up before I realized I forgot to tell you I was coming."

Gary Bushwright lit a cigarette while Packard helped Frank down from the truck. The corgi ran straight to the man who had rescued him from a filthy breeder's farm years ago and who always had dog treats in his pocket. "How are my favorite boys?" Gary asked, squatting to pet Frank.

"Busy," Packard said. "I need to board this guy for a few days. I just caught another homicide case. I think it's going to be long days and nights for a while and my dog sitter is on an Alaskan cruise. I also have a houseguest who's afraid of dogs."

Gary put fingers on either side of his mouth. "Is it a lover?" he asked.

"No, Gary. Not a lover."

Gary was of another generation. Late sixties, if Packard had to guess. Grew up in Sandy Lake before moving to California as a teenager. He'd been working as a florist when he picked up a trick at a bar who couldn't believe what Gary was packing and also happened to be a photographer. His nude photos of Gary ended up in magazines, which eventually led to Gary filming gay porn movies, working as an escort, and traveling around the world with rich men and their drugs. Gary saw the best minds of his generation die of AIDS in the eighties and nineties, and finally decided to get out of the scene. He was a truck driver for years. Eventually, he came home to take care of his elderly mother and open a dog rescue.

"How long will Frank be with us?" Gary asked.

"Just a few days, I hope. I'll pay for however long it ends up being."

"There's no bill. Frank doesn't get kenneled here. He'll be in the house with me and Baxter."

"Come on, Gary. You have to make money."

Gary's dog rescue and kenneling service was called Gary's Kids. He ran it out of a large aluminum building behind his house.

"Honey, I just got back from the Gay Adult Video Awards in Las Vegas. Do you know how many people will pay $75 to have a photo with me and a signed pic? Hundreds! A thousand people maybe."

"I didn't know you made appearances like that."

"I didn't for a long time. A couple of years ago I decided to embrace the current industry. A lot of people can't believe I'm still alive or that I used to be Johnny Hardwood." Gary ran his hand down his beard and gathered it together. "I don't want to brag but I'm a bit of a legend."

"You're the Bigfoot of gay porn."

"I'm the big something. Speaking of, I also got a nice check from an adult novelty company for licensing my likeness."

"What do you mean, your likeness? Pictures of you?"

"No," Gary said, looking down at his crotch. "My likeness."

Packard felt himself turning red and it wasn't from the heat. "I see. I got it," he said, coughing.

"In three months, anyone who wants a silicone version of Johnny Hardwood can buy one for themselves. They had me lie down and used lasers to scan my—"

"Okay, Gary. I can imagine."

Packard got down on his haunches and called to Frank who came over and let himself be hugged and scratched before beelining back to Gary for another treat.

"How's Cora been?"

They both looked at the blue house with the three-car garage just down the road from Gary's.

"We've established a fragile peace since her husband died."

Cora and Gary had been involved in a holy war for years. Cora was an evangelical who didn't like living next door to a flaming homosexual (and she didn't even know about his sex work). Cora lived with her daughter, Greta, who took after her dark, lumbering giant of a father. The two of them had taunted Gary with signs and vandalism and shouted Bible verses. Gary sassed 'em right back.

"Did you know they're both running the garage business now?"

"I did not," Packard said.

Gary lowered his voice and turned his back to Cora's house. "Turns out that shaved yak of a daughter of hers knows as much about fixing cars as her old man did. Cora's doing the books. I heard they're renaming the business Our Savior's Auto Repair."

Packard and Gary raised their eyebrows at each other and broke up laughing. "Good for them," Packard said. "I'm glad you're all too busy to harass each other anymore. I gotta run. I'll be in touch. Hopefully it won't be more than a couple of days."

"Honey, you know Frank is welcome here as long as necessary. Don't worry about him. You be careful out there."

Back to town after dropping off Frank. The air was yellow, same as the air quality rating.

When Packard got to the law offices of Wiley, Washington & Prentis, he found Lisa Washington behind her desk, dressed for court with a suit jacket over the back of her chair. Her thick brown hair was pulled back in a ponytail. She had on computer glasses and was glaring at her laptop. He closed the door and sat down.

"What are you working on?" he asked.

"The people out at the mobile home park have the biggest mess on their hands."

"They had a lot of damage from the storm out there," Packard said.

"Their connection to the sewer system got washed out and needs to be repaired. They're not supposed to be running water or flushing their toilets, but of course they are. Some of them are still without electricity." She took off her glasses. "Do you know who actually owns the park?"

"I don't."

"A private equity firm in Atlanta."

"What does private equity want with a mobile home park in Minnesota?"

"They want mobile home parks all over the place. They buy them, cut amenities, and delay repairs, all while slowly raising the rent on those who can least afford it. People in that park own their home but they don't own the land it sits on. It costs a fortune to move a mobile home, so when the rent goes up, they're trapped."

"Can you help them?"

"I can help them organize. And I can help them escrow their payments until these investor buttholes make the place livable again."

"Should be against the law to be a butthole," Packard said.

Lisa put her glasses back on, clicked her mouse a couple of times, then closed her laptop. "You didn't come here for a lecture on the evils of private capital. What do you need?" she asked.

"Ashley Turner."

Lisa nodded. "I know who that is."

"She was killed yesterday. Stabbed in the chest several times."

Lisa, who had seen and heard some shit in all her years as a public defender, looked genuinely shocked. "What on earth?" she said. Her head made a small movement side to side. "Any leads?"

"Working on it," he said.

He could see the cogs turning behind her eyes, spinning, spinning, wondering what he knew, comparing it to what she knew. "When I asked her husband, Tom, if anything out of the ordinary happened recently, the only thing he could think of was their son's car being vandalized."

Lisa nodded.

"I watched some of the video from the party. The report said Ashley wanted charges filed. Tom said she was thinking about suing the school district."

"I've seen the video. She's definitely got enough for a civil case against the three who did all the damage to the car. It's up to the county attorney to decide if there will be criminal charges. If charges are filed, it's likely going to be someone from our office who will end up on the defense."

"How would you defend those kids?"

"I would try to get a plea deal and keep it from going to court in the first place. The ones who are eighteen especially need to realize no attorney can get them off with what's shown in the video."

"I know one of them by name and reputation. He's getting a visit from me later today."

"Do you really think these car vandals could be responsible for killing Ashley?"

"It's been less than twenty-four hours since she was killed. No one is ruled out at this point."

"Killing her wouldn't have any impact on whether charges get filed."

"Do idiots who vandalize a car in front of a crowd filming everything with their cell phones know that?"

Lisa shrugged. "Probably not."

"How far did the talk about suing the school district get?"

"Not far. I did some research on existing case law. This incident happened off campus and after hours, and you can't hold the school liable for that. She said there'd been other incidents that were on school grounds. When I asked if I could meet with both her and Noah to talk about the incidents, she said he wouldn't cooperate. He was adamantly against what his mom wanted to do."

"Was that the end of it?"

"We had a couple of meetings. I told her my concerns. I think what she wanted more than anything was for the school to hold the kids accountable. She wanted there to be zero tolerance and some kind of consequences for bullying."

"Did you take any meetings with school administrators on her behalf?"

"Nope. We never got to the point where I was her lawyer or representing her in any way."

"Anyone reach out to you because they heard the school might get sued?"

"No."

"When was the last time you talked to Ashley?"

"Over a month ago. I can check my logs and tell you the date and time for sure if you need it."

"Email me," Packard said.

Lisa asked after Thielen and the baby, and Packard asked after Lisa's father, Ray Wiley, who opened this law practice on his own more than forty years ago. Lisa's sister, Robin, was married to Howard Shepard, which made Ray the sheriff's father-in-law. Packard's last big case—the death of an old woman and the use of her identity to commit fraud—had put him and Ray in opposing corners.

"Dad's not great," Lisa said. "His macular degeneration is getting worse. He can barely see but still thinks he should be able to drive. I'm trying to get his license revoked and he's furious at me. He's a car accident or a broken hip away from needing some kind of assisted living."

"He'll get plenty of assistance in jail if he kills someone with his car."

"I said those exact words to him!" Lisa said, leaning forward. "So frustrating."

"Sorry to hear that. I can ask patrol to keep an eye on him if they see him on the road."

Everybody in town knew Ray Wiley drove a black BMW with a personalized ATT RNY plate.

"That would be good. I'd appreciate it."

From Lisa's law office in downtown Sandy Lake, Packard headed south to where the county was a patchwork of boggy, uncleared land and farm fields. The

Johnson family lived off a dirt road in a dark-gray modular house set alongside a large shed that faced the road. A pair of dirt tracks ran past the shed and disappeared into the forest behind it. Packard knew the Johnsons had a private gun range back there wrapped in trees. Beyond that were fields of sugar beets.

Steel poles with metal chain strung between them staked out something of a weedy yard and directed Packard to the other side of the shed. Above the wide door and beneath the peak of the roof a red sign declared PRIVATE PROPERTY—NO TRESPASSING. The collection of stuff circling the building on all sides looked like a junkyard had a baby with a flea market. Packard saw stacks of wooden pallets, an old John Deere yard tractor, rusty lawn mowers, used tires, a trailer with a rotten wooden bed, garbage cans full of long tool handles, five-gallon buckets stacked and overturned, and blue tarps covering piles of who knew what. Behind the garage was a pontoon sitting on cement blocks and an old RV with flat tires and curtains pulled across its windows. Off by itself was a rusted burn barrel with smoke coming out of the top. Like the air wasn't dirty enough.

Packard stopped behind a pickup truck with a rear rack and aluminum ladders strapped to the top and a faded yellow DON'T TREAD ON ME bumper sticker. Just beyond the trailer, a tall pine tree that had once shaded the house had blown down in the storm. Rainwater filled the massive hole created when its roots let go.

Dennis Johnson came out of the trailer wearing splattered white painter's pants and a green T-shirt. He had a beer belly and wiry gray hair. He was a quiet but angry member of a growing demographic in the area of middle-aged white men who were fed up with contemporary living. They didn't fault the self-dealing politicians who were convicted con artists, who lied to their faces, and who manipulated the system to maintain their own wealth and power. Guys like Dennis blamed the Deep State, the Illuminati, Jews. They were primed to hate the Other—immigrants, Blacks, queers, trans kids—by the people with the power who were using it to push working-class men lower into the mud and hoard the wealth for themselves.

Law enforcement wasn't immune to this manipulation. Packard regularly saw how exposure to the worst of human behavior turned his fellow officers against the very people they had sworn to protect. Putting that kind of hate in a uniform gave it a dangerous legitimacy.

"Good thing the wind wasn't blowing the other direction," Packard said, getting out of his vehicle. "That pine tree might be sitting in your living room."

Dennis nodded. "Yeah, we got lucky for once. Could've been worse."

Packard was already sweating under the lightweight body armor he was wearing. He felt beads of perspiration form along his hairline. The foul air smelled like hot electronics.

"I'm looking for Darrel. He around?"

"In the house," Dennis said. He picked up a five-gallon bucket by the handle with both hands and heaved it into the back of his truck. Dennis had his own house-painting business. Packard had heard from several people that they'd never seen anyone cut around doors and windows cleaner or paint a room faster than Dennis Johnson.

Just then the screen door pushed open and Darrel Johnson leaned halfway out. He had a pistol in his hand pressed flat against the door. Packard's hand went reflexively to his hip and slid back the holster guard. He immediately thought about the last time he'd had to confront a man with a gun, back when he was working court security. He had to kill that man. He was ready to do it again if Darrel Johnson was planning something stupid.

"What the fuck do you want? Can't you read?" Darrel said, nodding at the sign over the garage.

Dennis spoke up before Packard could. "Boy, you better get back in that house and put that gun away before I come in there and break your other leg."

Darrel gave Packard a dead-eyed look. He had a wad of chew in his lower lip. He spit to the side and backed away. The door wheezed shut on its piston.

Dennis shook out a cigarette from the pack in his shirt pocket and lit it. Packard was still on high alert. He heard dragonflies hum in the air like a miniature military and felt his eye drawn to a trio of wasps with their pointy wings thrown up, drinking water collected in an overturned bucket.

“What’s he been up to lately?” Packard asked, nodding at the house. He reengaged the guard on his holster.

“He ain’t been up to shit. Dumbass got so high smoking his goddamn vape thing that he stepped off a ladder and broke his leg.”

“He been working for you?”

“Calling it work would be generous,” Dennis said. The smoke from his cigarette was thick as fog in the humidity and didn’t drift away.

“When did he break his leg?”

“Week ago. Been laying on that couch ever since he got home from the hospital. Good thing he can wipe his own ass ’cause I sure as hell wouldn’t be doing it for him.”

Laid up for a week with a broken leg made it unlikely that Darrel Johnson stabbed Ashley Turner and then crutched away. Packard wanted to go inside the house like he wanted to finish Dennis’s cigarette. He needed to see for himself just to be sure.

“You got another boy, don’t you?”

“Yeah. He’s in the Cities with his aunt. Robot camp. Lego something. I don’t know what the fuck. Kid’s too goddamn smart for his own good.”

Kid was going to have to be extra smart if he hoped to break away from here and not end up like his older brother.

“You mind securing that gun before I go in there?” Packard asked. “He’s less likely to shoot you than me if one of us walks through that door.”

Dennis looked like Packard had asked him to do his job for him. “It ain’t the only gun in there.”

“I know.” Dennis Johnson probably had more guns than he had empty five-gallon buckets and he had a lot of those. “If it’s the only one within reach, I’m fine with that.”

“All right then. But I ain’t got time to stand around while you two shoot the shit. Somebody has to work around here.” He tucked the cigarette into the corner of his mouth and climbed the four steps up to the door.

Packard heard him ask *Where’s that fucking gun at?* as the storm door eased shut behind him. A few seconds later Dennis stood at the top of the stairs while he released the clip and ejected the round in the chamber. He tried to catch it in midair but fumbled. The shell landed in the dirt at the bottom of the stairs. Packard picked it up and handed it to Dennis and then traded places with him in the doorway.

Darrel, unshaven, barefoot, and ripe-smelling, was stretched out on a pleather couch draped in a threadbare bedsheet. His broken leg was elevated by a shoebox with a towel folded on top of it. He had a greasy pillow behind his head and was wearing cargo shorts and a black T-shirt decorated with an American flag. A wheezing window air conditioner behind him was already losing the battle against the heat of the day.

"The fuck do you want?" Darrel asked. He pointed a remote at the TV.

Packard stood over Darrel with his arms crossed. He heard Dennis's truck start and the sound of its engine as he drove in a circle around the house and out to the road. "I was just thinking it's been a while. The last time I saw you was in Principal Overby's office when I was trying to find Jenny Wheeler and Jesse Crawford."

"So what? You come look me up now that I'm an adult so you can suck my dick?"

"The thought never crossed my mind. It's a thought that's never going to cross the mind of anyone with eyes. Look at you. You're a mess."

"You try showering with your leg in a cast."

"I'm not talking about showering. I'm talking about who you are. Who you've decided to be."

"Fuck off, why don't you?"

"I will. First we need to talk about the party from a couple of months ago. The one where you trashed that kid's car."

For just a second a wary worry broke through Darrel's tough-guy facade.

"I can tell you've been waiting to hear from someone about that."

Darrel shrugged. "We fucked up that faggot's car. It's all on video. No point in denying it."

"What were you even doing there? You graduated last year. Why are you still hanging out with high school kids?"

Darrel didn't say anything. He pointed the remote at the TV and scrolled through the channel menu.

"This is what I'm talking about. You're the guy who learned nothing in school, who barely graduated, and now has no job, which gives you plenty of time to crash high school parties in hopes that maybe someone there remembers you and still thinks you're cool. Pathetic, isn't it?"

"Packard, you wouldn't know cool if it slapped you in the face with its dick."

"You're right about that. I don't have to be cool. I don't have to know what's cool. I'm tall and good-looking and give zero fucks what other people think. You'll never know what that feels like."

Darrel pushed himself up with an elbow and half turned to adjust the pillow behind him. "Seriously, Packard. What the fuck do you want? I'm trying to watch this fucking movie."

"I want to know why that kid? Of all the people at the party, all the cars parked in that driveway. Why that one?"

Darrel ignored the question.

"It's because the skinny gay kid with the fingernail polish isn't likely to fight back. You're bigger than him. He's outnumbered in any setting. Am I right?"

"Sure."

The heat and the odor of the place were getting to Packard. It smelled like cigarettes and hot garbage and unwashed everything. Darrel's hate felt like something black growing in the walls. "What else?"

"I did it because I wanted to. Because it was funny. Flaming faggot like that around these parts is asking for it."

"No, he's not. He's asking for you not to be a piece of shit. He's asking to be left alone so he can have fun at a party with his friends like everyone else."

"Asked and answered, I guess," Darrel said. He pointed the remote at the TV to turn up the volume. Packard snatched it out of his hand and muted it.

"Someone stabbed that kid's mom to death yesterday."

Packard waited to see what Darrel would say. He just stared at the mute TV. His tongue probed the wad of chew in his lip.

"Where were you around one o'clock yesterday afternoon?"

"Where the fuck do you think I was? I was right here, doing exactly this. I can't drive with this fucking cast on. Haven't been out of this house in a week."

"What about the other two idiots that were captured on video messing with the car? They friends of yours? You seen them lately?"

"They've been gone all summer. One of them is driving a truck with his dad. The other one got a summer job down in Florida at a dive shop."

"Good to hear. They'll have money to pay the restitution the three of you owe Noah Turner for trashing his car."

"I don't owe anybody shit. I ain't been charged with nothing."

Packard chuckled. "You will be. Trust me on that. If you don't have the money, the state will garnish your wages and you'll work for free until you pay it off."

If Darrel could have sunk deeper into the couch, he would have. He sighed and reached down and picked up a Coke can on the floor beside him and spit into it.

Packard had what he came for. Darrel had saved him the trouble of following up with the other two vandals now that he knew they'd both been gone all summer. He could start looking elsewhere for Ashley's killer. There was just one last thing.

In front of the couch was a coffee table littered with empty cans, a dirty plate, an ashtray, and a bunch of wadded tissues. Packard hooked his boot around a spindly leg, yanked the table out of place, and stepped into the spot where it sat. Darrel tried to sit up but Packard quickly got both of his wrists in his right hand and pushed him back. He put his left hand on Darrel's cast right at the knee and leaned on it.

Darrel squirmed and cried out. "Heyheyhey!"

"The next time you feel like bullying a faggot, you come and see me. I'll beat your ass," Packard said, leaning in close enough that he could smell the peppermint flavor of Darrel's chew and his bad breath behind it. "Don't believe me? Fuck around and find out. I dare you."

He let go of Darrel and stepped back.

Darrel struggled to sit up and adjust his broken leg on its prop. "Someone's gonna kill you one of these days, Packard, and I'm gonna laugh when they do."

Packard pushed the front door open. It felt like it had gotten hotter out while he'd been inside. "You might be right," he said to Darrel as he put his sunglasses on. "Key word being *someone*. Not you. I don't have a thing to worry about from you."

CHAPTER NINE

Packard drove in a circle around the Johnson family home and back out to the dirt road. The inside of his vehicle had reached oven-like temperatures. He lowered the windows, turned up the AC, and stopped at a stop sign a quarter mile down the road.

He wasn't proud of his behavior back there. Keeping his cool was part of the job. So was treating everyone with respect. Sticking up for what he thought was right by being an asshole made him no different than everyone else in the world screaming in each other's faces. It wasn't like him.

He took out his phone and called Reynolds. "Sorry for running out on the shift meeting this morning. I know the woman who got arrested last night. I had to take care of that."

"No worries," Reynolds said. "Everyone got their assignments."

Reynolds said he and another deputy were slowly working their way through the list of people and places Ashley had recent contact with. Moms of kids her sons' ages. A party for homework tutors at the public library. A virtual meeting of her book club that was mostly friends from back in the Twin Cities. "I'm still making calls but no one has reported that anything seemed out of the ordinary with Ashley. She wasn't worried about anything, wasn't acting strangely. Didn't mention any alarming interactions or incidents with others."

Packard told him about his visits with Lisa Washington and Darrel Johnson. "I'm pretty sure the car vandals angle is a dead end."

"Suresh is uploading all the doorbell and security camera video collected yesterday. He said he's using AI to flag each vehicle and time-stamp its location. It should help distill hours and hours of video down to a manageable list that we can start to take apart. It would normally take him days to do this on his own. He thinks he'll have something for us by the end of today."

Ashley's body had been sent to Saint Paul for autopsy. Packard was about to ask Reynolds if there was any word from the coroner's office when Reynolds's phone beeped with another call and he put Packard on hold. Packard watched the wind move through the tall grass in the ditch. He counted three bullet holes in the stop sign. After the storm, all of Sandy Lake had smelled like wet, raw wood. Pine and cedar. The smell got sweeter as the debris piles dried out. Now all he could smell was wildfire smoke. The truck had started to cool so he put up the windows.

"Hey, that was dispatch," Reynolds said. "A dog walker found a knife wrapped in a towel about a mile from Ashley's house."

"Send me the location. I'll meet you there."

He beat Reynolds by two minutes. A patrol deputy beat both of them. An older woman in a tank top and shorts, with a pug on a leash, stood nearby smoking a cigarette and waving at gnats. Packard got a paper bag and an L-shaped photomicrographic ruler from the trunk of his vehicle. He waited and watched as Reynolds's car pulled up and crunched through the grit on the side of the road. The relentless sun pushed the shade cast by a row of wild birches and maples out of reach.

"Heard about that woman got killed the other day," the dog walker said.

Her pug had collapsed to the ground and was breathing heavily. "One of y'all came by our house asking questions. Said to call if we saw anything out of the ordinary."

Packard looked at the kitchen knife sitting in the weedy grass near the edge of the road. In his years on patrol, he'd seen a lot of things abandoned in ditches. The occasional body, of course. He was always more curious about the unlikely objects and how they got there. A twisted doll. An empty picture frame. A pair of broken eyeglasses. He'd seen a lot of single shoes, each one hinting at a different story based on its size and style. Who were all those dirty-footed children, he wondered, those wobbling women?

The blue-and-white-striped dish towel was pinned beneath the knife's hilt and stained with blood. Packard knew the knife was the missing one from the set in Ashley's kitchen, but he pulled up the reference photos on his phone just to make sure. He put down the L-shaped ruler and stood back while Reynolds photographed the knife from different angles. Reynolds put on a pair of black gloves and carefully picked up the knife and lowered it into the bag Packard was holding. The kitchen towel went into a separate bag. Reynolds put both in a plastic bin in the trunk of his vehicle.

They thanked the dog walker for the call, then stared at her wordlessly until she got the hint and moved on. The deputy left, too.

"Get that stuff checked into evidence. It's been outside in the heat and the sun. It was damp and humid last night. We might still be able to type it. The DNA should still be good."

"If it's Ashley's blood, we won't know much more than we do now," Reynolds said.

"We already know more than we did before this. We know which way the killer went after he killed Ashley."

He and Reynolds looked up and down the empty road both ways like they were watching a tennis match. The heavy scent of clover growing wild in the ditch was almost enough to mask the smell of the wildfires.

"He was headed west then," Reynolds said.

"I agree. I don't see him putting down the passenger window and throwing the knife wrapped in a towel across the inside of his vehicle and out the window. He threw it out his window, probably left-handed, and it probably didn't go as far into the ditch as he hoped."

"If he was really worried about it, he would have come back."

"He probably already knows he left blood at the scene. He knows he left behind DNA. It's more important for him to get out of there and get rid of this evidence."

Packard's phone vibrated in his pocket. The way Reynolds twitched, he could tell the same had happened for him. They both reached for their phones.

"Suresh—" Packard said.

"—has something for us," Reynolds finished.

"Let's go."

Back at the sheriff's office, Reynolds logged the knife and towel into evidence and then met Packard in the former interview room that had been converted into an office for Suresh, their digital forensics expert. Suresh was a young immigrant from India with a comb-over and a mustache that made him look years older than he was. His office had long tables arranged in an L-shape, six monitors stacked three across and two high, and more computers running more operating systems than Packard had heard of. Suresh was their expert on all things phones, apps, social media, the dark web, and encryption. The room smelled like warm air from dusty computer fans and the chai Suresh always drank.

"What have you got?" Packard asked.

"I am still working on the video analysis. This is the first time I am trying the program I wrote. In another few hours I should have a list of vehicles and locations and time stamps. Also make and model with 97 percent accuracy."

"Plates?" Reynolds asked.

"The cameras often don't have the resolution to capture license plates but I will grab them if they are visible."

Packard had Suresh pull up Google Maps on one of his monitors, and they dropped a pin on the road where they found the knife and towel. "The killer was driving west on this road. It's what...two miles from Ashley's house? He's a mile off the highway, maybe intentionally, maybe making his way in that direction. It's another data point to feed into your hive mind."

Suresh opened a Notepad file and made a couple of notes. "Okay, but this is not why I texted you. I have other information from Ashley's phone."

On another monitor he pulled up a scrolling list of text messages from Ashley's phone, opened a search box, and typed "not our son." The screen jumped to a text message from Ashley to her husband, Tom, almost four months old and time-stamped just after 10:00 p.m. Ashley had sent Tom a photo of two cell phones sitting side by side on the kitchen counter. One of the screens was illuminated with a text message on it from DAD that said, "I'm so fucking ready for you," and below that a photo of just a man's briefs with an obvious bulge in them.

From Ashley to Tom: Who was this intended for? Not our son surely?

"I checked her call log. He called her minutes after her text was sent," Suresh said. "I also checked the date of these texts against the family calendar on her phone. Tom was in Minneapolis that week."

"Interesting," Packard said. "So, Tom's having an affair. Four months after his wife finds out, she's brutally murdered while he's on a boat with the boys, giving him a rock-solid alibi."

Packard took out his phone and put it on speaker so Reynolds and Suresh could hear the call he was making. "Tom, it's Deputy Packard. I have a few more questions I'd like to ask you. Can you come down to the sheriff's office?"

"Can we do it over the phone?"

"I'd rather it was in person."

Tom sighed. Packard imagined him with his forehead in his hand, fingers in his hair. "Hang on a sec."

Packard heard the sound of a sliding door opening and closing.

"Have you gone through Ashley's phone?" Tom asked.

"We have."

"And you want to know about the affair."

"I do."

"I'll be there in an hour."

Packard told Reynolds about his plan to drive Symphony back to Minneapolis and asked him to cover the evening shift debrief meeting. He spent the next hour writing his notes from talking to Lisa Washington and Darrel Johnson and the visit to the location where he and Reynolds found the knife. He saved his work, then waited by Kelly Phelps's desk to greet Tom.

"I stopped by and saw Thielen and the baby yesterday," Packard said.

"She's cute, isn't she?" Kelly said.

Packard shrugged. "I don't know. Thielen's not really my type."

"I meant the baby, smart-ass."

"Right. Yeah, the baby's cute."

Kelly loved three things: hair spray, jewelry, and Barry Manilow, and not necessarily in that order. She had big bangs and her hair pulled back in a ponytail. Nails painted red, white, and blue for Flag Day. With a couple of recent retirements, Kelly was the department's longest serving employee. She ran the office's administration side with precognitive efficiency. She knew what people needed before they did. The election of Howard Shepard last fall had her seriously considering retirement, but she'd hung in there and now she bossed Shepard and his chief deputy around like they worked for her.

Kelly turned in her chair, took off her reading glasses, and gave Packard a look up and down. "If anyone should have a kid, it's you," she said.

"What would I do with a kid?"

"It would be good for you. Children pull you out of yourself. They make you see the world through new eyes. You're too much up here all the time," she said and tapped her temple.

Packard shook his head. "I don't understand kids. I don't know what to do with them. I don't know how to heal their hurts or—"

"Guess what. Nobody does. Nobody's ever prepared for kids. No one can afford kids. No one knows how to raise them. You just figure it out."

"I have a three-legged dog I can't even adequately take care of. I had to kennel him at Gary's this morning."

"You should do better."

Tom pushed through the door then, looking like he might be walking into an ambush. He was wearing cargo shorts and flip-flops and a baseball cap. Packard shook his hand and introduced him to Kelly before leading him through the secured door and back to an interview room. Tom declined something to drink.

"I'm fine. I just want to get this over with and get back home to the boys."

They sat on opposite sides of a small table. "All right. Let's get to it. I don't know the whole story from the texts, but I take it Ashley found out you were having an affair."

Tom stared at Packard like he didn't know whether telling the truth was in his best interest or the first step down the wrong path. His mouth made tiny muscle movements but no words came out. Packard waited.

"Yes, I was having an affair," Tom finally said. "I know you saw the photo. So fucking stupid. I had been texting my son earlier. I took that photo and sent it to the wrong person. The boys aren't allowed to have their phones in their rooms after nine o'clock. I was logging into our family cloud or whatever the fuck it's called, trying to delete the photo, but Ashley saw it right away. It makes me sick every time I think about it."

Last year Thielen was in disbelief when Packard admitted to having never sent a dick pic. Beyond just the ridiculous act of photographing your own genitals, he could think of a million reasons not to have photos of his junk on his phone. Accidentally sending one to the wrong person was near the top of the list.

Tom's eyes turned pink and brimmed with tears. The photo must have seemed especially absurd in light of Ashley's murder, all the fights and remorse related to it like scenes from a different movie than what was currently playing.

"Who was supposed to get the photo?"

"Her name was Cara."

"Who's Cara?"

Tom wiped his eyes with the back of his hand. "The company she works for was a client. I was the project lead for the installation of our software and worked in their offices for a few months." He shrugged. "We put in a lot of hours together. One thing led to another."

He made it sound like intercourse was included in the project's statement of work, that the affair was inevitable and not the result of a series of conscious decisions and escalating risks he'd taken that led to him and Cara taking their clothes off. Repeatedly.

"The affair started when?"

"About a year ago."

"What happened when Ashley found out?"

"I ended things."

"When was this?"

"Immediately after that stupid photo."

"How did Cara take it?"

Tom appeared reluctant to answer. He took off his hat and scratched the top of his head and put his hat back on. "She was… She thought Ashley finding out was for the best." He laughed at himself. "Easy for her to say."

"Meaning what?"

"Meaning that Ashley finding out could have been the start of something more serious for the two of us. Me and Cara. I think she was looking for an excuse to leave her husband and thought I was in a similar situation."

"Were you?"

"No. I said what we were doing wasn't supposed to be serious. It was temporary, like my work for her company."

Packard had a feeling this wasn't the first time Tom had cheated on his wife, just the first time he'd been caught.

"How did Cara take that?"

"Not great, initially. Eventually I had to cut off all contact. I sent another guy from our office to finish the job."

"When's the last time you heard from her?"

"It's been a few months. Things were intense for a few weeks but then they died down. Once she got over her emotions, I think she realized there was nothing serious between us."

"Any contact recently?"

Tom shook his head.

"I'm going to need to talk to her."

"Is that really necessary?"

"It really is," Packard insisted.

"And this is more important than finding out who killed my wife?"

Packard understood that people had their own ideas of how an investigation should be run. They imagined searchers strung out in a long line, marching through fields, climbing into attics with a flashlight. Roadblocks and helicopters. Finding a killer wasn't like locating a missing child.

"The search for Ashley's killer requires us to follow every possible avenue. The fact that you were having an affair that ended recently with a woman who didn't want it to end is very relevant to the investigation. Until we find something that conclusively points in one direction or another, I'm going to knock on every door in front of me."

"Cara didn't have anything to do with this. She might be unhappy in her marriage but she's not a lunatic."

"Were you unhappy in your marriage?"

Tom seemed taken aback by the question. He stared at Packard with an expression that was a mix of incredulousness and a plea for understanding, one man to another.

"Unhappy? Never."

"And the affair?"

"The opportunity was there and I took it. You ever have a coworker with a candy dish on her desk and you never give jelly beans a second thought in your day-to-day life, but every time you walk by her desk, you stick your hand in the bowl and you eat the fucking jelly beans without even thinking about it? That's what it was like."

"Hmm," Packard said. His standard response to bullshit.

Packard had never been in a relationship long enough that monogamy became a question. He was curious about how other couples made the choice that was right for them and felt no particular judgment either way. What he didn't like was dishonesty. He didn't like it when one player changed the rules of the game and didn't bother to tell the other.

"I wasn't unhappy in my marriage. I wasn't trying to wreck it or get out of it. I slept with Cara because I could. Because I thought I could get away with it. Because I'd done so before."

There it was. The truth.

"My affair didn't have anything to do with Ashley being killed," Tom insisted.

Affairs. Plural, Packard thought. "Let me determine that for myself."

Tom said he didn't have Cara's number in his phone anymore but he could find it. He gave Packard Cara's last name and the name of the company where she worked. Packard asked about other women, and Tom reluctantly gave him the name of a woman in New Orleans and another in Phoenix. He hadn't had contact with either in years.

Packard told Tom about the call from the dog walker and the knife and the towel they'd found. He pulled up the photos he'd taken and laid his phone on the table between them. Tom leaned in and turned his shoulder to look at the screen.

"That's one of our kitchen towels. The knife is from the set. Have you learned anything from it? DNA?"

"We just picked it up an hour ago. Testing will take a while."

Tom sighed. "Anything else? Any other questions? I want to get back to the boys."

"How are they doing?"

"Not good. Noah won't look up from his phone. Jake hasn't stopped crying. My parents are coming from Maine. I'm hoping Grandma and Grandpa can provide some comfort and familiarity. We're going back to the house in Bloomington unless you tell us we can't."

Packard couldn't think of any reason not to let them go. Making the boys stay in the house where their mother was murdered when they had other options seemed cruel and unnecessary.

"I know how to get hold of you," Packard said. "But if I need you to come back, you need to come back. Understood?"

Tom nodded.

Packard led him out to the reception area, listening to Tom's flip-flops flap as they walked. Kelly's desk was dark, reminding Packard it was the end of the day. He unlocked the reception office door and let Tom out and locked it again behind him.

He checked his phone. No messages or calls from Symphony all day. What that meant he would find when he got home, he had no idea.

CHAPTER TEN

The man flat on his back in Holding Cell 4 had been many things in his life.

A bartender.

A line cook.

A dreamer.

A poet.

He was wearing a black T-shirt and jeans, no shoes. His second toe stuck out of a hole in his sock. Red hair shaved close on the sides. Balding. He had a hard alcohol belly, something dead and dense inside, soaked in formaldehyde.

The cell had a concrete bench with a mat on top and a metal toilet. No window. The man stared at a fly on the ceiling and thought of the cages we keep ourselves in even when the doors are open. At one time, he'd considered writing a collection of poems about all the jail cells along the Atlantic Seaboard he'd known and the nights he'd spent there. Now he could add the Midwest if he ever got around to it.

He sat up and took stock. He couldn't see it but he was fairly certain he had an ax buried in his forehead, right between his eyes. A bandage on his forearm was held in place with medical tape matted into the red hair there. He didn't remember hurting himself or getting bandaged. His hands hurt more than anything. The heels of his palms were scraped and raw. He'd fallen down drunk enough times to know exactly how that happened.

He'd lost track of time. Didn't know how long he'd been in the cell. Couldn't remember where he'd been or how he'd gotten there. His fingertips weren't stained with ink, which meant he hadn't been printed. It gave him hope he might get out without charges.

He lay down again with a forearm across his eyes. His hand shook with tremors. The smell coming off him was rank and boozy.

Time passed.

He slept. He heard a buzzing sound and thought of the fly but no, it was the electronic lock of his cell being released. He opened his eyes. A long-legged, short-waisted female deputy with hair pulled back tight called to him from outside the cell.

"Checkout time, friend. We need to let housekeeping turn this room and ready it for the next guest who'd like to enjoy these fine accommodations." There was no humor in her face or her voice. He got up slowly. She stood back and left the door open and ushered him through one locked door, then another. She brought him to a counter and left him there in his stocking feet with one toe poking out while she retrieved a plastic bin with his belt and his boots.

"You had no other personal effects besides these," she said. "No wallet, no ID, no phone."

He usually left those things in the truck as he had a tendency to lose stuff when he was drunk.

"We got a first name out of you last night but that was it. Charlie, right? Is that your name?"

Charlie didn't say anything. The only reason they were letting him go was because they didn't know who he was. He intended to keep it that way.

He sat on a bench and put on his boots. Behind him was a rail that a handcuff could be affixed to. He had a sense memory of sitting with his arm pulled back and his wrist limp through the manacle. Could have been last night. Could have been any number of nights in any number of police stations exactly like this.

"Anybody out there who can pick you up?" the deputy asked.

"I can walk."

"Where are you staying?"

"The motel."

"Bob doesn't want to see you in his bar again. You'll get a beating if you so much as darken his doorway."

"Is he allowed to threaten people like that?"

The deputy stood with her hands on her duty belt. "I don't have a problem with it," she said.

He nodded. Put his hands in his empty pockets. Checked the time on the wall. 5:30 p.m. He'd lost a whole day.

The deputy followed him all the way out to the front steps. The sudden heat and humidity felt like god's judgment.

"Good luck to you," she said. "Make better choices."

They'd been doing roofs in the area for three weeks so he knew where he was going. He walked away from downtown until he came to the four-lane highway, then headed east on the shoulder. Even through the smoky haze, the sun was hot on the back of his neck and across his shoulders through the thin fabric of his shirt. Traffic picked up speed outside of town and buffeted him with hot wind and blew dirt in his eyes. No sunglasses. No hat. He was a man of few means and fewer options. The sticky, black-tar shame of it all.

The Tabard Motel was two miles outside of town, a dilapidated relic from an era of family vacations taken in station wagons filled with cardboard luggage and ugly kids. Dads and their gin. Moms and their amphetamines. The fear of nuclear annihilation hanging over everything.

A tall wall of arborvitaes hid this eyesore from people in town. On the other side, Charlie came to an L-shaped building held together with bent nails and a million coats of dark-brown paint. He walked off the road and into the gravel lot and saw the truck he'd been driving yesterday parked in front, meaning someone had found it and driven it back. Outside the doorway of the very last room in this place they called home, Matthias sat in a metal chair, reading the local paper. He was wearing a two-tone gray short-sleeved shirt, light in front, dark in the back. Embroidered logo in the shape of a house with a red roof that said Fredricksen Construction on the chest.

"You find yourself a woman and shack up for the night?" Matthias asked.

Charlie thought of the short-waisted deputy who told him to make better choices. "Something like that."

"And what? You spent all night and all day today making love? She was so good you missed a whole day of work, forgot you had the truck, leaving me and Juan to drive around and try to find it this morning?"

Charlie walked past Matthias on the narrow sidewalk in front of their rooms. The doors were sun-faded and fit loosely in their frames. A rusty number was nailed beside each. Across the parking lot he saw the rest of the crew gathered around a picnic table and a charcoal grill beneath a large maple. Wind and hail had shredded the tree's leaves. The shade beneath it was spotty and stingy.

"That's exactly what happened," Charlie said.

He opened the passenger door on the truck he'd been driving yesterday and got his wallet out of the glove box. His room was next door to Matthias's. Charlie unlocked the door with a key card from his wallet. The furniture was from the last century, creaky and sagging, the bed linens thin and stiff at the same time. The place smelled of dry rot and night sweats.

Finding the crew a place to stay was the first thing Matthias did when he arrived in a new town and started selling roofs. The Tabard Motel had eight units. Two guys who were in town taking down trees had the first room. Matthias made a deal with the owner to get his crew five rooms for $1,000 a week. He and Charlie each had their own room. The five guys on the crew were spread across three others. Each person's share of the cost came out of his pay.

Charlie stripped off his rank clothes and showered in the bathroom's moldy stall. He shaved and combed his wet hair back. The bandage on his arm was soaked and oozing. He pressed a towel against it. He still couldn't remember how he'd cut himself. He'd been drinking so hard for so long, his memory had as many black spots as a crossword puzzle. A brain that craved alcohol did whatever it took to get another drink. Erasing his humiliation removed the incentive to reform.

Outside under the tree, Luis was stewing chicken legs and potatoes in a pot on the grill. Cooking was supposed to be Charlie's job.

A case of Modelo Especial had been dumped into a cooler of melting ice, empties crushed in a pile next to it. Charlie opened a beer. Somewhere in the tree above them a cardinal sounded like a stuttering slide whistle.

Luis tasted the tomato broth in the pot with a finger. *Está bien.* The rest of the crew gathered around with paper bowls and plastic forks. Charlie hung back and drank his beer. He'd lost his cigarettes in the night. Luis's cousin, Juan, saw his searching eyes and twitching hands and extended a pack in his directions. *Gracias*, Charlie said as he took two, put one behind his ear, and lit the other one.

Luis, Juan, and Francisco had been with Matthias since last November when he pulled the crew together in Florida to work on houses after Hurricane Hannah. From there they spent two months replacing roofs southwest of Houston, then went to North Carolina in April, which was where Charlie met them. He'd been fired from his latest bartending job and was at the library clicking through help wanted ads on craigslist when he saw a post looking for a crew lead who could cook and travel. Charlie didn't just need money; he needed to get out of town. A job on the road that came with lodging seemed like an answer to a prayer.

The newest members of the crew were Miguel, a fourteen-year-old from El Salvador who was in the country by himself, and a local kid they called College Boy.

Charlie finished his beer and dished himself some food. The crew ate in silence. There was limited English among them. Charlie spoke Spanish but liked to keep that information to himself. He sat down across from Francisco, a brown giant covered in muscles and tattoos that crept across the back of his hands and up his neck and probably illustrated his scalp under his thick black hair. Francisco stared through Charlie as they ate. Indifference. Exhaustion.

Matthias finished his food first and stood at the head of the picnic table. Medium height, stocky build. He'd changed out of his work shirt into a Wisconsin Badgers T-shirt. Give him a whistle and he could have been a high school football coach. "We've been a merry band of travelers for a while now. Some of us have been together longer than others. I just want everyone to remember why they're here."

Charlie stared down at his food wishing he was invisible.

"Our goal is to come to these storm-ravaged areas, sell as many jobs as we can, and do the best work we can. The way we make money is by keeping our noses clean and our output high. Okay? We all need to show up for work and do our jobs. Does everybody understand?"

Charlie made eye contact with Matthias and nodded as if vigorous agreement could compensate for his fuckups.

"We all have our own reasons for being here. We all have families or dreams we're trying to support. My dad and I started this business and worked on roofs together until his health failed. It was my idea to go where the storms were. All the money I'm making is to help take care of my dad. The home he's in costs $6,000 a month. I gotta sell as many roofs as I can to make that note every month. I need a crew who's as committed to our goals as I am."

Charlie stood up from the bench. "I'm sorry for being MIA today. *Lo siento.* Things got out of hand last night. I know better and it won't happen again. Thanks for cooking, Luis. *Tu comida es deliciosa.*"

Francisco stared at Charlie and opened and closed his fists in front of him. The first three knuckles of both hands were tattooed with XIX. He pushed his empty dishes across the table toward Charlie, took another beer from the cooler, and called out to Miguel who was sitting under the tree doing something on his phone. Francisco nodded toward their shared room and Miguel got up reluctantly and followed him inside. The door closed and the room's ancient air conditioner started to wheeze.

The others got up and scattered. Everyone except Matthias. Charlie was still eating. He got sick if he ate too much or too fast.

"I'm not paying you to spend the night in jail," Matthias said when it was just the two of them.

"I wouldn't pay me either."

"I'm glad we're in agreement on that," Matthias said. He sat on the end of the bench and used the toe of his boot to uproot a dandelion growing near the picnic table. "What did you get into?"

"Don't really remember."

"Nothing?"

Charlie bit into a chicken leg. The meat came away easily, leaving just a bit of tendon at the top. The things he remembered were from a long time ago, not last night. Poems he'd studied in college and every criticism his writing had ever received from other writers. He remembered the look on a friend's face the first time she saw him again after drunkenly sleeping with him. The alcohol never let him forget that.

"I remember working on a bottle of whiskey as I made my rounds. Made sure materials had been delivered to the next couple of jobs. Confirmed with homeowners we were coming. One thing led to another." He shrugged as if the up-and-down motion of his shoulders told the rest of the story. "The deputy who walked me out said a guy named Bob doesn't want to see me in his bar again. Must've gotten into the worst of it there. Got a cut on my arm I don't remember. My palms are all scraped up."

Matthias didn't say anything.

Charlie tore at the chicken with his teeth. "I suppose they had Miguel up on the roof today since I wasn't there," he said.

"If you're not there to do your job, you don't get to complain about what happens."

Charlie stared at the closed door to Francisco and Miguel's room. They found Miguel, the *ruferito*, working on a dairy farm when they were doing roofs in Iowa. He was fourteen and had walked from El Salvador to the United States. His dad started the journey with him but got sick along the way and had to turn back. Miguel kept going on his own and crossed the border near Laredo and spent weeks living on the streets until he eventually hooked up with a crew of seasonal workers following a path across the Midwest to different farms.

They'd left him with a family in Iowa where he and two other workers shared a tiny camper that smelled like it was used as a litter box by every feral cat east of the Missouri River. When he was pleading with Matthias's crew to take him with them, Miguel said the family's teenage boys beat him regularly and were going to sacrifice him at the end of the summer to the king of the corn, who would cut his heart out and spread his blood across the fields to fertilize next year's crop.

Charlie had wanted to leave him there but Matthias felt bad for the kid.

His food eaten, Charlie lit the second cigarette he got from Juan, the one behind his ear.

Matthias said, "I'm starting to wonder if hiring you was a mistake."

"It probably was."

"I took a chance on you, Charlie. You said you needed a break. You said I could count on you."

"I did say those things," Charlie admitted. "I meant them."

"What happens if you're drunk and you total my truck? Or kill someone? You getting arrested in a strange town when we're all out here working without the necessary paperwork puts this whole operation at risk."

"I wasn't arrested. And by the way, you hired the crew. You hired the Mexican covered in gang tattoos and picked up the unaccompanied fourteen-year-old from Central America like he was a puppy at the pet store."

"Both of whom have done more work than you in the last thirty-six hours."

Charlie smoked his cigarette and ashed in his plate. The chicken legs had gone from appetizing to carnage in the act of being stripped bare. "I'll do better," he promised.

"I like you, Charlie. It's why I hired you in spite of everything I know about you. I need you to focus on the work. Think about the team. What happens if I have to let you go?"

"I'm fucked."

"Exactly. It's a long trip back to North Carolina, and there's nothing waiting for you there except a warrant related to that dead nurse."

Charlie sighed. "Please don't bring that up. You know I don't like talking about it."

"Manslaughter, isn't it?"

"Fuck you, Matthias."

CHAPTER ELEVEN

Symphony was gone when Packard got home.

No car. Nothing of hers in the house. The only thing that betrayed her presence was the robe he'd given her hanging on a hook in the guest bathroom. A hint of dampness and the faint scent of the body wash he kept in the shower made him think she hadn't been gone long.

He was disappointed but not surprised. Symphony wasn't obligated to accept what he was offering. She didn't owe him a thing. He wasn't even sure why he cared so much other than he was certain Marcus would have done anything for this sister, including respecting her wishes for no contact while she was in prison. But he wouldn't have left it there. When she needed him again, whatever she needed, he would have shown up.

Packard wanted to do the same. For Marcus. For her.

He changed into shorts and a T-shirt and was looking in the fridge for something to cook for dinner when he heard a car pull up. From the front window, he saw Symphony parked in the driveway, looking at her cell phone. He was so excited he went out the door without shoes. The hot cement burned the bottom of his feet until he stepped into the grass.

"You came back." He didn't even try to hide the joy in his voice.

Symphony got out of the car wearing large sunglasses and a fresh set of clothes. She had a new scarf wrapped around her head, bright as a parrot. "I went to get gas. Figured I should get a car wash, too. Get that police paint off the back window."

"So, you're ready to go?"

"Yeah. You driving? This was your idea."

"I am. I will. I need some shoes. I need to make a quick call," he said feeling his pockets. "Ten minutes and I'll be ready."

"You need to know I'm still not sure how I feel about all…this," she said, drawing a circle around him with her finger. "You and Marcus. It's not what I was expecting. It's not what I wanted to hear, and I got no problem admitting that. I'm allowed to feel how I feel."

"Agreed. It's not my intention to force you to change your mind. If you want to know the Marcus I knew, I'm happy to tell you. If you don't…" He let his voice trail off and shrugged. "I'll keep my memories to myself and you never have to see me again after this."

Symphony stared at him behind her giant sunglasses. "Get your shoes then. Let's go. It's a long drive."

In the car, Packard pushed the seat back as far as it would go and surveyed the dash's buttons and knobs.

"The car has AC but it don't work for shit," Symphony warned.

"Good thing we're leaving at the end of the day. It'll cool off."

He put the car in reverse and they headed away from his house, went east for a little while, and then started south on a winding two-lane road. He cracked his window and the one behind Symphony to let air move through. Symphony had her phone plugged into the car's cigarette lighter. She had long nails that sometimes clicked against the screen as she scrolled. The radio was off because the antenna was broken.

"Are there any CDs for the CD player?" he asked.

"There's one CD and it's stuck inside. It plays but you can't eject it."

"What is it?"

"Ginuwine."

"'Pony'? 'In Those Jeans'?"

Symphony looked him up and down. "You don't know 'In Those Jeans.'"

"I beg your pardon." Packard cleared his throat and sang in his best falsetto the song's most repeated line that asked if there was any room for him in those jeans.

"Oh Lord," Symphony said, pressing her fingertips to her forehead. "Let me guess. Marcus."

"You don't know the half of it."

What could he tell her? How Marcus had that song on his Getting Ready playlist. That he was usually naked or wearing only a towel while it played. How he used to come up behind Packard and wrap his arms around him and put his mouth by his ear and sing that line while undoing the top button of his pants, making them late for wherever they were supposed to be. That one time on a road trip to Duluth, Marcus singing the song, a hand on Packard's thigh, then higher, then Marcus wiggling out of his seat belt, Packard protesting *I'm trying to drive*, Marcus telling him *Just keep your hands on the wheel and your eyes on the road.*

Packard bit his bottom lip and shook his head. Symphony was staring at him. "I know you're not sitting there thinking impure thoughts about my dead brother with me right here."

"Sorry. Just remembering all the times I heard him singing that song. He loved it."

"Mmmm. I remember."

The road went up and down in rolling hills, past boggy wetlands and deer blinds and stands of pencil-straight pine trees.

"It's too many trees up here, not enough people. Makes me nervous," Symphony said.

"I love it for those very reasons," Packard said.

"How'd you end up here?"

He told her about his grandparents retiring to Sandy Lake and his childhood spending summers and holidays at their house on the lake. "We stopped coming after my brother went missing."

"What happened to your brother?"

"He died. In some ways, I had an experience similar to yours."

Symphony looked at him with suspicion. "Is this a real story? Not some bullshit you're trying to manipulate me with?"

Packard held up a hand like he was swearing an oath. "One hundred percent factual," he said.

"Go on."

He told her about Nick leaving home on a snowmobile one night when Packard was twelve, how Nick never came back, and how the sheriff's department eventually found his snowmobile in the lake but never found his body. He told her about the thirty years of not knowing and how it had impacted his whole family until last winter when he tracked down a woman who not only knew his brother but knew what happened to him.

"This woman lives in Paris now. I went there this summer and she told me all kinds of things about my brother I didn't know. I had an idea of him from when I was twelve years old. She told me about a whole different person. A person none of us knew. What happened to him was terrible but what we learned about him from her story was a gift."

"Did it feel like a gift when you were first hearing it?"

Packard thought back to that night sitting at a restaurant patio on a narrow Parisian street. "No. Not in the moment. It was heartbreaking. For a while afterwards, I was angry that I never got to know or grow up with that version of my brother. It was a lot to absorb."

"So you know how I feel," Symphony said. It sounded like an accusation, not something they shared.

"I do. I'm curious. Would it have made a difference if Marcus had been the one to tell you about who he was?"

"I don't know," Symphony said. She pulled her seat belt away from her body and rubbed a spot on her chest. "We grew up learning being gay was not acceptable. Not in our family. Not in our church."

"Imagine hearing that message over and over again when you know they're talking about the things you think and feel. It makes you want to hide."

"But I was his sister. He didn't have to hide from me."

Packard grunted in frustration. "Symphony."

"What?"

"Do you hear yourself?"

She took off her sunglasses and looked at him like she was daring him to say something to her face.

"When was he supposed to tell you? You cut off all communication."

Packard snuck a glance at her, then kept his eyes on the road. He let her sit with that while they kept driving. They hit Interstate 94 and headed on a southeast diagonal toward Minneapolis. The speed limit was seventy but the car shimmied too much above sixty-five. The sun came down big and orange behind them. In front of them, an endless haze that made him think blue skies were a myth.

Later, he asked her about where she lived and what she did for work. St. Louis, she said, and she had three jobs, one with a nonprofit that helped people with reentry after getting out of prison. She worked part-time in a retail store and sometimes waited tables in a waffle restaurant for extra cash.

"Did you have any contact with Marcus before he died?"

"No. He was dead almost a year before I heard about it. My lawyer found out and told me. When I got out three years ago, I wanted to know more, but they still had me locked down in a lot of ways. You live in a halfway house, you have a curfew. They got you going to parole meetings and counseling and job-training sessions. You're doing everything you can to convince people to give you a second chance."

Packard knew the recidivism statistics and how hard reentry could be. He knew how unforgiving society was to people with a record—refusing to rent them apartments or hire them for jobs. It created instability that increased the likelihood they would offend again. Packard also knew he contributed to the whole dysfunctional apparatus by arresting people and feeding them into the meat grinder of the U.S. criminal justice system.

"When I saw the five-year anniversary of Marcus's death was coming up, I had this urge to learn about him and his life before people started to forget about him," Symphony said, staring at her phone.

"What do you think would have happened with you two if he hadn't died?"

Symphony's finger paused on her phone. When she didn't answer, Packard looked and caught her looking out the window on her side. What had been shade earlier in the day and evening shadows after that had deepened to a purple dusk. Symphony used a folded paper towel to dab her neck and her forehead.

"I could ask you the same," she said.

It was Packard's turn to look away. He arched his back in the seat and leaned forward until his forearms were on top of the steering wheel. "I don't know," he said, falling back. "I have a hard time remembering the days and weeks right before he was killed. I don't know if we were good or things were coming to a head between us. I did everything I could to avoid serious conversations about the future."

"Why'd you do that?"

"Not ready. Afraid of the answers."

She looked at him without sympathy. "What's a white man with a police uniform and a gun got to be afraid of?"

Afraid was the wrong word. He knew now that what he felt back then wasn't fear. There was nothing to fear with Marcus. There was only the opportunity to be uncomfortable by being honest. What if a serious conversation revealed that they wanted different things? What if they wanted the same things but not on the same timeline, or not with each other?

"I didn't want things to change."

"You mean you wanted things your way. Never mind what Marcus wanted."

The truth hurt.

“You’re right,” Packard admitted. “Things changed anyway and in the worst possible way. People didn’t know about either one of us, let alone that we were together. I had to pretend I was mourning a friend and a colleague. We didn’t even share ourselves completely with each other. He didn’t tell me about you. I never introduced him to my parents or my other siblings.”

“’Cause he was Black?”

“No. Come on.”

“What? I don’t know your family.”

“I can tell you my mom would have loved Marcus. She lives in Arizona. My dad lives in Florida. For a long time me being gay wasn’t something I talked about with my family, and that’s the way I liked it. I worried that once people saw me as gay they’d never see me as anything else. It’s an idea I still struggle with personally and professionally. It was easier to keep it from being a topic of conversation if I never brought around a man I was dating.”

Why did it take so much time and tragedy to see how small he used to make himself in an effort to hide in plain sight? He was still doing it when he moved to Sandy Lake, until he realized there was no hiding in a small town. Everyone saw him for exactly who and what he was. He’d only managed to hide from himself.

“When Marcus died and I found out I was the beneficiary and executor of his estate, I was shocked. You don’t put someone in that role you’re just in a casual relationship with. He knew what he wanted. He was waiting for me to come around or be man enough to say this isn’t it.”

Symphony *hmmm*’d and held her phone in her lap. “There was a limit to his patience. You would have found that out eventually. For a long time when I was drinking and using, Marcus came running every time I called.”

“Of course he did. He was your brother.”

“Who wanted to change me and control me.”

“He wanted to protect you,” Packard said.

“He did until he didn’t. When I moved to St. Louis with a man we both knew wasn't good for me, he told me he was done. He told me I couldn't be in his life until I was sober. I hated him for that."

Packard made a noise in the back of his throat. "It must have been hard for him to let you go and accept the consequences, including that you might die and there was nothing he could do about it."

"I see that now. At the time it felt selfish of him."

"How did you finally get clean?"

"In prison," she said, like it should have been obvious. "My addictions were an attempt to quiet my mixed-up brain. It wasn't until I was in prison that I was finally diagnosed with schizophrenia. I needed to be on drugs, just not the shit I was buying on the street."

She told him how she and the man she was with had split up after their son was born. She and the baby moved around among friends and dealers and homeless shelters. All the while her mind continued to fight her. She thought she was being followed. She thought men in black motorcycle helmets wanted to steal her baby to do experiments on him. How she was high the night she put the baby in the tub and passed out and only came around when her friend started screaming.

"By the time Marcus heard about what happened with my baby, I was already in jail. He came to St. Louis to see me but I wouldn't see him. I had all his letters returned. My brain still didn't work. I told him he was dead to me and I was dead to me and stop trying to contact me. It took years to get me transferred outta prison and into a mental hospital. Longer still to figure out the right meds and the right doses."

"How long were you in?"

"Eleven years."

The car rattled around them as they passed all the exits for St. Cloud. Symphony told him about her job helping former inmates make the transition back to society. She said there were a lot of success stories but there were days when too much of her job was telling people no. There wasn't a bed or an apartment or a job or a check. She wanted to move from being a caseworker to a leader or a fundraiser. She knew she was good with people. She knew she had a story that could inspire others.

By the time they hit the outer limits of Minneapolis, it was full-on dark. Light from Symphony's phone lit up her side of the car. She tapped on the screen. Texting.

"Where am I taking you?" Packard asked.

"Get off on the Lowry exit. This car belongs to Ms. Rose. You're taking me to her house. She's holding a meal for us."

"Us?"

"Yes. She says she knows you."

CHAPTER TWELVE

The Folwell neighborhood of north Minneapolis was just west of where the Mississippi River flowed south before making its diagonal cut through the heart of the city. The house they pulled up in front of was a duplex with two metal doors side by side behind a wide porch. Satellite dishes grew like mushrooms from the roof and the side of the building. The lower windows had bars on them. Packard knew the area well from his time with the MPD. Something about this house triggered his spidey sense.

He knew this house.

They got out and he gave Symphony the keys and she knocked on the right-side door. Then they waited and listened to the sound of dead bolts being turned. The door whooshed as it swept inward. The woman standing there was Black and elderly, with hair that went up from her forehead and back in waves.

"You remember me?" she asked Packard. Rose Simmons was big in every dimension and wearing pink pants and a loose, flowery blouse. She had aged since he'd last seen her. Curly gray hairs swept across the top of her high forehead.

"Ms. Simmons. I remember you well."

"And I remember you. Course you was young and green back then. So determined. But you look the same."

"How's Ruby?"

"Come in and see for yourself. Make you a plate."

Inside, the house was bright and white. In the living room was a recliner with art on the wall above it that said *All I Need Is Jesus* in script. Two young men were playing NBA 2K on a PlayStation. An air conditioner with a hose venting through a side window kept the room a few degrees cooler than outside. "Boys, get off that couch and let Symphony sit down." One of them moved all the way over and the other slid to the floor without stopping the game. Symphony sat and sighed and let her head drop. Her hands hung between her knees.

"You all right?" Packard asked. "You need water or anything?"

"I'm fine. Just got lightheaded after sitting so long."

A teenage girl was sitting at the dining room table with a book open in front of her. "Ruby, say hi to Mr. Packard. He used to be a policeman around here a long time ago."

"Hello," Ruby said.

Packard felt something break off inside his chest and catch in his throat. Ruby was three years old when a stray bullet came through the side of this house, nicked a cast-iron pipe in the wall, and hit her in the back of the head. She was in a coma for a long time, and when she came out, there was little they could do but wait and see what damage the bullet had done. Here she was. A teenager. Healthy.

"It's nice to…" He paused. He didn't know if she knew his connection to what happened to her when she was a toddler or whether she wanted to be reminded of it. "It's nice to meet you."

"She got AP English this fall. Told her she better get a head start on her reading. Her teacher, Ms. Choi, don't play."

Ruby closed her book—*Beloved* by Toni Morrison. "Grandma, I read fifty pages. Can I have my phone now?"

Ms. Simmons reached into her blouse and produced the phone like she worked for Verizon. "This needs to be back in my hand in one hour. Do not make me come get it."

Ruby wiped the phone on her shorts and took her book and disappeared down a hall off the living room.

Symphony came off the couch and the three of them went into the kitchen while the boys yelled excitedly at the game. Ms. Simmons took a platter of spiral-cut ham from the fridge and a plate of sliced tomatoes and set them on the counter beside a basket with biscuits cooked that morning. She brought out butter and a jar of pickles and iced tea. Packard and Symphony put food on their plates and sat at the table with Ms. Simmons, who sat at the head with a half-empty bottle of Diet Coke and fanned herself with a folding fan she also produced from inside her blouse. If she pulled a coatrack out of there, he was leaving.

"How did you two meet?" Packard asked. He pulled a biscuit apart and made a sandwich with the ham and the tomato and some butter.

"Ms. Rose left a comment on Marcus's obituary that said beautiful things that made it sound like she knew him. When I googled her, her name came up in newspaper stories about Ruby. I reached out and said I was looking for people who knew my brother. She said if I could get up here, she'd help me." She pointed her butter knife at Packard. "I heard your name from a lot of other people, but I heard it first from Ms. Rose."

Packard thought he remembered the scene the evening Ruby had been shot, but in truth it could have been any number of scenes. Flashing blue and red lights, twisted yellow tape, officers in vests that said POLICE on the back. Little numbered tents set beside discarded shell casings in the street, the flash of photographers' cameras, and the bright lights of TV crews. The targets of the shooting had been walking by outside. One of them died at the scene. The other survived but ended up in a wheelchair.

Packard ate his sandwich and resisted looking over his shoulder for any evidence of where the bullet came through the wall. He suddenly remembered a stuffed yellow duck smeared with gore and a blood-soaked kitchen towel on the table where they were eating now. It reminded him of the bloody towel from Ashley's kitchen they'd found in the ditch that morning.

"It's nice you still remembered Marcus after all that time," Packard said.

Ms. Simmons lowered her forehead and fanned herself. "I didn't have to remember him. I saw him all the time. He came around to check on Ruby. I saw him at Juneteenth. Saw him at peace marches."

Packard knew her words weren't meant to shame him but he felt heat in his face anyway. Ms. Simmons was right—he'd been so green when they first met. He remembered the case for how little evidence or testimony they were able to collect. He had a lot to learn back then about the distrust between the Black community and the police, the long brutal history between them, the no-snitching part of the culture.

The teenager who'd been shot and lived wouldn't say anything about who was after him or what he'd seen. Usually, the beefs in this part of town were between rival gangs that controlled only a block or two of territory in the neighborhood. It wasn't until a month later that word started to get around that the shooter who hit the little girl might have been someone from south Minneapolis, that it was something personal between those involved, not a gang issue.

Marcus's precinct covered south Minneapolis. He was the one who brought Packard the news. This was long before they started dating, back when they were friends who had gone to the academy together, who sometimes met at the gym, who were still denying the attraction between them. He brought Marcus to the hospital to interview the boy who'd been shot, took him back to the neighborhood to talk to his family, while Packard stayed out of sight, knowing exactly what he was doing—hoping people might talk to a Black cop more than a white one.

They didn't.

It wasn't about the color of their skin. It was the color of their uniform.

He and Marcus visited Ms. Simmons together just once to find out how Ruby was doing and update her on the case—who they were looking at, who they'd been talking to. Ruby was still in the hospital. The hole in the wall still hadn't been patched.

Two months later, their main suspect was found dead in his car in a parking lot, his pockets turned out. Ballistics from a gun they found under the seat matched bullets collected from the scene of Ruby's shooting.

Case closed.

Even if Packard had wanted to stay in touch with everyone from every case he worked, it would have been impossible. He was never just working one case. There was always another murder, another body, another hot summer setting off violence like fireworks.

"I didn't know Marcus was still in touch with you and Ruby," Packard said. "He never mentioned it."

"He kept me updated on you. Said you were doing well. Promotions and cases solved. Said you two were close."

Packard caught a look from Symphony that Ms. Simmons didn't see while fanning herself. It was a warning.

"How come Symphony had to drive so far to find you?"

If Symphony hadn't known about his relationship with Marcus until she tracked him down in Sandy Lake, it made sense Ms. Simmons didn't know about it either. Symphony wanted to keep it that way. Let Ms. Simmons remember the Marcus she knew.

"Marcus and I were close," Packard said. "After he was killed, I decided I needed a change. I took a job with the sheriff's office up in Sandy Lake. It's a small town where I spent time as a kid."

"They got any Black folks up there?"

"Some. Not a lot."

If Symphony had looked refreshed after spending the day at his house, she looked exhausted now. She wasn't hungry. She'd moved her food around on her plate but hadn't eaten much. He could tell she wanted to get up from the table but was being polite.

"Thanks for letting Symphony borrow your car, Ms. Simmons. I'm glad she found me. And I'm happy to hear you and Marcus kept in touch. I can't tell you how great it is to see Ruby doing so well."

"She gonna be just fine. She got a little weakness on her left side but it don't slow her down at all."

The boys had finished their game and were slumped side by side on the couch looking at their phones. "Teddy, time for you to get home. Tarique, it's after nine. That phone belongs to me now."

The boys stood and Teddy said good night to Ms. Simmons. Packard took out his phone. "I should call an Uber."

Ms. Simmons laughed. "You gonna be waiting a long time for an Uber to pick you up in this neighborhood at this time of night."

Packard knew she was right. They were just a block off Lowry. It was a short walk to the Lowry Avenue Bridge and northeast Minneapolis on the other side of the river. A short walk but a world of difference in people's perceptions of the two areas.

Packard thanked Ms. Simmons for the meal and reminded her to renew her tabs.

Symphony walked him to the door and out onto the porch. It was cooler but still hothouse humid. "When are you heading home?" he asked.

"I gotta check the bus schedule. Tomorrow or the next day at the latest."

"Don't delay getting in touch with your PO. Those guys are not known for their sense of humor. If he needs anything from me about these last couple of days, have him call. You've got my number."

"I will."

"I have some things of Marcus's you might want. I completely forgot in our rush to get on the road. I think I told you I have his badge. There's also a family photo album. If you give me your address, I'll mail them to you when I get home."

He couldn't tell if the look on Symphony's face was exhaustion or wariness. He unlocked his phone and handed it to her. "Just type it in. Your phone number, too, if you don't mind."

She moved her thumbs and handed him back his phone.

"There's one more thing you should know. Marcus left money behind. A life insurance policy."

Symphony's mouth got small and tight. "Is that what you think I came here for? Money?"

"That's not what I think at all. I'm just telling you the facts. Stop—let me finish. I spent some of the money fixing my house, but it never felt right. The rest of it is invested and growing. We already talked about white saviors. This isn't that. The money is Marcus's."

"He's dead. It's your money now."

"If your lives hadn't diverged, it would have been your name in that paperwork. Not mine. If you ever need help from Marcus, the money is there. No questions asked."

Symphony shook her head. "I don't want his money. I don't want your money. I don't know why I did any of this." She turned and headed for Ms. Simmons's door. "Getting myself in trouble to come all this way and find out some shit about my brother I didn't want to know."

"Symphony," he said.

She shook her head and put a hand behind her in case he thought about coming after her. For the second time in as many days she slammed the door behind her.

CHAPTER THIRTEEN

The walk to the river took him along Lowry Avenue, an east–west corridor that cut through the heart of north Minneapolis. The same inequities and violence that led to Ruby getting shot all those years ago still persisted. It was easy to focus on the graffiti and the boarded-up houses and the chain-link fences and miss the small grocery stores, restaurants, and community spaces that endured, providing services to a neighborhood that too often found itself torn between pride and despair.

The arch over the Lowry Bridge was lit with blue neon. Below him, the wide, slow Mississippi boiled silently in the dark. He requested an Uber pickup at Tony Jaros's—a legendary northeast bar known for a drink called the Greenie—and the car pulled up just as he reached the corner of Marshall.

Packard climbed into the back seat, exhausted. Sandy Lake felt like an ocean away. When he closed his eyes, he saw piles of tree debris and Ashley Turner's empty gaze and the mess in his house. Air the color of a dirty cigarette filter. Why would a sane person go back? Where was the good in this life?

His driver carried on a conversation in Somali on a Bluetooth earbud while MPR played quietly on the radio. Packard softened into his seat. Out his window, the Minneapolis skyline glowed with lights blurred by low clouds.

He wished things had ended on a different note with Symphony. He thought about texting her and decided against it. She'd clearly had enough of him for one day. Nothing he said tonight was going to make any difference. Better to wait.

On the plus side, he felt the presence of Marcus in his life again in a way that he hadn't for years now. Some of his memories of their time together had started to feel like a dream he could barely recall, while others were worn smooth from handling, losing their definition in a different way. Symphony had reanimated her brother and given him a new history. Just when Packard felt like there was nothing new to know about Marcus, he was starting to realize that he might not have known him at all.

His driver took them south on 35W to 494 in the direction of the airport. When he got to the circular driveway in front of the address, Packard got out and entered a six-digit code that let him into the building. Up three flights of stairs to a door in a gray hallway with blue commercial carpet. He knocked. It was almost 10:00 p.m.

Detective Garrett Easton answered the door in nothing but a pair of red shorts that were too small to fully cover the wide waistband of the jockstrap he was wearing underneath. A body lean and lined. Chest hair trimmed as neatly as a bonsai.

"Finally," he said.

Gare took Packard by the hand and led him into the condo. Packard shed his clothes on the way to the bedroom, a trail of shoes and socks, his pants, a shirt, those short red shorts the last in the line, like punctuation, like a mark that gave everything that came before meaning.

An hour later, stretched out in a king-size bed on sheets as cool and white as winter, he turned to Easton with a sleepy grin on his face.

"That was worth the long drive."

Easton was sitting up in bed beside him, looking at his phone. "You didn't drive all this way just for that."

"No, but of everything I have to do while I'm here, that was what I was most looking forward to."

"I am a public servant. I aim to please."

He and Easton went way back, before Marcus even. A gym crush turned hookup that pivoted to friendship when Packard found out Easton had a wife he wasn't being honest with. They'd lost touch after Marcus was killed—despite Easton reaching out multiple times—and reconnected last winter when a dead body in Sandy Lake led Packard to an MPD missing person's report written by Easton. By then Easton was divorced, their friendship was a bridge burned, and they'd started over like this, drunk on each other's body, almost full circle back to where they'd begun.

Packard had been down to the Cities on vacation once since then, and Easton had come up to Sandy Lake once. He'd met Thielen and her husband while he was there.

Packard stared at the ceiling and wondered if old patterns weren't reestablishing themselves. He had avoided serious conversations about the future with Marcus. Was he doing the same with Easton? In some ways it felt too soon for such a talk. It had only been a few months since they'd reconnected. Packard also wondered if the distance between them—a three-and-a-half-hour drive—precluded the need to discuss long-term commitments. All he knew was that he liked being in Easton's company, that when they were together he wanted to eat the meat off his bones, that he missed him when he wasn't around.

Then there was Kyle. Bud Light, as Thielen had called him. Packard felt a connection developing there, a slow pattern of getting to know each other that hadn't crossed into the physical yet, and might never. And if it did, would it be as good as it was with Easton? Impossible to know.

He looked up at Easton, who was looking down into the bottomless depths of his phone. What if he just asked Easton what he was thinking, what he wanted? It would be so simple.

Instead, Packard did what he always did. Decided those were conversations for another day, one when he wasn't so tired. He closed his eyes, relaxed his whole body, felt himself giving in to sleep, his mind an empty canoe slipping from shore into dark waters.

CHAPTER FOURTEEN

FRIDAY

AIR QUALITY INDEX: ORANGE (UNHEALTHY FOR SENSITIVE GROUPS)

The laundromat in Sandy Lake was called the Sock Tumbler. It was empty when Charlie got there at 6:00 a.m. He sat alone in the middle seat in a row of chairs and scrolled through a list of calls on his phone down to the last time he called Matthias. He called again and left a message reminding him it was payday. The guys would be expecting their cash.

Against the wall, seven dryers spun like the insides of a watch. Friday mornings were a rare point in his week when he wasn't working, and he hadn't been drinking so he could try to write. In the notebook in his lap he wrote whatever came to mind.

Clean clothes, a dirty mind, the filthy air
Intimate as underwear
The Sock Tumbler
Machine rumbler

Man humbler
She forgot the soap, he brought the dope

He read it again, then scratched it out. Why was he trying to rhyme everything? Was that all he was capable of now? Kids' rhymes? He wrote:

She said give me the dope
I thought she said soap
I thought she wanted me to wash her back
She wanted the stuff that made her eyes roll back

He scratched it all out. Why did he even bother?

All seven dryers finished within a few minutes of each other. On Fridays every man left his laundry bag in front of his door and Charlie took them to the laundromat. One bag per washing machine, and if you left shit in your pockets or had stains that didn't come out in the regular wash, too bad. From washing machine to dryer and from the dryer back into the bag. He did a lot of menial shit for these guys but folding their underwear wasn't on the list.

It was 7:30 a.m. when he got to the current job site—a Methodist church with a steep gabled roof over the sanctuary. An addition on the building turned the roofline ninety degrees in the middle and connected to another smaller building with the same shape as the main part of the church. They were doing the whole roof, the porticos, even replacing the shingles cladding the steeple that shot sixty feet into the air. They'd replaced roofs on three homes belonging to members of the congregation and that's how Matthias was able to sell such a big job.

The church was on a corner lot in town with houses all around it. During the storm, the wind had come from behind the homes across the way and pushed every tree into the street. All that remained was a line of stumps down the block, cantilevered like cannons, each braced by a hump of soil and a tangled root ball big enough to hide behind.

It was their second day on the job. The underlayment they put down the day before was covered with slippery dust from everything in the air and made a dangerous job even more so. Charlie pulled up just short of the stop sign on the corner in time to see Miguel climb a ladder up the tallest side of the church with two packages of shingles over his shoulder. Above the ladder, scrap two-by-fours had been nailed to the roof creating bracing to help them climb the nearly forty-five-degree angle.

"Goddamnit," Charlie said, getting out of the truck. "That kid cannot be on the roof. He's not even wearing a harness. Are you shitting me?"

Francisco stood near the peak. A giant almost as big as the steeple. The sky behind him was the color of dirty water. He made Charlie think of an Aztec priest standing atop a temple, waiting for the blood sacrifice to be brought to him.

"He wants to do. I decide for him," Francisco said in halting English.

Working in kitchens on the East Coast for twenty years with Central and South American immigrants had taught Charlie plenty of Spanish. He'd decided early on not to let the crew know how much Spanish he knew. He liked that they talked freely in front of him, assuming he didn't understand. It was how he knew Juan, Luis, and Francisco all struggled to understand Miguel. Charlie didn't know if it was because the dialect was so different in El Salvador or because the language of children is indecipherable to adults in any language. Charlie also knew that Francisco knew a lot more English than he let on. He and Charlie were playing the same game, just in reverse.

"Francisco, you decide fuckall," Charlie said. The gleaming white building and the giant cross over the door did nothing to temper his language. "I'm the crew lead. I decide."

Francisco turned away and looked at something in the distance. He had one foot braced against a two-by-four, the other near the roof's ridge. Miguel was sitting on top of the shingles he'd just dumped and looking at his phone, an old Android with no SIM card that he used to record videos of himself singing pop songs and making signs with his fingers that Charlie didn't understand.

"Okay. Let's have a deal," Francisco said, staring down at Charlie. "You bring one package of shingles to me and I keep Miguel off the roof. For today and all the jobs next. I will carry all the shingles, just me."

Juan, Luis, and College Boy came up from the other side of the steep roof where they'd been out of Charlie's sight. The air quality that morning had gone orange and all three wore bandannas over the lower half of their faces like train robbers.

Charlie's job as the crew lead involved everything but getting on ladders and climbing on roofs. He told Matthias he didn't like heights when he hired him. Matthias assured him he'd stay plenty busy on the ground. Charlie did the shopping and the cooking and the laundry. He helped spread tarps to catch the old shingles as they were tossed down, and he loaded trash into the trailer and drove it to the dump. He ran errands, collected payments, and maintained the schedule in his notebook.

"Just one package?" Charlie asked.

"*Sí.*"

"Onto the roof?"

"*Claro.*"

Charlie stepped on his cigarette. Chest beating and dick measuring wasn't his style. He was a writer, a poet. Not a leader of men, or even a cheerleader of men. It was the thinnest of veneers that held this group together. If ICE showed up, the white guys would shrug and stand back. If someone got hurt and couldn't work, he'd be left behind.

Charlie saw the fatal blow his reputation with the crew had taken after his night in jail. He'd proven himself expendable. College Boy did his job yesterday picking up trash and driving to the dump. Luis had cooked. If the crew turned on him, he'd have nothing. If a fourteen-year-old, undocumented, unaccompanied minor fell off a building and took everyone down with him, he'd have nothing. Climbing a ladder just far enough to flop a bundle of shingles onto the roof seemed a small ask to keep the machine running and the kid on the ground. Charlie thought he should be able to do that much.

Three pallets of shingles had been delivered to the church. One was empty. Two of them were still wrapped in plastic. Charlie took the knife off his belt and sliced at the delivery wrap. He grabbed a long, narrow package and knew immediately he was in trouble. These were architectural shingles. The package weighed eighty pounds. Double what the three-tab shingles weighed that they used on most jobs.

He got the package over his right shoulder like he was burping the world's heaviest baby. With his left hand, he grabbed the ladder. Right foot on a rung. Left foot. Using his left arm to pull him up. The cut on his forearm he couldn't remember getting was pink and scabbed.

Up. Up again. As he rose, he stared straight ahead at the narrow, stained-glass window in front of him. A child in a tunic sat at the feet of Jesus, who was dressed in a white robe with what looked like a blue scarf that ran the length of him. Under the robe he wore red clothes that reminded Charlie of an Adidas tracksuit.

He was out of breath by the fifth rung. The bundle of shingles shifted slightly over his shoulder. How did Miguel haul two of these at once? One hundred sixty pounds was more than Miguel weighed. Charlie shrugged his shoulder and tightened his grip on the shingles. He went higher.

"*Donde está? Vamos*!" Francisco shouted from above. "Today, *por favor*!"

That was when Charlie made the mistake of looking up. The edge of the roof seemed to extend over him, to be pushing the top of the ladder away from it. When he looked down in a panic and saw he was ten feet off the ground, everything seized. His mind, his grip, his balls. He was frozen. He couldn't lift his foot or reach for the next rung. His body refused to accept the signals his brain was sending.

Directly in front of him, stained-glass Jesus was looking at a group of figures in the next window over with an expression like, *The fuck is this guy doing?*

Charlie closed his eyes. It only made his vertigo worse. The shingles slipped further. He tried raising his shoulder, gripping the package tighter, but gravity had the upper hand and the bundle slid down his back. It hit the ladder with a thud on the way to the ground, making Charlie cling even tighter.

Above him he heard groaning, then Spanish, then laughter. He heard Francisco say *pinche canelo*.

Eventually he loosened his grip and climbed down. The guys were still laughing. It didn't bother him. They could talk about him in Spanish or laugh right in his face. No one thought less of him than he did.

Charlie lit a cigarette and sat on the truck's bumper. The day emerged minute by minute. He checked his phone. Not 8:00 a.m. yet and already the heat and humidity felt like the sun had never set. Across the street, he saw a woman in a long housecoat and a KN95 face mask leaning on a cane and watching from her top step.

Miguel came down the ladder like it was a slide. He handed Charlie his phone and spoke in Spanish, then mimed that he wanted Charlie to film him climbing to the roof. Charlie put his cigarette in the corner of his mouth while Miguel heaved two packages of shingles over his narrow shoulder. At the bottom of the ladder, he looked back at Charlie to make sure he was ready with the camera.

"Yeah, fuck, go," Charlie said, watching him via the phone's screen. "Do whatever you want."

CHAPTER FIFTEEN

In Minneapolis, Packard woke with the weight of Easton's arm across his chest. He stared at the former marine as he slept. Long eyelashes. The chicken pox scar on the side of his nose. Bushy eyebrows. Packard turned the other direction and watched the morning flights take off from the nearby MSP airport through the bedroom window. Three hours from home, the air quality was no better. The sun shimmered like a lit cigarette.

Packard slid out of the bed and started the shower. Before he could finish, Easton was there with him under the needling spray. They made full use of the shower's bench, all their groaning, grunting weight pressed against wet tile, neck bites and leg cramps, clinging to each other like they were drowning.

Later, they stood over the island sink dressed in just their briefs, eating breakfast burritos. Easton was the type to never miss a meal. He prepped food in batches, built the menu around macro percentages, and packaged everything for the refrigerator or the freezer, food for a week or a month.

"You're throwing off my meal count," Easton said as he squeezed sour cream from a tube.

"Sorry. Maybe you should make a few extra in the next batch for occasions like this."

"I might have to."

Packard told the Minneapolis detective about Ashley Turner's murder, her bullied gay son, her cheating husband. "I need to stop by an office park in Eden Prairie and talk to the woman he was sleeping with. I don't have a car. You think you could drive me this morning?"

"I could. I will."

They finished eating and left their plates in the sink. Easton touched Packard's jaw. "You've got something on your face." He kissed the spot above Packard's top lip, then his mouth. Packard's eyes widened at the intimacy of the moment, the tenderness of the hand on his chin, the other on his waist. It felt like a message beamed directly into his brain. Were these the answers to the questions he couldn't ask? Was this Easton telling him exactly what he wanted?

Packard closed his eyes, felt himself stirring again.

"Come on. Don't get me worked up. There's no time. We got things to do," Packard said.

Easton pulled away. "Time is a made-up construct. There's time for all the things."

"Is that what you tell your sergeant?"

"Let me worry about my sergeant," Easton said, kissing Packard again and leading them back to the bedroom.

Easton drove them in his Highlander west on 494 and exited on a frontage road that took them to an office building not far from the old Minnesota Vikings training center. They took an elevator from the lobby to the fifth floor and stepped out into an open work area fronted by a long receptionist's desk beneath a sign that said Byerson Construction.

"We're here to see Cara Foster," Packard said.

The receptionist looked at her monitor. "Do you have an appointment?"

"We don't," Packard said, handing the receptionist his card. "But do tell her that I'm here and where I'm from."

They waited patiently while the receptionist typed and stared at her screen. "She's on her way."

The woman who came out to greet them was dressed in navy blue with a bright yellow blouse and high-heeled shoes. "I'm Cara," she said brusquely. "Follow me."

They went through a door beside the elevator and down a flight of stairs. She used a key card on a lanyard around her neck to open a door and they stepped inside an empty office, nothing but the carpet on the floor.

"I don't know what this is about but I don't appreciate two TV cops showing up at my place of work unannounced."

"TV cops?" Easton asked.

"You're too good-looking to be real cops. I don't like it." She looked behind her and then around them. "And I'm realizing I just locked myself in an empty office with two guys who could be anything but cops."

Packard had pocketed his badge to be discreet for Cara's sake. He showed it to her and she glanced at it impatiently while he introduced Detective Easton.

"So what do you want? There's only one person I know in Sandy Lake, and he and I don't speak anymore. Does this have something to do with Tom Turner?"

"Indirectly," Packard said. "Two days ago, someone killed Tom's wife in their home."

Cara's face froze but her eyes couldn't stay still: widening, darting, not blinking, losing focus. Packard could read her mind from each tiny muscle movement. The shock, the disbelief, the refusal to accept that it might have happened to her had she and Ashley switched places, then the realization it very well could.

"You don't… Tom didn't do it, did he? He couldn't have."

"Tom was on a boat with their boys when it happened," Packard said, taking out his notebook.

"So he's cleared."

"So we're pursuing every possible avenue in our search for answers."

Now a new understanding on her face. "And you're here because I had an affair with Tom and you think I might have had something to do with it?"

"I don't think anything like that. But I need to know where you were two days ago."

Cara had been clutching her phone the whole time. She pulled up her calendar and showed him the screen. "I work full time and then some. I was in meetings all day Wednesday, both here and in the office and online. In the evening, I went school shopping with my niece." She swiped the screen. "Thursday, more meetings, a long run with my husband after work. We're training for the Twin Cities Marathon in October." She moved to her photo app and showed him dated selfies and photos of herself and others. "Dozens of people can vouch for my whereabouts the last several days."

"Good," Packard said. "Have you had any contact with Tom recently?"

"No. When we ended things, we ended things."

"After he texted the photo to the wrong number."

Cara just stared at him.

"Tom said you thought there might have been an opportunity for both of you to leave your marriages and be together."

"I'm sure that's what he thought."

"And you didn't?"

"I simply asked the question that if we were so happy in our marriages, why were we sneaking around together?"

"What was your answer to that question?" Packard asked.

Cara sighed. "You ever been married?"

"I have not."

She looked at Easton annoyed. "Do you do anything besides stand there and flex?"

"No, ma'am."

"Listen, we were having fun," she said to Packard. "I told him to take care of business at home and maybe we could still have fun. It wasn't a goddamn proposal like you're making it sound."

"Did you ever meet his wife, Ashley?"

Cara thought about her answer. She touched her temple. "Yes. Once," she admitted. "Ashley showed up here unannounced. Just like the two of you."

"When was this?"

Cara looked at her phone. "I had big client meeting that day… It was a month ago."

"What happened?" Packard asked.

"I did the exact same thing. Brought her down here. Asked her what the hell she wanted."

"And?"

"She said she wanted to meet the woman her husband was fucking behind her back. I said, 'Take a good look and then I need you to leave.' She wanted to know who initiated things. I said it was mostly her husband but the attraction was mutual. She just stood there fuming. I could tell she wanted to hate me, to attack me. I think the feminist in her wouldn't let her put all the blame on the other woman. I told her I was sorry."

"What did she say?" Packard asked.

"She scoffed. 'You're sorry you got caught. Both of you. When the time comes, Tom's going to be the one who's sorry.'"

Packard wrote in his notebook. "Any idea what she meant by that?"

"No."

"Did you tell Tom?"

"No, we'd already cut off all communication. I didn't see a need to reopen it."

"Did Tom make any promises while you were together?"

"The only promises were in the project contract we signed. On time and on budget." She looked at her phone. "If there's nothing else, I'm late for a meeting."

Packard got her number, gave her his card, and they all went back to the stairwell. Cara went up; he and Easton went down.

Back in Easton's vehicle, Packard said, "She seems clean."

"Does this case read like a hit was involved?"

Packard shrugged. "Not really. When I think of a hit, I think of a gun from a distance. The attack on Ashley was up close with a knife. No sexual assault. I can't put my finger on it. It felt…unplanned."

"So what now?" Easton asked.

"Can you drop me off at the bus station?"

"What's there?"

"Uh…the bus," Packard said.

"You're taking the bus home?"

"I'm not hitchhiking. I can take a bus to Bemidji and have someone pick me up there."

"How long's the ride?"

"About five and a half hours."

"I wish I could drive you," Easton said, hand on Packard's thigh. "I should get to work."

"Really? What happened to there's time for everything? Time is imaginary."

"I made that up to get you naked again."

Packard turned and reached for his seat belt. "It worked," he said.

On the bus ride home, Packard had plenty of time to think about what he knew so far about Ashley's homicide. He'd followed all the obvious trails—it wasn't the bullies that vandalized Noah's car at the party, and it wasn't Tom, who was on a boat with the boys when it happened, and it wasn't his mistress, who was far from Sandy Lake. Neither Cara nor Tom seemed cunning enough to plot to kill Tom's wife. What would be the point if Cara was still married? Were they going to kill her husband, too? Unlikely. Whoever killed Ashley took a big chance taking her out at home with her husband and kids barely out of sight on a boat. That spoke to desperation, to urgency. Killing her before she…what?

And what about Ashley's comment to Cara. *When the time comes, Tom's going to be the one who's sorry.*

What did that mean? If anyone was plotting something, it sounded like it was Ashley. Was she mustering her resources in preparation for leaving Tom? Lisa Washington, the lawyer, hadn't mentioned anything about divorce conversations but Packard hadn't asked her about them either.

He texted Lisa.

> Did Ashley ask you to represent her in a divorce?

The bus had started full in Minneapolis and let off more passengers than it took on at each stop. Across the aisle, a young woman was lying across both seats looking up at her phone. Packard stared out the window beside him. He was sitting high above the road, high above the ditch and the fields of sugar beets that whipped past his window in rows of leafy stalks. He saw pro-life billboards and real estate billboards and casino billboards. Tall, beautiful, undamaged trees. They went under a bridge and a bicyclist loaded with gear who was following a state trail from one side of the road to the other.

His phone buzzed with a text from Lisa.

> I'm not a div atty. She didn't mention divorce. Didn't request a referral. We just talked about the vandalism.

He gave Lisa's text a thumbs-up and turned back to the window. The thrum of the bus and the bright afternoon sunlight had him longing for something he couldn't quite name. He thought about Easton and that kiss over breakfast. Wondered how he felt about it. Wondered how he was supposed to feel about it. The key, he knew, was to try to imagine he was a normal person who longed for more than work and a dog in his life.

He and Easton hadn't had a lot of tender moments like that. (God. Tender moments? Was he writing a country song?) What he meant was that their time together was usually short on romance. Less silhouetted lovers drinking champagne in front of a fireplace and more like a Greco-Roman wrestling match sponsored by your favorite water-based lube.

This wasn't unfamiliar ground for him. He'd dated a cop before. He'd been on the receiving end of romantic gestures from Marcus and felt just as confused about how to react. Intimacy made him feel uncomfortably seen, which ran contrary to his desire to be invisible. And if not invisible, then utilitarian. Useful as a car jack or a shovel but out of mind when not needed. With Marcus, he used to laugh or move in close, anything to break eye contact and avoid words.

Packard turned away from the window, wincing at the memory. Meeting Symphony had resurrected a lot of emotions, a lot of memories. Not all of them good. Now he had Easton to think about. That moment at breakfast might have meant something or nothing. The question was, would Packard act like he had in the past, or had he changed?

He was an hour out from his stop when he realized he hadn't arranged for anyone to meet him. There was no cab or Uber that was going to drive him to Sandy Lake. He texted Reynolds.

> Can you pick me up in Hackensack in an hour? Dinner on me for your trouble.

Reynolds responded almost immediately.

> Sure. I got news.

The bus dropped Packard off in a big parking lot next to a restaurant with an outdoor deck shaded by blue and white umbrellas that was completely empty because of the heat and the air quality.

He found Reynolds inside at a tall two-top not far from the bar. A waitress came just as Packard sat down. He ordered a beer and a cheeseburger. Reynolds got a Mountain Dew and a chicken tenders basket. The department's junior-most deputy barely looked older than a twelve-year-old. When his wife wasn't cooking, he ate like one.

While they waited for their food, Packard told him a little bit about Symphony and Marcus, everything about his interview with Cara, and nothing about how Easton had drained all his fluids.

Then it was Reynolds's turn.

"We got Ashley's phone records," he said after the waitress dropped off their food. "You noticed there was blood on her phone. DNA is still out but we typed the blood on the screen and it wasn't hers. So the killer used her phone."

"Any prints?"

"Nothing usable."

"So what did he do on the phone?"

"He deleted a text message."

Packard eyes widened. He had to move the bite he'd taken to the side of his mouth. "No shit."

"Yeah."

"So he texted her, then deleted his text from her phone, but her phone records show her receiving a text from a number that's not on her phone."

"Exactly."

"What do you know about the number?"

"Nothing yet. I'm working on the subpoena."

"Nothing in the databases?"

"Nope."

"You try calling it?"

Reynolds shook his head. "Wanted to see what you thought before I did anything."

"You have the number?"

"I do. I texted it to myself just in case."

Packard wiped his hands on the napkin in his lap and took out his cell phone. He looked at the number on Reynolds's screen and typed it into his. He turned the volume all the way up and hit the speaker button.

This is Red. Leave a message.

Packard ended the call. He ate a french fry with the puzzled expression of a philosopher.

"What are you thinking?" Reynolds asked.

"Just trying to imagine who Red is. If that's his real name or a nickname. How old he is."

"That area code isn't a Minnesota number."

"I noticed that, too. It's probably a burner. The area code could be from anywhere. What time was the text sent?"

"1:47 p.m.," Reynolds said.

"Any chance Suresh could recover the text?"

"He said no. Her cloud storage was full and not backing up. He also said something about the latest phone software not preserving deleted messages like it used to."

"What else did the phone tell him?"

"The last time the phone was unlocked was 1:59 p.m. Twelve minutes after the message was received."

"If he's getting blood on her phone, she's dead by 1:59." Packard took out his notebook and flipped back a few pages. "Her son Noah called 911 at 2:39."

"Forty minutes later," Reynolds said.

"Any other calls to or from Red's number on her phone?"

"No. No calls, no other texts."

"So the deleted text was first contact. He had to have her number in order to text her."

"Meaning he already had it or she told it to him at the time."

"We don't know what time he got there so he could have texted her to tell her he was on his way or he could have texted her while he was there."

"Why would you text someone you were planning to kill?" Reynolds asked.

"I'm guessing the killing was a spur-of-the-moment decision. She threatened him somehow. Or triggered him."

"He knows he's texted her from his number but he kills her anyway because she might…what?"

Packard nodded knowingly. "That's the exact question I was asking myself on the bus. We need to figure out the carrier for this number and get them a subpoena. I want to know who else called this number and vice versa. I want to know where this phone was sold."

Reynolds dipped a chicken finger into honey mustard. "I'll finish the paperwork tonight, send it tomorrow. If it's not a major carrier, it could take time to get anything back. We could be looking at a week or two."

"I know. Which means we have to find another way to figure out who the hell Red is."

CHAPTER SIXTEEN

The roofers finished the church job just as the sun started to set.

Back at the motel, they moved like the walking dead, heavy and hunched and hungry. Each man's pay for the week was in an envelope under the door to his room. They pocketed the money and left the doors open to let out the heat of the day trapped inside. There was a car in the lot—a maroon Chevy Malibu—Charlie didn't recognize. A new guest maybe. No sign of the tree guys. One of their trucks was gone.

Charlie got dinner started while the crew showered. Grilled corn on the cob with butter and Tajín. Bratwursts with peppers and onions. A case of Modelo. The sound of frogs as the first stars came out.

They ate together at the picnic table and drank beer and smoked cigarettes in the breeze that picked up as it got dark. It was Friday night, not that weekends meant anything to this group. They'd rather work than take time off. Time off meant less money. Time off meant sitting around with nothing to do but drink and imagine all the ways their lives could or should have been different.

Francisco went to bed first, followed by Matthias, who reminded the rest of them not to stay up too late. The kid, Miguel, leaned back in a chair outside the motel office where the Wi-Fi was strongest and there was an outdoor outlet to charge his phone.

Charlie sat at the picnic table with Juan and College Boy, who wasn't old enough to drink but had helped himself to a third beer and sat with it in front of him, his fingers barely touching it like it might be a booby-trapped golden idol. He rattled on about how steep the church roof was and how his calves were killing him. Juan sat on the bench with his back to the table and kept an eye on his cousin, Luis, pacing back and forth in their room while talking loudly in Spanish.

"*Como está su*…your cousin?" Charlie asked. "*Como está Luis*?"

Juan stared down at the beer can between his legs and shrugged. "*Su esposa no está contenta. Él lleva mucho tiempo desaparecido. Su bebé está creciendo sin padre.*"

College Boy looked at Charlie for help translating. He had rounded gym muscles that bulged out of the tank top he was wearing.

"His wife isn't happy. Something, something. His son is without a father."

Charlie knew Juan and Luis were from the same village in Jalisco. Juan came to the United States first and had spent years working on roofs. He could unroll underlayment with his feet on a steep roof and chase it with a stapler. He could balance a sheet of plywood sheathing on his knee and cut it to size with a circular saw without taking a single measurement. He was patient with the newbies on the crew and had the sad eyes of a man who lived in the past. Perhaps a clue to his heartache was how he got a certain look on his face at the mention of Luis's wife.

College Boy buried his chin in his neck and burped loudly. "At least Luis is working his ass off, trying to provide for them. A lot of families don't have that."

Charlie gave College Boy a sideways look. He knew almost nothing about him. Couldn't even remember his name. They'd been calling him College Boy since the first day. He was from the area but his parents' house had been damaged in the storm. They left on an RV trip while the house was under construction and told their son he could stay in town if he found a job and a place to stay.

"What do you know about what a kid needs?" Charlie said to him. "You're a kid yourself. I bet your dad was around all the time and somehow you still ended up being the only white boy I've ever seen on a roofing crew."

"I'm on this crew because I need a job and I don't have the best reputation around here."

"Why is that?"

"I hang out with the wrong people," College Boy admitted. He slumped a bit.

"Doing what?"

"Stupid shit. I don't want to talk about it."

"And what are you going to do when we leave town and you're stuck here with your bad reputation?"

"Maybe I'll come with you until I start college in the fall. There's still plenty of summer left."

Charlie shook his head. "The fuck you will. I'm not hauling an underage drinker across state lines." He snatched College Boy's can, squeezed it, and dropped it into the paper bag beside the picnic table.

"Motherfucker, you got so drunk you got arrested. You're giving me shit about a couple of beers?"

"I didn't get arrested. I was given a place to sleep it off. There's only room for one alcoholic on this crew. Go to bed," he said. "Five a.m. is coming soon."

"You say that like I haven't been up at five every day since I started."

College Boy pushed up from the table and Charlie and Juan watched him walk away. Charlie yelled across the lot at Miguel. "Hey. Bedtime." To Juan: "*Como se dice in español*?" How do you say it in Spanish? "*Va a la cama*?"

Juan shook his head at Charlie's terrible Spanish. "*Ruferito. Acostarse*," he said. Little roofer. Bedtime.

Luis was off the phone. He came over to the picnic table and reached into the cooler for a beer. Friday night traffic went by on the road behind them. A car with a thumping stereo. A pickup raised high on stupid tires.

Luis sat where College Boy had been sitting and talked in Spanish to the back of Juan's head. Charlie lit another cigarette and pretended not to understand their conversation.

Isabella wants me to come home, Luis said.

You've been gone a long time.

Aye. I know. Going back and forth is too risky.

That's why I don't go back.

Isabella says I don't love her. I say the money is my love. I'm working so hard for her and our son.

Juan grunted. *Maybe I'll go home and be with Isabella.*

That's not funny.

I was in love with her first.

But she chose me.

Juan sighed.

Charlie smoked. Deep in his brain he recalled something from his college reading days about cousins in love with the same woman. A story from *The Canterbury Tales.*

If he remembered correctly, they tried to kill each other.

Charlie couldn't breathe when he ran the air conditioner in his room at night. He put a fan by the window to cool his space and let the evening pass into night while he sat at the picnic table and washed each cigarette down with another beer like they were paired on a tasting menu.

He was still sitting there when the tree guys made a hard turn into the gravel lot in their pickup truck and came to a sudden stop in a cloud of dust and muffled country music. They got out of their truck. In between them was a woman who slid out on the passenger side and adjusted her skirt as the short one named Dustin stood behind the door, waiting for her to move so he could shut it.

The driver was Pete. He was tall with a black beard and a belly and big hands that looked like they'd been toughened against a brick wall. "Hey, Charlie. *Dondé* your *amigos*, eh? We brought tequila!"

Charlie sighed. He picked the corner of his mouth with his cigarette hand. "They're all in bed. We had a long day."

"Yeah, but it's fucking Friday," Pete said. He reached through the truck window, flashed his brights at the motel, and honked the horn. "*Muchachos*! Let's party!" More honking. Both he and Dustin looked like they'd showered and dressed for a night out. Jeans that hadn't been worn as work pants. A black polo shirt on Pete that had shrunk and just barely covered his belly. A clean Corona T-shirt for Dustin.

Both of them were unsteady on their feet. Pete came around the truck and threw an arm around the woman's shoulders while Dustin fell a step back. She was wearing a miniskirt and a pink tank top with spaghetti straps. A small purse hanging to one side. She put a hand on Pete's belly as they came over to the picnic table.

Charlie felt a sudden soberness come over him. Matthias's crew might have been in prison or on a submarine for as much female companionship as they'd had over the last months. Usually, long days and hard work helped maintain equilibrium in this camp of men without women. Now and then a funk came over the crew. They got sullen, more in their heads. They drank more. A woman walking into this scenario had the potential to create chaos.

"Who's your friend?" Charlie asked.

"Her name's Donna," Pete said.

"DARLA!" the woman said, slapping his stomach.

Pete kissed the top of her head. "Darla, my bad."

Charlie didn't care what her name was. He didn't want her there.

Dustin had a thin paper bag in his hand. He took out a big bottle of cheap whiskey, a big bottle of tequila, and a sleeve of fluorescent plastic shot glasses.

"We got a bottle for the three amigos. Firewater from the homeland," Pete said. "Tah-kee-LAH de Meh-hee-coh!"

Charlie hated guys like Pete. He'd served men like him at every bartending job he'd had. Guys who assumed that everyone was their friend, that casual racism was okay as long as your intentions were good. Guys who turned ugly real quick when their drunk feelings were hurt.

Juan poked his head out of his room. So did Matthias. College Boy came over barefoot in a pair of basketball shorts, no shirt, the bare-chested pride of youth. "Come here, motherfucker! Making the rest of us look bad with those abs," Pete yelled. He had Darla under his arm and he moved her like she was a log he was wrestling as he twisted around and fist-bumped the boy.

"What are we drinking?" College Boy asked.

"Only the finest," Dustin said, laying out the shot glasses. "White or brown liquor. You pick her."

Charlie stared at Darla, big phony smile on her face. She adjusted the strap of her top, and said, "Lemme pour. I used to bartend in a previous life."

"It doesn't take a degree from bartending school to pour liquid in a tiny glass," Charlie said.

She gave him a wink as she set two shot glasses side by side and quickly moved the whiskey bottle from one to the other. "You look like you want a double," she said, grabbing both glasses in one hand and moving them in front of him.

She poured shots for Dustin and Pete and College Boy.

"Get you some of that," Pete said to her.

She put the bottle to her mouth and threw her head back. The tree guys whooped in admiration. Charlie was the only one who saw the tip of her tongue plug the opening.

Behind her, the others came out of their rooms, slow and uncertain, sniffing the air. Only Francisco and Miguel's room stayed dark. Matthias, Juan, Luis. The group of men grew around the table. Seven of them, one of her. Snow White or another fairy tale full of hungry wolves.

CHAPTER SEVENTEEN

It was dark by the time Reynolds got them close to Sandy Lake. On the way, Packard had stared at the number they'd called from the restaurant, now logged in his recent calls. Having the killer's phone number and name—

This is Red. Leave a message.

—and not being able to take meaningful action with it felt like a stick in the eye. They needed an account name and address. Even if it was a prepaid phone with no account info, they could get its call log and find out who else the phone had called, then contact those people and find out who the number belonged to.

Packard kept mulling the order of events. The killer texted Ashley. Then he killed her and deleted his text a few minutes later. He wouldn't have texted her in the first place if the plan all along had been to kill her. What happened in that gap of time to make things take such a violent turn? What did Ashley see? What did she know about Red that cost her her life?

They drove by the brush drop-off site as they came into town. Mountains of shredded wood reached fifteen feet high and stretched the length of a football field. Enormous piles of tree limbs waited to be fed into the industrial grinder. A sign offering FREE MULCH felt like a bad joke.

They passed the Tabard Motel, with its red neon sign and below that another sign with slide-in letters that promised FRE W -FI. Packard's head turned as he spotted Darla Knoll's car in the lot. He saw a group of people gathered around a picnic table. The only reason for Darla's car to be at the motel was if she was turning tricks again. The last time he'd talked to her, she said she was working on her nursing degree.

He looked away and let it go. If whoever was on patrol that night was paying attention, they'd pull into the Tabard's lot and check on things. Darla was a known entity.

When they got to his house, Packard thanked Reynolds for the ride and unlocked the door, expecting Frank to be right there, ready for a walk. *He's with Bert*, Packard thought before remembering he'd dropped Frank off at Gary's house the day before. How was that only a day ago?

Packard locked the door, turned on some lights.

His phone buzzed with a text.

> Having some people over tonight if you're free. Be great to see you.

Kyle, the brewery owner.

Packard looked up at the giant hole where his living room ceiling used to be. It was hot in his house and it smelled like smoke. He wanted nothing more than to be back in Minneapolis in Easton's bed. Anywhere but here.

Yeah, he was free.

Packard pulled up to Kyle's just as a car was leaving. He was late but knew these things sometimes went late. He found two other people around the bonfire with Kyle—a local couple, David and Elizabeth, who supported themselves doing music gigs around the area and selling handmade soap and honey from their beehives. They had an eight-year-old daughter who was in the house watching something on her iPad.

Packard brought bottled root beer he'd picked up from Kyle's brewery and had a seat in a metal chair that rocked under his weight.

Kyle and David had guitars. "What do you want to hear, Ben?"

"Surprise me," he said.

Kyle looked down as he picked out a few notes. He swept his hair back only to have it fall again and curl around his forehead. He had a permanent five-o'clock shadow and a scar on his lip. "Remember 'Anchorage'?" he asked Dave.

Kyle played and Dave kept time with his wedding ring on the body of his guitar. Elizabeth sang a song about a woman writing to an old friend in Dallas and the reply coming from Anchorage, Alaska. The friend recalls their punk rock days and laughs at how she's become a housewife.

Packard didn't know the song. "You've never heard of Michelle Shocked?" Elizabeth asked when they were done. "She has a couple of perfect early albums. You won't find them on any streaming platform. You'll have to buy physical copies if you can."

They played another song by Shocked, "Come a Long Way." Elizabeth closed her eyes and sang without an ounce of inhibition. Packard smiled but also felt his mood sliding sideways. There'd been too much of the past on his mind lately, too much loss, and now there were these songs about getting older and life not working out the way you planned, beautiful but also elegiac. Packard was glad he wasn't drinking. Alcohol would have only made him more maudlin.

"Did you see the photo of Jill and Tim and the baby in the *Sandy Lake Gazette*?" Elizabeth asked.

"I didn't," Packard admitted.

"It was in the birth announcement section. Super cute pic of them," Elizabeth said.

"I can't imagine Thielen signing up for that. Someone must have black-mailed her into it."

They played more songs and chatted about the bees and an upcoming music festival Dave and Elizabeth were playing. No one asked him about Ashley's murder or the latest fentanyl overdose or the wrong-way drunk driver who killed an elderly couple on their way into town for bingo at the VFW. They didn't talk about all the ways people were still suffering since the storm. Out of work, out of their homes. The enormous bills. The things that could never be replaced.

After an hour, Dave and Elizabeth corralled their daughter, who gave Packard a shy wave on the way to their minivan, and left. Kyle threw another log on the fire, then went into the house. Packard watched fireflies blinking and reminded himself that his mood was up to him. Yes, time was the thief of all things. You had to enjoy the summer nights and fireflies while you could.

Kyle came back out with small paper plates holding diamonds of baklava Elizabeth made with Dave's honey. They ate and licked their fingers and threw the plates in the fire.

"What's new with you?" Kyle asked.

Packard told him about the surprise visit from Symphony and the shock of meeting someone with Marcus's face..

"It felt like seeing a ghost. I was thrilled to meet her, but she wasn't too happy to find out her brother was gay."

"She didn't know?"

"She'd been incarcerated for a long time and had cut off communication. They missed their chance to reconcile."

He told Kyle about her storming out of his house, her arrest in Sandy Lake for multiple moving violations, how they hadn't left on the best of terms after he drove her back to Minneapolis.

"I'd genuinely like to get to know her and help her know Marcus the way I knew him. He was an amazing man."

"And what do you want from her?"

Packard was taken back by the question. He picked at the label on his bottle.

"She reminds me of a different time in my life. Maybe a time I'm nostalgic for right now when everything feels like it's going to hell. My house is falling down. The weather is garbage. I miss my dog."

"You sound like a country song."

Packard laughed. "I had the same thought on the bus ride home today. More than the nostalgia, Symphony reminds me that there was unfinished business between Marcus and me when he died. Maybe I'm trying to use her to set things right."

"Is that even possible?"

"No. Marcus is dead. There's no changing the past. What I really want is to hear her stories and tell her mine so neither of us has to feel like the only one cradling the flame of his memory."

Kyle picked up his guitar again. "You could be a real boon to each other. I hope she comes around."

Packard nodded. "How's business?"

"Things started strong but have gone downhill since the storm," Kyle said and played a waah-waah sound on the guitar. "We have spotty good days but nothing like earlier in the summer. The air quality is making it worse. People are staying home. I have a lot of summer ale that's going to go bad in the keg if people don't start showing up again."

"I'm sorry to hear that," Packard said.

Kyle smiled and shrugged. He strummed something on the guitar that Packard recognized but couldn't name. He hummed a bit until the words came. "'Closer to Fine.' Indigo Girls," he said.

"You got it."

"How did you learn how to play guitar?"

"Just started playing with a friend when I was in high school. We were both into Dylan. Learned how to play by ear a little bit. Got some books. YouTube was just starting to become a thing and was a game changer."

"I always wanted to learn," Packard said.

"Why haven't you?"

"I don't know. Buying a guitar felt like a big commitment when I wasn't sure I was going to have the time or passion to dedicate to it."

"I have six guitars. You can borrow one. Come over here. I'll show you a few chords."

They had been sitting on opposite sides of the fire. Packard got up and had a seat on Kyle's left on the same bench. Kyle handed him the acoustic guitar. Packard marveled at how the dip in the body fit perfectly over his thigh, how his right arm draped over the top and his left hand reached for the neck. It felt organic, like an extension of him.

Kyle explained the names of the strings and the frets that went down the neck.

"Put your pointer finger on the third string, second fret, your middle finger on the bottom string, and your ring finger on the second string, third fret." He stood and took a green plastic pick from his pocket. "Use this."

Packard strummed the D chord a few times. Kyle showed him C and G. Taught him a few strumming patterns. Kyle stood behind him, leaned over while Packard tried to switch between chords. Packard leaned back, not really into him, just upright to keep from being completely hunched over the guitar. Kyle taught him how to pick out the first few notes of "Seven Nation Army" by the White Stripes, which was the first time Packard felt like he was playing something he recognized.

Kyle sat again, straddling the bench so that Packard was almost between his legs. "You do the chords and I'll strum," he said, scooting even closer.

After a few laughable messy chord changes, what almost sounded like Johnny Cash "Ring of Fire" came from the guitar. They played like that for a couple of minutes. Packard could feel the heat off Kyle's body on his right side. He wanted to look away from his fingers, look at Kyle, but he couldn't do that and change chords.

They finished with Packard holding the G chord and Kyle doing a quick strum and banging his knuckle against the guitar body.

"You played your first song," he said.

"I can't believe it. You're a great teacher."

For a brief moment they sat there, as close as two men not having sex with each other could possibly be. Packard stared at Kyle, looking for some kind of a sign of what should happen next. Kyle stared back at him and didn't move.

Thielen had made fun of him for coming out here and playing tambourine. Come back with a better story, she'd said.

Kyle still hadn't moved.

Shoot your shot, player.

Packard leaned closer and tilted his head.

Kyle pulled away. "Uh…wait. Whoa," he said.

Packard jumped to his feet. "Oh fuck," he said. "Fuck. I'm sorry."

He was holding the guitar just below the head. He didn't know where to put it. Setting it on the ground seemed like the wrong thing to do. Lying it on the bench where he sat? No. He held the guitar away from himself, pulled it closer. It was stuck to his hand like a piece of packing tape. *Throw it in the fire*, he thought. *Burn it down. Burn everything down.*

"I didn't mean to. I mean…obviously I meant to. Oh god…I'm sorry."

"Hey, hey, relax. I'll take the guitar," Kyle said.

Packard handed it over and Kyle laid it across the arms of a nearby chair. "Sit down," he said. "We're cool."

Packard didn't sit. He drew his hands down his face and walked to the other side of the firepit and stared up at the sky.

How had he read things so wrong? And why was he trying to kiss another guy when Easton had gotten him out of his clothes for the third time only twelve hours ago? It hurt being so stupid. It made him groan like he'd been punched in the gut.

He sat in a chair with the fire between them. "I'm sorry. That was uncalled for. I don't know what I was thinking."

"No, I've been sending mixed messages. It's all on me," Kyle said.

"I don't accept that. At no point did you say were gay or bi or interested in me or anything like that. I don't know if I assumed or if it was wishful thinking or what. I shouldn't have—" He couldn't say the words *tried to kiss you.* "I shouldn't have done that."

"I'm not really into labels. That's part of the problem," Kyle said. "I've been very physical with you."

That part was true. Packard thought of all the times they'd stood too close, shoulders rubbing, back of the hands touching. The long hugs, Kyle's mouth close to his ear.

"A few minutes ago I was all but wrapped around you. That wasn't just about showing you how to play guitar."

"Okay…I'm confused. What are you saying?"

"I'm saying I like you. I'm drawn to you."

"But what? No kissing?"

Kyle sighed and reached between his feet and yanked out a thick blade of crabgrass that he peeled into strips. "We've been hanging out and talking a lot. There's things about me and my life we haven't even touched on."

Also true. Their talks had covered a wide range of topics: their jobs, their aspirations, Kyle's sobriety, policing in America, politics and toxic masculinity, music and books.

One thing Packard had noticed was that Kyle was less forthcoming about his past. He just knew the highlights. That Kyle had grown up in Sandy Lake and left immediately after high school for the Cities. Went to trade school and community college. There was a lot of partying. Then the idea to try brewing with a cousin and, a few years in, the realization that starting a business to underwrite their drinking habit wasn't the soundest foundation on which to build their financial future. Finally, a bad car accident that made him realize everything had to change.

"You want to talk about it now?" Packard asked.

"Mmmm." Kyle made a sideways face. "No. I will someday. It's a lot. It's a long story."

"Whenever you're ready. No pressure. I enjoy our friendship exactly the way it's been. I'm not going to make a move like that again. I promise."

"Maybe I'll make the next move."

Packard shrugged. Honestly, he would probably be the one to pull away next time unless he knew more about what Kyle was withholding. If Kyle never wanted to tell him, that was okay, too.

"I'm going to go. Thanks for the lesson."

"Want to take a guitar home with you?"

"Not right now. Thank you. Work is crazy. I wouldn't know how to keep it tuned. Maybe I can get a few more lessons first."

"Any time."

On a normal night, they would have hugged. Packard couldn't stomach the thought. He grabbed his two remaining root beers and said good night. It was ten thirty. He texted Thielen to call him if she was still up.

On the drive home, he wondered what would make him take a chance like that. It wasn't sex. He'd just had plenty. Thank you, Detective Easton.

There was something about Kyle that intrigued him. This sober brewer. This amateur musician. This dark-haired mystery.

He drove by the Big Beaver, a bar that sat by itself off the two-lane highway. Not as many cars as he would have expected for a Friday night. He'd tracked a murder suspect there once, had a shovel thrown at his head, and wrestled the guy in the snowy parking lot, the memory of which was nowhere near as bad as that of Kyle pulling away as he leaned in.

Packard's stomach cramped again. It felt like this could be the end of him. The big, strong cop taken down by a shovel to his dignity.

CHAPTER EIGHTEEN

By midnight, everyone at the motel was drunk and hungry. A pile of logs and flames rose out of the firepit and the grill was lit again while the men made a list and threw twenty-dollar bills onto the picnic table like the ante in a poker game. College Boy and Luis drove a mile to the store and came back with cigarettes and another twelve-pack of Modelo to replace the one Charlie drank after dinner. They bought a stack of frozen burger patties and cheese and buns and chips. College Boy had wanted Top the Tater dip and had to explain to everyone what the fuck that was.

The tree guys had spent the day taking down a nearly eighty-foot cottonwood that was three trunks fused together at the base. It was no use trying to impress them with tales of the steep church roof Matthias's crew had worked on for the last two days. Dustin and Pete climbed higher and saw things a roofing crew would have to crane their necks to look up at. Weeks after the storm, damaged trees were still coming down on houses and across roads. When the tree guys went to a job with roof damage, they handed out Matthias's card, said they knew the crew and they did good work. Matthias did the same for them when he found a house that needed trees removed.

Charlie made himself useful at the grill, the air thick with the smell of burning charcoal and sizzling beef. Greasy flames flared like fireworks and the men tore into the burgers as quickly as they came off the heat, wiping their mouths with the backs of their hands. The levels in the liquor bottles dropped. College Boy picked up red and green shot glasses off the ground and tossed them in the firepit where they melted into tragic Christmas bulbs.

Charlie saved the last burger for himself and sat at the picnic table beside Matthias, who was looking at his phone. "Forecast has changed. Rain tomorrow. Starting early in the morning," he said.

"All day?"

"Looks like it."

"Can't tear off a roof in the rain," Charlie said.

Matthias looked at his crew drinking late into the night.

"The guys deserve a day off," he said. "I've got a few more days here of meetings with insurance adjusters. If everyone signs off, you guys should have two more weeks of jobs. I placed a materials order today. I'll do one more before I leave."

It was hard for Charlie to think about work. If the weather was going to keep them off the job, he wanted to give in to the whiskey, enjoy this brief window when the booze in his blood felt like warm relief, like pissing himself. He poured another shot.

"Where would we go next?" Charlie asked. He bit into the burger. Didn't taste nearly as good as the whiskey.

Matthias had his weather app open. "There was a tornado and some big hail in Arkansas. Pretty rural but that means not much competition. There's a hurricane building in the Gulf. Projected landfall is right up the ass crack of where Mississippi and Alabama meet. We could spend months down there if it's bad enough."

"We should rebuild the crew when we get there," Charlie said. "Too many kids working for us right now."

Matthias shrugged and stared at his phone. "The work's getting done. Everybody's getting paid."

"College Boy has to stay behind. We should figure out what to do with Miguel. Nobody around here is trying to foster a fucking fourteen-year-old." Charlie glanced at the only room in the motel with the door closed and the lights off.

"Maybe Francisco is," Matthias said.

"That tattooed motherfucker ain't nobody's parent."

Matthias shrugged. "He's done a good job keeping the kid in line."

Charlie reached for the whiskey, poured. "He could be raping that kid in there for all we know."

"That's not happening."

"How do you know?"

"Cause if that kid was getting raped, we'd hear it or hear about it. Miguel trusts Francisco," Matthias said. "I'm more concerned that my crew lead would think that was happening and just shrug it off."

Charlie didn't believe Miguel was being abused. He was suggesting it because of the way Francisco had taunted him to climb the ladder, because whiskey made him indifferent to things like the truth. "Kid should be in school. Learning English. Not tearing off roofs."

"You want him gone, you figure out what to do with him," Matthias said. "He can stay on the crew and take off roofs until he's eighteen for all I care."

They could leave Miguel behind. They'd done it before. Back in Oklahoma, there was a guy on the crew named Alberto who did less work and more complaining than everyone else. He got drunk their last night in town and wanted to fight Francisco over his gang affiliation. He came at Francisco with a knife. Francisco punched Alberto so hard he was unconscious before he hit the ground. To make sure he'd be of no further use to Matthias, Francisco stepped on his elbow and bent his arm the wrong way until it snapped. Charlie was glad to be rid of him. He dumped Alberto outside an emergency room and followed the rest of the crew to Iowa where a hailstorm had destroyed the early corn and everyone's roof.

Charlie shook his head, sat up straight and pulled his focus away from the tunnel closing in around him. The picnic table felt like a tiny island. He noticed Matthias was gone and the music had changed from country coming from the truck to the Latin music they normally listened to on the job. Juan and Luis had pulled chairs up to the firepit. Luis had his elbows on his knees, staring into the fire. Juan was leaning back, looking up at the stars.

Charlie looked around. It took him a minute to realize who else was missing.

The tree guys.

The woman.

Who else?

College Boy.

The trees guys shared the first room in the motel's long leg. A thin curtain was drawn across the window, the door closed. The yellow light inside created the silhouette of a man against the window. Looked like Pete, the bearded one. His shadow barely moved, like he was transfixed by what was in front of him.

Charlie took a deep breath. The whiskey's warm, pissed-pants feeling had been replaced by a cold, shivering emptiness. Too many nights ended this way. He remembered being young and writing poems about rivers and wild mushrooms. He was going to publish and get invited to speak at conferences and colleges and teach kids about finding the truth in everything they observed. Laughable now. What did a drunk know about the truth?

The door to the tree guys' room opened and College Boy scurried out, hands in front of his crotch. He went to his own room and slammed the door. There was movement and voices in the room he left. Charlie felt like he was watching a play, waiting for actors to emerge from the wings. After a bit, the woman came out alone, smiling at Charlie as she crossed the gravel lot and took a seat across the table from him.

"You want to party?" she asked.

Charlie blinked at her like a sleepy cat.

She put her little purse on the picnic table and opened it. "I got weed. Coke. It's clean—I tested it for fent. The other guys had some."

"Mmmm," Charlie said and shook his head.

"No drugs then. Let's go to your room. How long since you've been with a woman?"

"A long time," Charlie said.

"Let's do something about that. I could blow your mind, baby."

Charlie's feelings about the woman in front of him felt like a snake slithering under his clothes, too quick to get a grip on. The booze had him zoomed in on every blemish on her face, on the old acne scars constellated across her chest. He wanted to reject her but give her all his money to save her. He wanted to admire the bravery it took to do sex work and shame her for whatever she did in that room with College Boy while the other two watched.

"You were only pretending to drink," he said and stuck the tip of his tongue out.

She smiled and lifted the whiskey bottle and raised a questioning eyebrow. Charlie nodded. "I'm at work, sweetheart," she said and filled his shot glass. "A girl has to keep her head on straight if she's going to be alone with all these men in a motel."

"You meet the tree guys downtown?"

"That's my car over there. I came here looking for anyone who wanted to have some fun. We went downtown together, then brought the party back here."

"Is College Boy all right?"

"That boy thought he was going to put his hands around my throat and choke me. I had to teach him a lesson. He'll be fine."

Charlie drank the whiskey in front of him. He looked at her and at the bottle, and she poured him another. "You shouldn't be here," he said.

"Why not?"

"We got work to do. We don't need a woman…messing things up. Causing conflict."

"I'm not here to cause conflict. I'm trying to make a buck same as you guys. We're all just trying to eat."

"We're all whores," Charlie said. "But women are also liars. You say one thing and do something else. You make things up."

Old wounds. Old stories. A drunken night in college with a girl he liked. Both of them too drunk to fuck. The next day, her telling people he'd done things to her while she was passed out. She'd taken off her own clothes, got into the bed with him. She touched him, too. That's how he remembered it. Everyone turning away from him after that. People who told him how much they loved his poems wouldn't look him in the eye. Wouldn't believe his version of events. He dropped out after that year. It was the beginning of the end for good old Charlie.

"I don't know who hurt you, sweetheart. It wasn't me. Let's go to your room and lie down together. We can do whatever you want."

"I stopped wanting things a long time ago," Charlie said.

"I never met a man who didn't want something." She reached across the table and put her fingers under his hand and rubbed the back with her thumb.

"You never met me until tonight." He pulled his hand away and drank.

The last thing he remembered was her sad smile as she got up from the table, grabbed the tequila bottle, and moved like a cat over to Juan and Luis by the bonfire. She stood behind Luis, rubbed his shoulders, and leaned down to whisper something in his ear.

After that, only sounds. Only ideas.

Trying to stand up.

Trying to aim his body in the direction of his room.

Juan and Luis yelling at each other.

The woman screaming.

Francisco nearly naked, his body a treasure map of tattoos from head to toe. A giant XIX across his chest.

Someone had a knife.

They all had knives.

I'll fucking kill you.

After that, nothing.

CHAPTER NINETEEN

SATURDAY

AIR QUALITY INDEX: GREEN (NORMAL)

It started raining sometime in the night. Packard woke at 5:00 a.m. to the sound of water sluicing through the gutter by his bedroom window. He went to the living room with a flashlight to make sure his patched roof was holding. No water on the floor. A small win.

In the basement, he did one hundred pull-ups, two hundred push-ups, and three hundred squats. He texted Gary to see how Frank was doing. Gary sent him back a photo of Frank and Baxter staring up at a breakfast sausage Gary was holding above them. Packard wondered if Frank missed him as much as he missed Frank. Probably not if Gary was feeding him sausage for breakfast.

Packard showered and dressed. His phone rang as he stood in front of his bedroom closet looking up at a box on the top shelf. It was Thielen.

"I just saw your text from last night. What do you want?" she asked.

"I called to say goodbye before I disappear into the Boundary Waters with a Duluth pack and a canoe and never come out."

He held the phone between his shoulder and his ear as he carried the box to his bed and opened it. Inside, Marcus's badge and an album of family photos.

"Why? What did you do?" Thielen asked.

The only thing that made him more uncomfortable than the memory of last night was speaking about it out loud. "I tried to kiss Kyle."

"What?"

"You heard me."

"Why did you do that?"

"I don't know," Packard said, walking through his house. He put the photo album and the badge on the countertop beside the garage door so he wouldn't forget them when he left. "Because you told me my last story was boring. Because it felt like the opportunity presented itself."

"What do you mean, you tried to kiss him?"

"I mean I went for it."

"And what did Kyle do?"

"Pulled away."

"Oof. Ouch," Thielen said, chuckling like an old lech. "Did you have bad breath?"

"I don't think so. I was drinking his root beer."

"I bet you'd like to taste his root beer."

"I swear, Thielen. You've gotten filthier since having the baby."

"Listen, asshole, you have no idea the storm of hormones, medications, and emotions swirling inside of me. I feel like I've turned into this weird beast: half mom, half werewolf. I want to snuggle my baby and rip everyone's throat out at the same time."

"I heard your picture was in the paper."

"Ugh. I have not and will not look at that. Kelly was behind it."

"You're kidding. I thought maybe it was Tim's mom."

"Tim's mom could give a shit about a birth announcement. Kelly asked for the photo and permission to send it in. Said it was good news from the department, builds community. Some crap like that."

"She owes you one in that case."

"She'll owe me two if I bring her the news that you tried to rub your big, wet gob all over her nephew," Thielen said. She made a sound that he interpreted as her sticking her tongue out and trying to rub it all around.

The thought of this getting back to Kelly hadn't occurred to him last night. If she found out, she'd bear down on him like a runaway truck. He remembered a horror movie from when he was a kid that had a semi with a huge grinning goblin face on the front that terrorized people trapped in a gas station. He imagined that, only with Kelly's face and the sinister music coming out of the cab was Barry Manilow.

"Why do I tell you anything?" Packard said.

"It's a fair question. I'm a horrible person sometimes," Thielen said.

"Have fun coming back to work a month early since I'm resigning and moving to the woods."

"Okay. Nice knowing you."

When he got to the sheriff's office half an hour later, Packard was surprised to see Kelly at her desk. He approached warily, worried that Thielen might have carried through with her threat.

"What are you doing here on a Saturday?" he asked.

Kelly seemed a normal amount of annoyed at the sight of him. "Working. Trying to get ahead of things before I'm out of town next week."

"For Barry?"

"Yes. He's playing make-up dates in Seattle and Spokane. I'm meeting my girlfriends out there."

Kelly had followed Barry Manilow around the world and seen him in concert more than two hundred times. Pinned to the wall of her cube was a Barry Manilow calendar that showed him at a white piano with the word MANILOW in giant purple neon behind him.

“By the way, Shepard’s looking for you.”

“He’s in today, too?”

“Yes, and don’t ask me why. I thought I was going to come in here and get some work done, and now I got all you idiots bothering me like it’s a weekday.”

“I love you, Kelly. Never forget that.”

“Ugh. Go away,” she said.

Shepard sat leaning on the arm of his chair while he looked at something on his computer screen. The last six months being sheriff had taken their toll on him. He looked fifty pounds heavier than when he won the election. Big bags under his eyes. Packard still wasn’t 100 percent over the loss but was thinking more and more that he’d dodged a bullet. He’d clearly been the better candidate, but people wanted what they knew, what most resembled them.

So, not the six-foot-four gay guy.

“Packard, why the hell did one of my deputies request to take off early yesterday so he could personally chauffeur your ass back to town from a bus station?”

Shepard leaned back in his chair, hands across his belly. The buttons on his white uniform shirt were performing feats of strength. He was bald on top with a goatee that spread wide under his chin.

“It wasn’t Reynolds’s fault. I asked him to. I went down to Minneapolis to interview someone in relation to the Ashley Turner case.”

“And you couldn’t do this by phone?”

“I thought it was important to do it face-to-face. Eye contact and all that. You know how it is.”

Shepard didn’t know shit.

“Yeah, what I don’t know is how you got down there but didn’t have a way home and had to involve my deputy.”

“It’s kind of a long story.”

“Does that story involve the woman you had released from custody? The Black one.”

“As opposed to all the white women I let out of jail yesterday?”

Shepard looked confused. “What are you talking about?”

"Nothing. Never mind. That woman was Symphony Kendricks. She's a family friend that came to see me. She didn't realize she was driving a car with expired tabs."

"Did she realize she was driving without a valid license and was in violation of her parole?"

"She…did," Packard admitted.

"You need to quit acting like you run this place, Deputy. You don't get to do whatever you want or give my deputies orders."

Shepard kept saying "my deputies" like he was a mother hen and they were his baby chicks. The truth was he thought of them more as minions, there to do his bidding. He had a lot of things that needed delegating.

"That's not my intention," Packard said. "I'll mark the day I was in Minneapolis as PTO."

"You're damn right you will. And Reynolds is going to get docked a half day for his role in this. Maybe you guys will be more considerate of the shift schedule next time."

Packard nodded, asked if there was anything else. Shepard dismissed him with wave of his hand and went back to looking at his screen.

Just around the corner from Shepard's office, Packard found Suresh in his computer-filled room, also putting in weekend hours. The backgrounds on several of his monitors showed pictures of his eight-month-old son.

"I know you already briefed Reynolds, but I want to see everything you've learned from Ashley Turner's phone."

It was a lot of the same information he got from Reynolds, but it was nice to see the virtual copy of Ashley's phone as Suresh walked him through the details. Packard wrote down all the relevant numbers and times and actions in his notes.

"What kind of security did she have on the phone?"

"She had facial recognition enabled and a six-digit passcode," Suresh said.

"How was the phone unlocked when the killer deleted the text message?"

Suresh pulled up a document that listed every interaction on Ashley's phone that morning: the pickups, unlocks, apps accessed, durations.

"It looks like the phone was unlocked just one minute prior to the text message being deleted."

"Could her dead face have unlocked the phone?" Packard asked.

"There are only anecdotal stories of that being possible. Usually, the eyes need to be open and focused on the screen. It is possible she was dying, not dead at the time," Suresh said.

Packard imagined it. Wished he hadn't.

"Two more questions—can I get the names and numbers of Ashley's most frequent contacts based on calls and texts?"

"I knew you would ask. I already have that. I will send a list to your email."

"Thank you. Number two: How is the video review coming? You got any vehicle information for me yet?"

"A few more hours, please. I had to upload all the source files and time sync everything, which took longer than expected. Come back this afternoon. I will show you what I have."

"Thanks," Packard said, standing and pushing in his chair. "You have any playdates scheduled with Thielen and her baby yet?"

"Not yet, but my wife has had many phone calls with her. Prachi is happy to know another new mom. When I ask what they talk about, I am told to mind my business."

Packard remembered everything he learned about all of Thielen's problem areas the last time he was at her house. "It's good advice. You don't want to know."

Back in his office, Packard looked up Tom Turner's number and called him. "You got time to meet this morning?"

"You got news?"

"Some. Not much."

"I'm at the house packing some things for me and the boys. We're heading to Minneapolis today. We'll be there until… I don't know. Permanently maybe."

"I have a stop to make. I'll be there in half an hour."

His stop was the post office. It was still raining. He found a box that Marcus's photo album and badge fit inside, filled out a shipping label with the address Symphony had put in his phone, and took everything to the counter to pay.

The postal employee was an old woman with thin hair and thick glasses. She typed on her keyboard and squinted at a screen he couldn't see. She typed again.

"Are you sure this is the right address?"

He compared what he'd written to what was in his phone. "I think so."

"This isn't a valid St. Louis zip code. When I try to enter it without a zip code, I don't find this number and street name combination either."

Symphony. Even before she got angry at the mention of Marcus's life insurance money, she had decided she was done with him. If the address was phony, the phone number she gave him probably was, too.

Packard apologized to the postal worker and left with the box. He dashed through the rain to his truck and tossed the box behind the seat.

Heavy rain slowed him down on the way to Tom's. How it could rain and still be this hot was a mystery. Felt like a steam room. He had to keep wiping at the humidity fogging the inside of his truck windows.

At the Turner house, Packard parked close to the front door, ran under the awning, and waited until Tom let him in. Inside, the house was almost back to normal. The evidence tents were gone, the blood cleaned up. There was still a feeling in the air. The weight of grief. The vacuum of a missing life. When Packard glanced in the kitchen, he saw Ashley slumped beside the refrigerator even though the body had been removed days ago.

Tom had a wet-dog look to him, and not just from loading the car in the rain. Run-down, slumped, miserable. His clothes looked like he'd been wearing them for days.

They sat at the dining room table and Packard told Tom everything they'd learned from examining Ashley's phone, including that the killer had deleted a text message.

"You're telling me you have the guy's phone number?"

"We think we do. We're waiting for a response to our subpoena. If he's with a major carrier and has a phone plan in his name, we'll know something in the next few days to a week. If it's a prepaid phone with a small carrier, it would take a lot longer. It could also be a complete dead end."

"I thought you guys had databases where you can look up everyone's phone number."

"We do. We checked—the number isn't there. Tell me this. Does the name Red mean anything to you? Anything in relation to Ashley?"

Tom bit the inside of his cheek. "No. I don't know anybody named Red. I've never heard Ashley mention anyone named Red that I can remember."

They talked about Tom's plan for his family. "We can't stay in this house. Not anywhere near here," Tom said, looking over Packard's shoulder into the kitchen. Both boys wanted to go to school in Minneapolis. Noah had one year left and didn't care about being the new kid in a new school for his senior year. "That boy can't wait to spread his wings and fly away. I don't blame him. He's made the best of things here but it hasn't been easy."

"What will you do with the house?"

Tom shrugged. "I don't know yet. How do you list this place? Great lake views. Three beds, two baths, one murder?" Sounded like a joke but the pain on Tom's face wasn't funny. He sighed and blinked the tears out of his eyes.

Packard pulled up the list of contacts Suresh had emailed him and asked Tom to help him identify who the people were. He and the boys were at the top of the list. After that was her best friend, Natalie, who lived in the Bay Area. Another college friend in Chicago. Her sister in Wisconsin. Then a random mix of friends from Minneapolis and a few acquaintances in the area. "Neither one of us has done a good job of making friends since we moved here. It's not going to be hard to leave," Tom said.

"Does everyone at the top of this list know what happened to Ashley?"

"They do. I've been in touch with the people closest too her."

Packard leaned back in his chair. "Mind if I take a look around again?"

"Go ahead," Tom said. "It doesn't feel like our house anymore. I keep thinking this isn't even our stuff. Then I see her clothes in the closet, all her brushes and bottles in the bathroom. I smell her, like she just walked through the room."

Packard remembered his first time back in Marcus's house after he was killed. His body held the muscle memory of all the times and all the ways the two of them had inhabited those rooms together. The persistence of Marcus's things—the albums, the dog—argued in the face of his absence. Packard had grown furious at inanimate objects. The audacity of yellow bananas. A stupid toothbrush he'd pounded against the bathroom vanity until it bent and broke.

"I'm sorry," Packard said. "I won't take long."

"Take your time. I'm going to keep loading the car."

It was easier to see the family's patterns when there wasn't a body on the floor or cops crowding the space. Packard noticed dust bunnies collected around the feet of the barstools at the kitchen peninsula and food stains on the canvas seats. The fridge was covered in magnets and holiday photos and cards. Packard took a photo of the collection with his phone. In his last big investigation, a business card stuck to the fridge had helped him identify a dead woman whose face had been obliterated by a gunshot.

From the kitchen window he could see down to the lake. In the backyard, he noticed the downed tree sliced into rounds. There was a huge pile of branches cut down to size, covered in wilted, dead leaves. Packard never realized how much mass the average tree had until it was all down on the ground.

"Did you clean up this fallen tree?" Packard asked.

Tom stopped near the door with a box in his arms. "No, some tree guys took care of it. They didn't haul it away because the neighbor wants to split it and dry it. It's a maple."

"How'd you find the tree guys?"

"They came by and rang the doorbell."

"When was that?"

"Probably ten days ago."

"Can you pin it down more precisely?"

Tom looked down into the box he was carrying. His lips moved while he talked to himself. "Today is Saturday. They took the tree down a week ago today. A guy stopped by two days before that. So last Thursday. He came back with another guy and they did the job."

Ashley was killed on Wednesday. The tree came down four days before that. The tree guy first stopped by six days before. Nine days ago.

"Interesting," Packard said. Maybe it was, maybe it wasn't. It was another lead to follow if nothing else turned up. "Did you talk to him or did Ashley?"

"Ashley answered the door and asked for me to come talk to the guy."

"Was she around when they cleaned up the tree?"

"It was a Saturday. We both were."

"Remember what the guys looked like?"

Tom set the box at his feet. He closed his eyes and pushed on them with his thumb and forefinger. "One guy was tall. He had a dark beard. Probably a bit older than me. The other guy…I don't remember. They looked like you would expect tree guys to look. Tanned. Dirty clothes. That's all I remember."

"Names? Business card? Anything like that?"

"I don't think so. They gave me a discount for cash. I don't remember getting a receipt or anything."

"Hmm," Packard said, disappointed.

He went downstairs. The boys had their own rooms, the doors separated only by a thin wall. Jake's had a large table where he built Star Wars Lego sets. He had a Lego Millennium Falcon on top of his dresser. Noah's room looked like it belonged to a young professional. The wood paneling had been painted an eggshell color. He had neatly folded clothes stacked in a closet with no doors. The lower half of a bookcase had been converted into a desk. Packard saw nail polish and makeup pencils. On the shelves above, a bright stack of *Heartstopper* books and a ring light.

Packard had been thinking about how hard life was for queer kids in small towns who couldn't or wouldn't hide who they were. In a city, the whole world could feel gay depending on who you surrounded yourself with. There was safety in numbers. Not in Sandy Lake. When Packard was Noah's age, the majority of his mental energy was spent trying to hide that part of himself. It was the nineties. Not many role models. A culture he wanted nothing to do with that was focused on surviving AIDS and celebrating small wins like "Don't Ask, Don't Tell." He was still hiding who he was when he came to Sandy Lake. He could threaten all the Darrel Johnsons in town with an ass-beating but what he really needed to do was show up more, show these kids someone like them who was happy. Add to the numbers.

Back upstairs, Tom stopped him in the kitchen. "One more thing. I know you talked to Cara."

Cara was the woman he had an affair with in Minneapolis. "You know because I told you I was going to or because she told you?"

"I got a text from her. All it said was she was sorry to hear about my wife."

"Did you respond?"

Tom shook his head.

"Can I see your phone?"

Tom unlocked it, pulled up his texts, and showed Packard the message from Cara. There was no previous message history, no name associated with the number in his phone.

"Mind if I search for something?" Packard asked.

"Be my guest," Tom said.

Packard quickly swiped to the search bar and typed in the number he'd memorized that belonged to the killer. No history of Tom getting a phone call or a text from that number.

"All right. Thanks for telling me about Cara," Packard said.

"I'm going for one hundred percent transparency. I know how it is when a woman gets killed. All eyes are on the husband."

He looked resentful but they both knew he was right.

CHAPTER TWENTY

Packard spent the afternoon with Suresh, reviewing his AI-assisted database of vehicles that had been captured on the video they'd collected from around the area.

"The first problem is that some systems are wired to the internet and the time is set automatically. On some systems the time is set manually by the user and might be several minutes or even an hour off if it has not been updated for daylight savings. Other systems have no time stamp at all. I first sorted images by time and then had to do some calling to the owners to confirm the current time in their system, then adjust as necessary."

They were looking at a user interface that pulled up snapshots according to how they were tagged by either time or vehicle make and model. Suresh was able to display all the video from a single source, or all the photos stamped between 9:00 a.m. and 10:00 a.m., or all the photos of a black BMW.

On another tab, Suresh had a map of Sandy Lake County and the approximate location of each video source. He could click a camera icon for each source and pull the video from just that location. A green dot marked Ashley and Tom's house.

Packard clapped a hand on Suresh's shoulder. "Suresh. This is amazing."

"Thank you. I do my best."

"Okay. Where do we start?"

"What do you want to see first?"

"It looks like there's only one camera close to their house."

"Yes. The problem is that the camera that is closest to the victim's house does not show the road or any vehicles traveling at that time. It also only activates video when there is motion. Otherwise, it takes a photo every two minutes."

"So really nothing on that one."

"Correct."

"Let's come back to that. We know almost the exact time of Ashley's death from her call data and when the message was deleted from her phone. I want to see a list of vehicles that were approaching or leaving the area around Ashley's house within an hour before the call and within an hour after the message was deleted. I imagine after you kill someone you don't linger in the area. You want to get the hell out of there."

Suresh got a sly smile on his face. With his mouse, he drew a circle that covered approximately fifteen miles all around Ashley's house. There were eleven camera sources within the circle. A box popped up and he typed in a time range from 1:00 p.m. to 3:00 p.m.

"Are you kidding me? It's like you read my mind."

"It is my job to anticipate how to use the data. That is all."

"Don't underplay it, Suresh. You're brilliant."

What came back was a list of video freeze frames with links to the source video if there was one. Also a list of makes and models as determined by the AI. The list of unique vehicles was over three hundred.

"Can you make the circle smaller so we're not getting all the traffic in town? Also exclude the highway. Too many vehicles there."

Suresh redrew the circle. The problem was, most of their cameras were in or near Sandy Lake. If he drew the circle too small, there were no cameras. Roads near Ashley's house went in all cardinal directions, and some of the ways wouldn't encounter a camera until the vehicle hit town.

There were still more than one hundred cars this time.

"I have been thinking there is more work to do to eliminate cars that are captured on two different cameras within a time period that would not allow them to stop at the victim's house. Some cars would not be captured because they turned off and ended at a location without crossing the path of another camera."

"What do we have for plates?"

"The highest resolution and ideally positioned cameras are all in town. Two cameras that capture hundreds of plates."

"We can't run every plate. Let's map all the routes to Ashley's house from Sandy Lake and from St. Albans and estimate travel times, then back up from the time of death. We could narrow our window that way. The problem is, he could have come from anywhere and not necessarily driven through either town."

Suresh opened the computer's notepad and made a list of follow-up items.

"Let's take a look at the camera closest to Ashley's house. I just want to see what's on it."

Suresh clicked the camera icon and brought up a series of still images captured every two minutes. He opened several hundred of them captured during daylight hours and then clicked through them quickly. The view was of a bit of the lake to the left, the side of the neighbor's house, and beyond that some wind-damaged trees in the distance. The image didn't change much except for light and shadows.

"Wait. Go back," Packard said.

Suresh clicked the back arrow a few times.

"There. Do you see that?"

"I missed it."

"There. There's someone in that tree. Keep going."

Suresh clicked forward a few times while Packard noted the address of the camera and the time of the photos in his notebook. "Now that tree is gone. Keep going," he said. Forty minutes later, another tree dropped from the camera's sight.

"There was a tree crew at Ashley's house four days before she was killed. I'm betting those trees that came down are two, maybe three houses down from hers. You keep working on trying to filter down the vehicle data. I'm going to find out who took those trees down."

Packard left Suresh's office and walked down the hall to his own. There were times when police work required the latest technology, and there were times when you had to kick it old school. He slid open his desk drawer and took out a slim phone book for Sandy Lake County.

There was only one landscaping company listed. He called the number and got voicemail. He looked up the company online and found a Facebook page that listed another number. Also voicemail. He left a message at both.

Packard put his feet on the desk and stared at the ceiling. He knew from years of experience that crime could be entirely random. Someone had the bad fortune of being in the wrong place at the wrong time, the result of a lifetime of small decisions and dice rolls that brought them to that moment when their path intersected with a carjacker or a stray bullet or a drunk driver. Ms. Simmons's granddaughter, Ruby, was a prime example. What if she'd sat in a different spot at the table that night? What if the bullet hadn't hit a pipe in the wall? What if the gunshots had started a block earlier?

Then there were times when crime wasn't as random as it appeared. Sometimes the environment around the victim changed. New circumstances, new variables, new people introduced a chaos factor to the equation that produced a new result.

Ashley's son had been bullied at a party for being gay.

Her husband had an affair.

What about the storm? Hundreds of homes damaged. Thousands of trees down. Electricity out. Sandy Lake had been crawling with strangers over the last month. People going door to door. Tree trimmers. Landscapers. Insurance inspectors. Roofers. Waste haulers. Utility workers.

Chaos.

Packard was looking at the list of other calls he needed to make to people from Ashley's contacts when he suddenly remembered he'd met a landscaper recently.

He found the number in his phone and called.

"I didn't do it," Tess Reid said when she answered.

Packard couldn't help but laugh. He'd met Tess last winter while investigating the death of an elderly woman who supposedly fell down the basement stairs in her home. Turned out not to be the case at all.

"How's life, Tess?"

"You know—just waiting to hear if the federal government is going to send me to prison for the rest of my life. Typical bullshit everyone deals with."

"What's your lawyer say?"

"We're trying to keep our heads down and not poke the bear. I've cooperated fully. They were able to retrieve all the money that was taken. So far, the people they've been charging who defrauded the same program stole way more money and actually spent it. I'm hoping they'll forget about me."

"And how's Lady Gaga Pinot Grigio String Cheese Reid?"

Tess had named her dog, a cocker spaniel, after her favorite pop star, wine, and go-to road trip snack, as one does.

"She's good. Fat and sassy. Like her moms."

"What are you doing for work these days?"

"I'm in St. Cloud permanently now, living with Brenda. I don't have a criminal record yet since I haven't been charged, so it was pretty easy to get a job at a greenhouse down here."

"What was the name of the landscaping company you worked for up here?"

"It wasn't so much a company as it was one guy named Brian who had three hired hands and a list of loyal clients."

"So not Schmidt Landscaping?"

"No. Fuck those guys. Brian was a cofounder of Schmidt's and then Schmidt's son came on board and they squeezed Brian out so they didn't have to split the profits three ways. They're assholes."

"Does Brian's company do tree removal?"

"We did tree trimming but he didn't have the equipment or the crew to do whole tree removal. If people asked for a referral, he wouldn't even mention Schmidt. He'd just say, 'Look in the phone book.'"

"Anyone else in the tree game locally besides Schmidt?"

"Not that I know of. You might get someone from Brainerd or Bemidji all the way out to Sandy Lake but they'd charge a premium to come that far."

"I've got a guy who said someone knocked on his door and offered to take care of his downed trees. Paid in cash. No receipt."

"Doesn't sound like Schmidt. Your guy was probably dealing with storm chasers."

"That's what I was thinking. They could be long gone."

"Who knows? There's no shortage of trees that need to be cleaned up and not a lot of competition," Tess said.

"You get back up here at all?"

"Yeah, we meet the gals at the cabin pretty regularly."

"How did the trees at the cabin fare?"

"Not good. We've lost a lot of our shade. One tree came down and hit Susan's Subaru at just the right angle that the car flipped upside down and landed on top of the tree."

"Who did you hire to help with the cleanup?"

"Nobody. We're a cabin full of lesbians. Do you know how many chain saws and log splitters we collectively own? We took care of it."

Packard thanked Tess and told her good luck with her case. He liked Tess in spite of the fact that her supposedly victimless fraud had resulted in three homicides and a suicide. She'd been a dupe, as surprised as anyone when the smoke cleared and the ground was littered with bodies.

His next call was to Ashley's best friend in San Francisco. It felt like a long shot that someone so far away would know anything, but it wasn't out of the realm of possibility that Ashley had told Danielle something she wouldn't have told Tom. Seemed likely in fact.

Danielle didn't answer when he called but she called back five minutes after he left a message. He'd barely finished introducing himself before she landed the first question. "Do you think Tom killed Ashley?"

"I don't know," Packard said. "Do *you* think Tom killed Ashley?"

He heard Danielle take a deep breath through her nose. "I don't know either. If he did, I'm going to be so fucking furious that he evaded my radar. I work in the DA's office as a prosecutor. Do you know how many wife killers I've sent to jail?"

"No idea."

"A lot. I liked Tom."

"What about after the affair came to light?"

Danielle scoffed. "No woman is allowed to be surprised by news that a man cheated. He was unfaithful? You don't say. It's not a shock when it's your favorite celebrity couple or your parents or even your own husband."

"Was she planning to leave Tom?"

"She said they were trying to work things out but she was prepared for any eventuality."

"What does that mean?"

"It means we'd talked a lot about how a divorce might affect the boys. Whether she could afford to be a single mom. What a settlement between them might look like. I told her to get statements from all their accounts in case Tom tried to misrepresent what was at stake. I shared a link to my Dropbox where she could upload stuff. I haven't looked at any of it out of respect for her privacy but I have it all if it's needed."

Minnesota was a no-fault state, meaning Tom's infidelity wouldn't impact the division of their assets. They had two homes and three cars and a kid a year away from college. If they were saddled with debt, there might not be enough money to support two separate households. Ashley stood to lose her health insurance and half or more of any retirement savings.

What was the bigger pill to swallow? The loss of trust or the financial hit? Maybe they were the same size and you choked on both.

"Did Ashley mention anything about men working to clean up trees on the property?"

"No. I know they had some storm damage. I think she said a tree took out their air conditioner. That's about it."

"What about the name Red?"

"Red who?"

"Red I Don't Know. A man named Red."

"No. I don't ever remember hearing about a Red."

He had a few more basic questions about her relationship with Ashley, how long they'd known each other, the last time they saw each other. He was probing. Looking for anything.

"I'm coming back for the funeral as soon as I know the details. If you need a lawyer or a trained kickboxer, let me know. I will fuck someone up for you." There were angry tears in her voice.

"I appreciate it, Danielle. I'm very sorry about Ashley. I'm going to find out who did this."

He took a break to stretch his legs, get a glass of water. The next person on his list to call was Ashley's sister, Vanessa. This time, the tears were in her voice from the beginning.

"I'm still picking up my phone wondering why Ashley hasn't texted me back. We texted every day."

Packard knew as much. Suresh had downloaded the texts from Ashley's phone, and Packard had read through all the messages between Ashley and her sister, all the texts between Ashley and Danielle, too. The digital receipts from long relationships: blue and white bubbles that captured the minutia of daily life, parenting, partner squabbles, the outrageous cost of things, memes, and emojis. Packard remembered reading back through his texts from Marcus after he died. How little they said and yet how reading them again was almost enough to conjure the man in the flesh.

Vanessa lived in Stevens Point, Wisconsin, where she and Ashley grew up.

She was ten years older than Ashley, married, no kids. Her husband, John, was a cabinetmaker and a part-time firefighter. She was a nurse. They were making plans to tour the country in their fifth wheel and for Vanessa to work as a travel nurse wherever they landed. John could do handyman jobs.

Packard asked her a lot of the same questions he asked Danielle. "How were things between her and Tom?"

Vanessa's silence spoke volumes. "It was a work in progress."

"Do you think they were going to make it?"

"Honestly? No."

"Did Ashley feel the same?"

"She never said it in so many words but I could hear the sadness in her voice for what had been lost. I think she still loved Tom but she didn't trust him anymore. I'm sure he loved her. He just wanted to have sex with other women on the side."

"Was Ashley worried at all what life would be like if they got divorced?"

"She was more worried about the boys. Noah's had a rough go of things up there because of his…inclinations, if you know what I mean."

"I know what you mean."

"Not that there's anything wrong with that. Anyway—the boys are almost not boys anymore. They've been through a lot with COVID and the bullying and what-not. She was worried what a divorce on top of that would be like for them."

"Would the divorce have been amicable, do you think?"

"Probably," Vanessa said. "I don't want to give Tom too much credit because he is literally a dumbass for ruining the great thing they had. But I don't see him trying to leave his wife and kids out in the cold."

Packard told her in vague terms about the evidence they'd collected and the leads they were following. He told her about the deleted text from Ashley's phone.

"Wait. You have the killer's phone number?"

"I have a phone number. I don't know yet who it belongs to. We're waiting for records from the cell providers. There's a chance it might be a burner phone with no name or payment details linked to it."

"That's…frustrating."

"It is," Packard agreed. "I'm going to say a name to you, and I want you to respond with the first thing that comes to mind."

"Okay."

"Red."

"Just Red?"

"That's all I got."

Vanessa was quiet. "Nothing comes to mind. No names. Red, white, and blue. Red rum. Red state. Red snapper. I don't know. Sorry."

"Don't be sorry. That's the name on the phone's voicemail. Just Red."

"Let me think about it and get back to you. I can tell you Ashley never mentioned anyone named Red. I would remember that."

Packard thanked her and spent the next hour updating his report. He got a call back from a woman at Schmidt Landscaping who told him right away all their crews were booked fully into November.

"I don't need a crew. I'm wondering whether you can confirm if you did a tree removal at a specific address."

"You're with the sheriff's department?"

"I am."

"What's the address?"

He told her and she said they had no paperwork for a job at that address.

"Are you aware of non-local crews doing tree work in the area?" Packard asked.

"I've heard that's the case. It was a big storm. There's a lot of need out there."

"Have you met any of those crews or do you know any of the members?"

"I haven't personally. I just work in the office. I could have Dean or Victor call you. They might know more."

"Please do."

CHAPTER TWENTY-ONE

Charlie ran out of cigarettes by midafternoon. He'd spent the day alone in his room, watching TV and working on what remained in the whiskey bottle from last night.

His mood was as sour as his stomach. It was raining too hard to tear off a roof, and no one wanted to talk about what happened the night before. He'd woken up stripped out of his boots and his pants with a huge bruise on his ribs. Another mystery injury to go with the cut on his arm he couldn't remember getting.

When he checked his wallet, all his cash was gone. His whole paycheck from the last week.

He couldn't imagine anyone on the crew putting him to bed. Had to have been the whore. He wanted to strangle her for taking advantage of him. There ought to have been a code among those who made their living on the fringes, who threw their bodies into the furnace of manual labor until they were used up. He wanted to find her and get back what was his, but he couldn't remember a thing about her. Even her face was a blank in his memory. He thought he remembered her saying her car was there but when he closed his eyes, he couldn't recall the make or model. Red. Maybe white.

The timing of the rain couldn't have been worse. Work would have given the crew something to do. They needed each other when they were on a roof. Without that, Charlie felt like he was sitting in his filth from last night. Luis told him to fuck off when he asked what happened with the woman. Charlie could tell he and Juan weren't speaking to each other by the way Luis was sitting in a chair outside their door and staring at the rain like he could will it to stop.

Out of cigarettes and low on whiskey, Charlie knocked on Matthias's door. Matthias was lying on top of his made bed, barefoot, the itchy comforter beneath him, pillows bunched behind his head. On the room's television was a show about guys competing to make knife blades.

"I need to borrow some money," Charlie said.

"How is that possible? You got paid yesterday and haven't left the motel since."

"That woman took all my money."

"The whore?"

Charlie shrugged.

"What the hell did you ask for? The Russian Over Under? A Tijuana Twister?"

"I don't know what that is," Charlie said.

"I hope she was worth it."

Charlie pressed on the tender spot on his ribs. "I don't remember what happened last night. I thought there was a fight. Did anyone get hurt?"

"Don't ask me," Matthias said, staring at the TV. "I went to bed after you stopped holding up your end of the conversation. I slept through the rest."

"Someone was screaming. Something about a knife."

Matthias turned his head on the pillow. "Is there a dead hooker out in the parking lot?"

"No. Her car's gone."

"Lucky for you, Mr. Manslaughter."

The word *manslaughter* made a knot in Charlie's guts. "Fuck off, Matthias. Can you spot me a hundred or not? You can take it out of my next check."

"Won't be a next check until this rain lets up."

"Forecast says clear tomorrow."

Matthias winced as he rolled toward the nightstand between his bed and the unused one next to it. He teased a hundred-dollar bill from his wallet like it was a delicate tissue and held it out to Charlie, who had to come from where he was leaning in the doorway over to the bed to receive it. Charlie felt like he should get down on one knee, bow, and hold his hands out. Every time he thought he found the basement of his humiliation, the floor gave out and he dropped lower.

"What are you gonna do with your newfound wealth?"

"Go to town and get cigarettes."

"And a drink?"

Charlie touched his chin and raised his eyebrows like the thought hadn't occurred to him. "Who's got all our trucks?" he asked. "Two of 'em are gone."

They had three vehicles. A van with all their tools. A pickup truck with a trailer attached. Another pickup that Matthias drove.

"I don't know who's in the van. I told College Boy he could take the truck. He wanted to go to the doctor. Said his balls hurt."

Charlie remembered something from the night before. College Boy running from the tree guys' room holding his crotch.

"Can I take your truck?"

"No, you cannot," Matthias said. "You can walk. Last time I let you take the truck, you ended up in jail. I'm gonna need it when I go to town later."

"Wanna go now?"

"No. I'm watching this show."

They both stared at the TV. A man in a pair of safety goggles cut a pig carcass hanging from a hook in half with a single slash of a huge knife. "Your blade will kill," he said.

Charlie pocketed the hondo and started the walk to town in a light drizzle. He wore a cap to keep his head dry. A green BP station a mile from the motel sold cigarettes. No beer, no liquor. He'd have to keep walking for that.

He came out of the gas station, walked around to the side of the building, and smoked a cigarette pinched between his thumb and forefinger, the rest protected by his cupped hand. He remembered when he first started smoking in college: how much time he spent playing with a cigarette. Holding it, setting it down, picking it up. Tapping, flicking, rolling the tip. It was a whole fucking show he put on, part of his persona that included his unshaven face, his paint-spattered T-shirt (poetry/political science double major, art minor), his dirty jeans, and work boots. He spent more time pondering how he appeared to others than he did writing.

Charlie dropped his head. Rain dripped off the brim of his hat. He felt like he'd spent the decades since college in pursuit of something that was always over the next horizon. Childe Roland in search of his Dark Tower. What even was his tower? The perfect poem. Stability. A reason to quit drinking. Those were ideals without substance. No wonder he never arrived. There was no tower—just an endless road across a blasted wasteland, a river of burning alcohol, and now manslaughter charges for the dead nurse. The warrant with his name on it shrieked in his imagination like a circling hawk. What else would he do while he was too drunk to remember before it caught up to him?

The rain clouds pulled apart to reveal of glimpses of hazy sky. Charlie watched Matthias's truck go by just then in a nimbus of road spray, wipers slashing. That motherfucker couldn't have told him to wait thirty minutes and then driven both of them to town?

Charlie flicked his cigarette butt into a puddle and walked back to the road in search of a drink and a ride home, preferably in that order.

CHAPTER TWENTY-TWO

Packard headed back to Ashley Turner's neighborhood one more time before calling it a night.

He had the address of the house with the video doorbell closest to Ashley's house. When he got to the road, he saw Ashley's house on the corner on the right. This house was two down on the left and sat closer to the lake than Ashley's.

Packard parked on the side of the road and rang the doorbell. After a minute, an older woman with short gray hair and a pink sleeveless blouse answered the door. The smell of fried meat—a hamburger or a pork chop—came from the inside of the house.

Packard introduced himself. "One of our deputies collected the video from your doorbell. I just wanted to see the location myself."

"There's the doorbell," the woman said. Her name was Sylvia. "It looks at the same thing all day every day. Your deputy had to help me figure out how to get the pictures from it. Never looked at 'em myself."

From where Packard stood, he looked across several yards. There were shattered tree trunks at houses that hadn't dealt with the damage yet. He saw formerly green grass burning in the sun now that the canopy had been torn down. Ashley's house wasn't in view of the camera. He saw a house on the other side of hers and a row of arborvitaes beyond that. Looking higher, there was clear evening sky where he'd seen the damaged trees coming down in the photos.

He looked around Sylvia's property. "Looks like you didn't have many trees to get damaged."

"We had elms thirty years ago. My husband took them all down when Dutch elm disease was raging. Replaced them with ash trees and took them down a few years ago when they got ash borers. If it ain't one thing, it's another."

Packard was going to suggest American elms as a possible replacement but Sylvia didn't look like she had enough years left to wait for new trees to grow back. He bit his tongue.

"You catch the killer yet?" Sylvia asked.

"Not yet," Packard admitted.

Sylvia scratched her bare arm. "I wish you would hurry up. My husband died last winter of a stroke. I'm out here all alone. Every little noise at night now has me jumping like a cat."

He assured her many people were working hard, thanked her for her time, got in his vehicle, and turned around in the road. He drove past Ashley's house. No cars. No lights. Tom and the boys were probably in Minneapolis by now. The third house beyond Ashley's had two fresh stumps nearly level with the ground. The garage was open, a car parked inside. Packard crawled by one more house and saw another stump there. No lights in that house. He made another U-turn and parked across the driveway of the first house.

A big, bearded man in shorts and flip-flops came out of the garage's shadows holding a cigar in one hand and a Coors Light in the other. "Evening, Deputy," he said.

They shook hands. His name was Adam and his cigar smelled like burned leather and old mud.

"Wanted to ask you about the tree work you had done," Packard said.

"This have to do with Ashley Turner or something different?"

"Just trying to establish who was in the area when Ashley was killed. Were you home that day?"

"I was at work. I'm a store manager at Wellards." Wellards was the big-box home improvement store in Sandy Lake.

"You had a tree crew here that day?"

"They were at my house the day before. They took down two big ash trees. They got here just before I left for work and were gone when I got home. They came back the next day and did the job next door. That was the day Ashley was killed."

"Local guys?"

"I don't think so. They came by a few days earlier. I negotiated a deal for me and my neighbor." He jabbed his cigar in the direction of the house next door. "They're not around as often since their kids grew up."

"Did you get a name or receipt from those guys?"

"I paid cash for the whole job. The guy gave me a handwritten breakdown of the cost."

"Did it have a company name or anything on it?"

"Lemme check." He stuck the cigar in the corner of his mouth and the beer in the crook of his elbow and took out his phone. "I took a photo of it to share with those guys," he said, tipping his head in the direction of the neighbor's.

After a minute, he turned the phone and showed Packard a photo of the bill. No letterhead. Just a blank sheet of white paper. It had the date on the top and each address written down with a description of what the job included. Two trees at Adam's for $1,800. One tree next door for $900. At the bottom was a scrawled signature. Indecipherable.

"How many guys on the crew?"

"Two."

"Any names or logos on their trucks?"

"Not that I noticed."

"You take any photos the day they were working?"

"No."

"Talk to them at all about where they were from?"

"Nope."

"Have you seen them since? They been into Wellards?"

"I haven't seen them. A lot of people come to Wellards every day. I can keep an eye out if it'll help."

"I'd appreciate that."

Adam said he was friendly with the Turners in a head-nodding sort of way when they saw each other on the water. He saw Ashley at the lake association meetings. He'd heard from another neighbor about the son's car being vandalized but hadn't seen it himself, didn't know the story behind it.

Packard had Adam text him the job receipt and thanked him for his help. He was frustrated by how hard it was to track down these tree guys. He didn't believe they were trying to hide or keep a low profile. The cash economy was predicated on a certain amount of anonymity and a scarcity of paperwork. If they didn't leave a name or a number, they couldn't get complaints. Couldn't get referrals either, but there was enough work that they probably didn't need them.

At home, Packard changed clothes and put on a Lucinda Williams album. He opened a can of tuna, mixed in Greek yogurt and diced pickles, salt and pepper, and made a sandwich. He ate more yogurt and more pickles while Lucinda sang about waiting in her car, waiting at this bar. A couple of songs later when she sang about taking a bus to Baton Rouge, he thought of his own bus ride from Minneapolis, and he thought of his night with Easton. The morning in the shower. He didn't know how to put into words what he was thinking or feeling, so he texted Easton a GIF of a smiling, winking Jimmy Fallon and then almost instantly regretted it. What an idiot.

Easton FaceTimed him five minutes later. He was shirtless, folding laundry.

"Hey, I remember those red shorts. Do you have any clothes that aren't gym clothes?" Packard asked.

"This is a load of just gym stuff, but yes I do."

"I mostly see you in your uniform or naked."

They talked about their days. Packard went to the kitchen and opened a beer. He lay down on the couch, didn't like how his chin looked on the camera, sat up again. That's when he noticed the moisture on the wall above the wood-burning stove. He turned his camera around, told Easton about the rain they'd had, and gave him a tour of his current living conditions: the jumbled furniture, the missing ceiling in the living room, the damaged flooring. Now more water coming in.

"It's just one thing after another," Packard complained. "Our county has been wiped out by this storm. The recovery costs are unbelievable and federal disaster funds aren't going to come anywhere near covering it. The county budget for things like public works, the sheriff's office, the library are going to be impacted for years. Then there's what everyone has to pay out of pocket to clean up their property or their trees or fix their roofs. People around here are hurting and there's not a damn thing I can do for most of them. I've got a woman murdered in her own home that's got me working fourteen-hour days. You can't breathe the air outside. I miss my dog. And now water is getting in."

He kept the part about Kyle pulling away to himself. The list was long enough. Speaking it out loud seemed to manifest the weight of everything. Packard was suddenly weary to the bone. "I'm sorry for whining," he said. He propped the phone against his beer bottle and sat back from it.

"You're allowed to be frustrated and run-down," Easton said. "Where do you think the water is getting in?"

"Looks like it's coming in around the damaged chimney."

"Do you have a tarp on it?"

"I do but I probably need to adjust it. I don't know what I'm going to do if the whole chimney needs to be rebuilt."

"If the foundation under it is okay, you can fix the lean in the chimney with straps. I can help you with that. And I can rebuild the part that fell off."

"You know how to lay bricks?"

"I do. My dad was a contractor. I worked with him for years growing up. I can do cement, bricks, framing, drywall, finishing. All of it. Catch your killer and I'll come up and help you with your house."

"You don't have to do that."

"I want to do that. I want to see you. I miss you when you're not around."

Packard looked at Easton staring back at him through the phone. Thought of Easton kissing him last time they were eating breakfast over the sink. Remembered what it felt like to share space with someone else. To wake up to another face. To sit in easy silence.

He didn't know what to say. "Gare," he said.

"Am I adding to your list of troubles?" Easton asked.

Kind of.

Packard looked away from the phone. "No. I just… I feel the same way. It would be so easy to catch feelings but to what end? We live three hours away from each other."

"Why are you worried about the end? We're barely at the beginning. Why not just enjoy ourselves and see what happens? Turn off your cop brain. Stop scanning for entrances and exits."

Packard laughed. "When's the last time you turned off your cop brain?"

"Last time I was with you."

The phone screen changed to show that Reynolds was calling.

"I gotta get this. It's work. Thanks for the offer to help. I want to see you, too. And get you up here soon," Packard said in a rush. A jumble of words that didn't convey what he really wanted to say.

"Later," Easton said.

Over to Reynolds. "What's up?" Packard asked.

"Hey, I caught a body tonight."

"Another one?"

"Yeah."

Packard stared at the water stain on the wall above his woodstove. "You got it, though, right?"

"I got it but I think you'll want to see this."

"I can assure you that I don't."

"We've got a white male in vehicle outside the Silver Dollar Saloon. He's got bruises around his throat and knife wounds to the chest."

Just like Ashley Turner had been killed.

Packard put his forehead in his hand. "I'm on my way," he said.

CHAPTER TWENTY-THREE

Moths and gnats churned beneath a bright light high on a pole that shone down on the busted asphalt parking lot behind the Silver Dollar Saloon. The few remaining cars were covered in humidity as the heat of the day ceded to the chill of the night. Another light hung over the restaurant's back door, where a man in a dirty apron was smoking a cigarette next to a pair of green dumpsters. Yellow police tape blocked access to the parking lot from the road in front and the alley in back.

Packard got the details on the drive over. Gerald Hall. Sixty-two years old. Bit of a known entity in town for his drinking, his conspiracy theories, his monochrome zippered coveralls. Last seen inside the bar sometime around 4:00 p.m. Likely dead in his car since then. No one noticed him until some kids getting in on the passenger side of their car asked if the man next to them was bleeding.

A privacy tent open on two sides had been erected around the car. "'88 Buick Park Avenue," Packard said as they stood under the cover of the tent. The car was ruby red with a white pinstripe the length of the body. The driver's door was open, the seat reclined and Gerald half sitting, half lying in a red leather chair saturated with his blood. The smell of his bowels was heavy in the air.

"Woodgrain dash, carpeted door panels, AM-FM radio. Auto Reverse cassette deck. This was a luxury car back in the day."

He shone his flashlight on the floorboards and crept up the body with it, from the light-blue coveralls stained brown with blood on one side, up to the bruised throat and the open eyes.

"There's a cigarette on the floorboard that's burned a hole in the mat where it landed," Reynolds said.

"I see that."

"I assume it belongs to Gerald but I'll make sure it gets bagged."

"Are the staff on duty the ones who were working when he was in the bar?" Packard asked.

"For the most part. The bartender who was working when Gerald was drinking inside is still here."

Packard walked around the back of the building. The patio on the other side was empty, the shade umbrellas all shut like flowers at night. On the front door he found a sign announcing the restaurant was closing early.

Inside, a high school kid was running a vacuum cleaner near the booths. Packard walked past the bar to a room in the back with two pool tables covered in red felt. Music came down from the ceiling: a white guy covering "Fast Car" by Tracy Chapman. Packard preferred the sound of the vacuum cleaner.

Chip Meyer, a heavyset man in camo shorts and a Vikings jersey was playing pool with a woman in a white blouse and tight black jeans. Chip was the owner of the Silver Dollar. It took Packard a minute to remember how he knew the woman.

"You're Kristie Capote, right?" he asked after she finished her shot that hit cushions on two sides and no balls. They shook hands. "Friends with Sherri Sanderson. I remember you from Bill's funeral."

Kristie gave him a small smile, turned the wrist of the hand shaking his and showed him her forearm where she had the word *Sherri* tattooed in script.

"I was fond of her myself," Packard said. "She was kind of a pain in the ass but she deserved way better than what happened to her."

"That was pretty much the story of Sherri's life," Kristie said.

"*You* thought she was a pain in the ass?" Chip asked as he stroked his cue between two fingers pressed against the rail. He knocked the cue ball into the three ball. It wobbled along the rail but stopped short of the pocket. "You should have tried being her boss. That woman is why I drink so much."

"Sherri's been dead for a year," Kristie said. She was drinking a Miller Lite. Chip had a short glass half-full of brown liquor. "What's your excuse now?"

Chip took a big drink. "How about business this summer being down 30 percent over last year? Storms hitting all my customers in the wallet. People with cabins up here deciding maybe they don't want to drive three hours closer to the fires. A murder in the parking lot sure as shit isn't helping matters."

"Sorry you're having to deal with this," Packard said as he took out his notebook. It was just like he'd told Easton. Everybody was suffering since the storm. If it wasn't damage to their property, it was an impact to their business or their health. There didn't seem to be any relief in sight. "Let me ask you a few questions so we can catch whoever did this."

"I'll cut to the chase," Kristie said. "Gerald Hall is the definition of a pain in the ass. I hated seeing him at my bar whenever I came to work but I certainly didn't want him murdered. Just go drink somewhere else. Annoy some other bartender."

Packard didn't know if Kristie was trying to absolve herself of her actions or her thoughts.

"What time did you get to work?"

"Three thirty."

"Gerald was at the bar?"

"Yes. I gave him a beer on the house and told him he had to finish it and get the fuck out by four. That guy at my bar will ruin the night. My regulars come in and see him sitting there and they make a face like they stepped in dog shit. Then they ask for a booth."

"What's so bad about Gerald?"

"He doesn't smell great for starters. Put a few beers in him and he'll get going about the lizard people infiltrating our government. He thinks the earth is hollow and there are secret bases in Antarctica. UFOs. Portals. A whole bunch of crazy shit. If you've ever been on the receiving end of one of Gerald's tirades, you don't forget. And you also don't sit by him again."

Packard remembered all the conspiracy posts on the department's Facebook page related to the storm. When the world felt out of control, people demanded a reason. If you gave them one they didn't like, they'd make up their own. It was the deep state. Or space lizards. Obviously.

"Was there someone at the bar he was talking to this afternoon?"

"Yes. I know you're going to want to know what the guy looked like but I just don't remember. After it stopped raining, the patio filled up. I was busy making drinks. It's pretty much in my job description to ignore Gerald until he leaves so I wasn't paying attention to either of them really."

"That's all right," Packard said. "Did you hear what they talked about?"

"I didn't hear how it started. It ended when Gerald started yelling, 'Are you legal? Do you have papers?' Shit like that."

"What do you think he meant?"

Chip chimed in. "Gerald had aliens and illegal immigrants all knotted together in his pea brain. He liked to say all the talk about Mexican and Salvadoran gang members coming to this country was meant to distract us from the real invasion happening by lizard men who can disguise themselves as human beings."

"So the guy at the bar. He was…not white? Spoke Spanish?" Packard asked.

"He had a hat pulled low. I didn't get a good look at his face or his hair. Nothing," Kristie said.

"Would Gerald ask a white guy if he was legal or had papers?" Packard asked.

"I don't know. He might have been Hispanic. I just don't remember," Kristie said.

"What was he drinking?"

"Modelo and a shot of whiskey."

Chip looked at Packard like there was his answer.

"Do a lot of people order Modelo?" Packard asked.

"Enough to keep it stocked," Chip said. "It's a good cheap beer for people who rightly think Miller Lite tastes like it was wrung out of a bar rag."

"Whiskey tastes like someone pissed in a gas can," Kristie shot back. She leaned over and hit the cue ball too low, making it jump across the table.

"Am I supposed to infer that the people who order Modelo are mostly non-white?" Packard asked.

"We don't have much of a non-white clientele. This is Sandy Lake, Minnesota," Chip said.

"So the Modelo doesn't imply anything about this guy's nationality."

"Not to me," Kristie said. "I'm sure Gerald read something into it."

"Had you seen the guy in here before?"

Kristie pointlessly rubbed chalk on the tip of her cue. She hadn't made a single shot. "No. At least not often enough for me to recognize him. Someone comes in twice in a short amount of time, I'll remember them. I'll remember their drink after the third or fourth time. There was nothing familiar about this guy."

"Any tattoos or scars or rings on his fingers that you noticed?"

Kristie shrugged.

"How did this guy pay?"

"Cash."

"Of course," Packard said. Gerald had paid with cash, too.

"Did this guy leave the same time as Gerald?"

"I don't remember for sure. Probably within five or ten minutes."

"I noticed cameras as I was walking through. Is there video?"

Chip missed an easy shot, shook his head. "There's no video. Those cameras require a subscription and I canceled it during the pandemic. I had to cut expenses everywhere I could. Still can't afford to turn them back on."

Packard realized they were going to have to go back to the same sources of video they had collected for Ashley's murder to see if any of them captured vehicles near the Silver Dollar shortly after Gerald's estimated time of death. If they were lucky, they might see the same vehicle on both days. It was going to take time to collect it all and for Suresh to run his AI again.

Packard asked for a list of the staff who had interacted with Gerald or the stranger at the bar, also a list of customers who paid with credit cards around the time Gerald was in the bar in case any of them had noticed the stranger.

Chip and Kristie could have been playing badminton instead of pool the way they kept swinging and missing at everything on the table. Chip was too drunk to hit anything and Kristie was probably a great bartender but she was terrible at pool. "You mind?" Packard asked her and held his hand out for the cue.

"Be my guest," she said.

Packard staggered his feet, bent at the waist, and hit the nine so hard the crack and the thunk into the pocket were almost simultaneous. He ran the table after that, every stripe in order. For his final shot, he banked the cue ball off the side so it came back and just kissed the eight ball, making it dizzy, making it fall like a lover into the embrace of the corner pocket.

Chip whistled. "Shark! Where'd you learn how to play like that?"

"I played for beer money in college," Packard said.

"Just beer money? You could've paid your tuition shooting like that."

"Might have been a bit of both."

Packard stayed on the scene at the Silver Dollar until they finished photographing the body and loaded it into a dark, quiet ambulance for the ride to the hospital. In the morning it would get sent to Saint Paul for the autopsy.

At home, just before midnight, he shed all his clothes and crawled into bed. It was too hot for covers. He pulled the sheet to his waist and let one leg hang out. He was too tired to sleep, or too wired to be tired. Something.

He had two bodies in or on their way to Saint Paul. Both killed in the same manner. First Ashley, then Gerald. It was too early to tell if there was any connection between the two. He'd learned that Gerald had been a custodian at the high school before he retired. Ashley had a kid in that high school who had been bullied. She'd been thinking about suing the school. The connection seemed tenuous at best.

Packard turned on his side, balled the pillow under his head. He was angry with himself for not moving fast enough to catch Ashley's killer before he killed again. What was driving this guy? If Ashley's killing was desperate, Gerald's felt…retaliatory. Or was it the opposite? Had he killed Ashley in a moment of fury and killed Gerald because he had to? If the killer was indeed the guy from the bar, he had taken a big chance killing someone he'd been seen talking to just moments earlier. Doing it in broad daylight meant this guy felt invisible or invincible.

Which was it?

Just as he was about to fall asleep, his phone rang.

"You up?" Thielen asked.

"Kind of. What are you doing?"

"Feeding this titty monster."

"Yeah? Did I need to know about that?"

"No, but it's what I was doing while I was scrolling through the dispatch logs."

"Why are you looking at dispatch calls when you're on maternity leave?"

"I like to know what's going on. I like to think about all the shit you and Reynolds are dealing with and laugh and laugh. It makes me pee a little bit now that I've had a baby but it's worth it."

"There's so much about your pregnancy I wish I didn't know."

"You'll want to know about this."

"What?"

"This afternoon I was driving home from running errands and I drove down the alley behind the Silver Dollar."

Packard sat up.

"And?"

"And I might have seen who killed Gerald Hall."

CHAPTER TWENTY-FOUR

SUNDAY

AIR QUALITY INDEX: RED (UNHEALTHY)

Sunday morning. Hazy skies and already eighty degrees before the sun came up that morning. A day after the rain, everything was damp, everything gave off steam. The job site was a small lake house with no tree canopy left. Every trunk still standing looked like a broken pencil.

The guys worked in silence except for the scrape of roof forks and the squeak of nails being pulled. The old roof came down in sheets of jagged shingles and old tar paper that Charlie loaded into the trailer. Miguel went up the ladder with a leaf blower and cleaned everything before they started unrolling the underlayment. When he was done, he stood with one foot on either side of the ridge line and filmed the sun rising across the lake. Charlie paused to see what he saw: a saffron yolk in a dirty white sky. Across the lake the splintered, broken trees looked apocalyptic in the haze.

They waited until nine to turn on the radio. Latin pop from the 1990s and 2000s. The music seemed to lift the mood. There was more chatter after that. Charlie watched to see if Luis and Juan had gotten over their beef, but it was hard to tell. They both seemed more deferential to Francisco. Whatever happened the other night after Charlie blacked out, it had been enough to bring Francisco out of his room nearly naked. He was always fully covered on the job. Turning his back even, when lifting his shirt to wipe his face. None of them had seen all his tattoos up to that point. Perhaps it was the sight of all the ink on his chest and back and legs dedicated to a violent Mexican gang that made them keep their eyes down.

Around noon, Charlie found a bit of shade on the side of the truck and slumped to the ground to smoke a cigarette. He took off his hat and poured water from his bottle over his head and settled the hat low again. He hadn't had time to shower that morning and could smell last night's drinking on himself.

After buying cigarettes at the gas station yesterday afternoon, he'd walked under clearing skies into town and stopped at the first bar he came to for a drink. It was twelve dollars for a double shot of rail whiskey so he left in search of a liquor store where the hundred dollars he got from Matthias (minus the twenty he'd spent on cigarettes) would go further. A half mile later he came to the municipal package store and came out with a liter of whiskey in a brown bag.

On the long walk home, Pete, the bearded tree guy, passed him driving fast out of town. Didn't stop. Charlie remembered that asshole showing up at the motel with the woman who stole all his money. He wondered if Pete had any way of contacting her. Did whores give out their cell phone numbers? Charlie didn't know.

When he got back to the motel, there was no sign of Pete or his truck. Charlie's feet were killing him.

Nothing a drink wouldn't fix.

The crew took their time in the heat and roofed the small house and called it a day. Charlie left early to go to the dump and get a head start on cooking.

Back at the motel, the crew showered and gathered around the picnic table where Charlie had spread out the ingredients for dinner. Chicken breasts, onions, peppers, black beans, tortillas. It was still uncomfortably hot. They cracked beer cans, sucked at the foam.

College Boy tried to tell Matthias about the job site, but Matthias was only half listening, engrossed by something in the local paper.

"You could literally see the edge of where the storm came through," College Boy said. "This house and everything to the south had no trees. Hundred yards to the north, trees were still standing."

"Listen up, everybody," Matthias said, ignoring College Boy. He tore something out of the paper and put in his pocket. "Here's where we're at. I've sold all the roofs I'm gonna sell in this area. I've got insurance estimates and down payments for the roofs you guys are going to work on for the next ten or twelve days. Tomorrow or the next day, I'm leaving. I'm going to stop at home and see how my dad's doing, then head for southeast Arkansas. They had big storms a few days ago. The heat map shows a wide band of damaging winds and tennis-ball-sized hail. I think we can finish the summer down there."

Juan understood more English than he could speak. He translated what Matthias said into Spanish for Luis. Francisco looked like he understood just fine. Miguel was on his phone and didn't even look up.

Charlie stirred the onions and peppers on the grill. If it was this hot and muggy in northern Minnesota, how miserable was it going to be in southeastern Arkansas? At least the air would be clearer down there.

He allowed himself a moment to fantasize about staying in Sandy Lake, abandoning this rootless existence that offered him nothing but lots of time to drink. What if he stayed and got a real job and got sober and back to writing? He'd written thousands of poems in his head over the years. Volumes. An imagined library. He just needed to get them out.

Easier said than done. All of it. The whole fantasy. He had less than a hundred dollars in his pocket. This job came with cheap housing, which was the only housing he could afford. If he stayed behind, he'd be destitute within days.

There was also the matter of his outstanding warrant. The longer he stayed in one place, the more likely it was to catch up to him.

"Are you going to pay us before you go?" Charlie asked.

"You'll get paid for this week before I leave. When you drive my trucks and gear down to Arkansas, you'll get paid the rest."

Charlie caught an inquiring look from Juan to Luis. Luis ignored him. Charlie had a feeling Luis wasn't going to make it to Arkansas.

College Boy looked glum. He knew there was no moving on with this crew. His short-lived summer job was near its end.

When the food was ready, they ate in silence. Matthias chewed with a look on his face like he was doing math in his head. Luis and Juan sat on opposite sides of the picnic table but kept their heads turned so they didn't have to look at each other. Miguel ate with his right hand and tapped the screen of his phone with the left.

After dinner, Francisco said something about *zapatos*, shoes, to Juan. Charlie looked at Miguel's feet and saw his big toe poking through a hole in the top of his shoe. Juan threw Francisco the keys to the van, and he and Miguel left together.

Charlie did the dishes. Picked up the trash from dinner, then opened another beer, his last before he started on the whiskey in his room. His eyes crossed as he took a long drink, staring at the end of the can. When he lowered it, he saw a sheriff's vehicle pull into the motel's lot.

"Ah fuck," Charlie said.

CHAPTER TWENTY-FIVE

Packard spent the morning at Gerald Hall's house looking for anything that might indicate Gerald had a previous interaction with the man from the bar. The same man Thielen claimed to have seen when she called the night before.

"I saw a tan white guy in a baseball cap standing over Gerald's car," Thielen said. "Might have been Native or Hispanic. I wasn't that close. But I know Gerald's car because my first car in college was an old Park Avenue that I got from my aunt. Same color and everything. I also pulled Gerald over for DUI back when I did patrol. I know that car."

"How tall was he?"

"Mmm…not as tall as you. Maybe six feet. Five eleven."

"What else?"

"He was wearing work gloves," Thielen said.

"You noticed his gloves?"

"I did. He had his forearms on the roof of the car. I thought he was wearing gloves because the top of the car was so hot but that doesn't really make sense. I just noticed the gloves."

"Why were you going down the alley?"

"Because I stopped at the thrift store to look for baby clothes and it's easier to park in back. When I left, I went down the alley."

"Did this guy see you?"

"I don't know. He had a hat on. We might have made eye contact."

Thielen hadn't noticed any of the other vehicles in the lot or anything else about the guy. She saw his head and his hands and that was it. Thielen thought it was sometime between four and four thirty, which lined up with what Packard had heard from Kristie the bartender.

What Packard found at Gerald's was a small house full of battered and beaten furniture. It smelled like a cat used to live there. In the living room he found a computer that was yellow with age and cigarette smoke. The password was written on a piece of scrap paper sitting beneath the monitor. According to his browser history, Gerald was into fringe news sources and cryptid message boards and porn hubs. His email inbox was full of spam, and his outbox contained long, rambling messages to newspaper editors and other random individuals about the secret invasion of lizard people.

Gerald's idiotic beliefs might have contributed to his death, but Packard was fairly certain their main suspect wasn't a lizard man. What had Gerald said or done that led to a confrontation in the parking lot? It seemed likely the man who killed Ashley also killed Gerald. Both of them choked, both stabbed between the ribs with a knife that pierced the heart. That was no coincidence.

They were looking for a white possibly Native, possibly Hispanic, guy in a baseball cap. Around five ten to six feet tall. Indeterminate age. A description that matched 90 percent of the men in town.

Packard peeled off his black gloves and gave Gerald's place one last look. How many houses like this had he been in over the years? Lonely old men and their sad things. It made Packard think of the current state of his house, which was a bigger mess than Gerald's. What stood between Ben Packard and a time when someone looked around at what he'd left behind and felt sorry for him?

Not much. A shrinking number of days.

His phone rang. It was Dean Schmidt from Schmidt Landscaping.

"I'm trying to track down a tree crew working in the area," Packard said. "Not your guys from what I've been told. Know anyone like that?"

"I think there's some guys staying at the Tabard Motel. I've seen a Kubota tractor with a log grapple on a trailer there the last couple of weeks."

"Have you had any interaction with these guys?"

"None. Couldn't tell you a thing about them other than I'm pretty sure they're not licensed or bonded or carrying the right insurance. If there wasn't so much work to go around, I'd be more inclined to chase them out of town. Good luck to you if they drop a tree on your house or someone gets hurt on your property."

"I'm not trying to hire them. I just want to ask them some questions," Packard said.

He waited until what he hoped was the end of the workday before stopping at the motel. The place was a dump, the rooms transactional or transitional. Customers stayed only as long as necessary or couldn't leave because they had no other options. It wasn't uncommon for them to scatter at the sight of law enforcement. Even people without options had plenty to lose in an encounter with police.

Packard got out of his vehicle. His shirt was immediately damp on his back. He watched a man in a hat hurry from the picnic table with a beer in his hand and disappear into a room near the end of the building. Two other guys stayed at the picnic table and regarded Packard with curiosity.

"Any of you guys tree trimmers?" Packard asked the men at the picnic table.

"Not us. Corner room," one of them said.

A truck with a trailer and the tractor Dean Schmidt mentioned was backed up against the front of the building with another truck and trailer parked side by side. More trucks and a van in the lot. One of them had a logo on the side with the words Fredricksen Construction arranged in the shape of a roof.

Packard knocked on the door to room number one. There was an inch gap under the door. An air conditioner with duct tape sealing it in place wheezed in the window. Thick cobwebs and dead bugs choked the corner where the building made a right angle.

A man with a dark beard answered the door in boxer shorts and a white tank T-shirt. He was hairy up to his Adam's apple, with ape-like arms and shoulders. He had a cigarette in one hand. Behind him, Packard saw a shirtless man wearing cargo shorts and looking at his phone on the bed farthest from the door. Packard caught a whiff of the room: unwashed bedsheets, men sleeping and smoking.

"You guys do tree removal?"

The bearded man looked him up and down. Packard was dressed in black pants and a black short-sleeved shirt with a sheriff's office emblem on the chest. He had his badge and his gun on his belt.

"We do," the man said.

Packard introduced himself. The guy at the door was Pete Hawkins. The shirtless guy on the bed was Dustin Weir.

"Is there a problem?" Pete asked.

"No problem. Just have a few questions for you guys. How long have you been in town?"

Pete looked over his shoulder at Dustin, like he had all the answers. "Ten, twelve days now, I think," Pete said.

"Where you from?"

"We're both from North Dakota," Pete said. "Dustin's my cousin."

"What brought you to Sandy Lake?"

Pete said he had a tree business back home but business had been slow lately. He saw news about the storm and thought the people of Sandy Lake could use his services. They were planning to stay another four or five days at most.

"Did you guys do some jobs over on Wood Lake?"

Pete shrugged. "I don't know the names of the lakes around here."

"You got an address?" Dustin asked from the bed.

Packard flipped back in his notebook to Ashley's address. "510 Fog Trail."

Dustin thumbed his phone. "Yeah, we were over there. We did three jobs on that street. Not all on the same day."

Packard took out his own phone and showed Pete a photo from the doorbell camera near Ashley Turner's house of what might have been a man in a distant tree. He swiped to the next photo where the tree was gone. "Which one of you was in the tree?"

Pete squinted at the photo. "Hard to say but probably Dustin. We both go up but he does more than me."

"You guys hear the news about a woman who was killed here recently?"

An odd look flashed across Pete's face. Nervousness. Uncertainty. Like he was trying to recall what women had he been around lately and who had seen them. Dustin was staring holes into the back of his head.

"Who told you we were at this hotel?" Pete asked.

"Does it matter?" Packard said.

"If someone has accused us of having something to do with a woman getting killed, I'd like to know who it was."

"No one has accused you of anything. I came to find you guys because you took down a tree at her house and were working in the area again the day she was killed. I want to know if you saw anyone else while you were there."

"We don't know anything about a woman getting killed. We work all day, come back to this dump and sleep, go out and do it again. A few drinks at the bar every now and then but that's it. We don't know anyone around here."

"I get it," Packard said. He looked past Pete. "The second time you were on Fog Trail, what time did you guys get there?" he asked Dustin.

Dustin was up on one elbow with his phone on the bed in front of him. "We did 510 Fog Trail a week ago Saturday. We were back on that street again three days later, two days in a row. We got there around 7:30 a.m. both days. We were there all day for the house that had two trees. The house next door with one tree only took half a day. I would guess we were done there by 2:00 p.m. or so."

Ashley had lunch with her family at 12:30. Tom and the boys went back down to the lake at 1:00. Someone sent Ashley a message at 1:47 and deleted it at 1:59. The call to 911 came at 2:39 and first responders were there within fifteen minutes. These two were there most of the day but were gone before police arrived.

"You guys work together, or do you split up and work separate jobs?"

"Taking down trees is a two-man job. Three would be better," Pete said. His cigarette was burning down. He flicked the ash onto the sidewalk in front of their room.

"While you were there, did you notice anyone drive by? Walk by? Any boats pull up?"

"There's not a lot of gawking in our line of work," Pete said. "You lose focus, cut the wrong spot, don't know what's going on over your head, you can get killed."

"I can imagine," Packard said. "Dustin, you see anyone when you were all the way up in that tree?"

Dustin bit his lip and pushed a button on his phone that made the screen go dark. "I didn't," he said.

He was lying. Packard knew it like he knew this motel room had a tiny, filthy bathroom with no fan and a pair of dirty underwear kicked into one corner.

"Someone killed Ashley Turner three houses down from where you were working while you guys were there. It's too bad you didn't see anything."

"Killed her how?" Dustin asked.

"Choked her. Stabbed her."

Packard saw Dustin's gaze fall on Pete again. Pete was staring down at the tip of the cigarette in his hand like he was bored by the whole conversation.

Dustin gave an awkward shrug with one shoulder. "Sorry," he said.

Packard got their addresses back in North Dakota and a cell phone number for each of them. He left his card. "Think back to that day. Call me if you remember anything."

Pete stared down at the card, turned, and pushed the door shut with his saggy-ass shorts. A second later the fan on the air conditioner cranked up a notch and the noise drowned out any chance of Packard hearing them talk to each other.

The guys at the picnic table were gone. Packard got back in his vehicle. In front of him were eight closed doors. Like a game show.

He felt a tingle behind his ear, the whisper of intuition.

Pick a door, it said. *Any door.*

CHAPTER TWENTY-SIX

MONDAY

AIR QUALITY INDEX: MAROON (HAZARDOUS)

The next morning, Charlie smoked a cigarette at the picnic table, waiting for the motel doors to open and discharge the crew. The morning air was warm and dewy and already the color of ash. He blew smoke at the early mosquitoes and waved a hand by his ear.

He felt like he'd used another of his nine lives yesterday, sitting in his room, waiting for the cop to bang on his door. Somehow they'd figured out who he was. They knew about the dead nurse. He'd contemplated hiding under the bed or crawling out the bathroom window. He smoked what he thought was his last cigarette. Drank his whiskey.

No knock.

He'd waited almost an hour before daring to disturb his curtains and look outside.

The cop was gone.

A miracle.

Things were getting dangerous here. Two close calls with local law enforcement were two too many. He felt a net he couldn't see slowly coming up around him. He looked at the cut on his arm, the bruise on his ribs, wondered what else he'd done that he couldn't remember.

The biggest threat to his ongoing freedom was Matthias knowing about his warrant. As soon as he decided he'd had enough of Charlie's bullshit, a quick phone call to the local PD with his name and room number would fix that problem. Charlie was a fool if he didn't think things would eventually get to that point. He needed an exit strategy.

Luis, Juan, and College Boy all came out of their rooms, yawning, stretching, and got into the van. Charlie stepped on his cigarette and got behind the wheel of the pickup. A minute later, Miguel climbed in on the passenger side. The boy looked at his phone while he still had Wi-Fi this close to the motel. He was wearing new shoes.

After two minutes, Charlie asked Miguel in Spanish what was going on.

Where's Francisco?

I don't know.

What? Is he in the room?

No. He didn't come home last night.

"What the fuck?" Charlie muttered to himself. He got out of the truck, intending to check Francisco's room for himself. He stopped.

Did you both come back to the motel after you bought shoes?

No. He left with some men at the store.

How did the van get back here?

I drove it. He gave me the keys and said to go home.

"Oh my god," Charlie said. A fourteen-year-old driving a van with all the gear inside it. If the sheriff's deputy saw that, they'd all be under arrest.

Charlie walked over to the van. Luis rolled down the window.

"Francisco is gone."

"Eh?"

"Miguel says he met some guys at the store last night and never came home."

A minute later, they were all on the sidewalk in front of Francisco's room, the door open. They looked inside like disbelievers at the tomb. Luis asked Miguel exactly what happened.

We went to the store and bought shoes. There was a van parked next to ours when we came out. Two guys got out and said hi to Francisco like they knew him. Another guy was driving. Francisco told me to get in the van. He locked the doors and threw the keys in my lap and said go home. See you later.

Who were the guys?

I don't know.

Gringos?

No. Mexicans. One had a tattoo on his neck like Francisco's.

Juan and Luis looked at each other. Three guys from Francisco's former gang didn't come all the way to Minnesota to catch up on old times. Francisco had something they wanted. Maybe it was Francisco they wanted.

What happened next?

Francisco got in the van with the two guys. They left.

"This is fucked," Charlie said. He took his hat off and ran a hand over his freckled head. "This is a big fucking job today. We need our crew."

He walked down to Matthias's room and banged on the door. Matthias answered after a minute, wearing his pants pulled up to his navel and no shirt. "Trade rooms with me," he said before Charlie could say anything.

"What?"

"Trade rooms." Matthias fished his key card out of his pants and handed it to Charlie. "My AC quit working last night. You don't even use yours."

"Fuck. Fine." They traded room keys. "Have you heard from Francisco?"

"Why would I hear from Francisco?"

"He's gone. He got into a van with some guys last night and never came home, according to Miguel."

"Okay, then you need to adapt. He'll be back later or he won't."

"We got a big job today. And look at this air quality. It's horseshit."

"If you want to sit in your rooms and wait for Francisco or wait for the air to get better, it's up to you guys," Matthias said, rubbing a hand in his armpit. His suntanned arm across his pale chest looked like it had been transplanted from another body. "No one gets paid in that scenario. Half of this crew smokes. The air quality right now is still better than every breath you take through a cigarette."

Charlie knew he'd walked right into that one. "We're down too many men," he complained.

"Then maybe you'll need to do some actual work, Charlie. Get on the fucking roof."

"Fuck you, Matthias. I do plenty on the ground. You don't pay me to climb ladders."

"I pay you to run the crew. I don't pay you to get drunk every night, or come whining to me when things go wrong. Figure it out. You're the crew lead."

"This is bullshit," Charlie said, walking away, then turning around again. "I can't run a crew when there's no fucking crew!"

The job was a barn that had been turned into an event space for weddings and family reunions. According to Matthias, the owners were involved in a nasty divorce and the business was idle. Charlie walked around the cavernous inside, imagined happy couples dancing under overhead lights that zigzagged on strings while the two people running the show stood in the shadows staring daggers at each other across the room.

Someone had come out and mowed around the barn so they could lay down their tarps. Outside the circle, wind moved through the waist-high grass and a field full of wildflowers that bobbed behind a pergola where couples would have made their vows.

An addition ran the length of the barn, enclosing a kitchen and prep space. The gambrel roof, shaped like a bell with near-vertical sides, had blue tarps nailed down with two-by-fours over the damaged areas. A cupola in the center of the roof had been ripped away by the wind. The owners wanted the hole patched and shingled over.

Most jobs, they didn't bother with the fall protection system. This job, there was no getting away from it. Luis went up first and pounded a dozen nails into a pair of hinged metal plates draped over either side of the roof's center line. Then did it again two more times. One each for him, Juan, and College Boy. They put on harnesses and connected themselves to the roof with heavy ropes that clipped to the metal plates and to a ring on the back of their harnesses.

By mid-morning the sky was the color of fire. From another planet. A hot wind bore down on them like it came from the sun itself. Juan and Luis wore long-sleeved shirts and wide hats cinched under their chins, bandannas over their noses and mouths. College Boy had pulled his arms out of his T-shirt and wore it bunched around his shoulders and pulled up over his nose like a mask. The three of them hunched over on top of the barn and peeled up the old shingles with pitchforks. The decking beneath was sheets of plywood, the original barn wood long gone.

Inside the barn, tables and chairs were stacked to one side and covered with drop cloths. Stairs went up to a loft that covered the back half of the barn. The front half was open all the way to the timbered joists that held up the domed roof.

Charlie and Miguel hauled an aluminum ladder to the loft and pushed the top of it through the hole in the roof left by the cupola. Climbing the ladder meant going over the empty space where the loft didn't reach. Nothing below but a concrete floor. They braced the bottom of the ladder with a package of shingles to keep it from slipping. Charlie took one look at the setup and felt his butthole tighten. Matthias thought he should get on the roof. Like hell he would.

They only had three harnesses so Miguel worked without one, tossing stacks of old shingles over the side. Charlie wore a hard hat and loaded the debris in the trailer. He saw a mouse scurry along the barn's foundation and watched grasshoppers jump in and out of the tall grass like they were running from a prairie fire.

Charlie stoked his anger at Matthias throughout the morning. The whole crew, what was left of it, was getting screwed on this job. Every roof was measured in square feet, and it was by the square foot that the crew got paid. The price per foot they'd agreed to was based on a full crew. The bigger the crew, the faster they worked, the more square footage they replaced, the more they got paid.

Since Francisco broke Alberto's arm in Oklahoma, they were down two experienced roofers. College Boy and Miguel worked hard but they couldn't make up for what was lost. They'd get paid their square footage rate for this job, but with fewer workers, it would take them more hours to earn the same amount of money.

Fucking Matthias. He wanted them to believe they were all on the same team. Bullshit. His share of the take actually increased when he had fewer workers to pay. So what if they didn't like it? Juan and Luis were relatively safe from ICE raids out in these rural areas, an incentive not to rock the boat. Charlie was on the run and had nothing without this job.

This wasn't a team. It was a serfdom.

Charlie wiped the sweat off his face with a rag from his back pocket. He thought about the size of this job, about Matthias leaving town tomorrow.

About what a mutiny might look like.

Charlie tied a tarp over the trailer and made the first run to the dump just before noon. When he came back, the wildfire smell in the air was strong enough that he could taste it. Lunch was leftovers from the night before. Chicken and peppers and onions. Cold tortillas and oranges.

Late in the afternoon the guys got on their hands and knees and started pulling out hundreds of old nails. As the sun went down, they had the steep sides covered in underlayment, each nail surrounded by a green plastic disk.

Charlie made a second trip to the dump, wondering the whole way how he could get the rest of the crew to turn on Matthias. Francisco being gone, he realized, was a benefit. Had he still been there, Juan and Luis would follow his lead, and Francisco had never been on Charlie's side when it came to anything.

He needed a plan that would get them all the windfall they needed to move on to the next chapter in their lives. Enough money to send College Boy off to school and for Luis to go home and be with his family. Juan would have no trouble finding another job as a roofer if he wanted it. Charlie just needed enough to give himself some breathing room while he figured out his next move.

Back at the barn, he started packing up the van. He lit a cigarette and watched a rafter of twelve wild turkeys emerge out of the haze in a staggered line and come down the driveway, pecking the ground. These ugly alien birds, the orange sky. They really could have been on another planet.

From on top of the barn came the sound of Miguel dropping a package of shingles onto the stack he'd been building near the ladder. Tomorrow, Juan and Luis would start shingling the barn's sides, starting at the bottom. Miguel would hand them shingles as they worked their way up, then when they got high enough, slide shingles down from above for them to catch.

In the plan coming together in Charlie's mind, he still hadn't accounted for what to do with Miguel. They couldn't all scatter and abandon him in Sandy Lake. Or could they? The kid had made it this far, all the way from El Salvador, on his own. Charlie wondered if he could convince Juan to take care of him.

Miguel dropped a last package of shingles onto a pile stacked four high. He took out his phone and climbed the stack, filming himself with the fiery sky behind him. He said something to the camera that Charlie couldn't hear, pointed his fingers in a sideways V.

Later, Charlie would recall the barn groaning right before the plywood gave way beneath the weight of two hundred pounds of shingles and a fourteen-year-old boy. Maybe the groan came from him. A premonition. He'd known in his bones that something like this was going to happen. He'd tried to prevent it by accepting Francisco's challenge to get on the roof but had failed.

The wood near the hole from the old cupola must have been wet and rotted.

A hole opened beneath the stack of shingles, swallowing them, swallowing the boy like the mouth of a whale.

The barn seemed to recede away from Charlie as he ran toward it. On the way, he became a believer in miracles. Certain this boy who'd climbed roofs all summer like a spider monkey would be able to leap and grab something, dangle by one hand from a rafter, swing and reach for another, and land on his feet.

Inside the barn it was dark. Charlie heard College Boy pounding down the ladder in the loft and calling Miguel's name.

On the concrete dance floor: packages of exploded shingles, pieces of plywood, strings of overhead lights and shattered glass bulbs. In the middle of it all, a very still boy who'd walked all the way from El Salvador to Texas.

College Boy was there with his hands in his hair—*Oh fuck fucking fuck*—and behind him the sound of Juan and Luis running, stopping, praying in Spanish. Charlie moaned as he scooped Miguel from the ground, held him against his chest, and looked up at where he had fallen from, at the tattered black underlayment hanging from the hole, at the orange eye looking down that cared nothing about them or the noises they made.

Charlie stood up, clutching Miguel. The boy weighed almost nothing, an armful of shadows.

CHAPTER TWENTY-SEVEN

"The depth of the wounds is very similar to the wounds on Ashley Turner," the Ramsey County medical examiner told Packard over the phone. "I can't be one hundred percent certain it was the same knife or object in both cases, but I'm comfortable saying a similar blade was used."

"Anything specific you can tell me about the blade used?"

"Single-edged, non-serrated. At least six centimeters long, based on the depth of the wounds."

"What else?" Packard asked.

"Both victims had stab wounds that penetrated the right ventricle. They both experienced tamponade, which is when fluid fills the sac around the heart and prevents it from relaxing. Both were choked, resulting in bilateral bruising to the neck and, in Ashley's case, the posterior neck. The killer used his left hand in both cases. You can tell by the prominent thumb bruise on one side. Measurements of the distance between bruises is similar in both victims."

"Choked them with his left hand, stabbed with the right then."

"Exactly. Multiple stab wounds in both cases but not frenzied. He had the upper hand in both cases and knew exactly what he was doing."

"Anything else?"

"Yes. I saved the best for last. The tip of the knife broke off in the male victim's chest. It's just the smallest piece of the blade left behind in the rib. If you find your killer and find the knife, you should be able to make a match."

Packard agreed it was good news but listening to it while he looked out the window at a burnt-orange sky made it feel unimportant. What did good news matter when they were being told to hide in their homes? What did good news mean when the world was burning and the air was made of ash?

After talking to the ME, Packard turned away from the window and ran Pete Hawkins and Dustin Weir—the two tree guys from the motel—through the databases to see what came back. He got multiple hits on Pete. Possession of methamphetamine. Solicitation of a prostitute twice in two years. The charges were eight years old and came from the Williston Police Department. Williston was a small town in western North Dakota, best known for being near the Bakken oil field.

If Pete was working in the fields back then and lost his job for any reason, getting hired by another company would have been almost impossible with his criminal record. Maybe that's why he came back to the east side of the state and went into business for himself. The fresh start didn't mean he'd stayed out of trouble. Eighteen months ago he'd been charged with domestic assault and terrorizing with a dangerous weapon. Three months later he was charged with violation of a domestic violence protection order.

Charmer, this guy.

Weir came back clean. Public records showed he was divorced in 2019. No business filings in either of their names with the North Dakota Secretary of State. If they were running a tree-trimming business, it was new or they were doing everything off the books.

Pete's solicitation charges reminded Packard of seeing Darla Knoll's car parked at the Tabard Motel when Reynolds gave him a ride home the other night.

Darla Knoll was in her late thirties and making bank with her body while she could. Packard had a soft spot for her, despite her disregard for the state's prostitution laws. A couple of years ago she had come to him with a sob story about falling in love with a guy named Chuck and thinking she was finally done with sex work. After a couple of head-in-the-clouds months, things got dark. Turned out Chuck didn't want to be her boyfriend; he wanted to be her pimp, and he gave her a beating when she tried to leave him. Told her he'd make her look a lot worse if she didn't do what he said. That's when she came to Packard for help.

Chuck was a personal trainer, five foot seven with a ridiculously overdeveloped upper body. Packard paid him a visit late one night, flashed his badge and pushed his way inside Chuck's condo and suggested he have a seat. Packard wandered around the place, dumping out all the contents of the kitchen drawers, pulling things out of cabinets and closets while he calmly listed the penalties for assault and promoting prostitution and sex trafficking. "Now that I know you're Darla's pimp, I'm going to be back here making a mess every time I see her car at the motel. Every time she gets arrested, you're going to get arrested."

"I'm not her pimp. I'm not anybody's pimp," Chuck whined. "She's lying."

"I don't believe you," Packard said. "And I'm going to tell you this only once: If another woman comes through the sheriff's office with bruises on her body and your name in her mouth… Buddy, I'm going to ruin your life. Believe that."

The last he'd heard, Chuck had lost all his personal training clients and moved to Omaha.

Packard had Darla's number in his phone. He called her but she didn't pick up. He left her a message.

He called Reynolds. They talked briefly about the findings from the ME. Packard was already certain Ashley and Gerald's cases were connected. Now they had the evidence to link them.

"Where do you go from here?" Reynolds asked.

"I honestly don't know." Packard made a frustrated grunt and shut down his computer. "How can we be so close to this guy and not know who Red is? We have his phone number. I've heard his voice on his voicemail. We have a bartender who served him drinks. Thielen made eye contact with him while he stood over Gerald's dead body. He's like an optical illusion you can't see while looking at it straight on. You needed to squint and let things go out of focus."

"Maybe you should go home and have a few beers. That'll blur things."

The mention of beers made Packard think of Kyle. More unresolved business.

"Things are blurry enough with all the smoke in the air. Maybe one beer," Packard said.

"Sleep on it. I'm on a call tonight. I won't bother you unless it's an emergency."

"Don't bother me even if it is."

CHAPTER TWENTY-EIGHT

Charlie laid Miguel on the dropped tailgate of the pickup truck and bent the boy's knees to one side. The back of his head was caked in blood. An arm dangled off the end.

The four of them stood around the body. Wind hissed through the tall grass. Juan was mumbling a prayer in Spanish and crossing himself. They kept looking at one another. Four sweaty faces as the sky turned black.

College Boy lifted the hem of his shirt and used it to wipe his face. "We have to call the police."

Charlie caught the look of terror on Juan's face at the mention of the police.

"No. No cops. Are you crazy?" Charlie said.

"Why is that crazy?"

"We've got two undocumented workers on our crew. We've got a job site without enough safety equipment for everyone. We've got a fourteen-year-old boy, also undocumented, not old enough to be working on a roofing crew. None of us know a thing about him. We've been letting him share a motel room with a guy covered in gang tattoos, and now he's dead on our watch. Can you not count all the ways that's fucked up and maybe not something we want to take to the police?"

"Listen, I just work here," College Boy said. "I'm not the boss. I didn't hire Miguel or have any sort of responsibility for him."

"And if they arrest Matthias and me, how are you going to get paid?"

That gave College Boy pause. He wiped his face again and turned away from Miguel's body. Charlie translated what had been said so far for Luis and Juan. He didn't bother hiding how well he knew Spanish. There was no more time for games.

"What are we going to do? Just dump him somewhere?" College Boy asked.

"We're not going to dump him. We're going to bury him," Charlie said. He'd dig the hole himself if he had to. It was the least he could do for the boy he had failed.

"What about Francisco?"

"What about him?"

"He's going to want to know where Miguel is."

"Do you see Francisco here? If he'd shown back up at the motel at some point today, Matthias would have driven him out here. He's not coming back."

"He could still come back," College Boy said. He tried to sound like he believed it but his faith left him before he finished the sentence.

"Francisco is not coming back. Three guys showed up out of the blue and ordered him into a van. That's never led to anything good in any of the movies I've seen."

"This isn't a fucking a movie!" College Boy protested. "It's our real lives. Oh my god. Why am I even here?" He reached into his shorts for his phone. "I'm calling the police. We have to do this right."

Luis put his hand on College Boy's shoulder and gently took away his phone. "*Amigo. Por favor. Quiero volver a Mexico con mi esposa y mi hijo. Por favor.*"

"What's he saying?"

"He wants to go home to his family," Charlie said. He took the phone from Luis and handed it back to College Boy. "Listen to me. If we do this right, we can all go home after this."

Not far from the barn was another building that looked like it might have been a stable at one time. It was open on the front and underneath its tin roof were stalls where a minibus and a carriage and a flatbed trailer were parked. Out of sight behind the building they found a three-sided bin where the groundskeepers dumped all the grass clippings and leaves for composting.

Luis drove the pickup and Charlie rode on the tailgate with Miguel's head in his lap. The other two walked with flat shovels over their shoulders.

In the compost pile, they cleared away last fall's leaves that had settled into a thick, damp mat and started digging. The ground was soft and rich. They worked quickly without speaking, trading off as necessary until they had a rectangular hole four feet down.

It was dark by the time they finished digging. In the harsh light from the truck's headlamps, Charlie held Miguel's feet and College Boy held his arms and they lowered him into the hole.

The grave.

Now it was a grave.

No one moved. No one wanted to toss the first shovel of dirt onto Miguel's face. His open mouth. His new shoes.

Charlie picked up a shovel, scooped the heavy earth, and closed his eyes as he tossed it into the hole. He kept scooping and shoveling and didn't look down until Miguel was covered. When they were finished, they pulled the leaves back over where they had dug. Juan said a prayer in Spanish.

It was done.

They were starving afterwards.

In the parking lot of the grocery store, Juan and College Boy sat on the tailgate with a pizza box and a twelve-pack of Modelo between them. Lights lit the pollution in the air and made it look like a gauzy curtain had been drawn across the bright front of the store.

Charlie decided it was time to share the plan he'd been thinking about all day.

"Listen, Matthias is leaving for Arkansas tomorrow," Charlie said, reaching for another slice. "I don't know what you guys are thinking, but I'm not going to fucking Arkansas. I'm done after this. *No voy a* Arkansas."

College Boy knocked his shoes together where they dangled below the tailgate. "I think I'm done, too. After today…I don't know, man. I should get ready for school."

"*Y ustedes*?" Charlie asked Juan and Luis. And you?

The cousins didn't need to look at each other to confirm anything. They were both done. Luis needed to go home and see his wife and kid. Juan said he might go with him. Or he might stay in the country and look for work on a different crew. Far from Minnesota. Far from the bad things that happened on this crew.

What about Matthias's trucks? Luis asked in Spanish.

"Fuck his trucks," Charlie said. That needed no translation. *You can drive his trucks to Mexico for all I care.*

"No," Luis said. Then he realized Charlie was serious. "*Sí*?"

"If Matthias leaves tomorrow, he's going to have to leave cash behind so that we get paid on Friday. That's four days away. Let's finish the barn job and I'll offer the owner a discount for cash. I'll pay out the week's wages; we'll split the barn money and all go our separate ways."

He translated for Juan and Luis.

Juan looked at him funny. *How'd your Spanish get so good all of a sudden?*

Charlie smiled and shrugged.

Juan shook his head, grinning but shameful, realizing Charlie had understood everything he'd said in his presence the whole time they'd been together. "Where you learn Spanish?"

"In restaurant kitchens."

"*Claro*."

"What about the rest of the jobs Matthias has lined up?" College Boy interrupted. "There's another two weeks of work."

"I'm out," Charlie said. "Matthias's intention is that you will have to drive his trucks to Arkansas if you want to get paid for those next two weeks. That's how he keeps us on the hook and makes sure his shit shows up at the new location. You want to drive eighteen hours to go pick up the money owed you?"

"No. But those people paid for a new roof."

"Fuck those people. They paid a storm chaser with a clipboard and a shit-eating grin to replace their roof. If they wanted guarantees and no risk, they had other options. We're not the ones who took their money. Matthias can return it if he wants, but I have a feeling they'll have a hard time getting ahold of him once he realizes we're all gone."

College Boy wasn't convinced. "It's one thing for you guys to be like, let's steal everything that's not nailed down and disappear into the wind. I live here. What if he comes back looking for my ass?"

Charlie lit a cigarette and opened another beer. "You think Matthias knows anything about you? I don't even know your first name and we've been together all day every day for three weeks. Take the money. It'll be gone before you know it. College is great at robbing you blind and making you think you're getting something valuable in return."

"Says the guy dumb enough to major in poetry."

"It was a double major in poetry and political science."

College Boy rolled his eyes. "Whatever. I don't know if I can go back to that barn tomorrow. I feel like if I look over by the garage shed, I'm going to see Miguel peeking around the corner at us and he's going to be all covered in mud and blood," College Boy said.

Charlie looked at the blood on his jeans from cradling Miguel's head on his lap. "You can go back and you will," he said. "We're going to finish that job. One more day and we don't have to talk about what happened ever again."

As soon as he said the words, Charlie knew that couldn't be the end of the story for Miguel. The boy had a family who would want to know what happened to him. If they didn't know the truth, they would spend their lives imagining the worst.

"I have his phone," Charlie said. "Maybe after we're all gone, I'll mail it to the police and tell them where to find the body. Explain what happened. They can figure out how to contact his family."

He repeated it in Spanish for Luis and Juan who nodded grimly.

"Can I see his phone?" College Boy asked.

Charlie pulled it from his back pocket. The screen had shattered in the fall.

College Boy poked at the screen. "I saw him swipe his password enough times but the screen doesn't work. I'm thinking about all the videos he made. We're probably all on here."

"You can't delete them?"

"I can't do anything. The screen is busted. I see he has TikTok on here. Give me a minute."

College Boy took out his own phone. Opened TikTok and started searching. "This is not good," he said.

"What's the problem?"

College Boy stared at his phone, thumbs moving. Juan leaned over to look at what was on the screen.

"He's been posting TikToks all summer long. Hashtag #ruferito. He's got more followers than I do."

"I don't understand half the words coming out of your mouth," Charlie said.

"He's been posting the videos he's been taking online. We're all on here. The motel's on here. He's got thousands of likes. Crazy comments."

"Delete it," Charlie said. "Can you do that?"

"I can't. I could delete it if I could get on his phone but I can't."

"Give me his phone. I'll figure out what to do with it," Charlie said. "This doesn't change the plan. Are we all in?"

It was almost ten by the time they returned to the motel. As Charlie walked to his room, he noticed the light was on and the air conditioner running. He could hear the TV inside. Matthias had asked him to switch rooms that morning and had already moved in.

Charlie walked to the room on the end and used Matthias's key card to unlock the door. Inside, Matthias's things were still everywhere. The far bed was unused. Charlie dumped his pockets on the nightstand, then remembered what else he needed to do.

He left the door open and walked down to the room Francisco and Miguel had shared. He knocked and waited in case Francisco had returned.

He hadn't.

Charlie used the key he'd taken off Miguel. Both beds were unmade. Miguel only had enough clothes to fill a single drawer in the dresser below the TV. Charlie swept everything into an empty grocery bag, grabbed the phone charger from beside the bed, and locked the door behind him. He had to walk all the way around the building to the back where the dumpster was. Somehow, throwing away the boy's clothes felt almost as bad as lowering him into the hole.

He knocked on the door to his old room and waited for Matthias to answer.

"How come you didn't move any of our shit if you wanted to trade rooms?" Charlie asked when Matthias opened the door.

"I meant to but then I locked myself out of my room and decided we'd manage for one night," Matthias said as he sat on the edge of the bed. He was shirtless and shaped like a barrel through the middle. His arms and neck were nut brown, his torso pale and hairless. "You guys were out late."

"It was a big job and we're a small crew," Charlie said. "I take it you never saw or heard from Francisco today."

Matthias dropped his chin and scratched the back of his head. "No."

"I just checked his room. His stuff is there but he's not."

"They come and go, these guys. If there's more money or better work somewhere else, that's the end of it."

"He just takes off without his things?"

Matthias's attention was drawn to the television. "What are things to a guy without a place to keep them? If he needs new clothes, he can buy them."

"The kid's gone, too."

Matthias looked back at Charlie. "Where?"

"I put him on a bus back to Texas. He said he had relatives in San Antonio."

"Well, good. I guess. It had to be done eventually."

Charlie walked over to the nightstand in between the beds and grabbed the whiskey bottle from the lower shelf. The real reason he'd knocked. "We're going to finish the barn tomorrow. Maybe. Shingles have to be nailed and glued because of the steep pitch. It's a big job for just three guys. And before you say anything, I'm not getting on the roof. You knew I didn't do heights and you hired me anyway."

"Charlie, it's late. Just get the job done."

"The square-foot rate should go up. You were paying Francisco and even the kid a few bucks. Now you're not. That money should get redistributed to the guys who have stuck by you."

"The kid primarily helped you on the ground, and I didn't cut your pay when your helper came on board. Now he's gone and you want a raise? Come on, Charlie. You guys have only worked one day so far with the diminished crew. Let's see if the jobs actually take longer or if there's been unnecessary slack in the schedule."

Of course, Matthias had no interest in raising their wages. That wasn't how you maximized profit off the labor of others. As long as their wages stayed flat, Matthias's costs went down. If they had to stay an extra week in the motel to finish all the jobs, that cost came out of their wages. He wouldn't feel the pinch until he needed a crew to work the jobs he sold in Arkansas. Even then, he could hire brand-new people if he had to. There were always guys who had their own trucks and gear looking for work.

"Are you still leaving tomorrow?" Charlie asked as he unplugged his fan from below the window.

"That's the plan. I'd like to make it to Kansas City and spend the night. Eat some barbecue."

"Make sure you leave our wages."

"Everyone will have their wages. You guys have never not been paid on time."

"Let's keep it that way."

"Do you want your toothbrush or anything?" Matthias asked.

"I got what I came for," Charlie said and held up the bottle. He pulled the door shut behind him, twisted off the cap, and had a healthy swig on the short walk back to where his room door was still standing open. The heat hit his belly just as he found College Boy standing between the beds, his back to the door.

"What's up?" Charlie asked. He dropped the fan on the unmade bed.

"I knew there was something sus about this operation," College Boy said, staring at something in his hands. "What are you guys up to?"

"I don't know what you're talking about."

College Boy threw a wallet on the bed where it flopped like a dead bird. In his hands he had two driver's licenses.

Charlie looked from one to the other and back again. He looked at College Boy, then went back to the door and turned the bolt.

"Sit down," he said.

CHAPTER TWENTY-NINE

TUESDAY

AIR QUALITY INDEX: ORANGE (UNHEALTHY FOR SENSITIVE GROUPS)

At the shift meeting the next morning, the supervisor started with some good news. There was rain forecast in Canada and a change in the wind direction. They might see clear skies within the next day or two.

"Next item on the agenda. Any more details on our headless friend?"

Packard thought he was hearing things. He looked up from the pad where he'd been making a list for the day. "Sorry. Was that directed at me?"

"No, Reynolds," the supervisor said.

Packard looked over his shoulder at Reynolds, who was standing in the back of the room. He looked like he hadn't slept at all.

"I looked up his tattoos in the database. I think we have a pretty good match. Need to go the hospital and take a closer look to be sure," Reynolds said.

Packard sat impatiently through the rest of the meeting. No new leads on Ashley Turner. Packard kept his call with the ME to himself. If word got out that Ashley and Gerald were killed by the same person, people might start throwing around the term *serial killer*. Likely the same people commenting on the department's Facebook page that the fires had been set intentionally by space lasers.

A deputy reported he was still collecting video from other businesses near the Silver Dollar. No one had a camera directly on the parking lot, unfortunately. Everything they had collected so far had been given to Suresh. Packard added a note to his to-do list to drop by Suresh's office.

After the meeting, Packard ran to catch up with Reynolds.

"Before you jump up my ass, you said not to call."

Packard looked at the department's most junior detective. He was coming into his own as a deputy. He had Packard's sense of duty and Thielen's filthy mouth. This must be how proud parents felt, Packard thought.

"Did Simpson say 'headless' during the meeting?" Packard asked.

"He did."

"There's a headless body in the hospital right now."

Reynolds nodded grimly. "Have you ever seen a headless body before?"

"I saw a really bad car accident where two-thirds of the head was missing. Just lower jaw and teeth left. It was pretty horrific."

"It's not any better when it's the whole head," Reynolds said.

When Ben Packard was a young boy, his grandfather took him and his siblings to a farm not far from their house on Lake Redwing. His grandfather told them the farmer's family was cleaning chickens, which had something to do with getting them ready to eat. Ben imagined them getting a sudsy bath and perfect drumsticks twisting off the same way a GI Joe's leg could be popped out of its socket.

At the farm, Ben watched a teenage girl come out of a fenced area with a nervous chicken clutched to her chest. She was petting it like a puppy. She brought it over to a stump and struggled for a moment to keep its head down. When Ben saw the short-handled ax go up, he still didn't know what was about to happen. It wasn't until the head flew off and his eyes followed it to the ground *littered with chicken heads* that the shock hit him. From there, everything he saw only added to the horror.

A barrel full of headless chickens still flapping and spraying blood. Boiling cauldrons where the headless chickens were soaked. A rubber-nubbed machine that spun and ripped off the wet feathers. A table where the bodies were sliced open and the guts pulled out in a loopy pile.

It was his first experience of numbing himself to the ugliness of life in order to do his job.

His job back then being to eat drumsticks.

Reynolds drove the two of them to the hospital and parked in the back. A nurse in purple scrubs met them by a secured door and led them down a hallway to another door that needed her badge to be unlocked. The nurse's name was Karen Roth, and back when Packard was new in town, she'd asked him on a date and given him her number. He said he'd call and he never did, a fact she liked to remind him of every chance she got. It pained him to remember these small acts of cowardice.

Karen opened a large metal door and they stepped inside a refrigerated room. She looked at her tablet and led them to a metal table on wheels with a light-blue plastic bag on it. Packard stood at the head of the table. As Karen reached to open the bag, she looked up at him and raised her eyebrows. "I always wanted to pull your zipper down, Deputy," she said in a breathy voice. "I never imagined it would be like this."

Packard felt the heat in his face even in that cold room. He made the mistake of looking at Reynolds standing at the other end of the table, fingers curled around the top of his vest, mouth open in disbelief.

"A missed opportunity on my part for sure," Packard said.

"Also, please note the ring," Karen said, wagging her fingers.

"Engaged?"

"Mm-hmm. But say the word," she said and ran a finger up the side of her body. "This could all still be yours."

"He's a lucky man."

Reynolds had been up all night and was tired. "Can we get on with it, please? This guy's head will grow back before Packard takes you up on that offer."

Karen gave Reynolds a look, then pulled the zipper down and around and folded back the corner of the bag.

There it was: a wide set of muscled shoulders and a stump of a neck with a ragged cut just above the Adam's apple. The exposed vertebra looked like it had taken several hacking blows. The gullet was wide open and obscene.

Packard had seen enough dead bodies not to be shocked by the coldness of flesh without a soul. He'd seen enough dismemberments to know we all come apart at the joints like meat. But the violence it took to remove a man's head was new to him.

"He's missing all ten fingers, too," Reynolds said.

"Can you identify him without fingerprints? Or dental records?" Karen asked.

"We can," Packard said. "There's a database that collects identifying marks, scars, and tattoos of people who've done time in prison. Reynolds already has a good idea who this is, based on his tattoos. The guys who did this weren't trying to slow us down. They were torturing him."

"Deputies are still searching the area for the head," Reynolds said. "No luck yet."

"Great," Packard said. "We have that turning up to look forward to."

Reynolds told them about the call that came in just before 2:00 a.m. A driver found the naked, headless body spread out in the middle of a quiet county road, like it had fallen off the back of a truck, which it probably had. The caller gave the exact location but said he'd been drinking and didn't plan to be there when the police arrived. The first deputy on the scene thought it might be a prank. It didn't take long to realize there was nothing funny about it.

Packard pulled the bag open a little further. The chest was missing a huge flap of skin. "They skinned him," Packard said.

Reynolds's complexion had paled. He looked green. "If I've got the correct guy, he had a huge tattoo of the number nineteen in Roman numerals across his chest. XIX."

"He was a member of the 19 Knights," Packard said. "It's a Mexican cartel gang. Ran into some of their guys during my days on the Minneapolis PD. Texas, Arizona, California are their main territory."

"What was he doing in Sandy Lake?" Karen asked.

"Good question. Hiding, maybe, if he had any idea that this might be his fate someday," Packard said. To Reynolds, "You said he was naked. So no clothes, ID, wallet, anything?"

Reynolds shook his head. He was looking at photos on his phone. He came around the table to get a closer look. "This is him. He's got the same Santa Muerte tattoo on his right arm," Reynolds said indicating the skeleton wearing a shroud and holding a Catholic rosary. "His name is Francisco Ayala. Born in Zacatecas, Mexico. Immigrated to the U.S. in 1995. Arrested in Bakersfield, CA in 2012 on multiple charges—attempted murder, arson, racketeering. In exchange for a reduced sentence, Ayala testified against an attorney who was helping incarcerated members of the 19 Knights run their organization from inside prison. The attorney was convicted of racketeering and money laundering. Ayala did seven years and was released in 2019."

"He'd definitely have a price on his head after that," Packard said.

"You can close the bag," Reynolds said to Karen, looking away from the table. "If he was trying to lay low, you can't get much farther from Mexican gang territory than northern Minnesota. Somehow, someone found out he was here."

"It gives me the chills to think the people who did this are just walking free," Karen said.

Packard didn't have the heart to tell her that even if they caught the guys who did this, there were hundreds more ready to take their place. Contract killers from across the border were a dime a dozen.

"Reynolds, you need to figure out where this guy has been living. How long he's been here. What he's been doing. Who knew him. There's probably a really gruesome location we've yet to uncover where they tortured this guy. I'm hoping it's an empty house and that we don't find out they kicked in the door where people were home and killed them, too, so they'd have a quiet place to work."

They said goodbye to Karen and found their way out of the hospital and back to their vehicle. Reynolds got behind the wheel. The clock on the dashboard said 8:00 a.m.

"You're going to run lead on this one," Packard said. "I've got too much on my plate already with Ashley Turner and Gerald Hall."

"I figured. It's why I didn't call last night," Reynolds said.

"I mean…you could have called. It's not every day a guy gets his head cut off around here. I wouldn't have been mad."

"Would Thielen have called?"

"Yes, even if I told her not to. And if I said, 'Take care of it. I'm going back to bed,' she would have shown up at my house, stuck four fingers in my mouth, and pulled me by the jaw into the car."

"You and Thielen have a weird relationship."

"I know."

Packard's phone rang. "And now I've got Shepard on my ass." He silenced the ring and pocketed the phone. "Let's go back to the office. I'll deal with him in person."

Back in the office, he stopped to talk to Suresh first. "Tell me that the AI has found our killer."

"I wish I had better news. I have a lot of data. Nothing conclusive."

"Tell me more."

"There are too many variables. We do not have any video close to the first victim's house. The first video source is three miles away and there are three different routes the killer could have taken from her house. I have done test driving from the center of town to her house, once going the speed limit, once going slower, once going a bit faster. I did the same test using different routes. Since we know what time the text message was deleted from her phone, I used those times to extrapolate when a vehicle might have left Sandy Lake prior to the killing or returned to Sandy Lake after the killing."

"We're assuming Sandy Lake was the killer's origin or destination."

"Exactly. He might have gone home and not crossed paths with any of our cameras. I can show you lots of vehicles but nothing that makes me think that one is the one."

Packard felt his phone buzz with a text message in his pocket. He saw a partial text message from Kyle on the screen.

> Sorry about the other night. I owe you
> an explanation. Let me know…

Packard put the phone away. He said, "We have another data point now, though, with the second killing at the Silver Dollar."

"Yes, on a weekend afternoon in the summer. I am still checking to see if any vehicles come up in both. There are a lot of gray Ford F-150s in this area, you know."

"I did know that."

"A lot of gray vehicles in general. Why do Minnesotans like gray so much? In India it is white."

"Gray hides the dirt and road salt better."

"Ah. Makes sense."

"Keep checking. I heard in the shift meeting this morning they're pulling additional video today. Let me know if anything comes up."

Packard stopped in the hall outside Suresh's office and read the rest of Kyle's message.

> Sorry about the other night. I owe you an explanation.
> Let me know when you have time to get together again.
> I'd like to see you and tell you what's been on my mind.

Packard tried to think of how to respond. He didn't know when he'd be available again. Didn't know that Kyle could say anything that would make him feel less foolish for taking his shot and having it smacked down.

Shepard burst out of the bathroom at that moment with a gun magazine under his arm. "There you are," he said. "Get in my office."

Packard followed and had a seat. Shepard tossed his magazine in a desk drawer and slammed it shut. "I don't know why but I want to blame you for all the shit that's going down lately," he said.

"For all the homicides, you mean?"

"Yes, all the homicides."

"That seems fair."

"I don't give a shit about fair. I give a shit about people emailing me and asking why it isn't safe to live here anymore and what I'm doing about it. You're the lead investigator. A job you begged to have back, if you remember."

"Reynolds and I are working around the clock."

"To what end? Why is there nobody in any of our holding cells right now?"

Packard sat up and held out his hands. "The way it works is, if you don't catch them red-handed, you have to get an arrest warrant. Judges are kind of particular about requiring a preponderance of evidence before they'll sign one."

"Don't be a smart-ass, Packard. How close are you to catching this guy?"

How close? Not close at all. He had two related killings—it would take a lot to convince him otherwise—and no obvious suspects. Ashley's husband couldn't have killed Gerald Hall. He was in Minneapolis with his kids. There was plenty about Pete Hawkins, the tree guy, that Packard didn't like, but what bothered him more was that no one describing the guy in the bar with Gerald that day mentioned a beard. Not Kristie, not Thielen. Both the tree guys were unshaven. Of course it was possible that a person not paying attention or viewing from a distance might fail to notice facial hair. It still bothered Packard.

And their friend without a head? That was a whole other mess.

"I think there's multiple guys. The two stabbings are completely unconnected to the body we found last night. That's cold-blooded cartel work if I've ever seen it. I'd bet money that whoever tortured that guy is long gone. They were told where to find him, they scooped him up, did terrible things to him, then went back to wherever they came from. You wouldn't stick around after something like that."

"I don't care if they're related or not. I need to be able to tell people we've made arrests. I need you to arrest someone. Got it?"

Shepard turned away from Packard and looked out the window. "I don't understand this world anymore. Everything is on fire. You can't breathe fresh air. Even the fish don't bite like they used to. Now we got headless bodies dumped in the road. No wonder people are up in arms."

Packard's phone buzzed with a call in his pocket. He ignored it.

"One thing that could help with the public is keeping a tighter lid on what we're dealing with," Packard said. "There's no reason that people need to know we found a guy with no head last night. If you need to, remind everyone under your command that confidentiality is part of our job."

"People are already discussing what happened last night on our Facebook page. Why do we have a fucking Facebook page is what I'd like to know."

"That was Stan Shaw's doing. If you take it away, people will claim we're hiding something. What we don't need is anyone talking to Ray Hanson."

Shepard stopped rocking in his chair.

Packard groaned. "You already talked to him, didn't you."

"He's a friend," Shepard whined, turning around. "We talk."

"He's also the publisher of the *Sandy Lake Gazette*. He's not your friend when he calls you looking for inside information about the department. He's going to have whatever you told him on his website before noon if you don't call him back. Then watch the Facebook page go crazy. Call him back. Tell him it was off the record. If he's your friend, he'll respect your wishes."

"I don't know if he's that good of a friend," Shepard admitted.

Packard's phone buzzed again. Thielen.

"Thielen's calling me."

"When is she coming back from her lady leave?"

"She's out for three more weeks." He couldn't wait to tell Thielen Shepard called it her *lady leave.*

His phone stopped vibrating, then started again. Thielen again. Packard was suddenly aware of a buzz growing outside of Shepard's office. Voices, footsteps. Something pinged on Shepard's computer.

Reynolds stuck his head in Shepard's office. "Packard, we gotta go right now. We've got an all-hands."

"What is it?"

"Someone attacked Thielen in her house."

CHAPTER THIRTY

Packard drove faster than he should have, full lights and sirens, all the way to Thielen's. Reynolds had already confirmed she and the baby were okay. It didn't slow Packard down at all.

Thielen and her husband lived in a gray ranch built on a hill with a two-car garage tucked underneath and a large side yard. An ambulance idled in the driveway. Three patrol cars were parked on the street. A deputy stood at the front door and asked them not to touch it.

It felt strange to have been to Thielen's house so many times as a friend and to see it now as the scene where the worst thing he could imagine had almost happened. Worse than the guy without his head. Worse than what happened to Ashley or Gerald. Because this time it was personal.

Thielen was sitting on the couch, with Emelia in her arms drinking a bottle. The baby's eyes were wide and very interested in all the activity around her.

"You all right?" Packard asked.

"I'm fine," Thielen said. Packard could feel her vibrating with rage. She wanted to be in uniform, badged and strapped and chasing after this guy.

"Where's Tim?"

"He's in Boston at a conference. He's trying to get on the next flight back."

"I want to look around for a minute," Packard said.

He followed the sound of voices through the house, down the hall to a room where the doorframe had splintered around the lock. Packard eased around a deputy and looked in Thielen's bedroom long enough to put a story together in his mind.

He came back to where Thielen and Reynolds were sitting in the living room.

"I think I know how it ended. Tell me the rest."

"The doorbell rang. I was carrying Emelia and she was fussy. He was standing on the front step with his back to the door. White male, 5'11", hundred ninety pounds. Late forties, I think. Maybe fifty. He was wearing a baseball hat and carrying a heavy clipboard. He turned around and smiled and asked if I'd had any roof damage from the storm. I immediately had a feeling that I'd seen him before. Like maybe he'd already come by here or we'd had some kind of interaction somewhere else. The storm door was shut. He stepped back and said something I couldn't quite hear because the baby was crying. I opened the door and instantly knew I'd made a bad choice."

Packard knew the feeling. Time stopped in that moment after you realized your mistake. You could see the future, the way all the possible outcomes spooled out in front of you. It felt like you had an eternity to regret your actions and only a microsecond to react.

"He stepped forward and I knew immediately this was the guy I'd seen standing over Gerald's car. The size and shape of his upper body came back to me. I also noticed he had a knife on his belt in a nylon holder."

"He killed Ashley Turner, too," Packard said. He was imagining this exact same scenario playing out at Ashley's house. The area had been crawling with guys like this since the storm. Guys who wanted to give you an estimate on repairing your roof, or replacing damaged siding, or taking down trees.

This guy had a clipboard. Ashley had been hit in the face hard with something that left an indentation across the bridge of her nose. It would have been incredibly shocking and painful and it would have given him time to pounce on her with the knife.

"I had the baby in my right arm and was pushing the door open with my left. He yanked the door and pulled me off-balance. Instead of fighting momentum, I went with it and shoved the door harder in his direction. He stumbled off the front step and it was enough time for me to turn, kick the front door shut, and take off running."

Thielen looked down at the baby in her arms and tickled her chin. "He's lucky I'm your mommy now and was holding you. Otherwise I would have stomped his ass on the front porch." The baby smiled around the bottle's nipple. "Yes, I would. I would have beat his ass for all the neighbors to see."

Packard had no doubt that Thielen would have fought this guy. She was barely five feet tall out of her boots, but inside that small package was a spring under tension always ready to explode. He'd lost count of how many Ironmans she'd completed. She was trained in grappling and defensive tactics. Was it enough to take down a guy with a knife once he'd lost the element of surprise? Probably. Maybe. Packard was glad it hadn't come to that.

"You ran for the bedroom," Packard said.

"Yeah, it's a solid door. It's got a lock on it. It's also where I keep my gun locked."

"He was right behind you?"

"Pretty fucking close. I literally threw Emelia on the bed like she was a gym bag and was punching the numbers on the safe when I heard him try the handle, then hit the door."

Packard had seen the safe in the drawer that was part of a built-in armoire in Thielen's bedroom.

"I yelled, 'I'm a deputy with the sheriff's department. I'm going to shoot you through this fucking door.' I don't know if he believed me or not. He hit the door pretty hard just as I was loading the clip." Thielen's right hand came out from under the baby in a fist. She hit the bottom of it with the palm of her other hand, then mimicked releasing the slide.

"I paused for a second to throw a blanket over the baby. I could hear something on the other side of the door. Might have been him running away. One more hit and he would have been through and I would have shot him. Nothing happened. I waited for a minute. No sound. Another minute. I wrapped Emelia in a blanket and put her in the bathtub and pulled the bathroom door shut. Then I opened the bedroom door, checked every room. Called it in."

Packard asked Reynolds to pull the laptop from their vehicle.

"You and the baby should stay at my house tonight," he said to Thielen. "Tim might be really late getting home. He might not get a flight."

He wasn't thinking she needed her husband to be safe. Tim was a decade older than Thielen, tall and lanky, and as useful in a fight as a cardboard tube. Thielen was running on adrenaline and anger. Eventually she was going to crash. Eventually she was going to realize how close she and her baby had come to being victims. Packard didn't want her to be alone when that happened.

"We're fine," Thielen insisted. "I'd love nothing more than for that guy to come back and try again. I wish the motherfucker would."

Reynolds returned with the laptop.

"I want to show you a couple of guys," Packard said. "Tell me if it was either one of them."

He showed her Pete Hawkins's most recent mug shot. He was the tree trimmer with the dark beard who'd answered the door when Packard stopped at the motel.

"Not him," Thielen said.

He showed her a driver's license photo of Dustin Weir, the guy on the bed who looked like he'd known more than he was letting on.

"Nope. Who are they?"

"Tree guys. They're staying at the motel. They were working a few houses down from Ashley Turner's house on the day she was killed. Both claimed they didn't see anything that day."

"It wasn't either of them."

"You still don't have a video doorbell."

"No. Neither do you."

"I'm reconsidering in light of recent events," Packard said.

"Same."

A deputy came through the front door. "Sorry to interrupt. I think we have an ID on the vehicle he was driving."

"How?"

"Next door has an outdoor camera."

Thielen put her head in her hand. "Of course, they do. Why is my brain not working? I knew that and should have thought of it immediately."

The deputy showed them some video he recorded on his phone of a woman showing him the video from her security system on a touch screen in her kitchen. "Here we go," the woman said. She had an old finger with chipped nail polish. A white pickup truck drove by on the screen. "He goes by in that direction. If you go all the way to the end of the road, it makes a sharp left and you can go back out to the main road. Looks like he turned around instead."

After a few seconds, the white truck went by again in the other direction.

"Go back for a second," Reynolds said. "There. Pause it. Looks like there's a dirt outline on the door there. Maybe where a magnetic sign would go."

"That he takes off when he goes out murdering," Thielen said. "Piece of shit."

The deputy played the video again. The edge of the camera's view caught the back end of the truck where it stopped by the curb behind a lilac bush. The taillights flared red. The truck sat there for almost five minutes before driving away.

"Get the video from her device," Packard said. "Send it to Suresh. Have him confirm the truck's make and model. See if he can zoom in and get a plate or a partial. Check if anyone else down the road has a camera with a different angle. I want a BOLO out immediately on that white truck. Make sure it mentions a possible door magnet or the outline of one."

The baby had fallen asleep in Thielen's arms. She went to put her down. There was a deputy trying to get prints off the front door. Another one in the bedroom taking photos. "Just don't open the nightstand. It's private," Packard heard Thielen say before she rejoined him and Reynolds in the living room.

"We have to assume this guy saw you drive down the alley the day he killed Gerald Hall. You were in your own car. He would have had no idea you were law enforcement," Packard said. "To him you were a potential witness to what he'd done. Someone who could identify him once word got out about Gerald being killed in the parking lot of the Silver Dollar."

"But how did this guy know who you were and how to find you?" Reynolds asked. "You were a random lady driving by."

"The birth announcement," Packard and Thielen said simultaneously.

"What are you talking about?" Reynolds asked.

"There was a photo of me and Tim and the baby in the *Sandy Lake Gazette* a week ago. Gave our names. Didn't say anything about me working for the sheriff's department. If he recognized me from that, he could have found my address in the phone book."

"Do we think he's really a roofing contractor or is that just a cover to get into people's houses?"

"A guy with a clipboard can claim to be anything and most people won't question it," Thielen said. She had to include herself in that category, and Packard could see it pissed her off.

His phone buzzed in his pocket. It was Darla Knoll, everyone's favorite working girl. "I need to get this," he said to Thielen and Reynolds. He stood up and walked out the front door and over to Thielen's side yard.

"Darla, it's Ben Packard."

"I know, sweetie. You looking for a good time?"

"You're going to get yourself in trouble talking to me like that."

"Come on, I'm kidding. I'm going through the car wash to get all the ash off my car. What do you need?"

"Same car I saw at the motel the other night?"

"You sure you saw my car and not someone else's?"

Packard heard the whir of motors rotating the wet brushes against Darla's car. "I know your plate, Darla." He didn't but she didn't need to know that. "You entertaining clients again?"

"Are you seriously asking me to incriminate myself?"

"I'm asking you a serious question. I thought you were going to nursing school."

"And where do you think tuition money comes from?"

"There's lots of other jobs, Darla."

She scoffed. "Deputy, did you call to give me guidance counseling or was there something else?"

Packard walked closer to the house where there was still a narrow band of shade. He could feel the hazy air in his lungs, which still hadn't fully healed since he was trapped in a house fire last winter. "I'm not trying to hassle or hustle you, Darla. I want to know who you saw at the motel when you were there."

Thielen had ruled out both of tree guys as her attacker. He didn't know for certain Darla had been at the motel with the tree guys. Could have been someone else staying there.

"Let me think of how to put this," Darla said. "I haven't met any gentlemen at the motel recently but my friend Carla may have."

"I got you."

"Carla may have gone out there to see if anyone wanted to buy her a drink and had a couple of guys take her downtown."

"What did these guys do?"

"Something with trees. Lumberjacks or some shit like that."

In the background, Packard heard the sound of the heavy wet sponge curtain slapping against her windshield and roof. "Did Carla have any trouble with these guys?"

"Carla spent some time in a truck with one of them. He grabbed the back of her head and got aggressive with her while she was trying to…do her job."

"Mm-hmm. How did she handle that?"

"She wrapped a perfectly manicured claw around his balls and suggested that if he wanted them to stay attached to his body, he should let go of the back of her head."

"Did this guy have a dark beard?"

"He might have."

"What else?"

"The three of them went back to the motel and partied a little bit."

"Drugs?"

"Mmm…no comment."

"Darla, you know that if you get busted with drugs on you, this whole friendly back-and-forth we got going on will be out the window. I won't be able to do a damn thing for you."

"I understand. So yeah—in a room with the two tree guys and another young guy who was staying there. That kid tried to put his hands around my throat and got a kick in the balls for it."

Packard thought about Ashley and Gerald being choked.

"Damn it, Darla. You need to be careful."

"I handled it. I was never not in control of the situation."

"I don't believe that. You were alone in a hotel room with three guys and one of them tried to choke you."

"Don't worry about me. I always have an exit strategy."

Packard stepped out of the shade and felt the wrath of the sun. Not light or warmth. Suffocating and radioactive down to his bones. He rubbed a spot on his forehead. "All right. No lectures. Anything else happen out there?"

"The place looked full. A bunch of guys were drinking around the firepit. I think a crew of roofers has all the other rooms."

"Roofers?" Packard perked up. "What makes you think that?" He tried to remember the other vehicles he saw in the motel lot when he was there talking to the tree guys. Something Construction. Was it a white pickup truck? Was the sign a magnet? He couldn't remember.

"I heard something about storm damage and shingles. I think I heard someone say 'rooferito.' Several of the guys spoke Spanish. I tried to get something going with one of them and his buddy got really upset. Called me a *puta*. Grabbed my arm and tried to smack me. Had to show him my knife."

"You had to fight off three guys in one night and you think you're in control?"

"I'm still talking to you, aren't I?"

"Back to the guy who tried to choke you. Was he on the roofing crew?"

"Yes."

"Did you get his name?"

"Come on now. Be serious," Darla said.

"What else did you notice about the roofers?"

"There was one guy I wanted to climb like a beanstalk. He came out of his room to break up the fight between me and the two Mexicans. Black hair, ripped. Covered in tattoos." She said something else but the sound of the car wash's dryers drowned her out.

"What did you say?" Packard asked.

"I said he was covered in tattoos," Darla shouted. "Two big Xes on his chest."

Packard felt a chill despite the heat of the sun. "Wait a minute. Wait a minute. Wait a minute," he said. His head was spinning. Things coming together in unexpected ways felt like a shot of caffeine right to the heart. "Darla, I need you to start over."

He was still buzzing ten minutes later after getting off the phone with Darla. Back in the house, he and Reynolds and Thielen stood in the kitchen.

"Reynolds, I was about to cut you loose to focus on your headless horseman, but now I think it's all connected," Packard said.

"How so?"

He told them about his call with Darla. About her entertaining the tree guys who were in the area the day Ashley was killed, how another guy tried to choke her the same night. About who else she saw there.

"Our friend who lost his head was staying at the motel. He's part of a roofing crew that's staying there."

"Roofers," Thielen said.

"Exactly. You said your attacker was white, right? Not Hispanic."

"He definitely didn't look traditionally Hispanic, if there is such a thing. And there was no accent that I detected."

"You said forties to fifty for the age."

"Yeah. I didn't get a good look at his face. He was wearing a hat pulled low again and everything happened so fast. I took off running before I got a good look at him."

"You've eliminated the two tree guys. Darla said there are some Mexican guys staying at the motel. She thought three at least. If we can eliminate them, then we can see who's left. She said the guy who tried to choke her was young, which doesn't align with what you've said, Thielen, so maybe that's one more we can eliminate."

"Does knowing our tattooed guy was staying at the motel change your mind about who might have killed him?" Reynolds asked.

"Good question. I don't think the same person killed him and killed Ashley and Gerald. The methods are so different. Ashley and Gerald were killed swiftly with knife stabs through the ribs into the heart. Whoever killed your guy tortured him. They skinned him alive."

"They did what?" Thielen asked.

"He had a big roman-numeral nineteen on his chest. Ex eye ex. It's gone," Packard said.

"For god's sake."

Reynolds looked like he still needed convincing. "Just to be clear. The tree guys are at the motel. Darla has been turning tricks at the motel and says there's roofers there. Our headless guy was at the motel. A guy asking about her roof attacked Thielen. But we don't know that a roofer killed Ashley or Gerald Hall. Or that our killer is at the motel. Or that a roofer at the motel is the killer."

"Reynolds is right," Thielen said. "If Ashley and Gerald's guy was a roofer, it doesn't mean he's part of the motel crew. There's probably storm chasers staying all over the area. In RVs, at campgrounds, rental cabins."

Packard put on his sunglasses. It was time to move. Enough talk. "I'll get other deputies to follow up on all those possibilities. Right now the motel is the best lead we've had since the beginning. I want to know everything about everyone who's staying there. If they're clean, we'll move on. Reynolds, let's get back to the office and make some calls. Thielen, I think these deputies are going to be here for a while. I'll stop by tonight."

"You don't have to."

"I'm going to."

Thielen walked them to the door. "Make sure you guys wrap all this up before my maternity leave ends."

"Shepard called it your 'lady leave' this morning," Packard said.

Thielen was not amused. "I'm gonna lady leave my foot in his ass."

CHAPTER THIRTY-ONE

Charlie spent the morning in town and arrived back at the barn just before noon. He hauled a sheet of plywood out of the back of the pickup to patch the hole Miguel fell through, laid it across a pair of sawhorses, and ripped it to size with a circular saw.

He yelled up to Luis that the wood was ready and went inside the barn where it was hot and airless. Above him, the sound of nail guns. *Bat bat bat, bat bat.* On a trembling stepladder, Charlie went from one side of the room to the other and hung replacement string lights that matched what had been hanging before Miguel crashed through them. With any luck, the next time people danced on the concrete floor, they'd have no idea a boy had fallen to his death in that very spot.

With every task checked off, Charlie felt a little lighter. His plan was coming together.

Matthias had seen them off early that morning. He'd traded one cheap cell phone for another with Charlie so Charlie could take any calls from locals about upcoming jobs. A stack of hundreds was for paying the crew. The same rate as before. Nothing extra since Francisco and Miguel had left.

College Boy was gone, too.

At the end of the day, the barn's owner was going to stop by to see the roof. Charlie had already called him and offered a discount for cash. The guy welcomed it.

Matthias would expect him to deposit the barn check as soon as possible. It was a big job and a big payday. Charlie figured he could stall for two days. When he'd asked Juan and Luis if they'd do two more small jobs after this one—ask for payment in cash again and split it—they looked nervous. Didn't say yes or no. The wheels were coming off this thing and they knew they had to jump soon.

Charlie sweetened the offer by telling them they could have the white pickup. Trailer, too, if they wanted it. Drive it all the way home to Juareverthehell, Mexico, and sell it. He was keeping the van. It would be easier to sleep in once he pulled out all the racks and sold off all of Matthias's equipment. With wheels and a pocketful of cash, he could go anywhere he wanted.

Charlie lit a cigarette and leaned against the side of his truck, watching the cousins work on top of the red barn. It might have a new roof and been modernized inside, but the classic shape and color of it harkened back to what it once was—shelter, storage, a family's fortune and future. A relic from back when your labor afforded you a place like this. He imagined it in winter, a man in suspenders and a wool hat moving inside, wind-whipped snow coming through the door. Horses' breath steaming from their nostrils.

He heard the sound of a vehicle approaching. Two vehicles. A black SUV that looked like an unmarked police car and behind it, Matthias in the other white pickup. Charlie felt every hair on his body stand up. Matthias was supposed to have been long gone.

A man got out of the SUV. "Goddamn, that looks nice," he said as Matthias joined him looking up at the barn. Charlie recognized the man's voice. It was the barn's owner, a guy named Lyle. The fancy SUV was probably for chauffeuring people out to the wedding site.

Lyle shaded his eyes and craned his neck to see his nearly complete roof. Luis was folding shingles over the center line and nailing them down, working backward toward Juan who was gluing and nailing down the last rows of shingles at the other end.

Matthias shot Charlie a look as he followed the owner around the barn, their voices disappearing. A few minutes later, they came around on the other side and went inside. Charlie stepped on his cigarette. The organs keeping him alive felt like they were pumping bile and acid.

The men came out of the barn. "I'm real pleased," Lyle said.

"My guys will be done later today. You agree, Charlie?"

Charlie had to break his feet loose from where he was frozen to the ground. He rubbed the back of his neck. "Sounds right to me."

"Why don't we settle up and you can be on your way," Matthias said.

Lyle pulled an envelope from his back pocket fat with bills. To Charlie, "You said 10 percent discount for cash, right?"

Charlie didn't say anything. He squinted like he had sweat in his eyes. Wiped his nose.

"If that's what Charlie said, then that's the deal," Matthias said. He looked at Charlie as Lyle counted hundred-dollar bills into his palm.

"Appreciate it," Lyle said. "Now if we can get this place sold, I'll never have to talk my ex-wife again. Charlie, you guys do good work. Thank you."

Charlie smiled weakly. Everything hurt.

"Good luck," Matthias said. He stood with his hands on his hips, smiled, and waved as Lyle drove off in his SUV. He turned to Charlie, still smiling. "Give me your keys," he said.

Charlie knew he was done. He lit another cigarette and watched as Matthias climbed three different ladders until he was standing on the roof with one foot on the ridgeline like he was about to plant a flag. He talked, Luis on one side of him, Juan on the other. Head going back and forth. They held out their hands and he put money in them and handed Luis Charlie's keys.

Back on the ground, Matthias stood on the opposite side of the truck from Charlie, his hands clasped over the truck bed.

"Ten percent discount for cash, huh."

Charlie didn't say anything. He flicked ash from the end of his cigarette.

"I was sixty miles down the road when I called Lyle and told him I had to leave town and he'd work with you on the final inspection. He said he'd already talked to you and that he appreciated the cash discount. I thought, 'Cash discount? Why would Charlie offer a discount and ask for cash unless he was planning to fuck me?'"

Charlie's brain scrambled for an excuse. Anything. It had been hard enough coming up with the plan. There was no fallback. All he could think was that he wanted a drink. He wanted all the drinks.

"So I turned around. Made it back to the motel. Got into your room and took back the payroll I gave you this morning. That 10 percent discount just came out of your wages. I paid Luis and Juan up there. Gave 'em a real nice bonus, too. We're walking away from the rest of the jobs. The upfront money those people paid covered the cost of materials, which are sitting in their driveway or scheduled to be delivered. They can find someone else to do the work. We could have kept going, Charlie. This was a good thing but you ruined it for everyone. Now we're done. The whole crew is done. The motel is paid for through the end of the week. After that you're on your own."

"I don't have any money," Charlie said.

Matthias laughed. "I know you don't. You don't have anything in this whole world that belongs to you, Charlie. You drank it all away. You drank until you convinced yourself you were the smartest guy in the room. I bet you thought you had it all figured out."

Behind Matthias, Charlie saw the bobbing turkeys from yesterday creep down the driveway. They stepped tentatively, like the ground was covered in ice. Twelve of them. A jury of his peers coming to tell him he was fucked.

"Got anything to say for yourself, Charlie? Anything that might convince me not to call the sheriff's department and let them know where to find you?"

Charlie opened his mouth. The words that came out surprised him. "What about your dad?"

"What about him?" Matthias asked.

"You said you were going to spend a few days with him. Now you're heading right to Kansas City for the BBQ and Arkansas after that. What happened to seeing your dad?"

Matthias looked incredulous. "Don't worry about my dad. My dad should be the last thing on your mind."

Charlie took his time shaking out another cigarette. "Your poor dad in the nursing home. Everything you do is for him." He scratched his lighter. "You know what I think? I think everything you've told us about yourself is bullshit. Including your name."

Matthias's mouth got small and tight.

"You left your wallet when we swapped rooms. College Boy and I saw your driver's license. You've been lying to us about who you are this whole time. You want to sic the cops on me? Go ahead. We'll see what they think about your fake identity."

"Going by another name isn't illegal, Charlie."

"Probably not. But you also have another man's ID in your wallet. He could be the dad you've been talking about but you guys don't have the same name. You've got his credit cards, too. I'm guessing these vehicles are his and not yours. It's all pretty fucking suspicious."

They stared at each other across the truck's bed. Matthias's face was red as he opened and closed his fists. "I'm getting real pissed off," he said.

Charlie shrugged and blew smoke at Matthias across the back of the truck. Up on the barn, the nail gun went *bat bat bat, bat bat.*

CHAPTER THIRTY-TWO

Back at the office, Packard called the owner of the Tabard Motel. Grant Tabard had a history of turning a blind eye to all kinds of behavior at his motel. He usually waited until things got really out of hand before he'd request help from the sheriff's department.

"I want all the personal information you have on the people currently renting rooms at the motel," Packard said.

"Yeah? I want a nineteen-year-old girlfriend who can put her ankles behind her head. I think we're both destined to be disappointed."

Tabard was in his early sixties, stringy hair, pockmarked skin. He had abused his body in every way imaginable. When he sat in a chair in the motel's office, it was hard to tell if it was him or a pile of filthy bedsheets.

"I'm not kidding, Grant. I'll get a warrant if I have to."

"You don't already have one? Then why are you calling me? I'm not giving you anything without a warrant. I got a reputation to protect."

"I could wreck your motel's reputation in five minutes by posting sheriff's department data to your Facebook page about all the incidents out there. The prostitution busts, the drug overdoses. You've had a suicide, a murder-suicide."

"Fuck you, Packard. Me asking for a warrant is me following the law. You're the law. Do your fucking job if you want what I got. Until then, piss off."

It was worth a shot. Getting the warrant wouldn't be a problem. Having a dead body with no head whose last known address was the motel would get him what he needed. It was more about the time it would take to write everything up and find a judge to sign it.

Packard remembered seeing Deputy Baker in the shift meeting that morning. He called the deputy's cell phone. "Do me a favor and grab the make, model, and plate of anything parked at the Tabard Motel right now."

"Can do. Anything in particular you're looking for?"

"I don't know yet."

"Been keeping an eye out for that white pickup on the BOLO," Baker said. "Any plate on that yet?"

"Not that I've heard."

"Okay. I'll get back to you with what I find at the motel."

Reynolds had all the info on the overnight homicide so Packard put him on writing the warrant for the motel's records while he looked through the dispatch logs to see if there had been any calls for service to the motel in the last couple of weeks. Surprisingly, things had been quiet.

Then he got a hit.

A 9:00 p.m. call to Bob's Bar for a drunk patron who needed medical assistance after falling on top of a table on the way to the bathroom. EMTs bandaged a cut on his arm. The man was too intoxicated to give any identifying information other than a first name—Charlie. They kept him overnight in a holding cell to sleep it off, no charges filed. Upon release, he declined to give his full name but said he was staying at the Tabard Motel.

The date of the incident was the same day Ashley Turner was killed.

Packard made a list of everyone he knew was at the motel or had been there recently.

Pete Hawkins and Dustin Weir—tree guys; at least one of them fond of prostitutes.

Francisco Ayala—former gang member, headless resident of the Sandy Lake morgue; roofer?

Charlie (last name unknown)—picked up for D&D, roofer?

He got a call back from Baker. "The lot at the motel is empty except for a rusty Toyota Sienna minivan. The back is open and full of cleaning supplies. There's a cart in front of one of the rooms so I think she works for the motel. Got the plate if you want it."

"I'll take it just in case. Swing by again before the end of your shift, if you can. People might be out working. I'll have someone on the next shift look, too."

Toward the end of the day, Reynolds emailed his warrant to Packard and they went over it together in his office. "I emailed the courthouse earlier and told them we'd likely have a warrant late today. Judge Westin said to email her and she'd take a look. We might still get it signed today."

"It's good. Run with it. Text me when you get a signature." He gave Reynolds all of Grant Tabard's personal info so he could deliver the warrant later that night or first thing in the morning. "Stay on his ass until you get what we want. Names, addresses, payment method, check-in dates of everyone at the motel."

Packard stayed for the second-shift meeting. There had been no sightings of the white pickup they had on the BOLO. No other usable video had been collected near Thielen's place. Packard put out his ask for another deputy to discreetly get the license plate info of any vehicles at the motel.

He went home and sat in his dark living room and stared at the hole in his ceiling. He thought about the three homicides in the last week. An attack on a law enforcement officer in her own home. Something was about to break in one of these cases. He could feel it coming like a change in the weather.

Packard looked at the time on his phone. He'd been on duty for fourteen hours. There was a sourness in his stomach from not eating.

He texted Thielen's husband, Tim, to find out where he was on his journey home.

Took off an hour ago from BOS. Probably not home before midnight.

I'll be there when you get home. Heading over now.

Thank you.

Dinner was a sandwich with sliced chicken breast and cheese and pesto. Tater tots cooked in an air fryer his mom had sent him. He hadn't had time to find any other uses for it.

On the drive to Thielen's, it had cooled enough that he could put the window down. The air smelled more like wood than smoke. He hadn't found any music that matched his mood lately besides Lucinda Williams. She streamed from his phone through the truck's stereo. A mournful slide on a steel guitar while she sang about that night in Minneapolis.

When he got to Thielen's, he parked in the driveway and ran up the steps to the front door where a moth was battering itself against the porch light.

Thielen answered the door. He knew right away that she'd been crying. She tried to smile at the sight of him, but her face cracked and she collapsed into his arms. Sobbing. Shaking. Exhausted.

Packard held her up. "I know. I know," he said with his chin, then his cheek on the top of her head. "You're going to be all right. Everything is going to be all right."

CHAPTER THIRTY-THREE

WEDNESDAY

AIR QUALITY INDEX: YELLOW (MODERATE)

The next morning Reynolds had everything Packard had requested from the motel's owner, which turned out to be less than he was hoping for.

The whole motel was booked—save for two rooms out of commission for renovations—but Tabard only had registration information for two people. One was Pete Hawkins, whose info Packard already had. The other was Matthias Fredricksen, who had rented five rooms for his crew. No names for any of them. No info on who was staying in what room, other than Tabard was pretty sure Matthias was in the room on the end.

The evening shift deputy didn't catch sight of anyone outside the motel but he got the plates on a Ford Super Duty pickup and a white cargo van. Both plates came back registered to Otto Fredricksen, who had an address in Rustler, Wisconsin, and whose recent record included operating a vehicle while intoxicated. Spotlighting deer. Hunting without a license. Possession of a deer carcass outside of the season. He had an outstanding bench warrant for contempt of court and a driver's license that had expired six months ago, according to records.

Packard tried to remember if it was Fredricksen Construction he'd seen on the side of a white pickup truck in the motel parking lot. It felt familiar. He googled it and found a single page website that looked like it hadn't been updated since the early 2000s. The business specialized in new and replacement roofing and was established in 1985 by Otto Fredricksen. There was a small picture of Otto already looking weathered and old. Another website had a long list of good reviews for Fredricksen Construction that praised the quality of its work and Otto's years of experience. He was seventy-one years old, according to records. Too old to be Thielen's attacker based on her description of him.

Packard ran Matthias Fredricksen through his databases. Nothing. No driver's license. No criminal record. No known previous addresses. That was curious in itself. Were Otto and Matthias the same person? With an outstanding warrant, maybe Otto was using Matthias as an alias.

Packard still didn't know anything about Charlie, the guy who spent the night in the drunk tank and said he was staying at the motel. So if the murderer wasn't Otto/Matthias and it wasn't either of the two tree guys, it had to be Charlie unless there was someone else on the crew they didn't know about yet. The headless gang member was part of this crew but he was already dead when Thielen was attacked. That ruled him out.

The other option was that Packard was barking up the entirely wrong tree.

He was curious about Otto's bench warrant so he called the sheriff's department in Otto's home county, asked for the civil division, and introduced himself to a deputy named Wendy Harker.

"What happened when you tried to serve Otto Fredricksen with his warrant?"

"Let me check the notes," she said. "Uh...yeah. When I went to the address on file, I talked to a young woman who said she was renting the place. She moved to the area for a teaching job at the elementary school. Said she only met Otto once when she signed the lease and hadn't seen him since. She gave us a cell phone number for him. My notes say I called it, no response. You got eyes on him?"

"I've got some vehicles registered to him at a motel in Sandy Lake and a room reservation under a Matthias Fredricksen. Might be your guy," Packard said.

"I can send you the warrant if you want to serve him. It's related to an arrest that was made by the Stevens Point Police Department, not us. They might have more details."

"Did you say Stevens Point?"

"Yeah. It's our county seat. About eight miles from where Otto lives in Rustler."

Packard heard bells ringing. Stevens Point had come up before. He asked the deputy to hold a minute while he flipped through his notes.

Stevens Point, Wisconsin, was where Ashley and her sister, Vanessa, had grown up. Ashley's sister still lived there.

"Did you get contact info for the renter?"

"I did." She gave him a name and number that he wrote down. She gave him the number she had for Otto from the renter. It was different than the number that had appeared in Ashley's phone records.

Packard thanked the deputy and tried calling the renter, whose name was Julia. His call went right to voicemail. It was summer and she was an elementary school teacher. Probably working at her second or third job.

He went back into the database and got the name of the officer who'd arrested Otto and left a message for him with the Stevens Point Police Department.

In his mind, he visualized tumblers in a giant lock slowly turning, pins starting to drop that would ultimately allow the key to be turned. He took out a yellow legal pad, flipped to a clean sheet, and started writing. Names and dates. Events. Times. Locations. He sketched the motel and put a name over who he knew to be in which room. His doubts faded as the ink filled the page. In the middle he wrote Stevens Point, WI with an arrow to Ashley on one side of the page and an arrow to Otto Fredricksen on the other.

Not a coincidence. He didn't believe in coincidences.

Half an hour later, he got a call from the police officer. "I remember that guy. I pulled him over for speeding and found a deer in the bed of his truck. Empty beer cans on the floorboard. Spotlight and a loaded rifle. Unfortunately for him, I used to work for the DNR and I got zero tolerance for people breaking our hunting laws. I wrote him up for everything I could think of. He refused a Breathalyzer so we arrested him and he tested over the legal limit. That got him an OWI on top of all the hunting offenses."

"Is this guy known to law enforcement?"

"Not necessarily to law enforcement. A lot of people know him or know his story. You'd have to have been around for a while to remember his son and daughter who were killed in an accident the night of homecoming."

"How long ago was that?"

"Probably twenty-five years ago. I can get you the exact date if you need it."

Packard looked at his notes. Twenty-five years ago Ashley would have been in high school. Close in age to Otto's kids. A sophomore or junior. Her sister was older and probably would have already graduated.

Something else stuck out to him. "Did Fredricksen have any aliases or nicknames?"

The officer was quiet for a minute. "In my report I have a note that he told me his name was 'Red,' which was different than the name on his license."

There it was. Packard could see 'red' was part of Fredricksen's last name. 'Red' was the name on the voicemail of the number that had been deleted from Ashley's phone.

He thanked the officer for his help and went to a paid newspaper archive site that had text searchable articles going back a hundred years. The late 1990s weren't that long ago, even if they felt like it. He entered the words *homecoming Stevens Point accident* and got the information he was looking for.

> Two Stevens Point high school students were killed on Thursday night in a one-car accident. Police have yet to release their identities but friends have identified them as Matthias and Marieke Fredricksen of Rustler, WI.
>
> The cause of the crash is still under investigation.

A couple of weeks later, there was another short article.

> Stevens Point Police revealed that alcohol and speeding were factors in a one-car accident that killed high school students Matthias and Marieke Fredricksen of Rustler, WI. Matthias, the driver of the car, had a blood alcohol over the legal limit.
>
> Measurements taken at the scene indicate the car was going in excess of eighty miles per hour when it left the road. Weather may have also been a factor as freezing temperatures were recorded for the area and contributed to poor road conditions.

Packard wrote down more names and dates on his Yellow Legal Pad of Truth. Ashley being the same age as Otto's kids was an interesting wrinkle and added another layer to their Stevens Point connection. He was also curious how Matthias had rented rooms at a motel in Sandy Lake when he had died in a car accident almost three decades ago.

He looked up the number for Ashley's sister, Vanessa. "Tell me, does the name Otto Fredricksen mean anything to you?"

"Well, yeah."

"In what way?"

"He lives in the area. He had two kids who were Ashley's age. Marieke and Matthias. Ashley was friends with Marieke and she dated Matthias for a while. He and his sister died in an accident. God, it was homecoming and just the worst kind of tragedy. Ashley was in a daze for months after. I used to—" She stopped and took a deep, shuddering breath.

"You used to what, Vanessa?"

"I used to get chills thinking about what might have happened if Ashley and Matthias were still dating at the time of the accident. She could have been in the car with him. I was so grateful she was safe." She paused. "Something got her anyway."

Vanessa wanted to know why he was asking about Otto but he couldn't tell her. He asked for her patience and said he'd be in touch again soon.

Lunchtime came and went. Packard was still making notes when he got a call from Julia, the elementary school teacher renting Otto's house. "I rented the place after I found an ad on craigslist. He gave me a tour and it was about the only thing I could afford on my own so I signed a lease on the spot."

"Can you describe him for me?"

"Middle-aged, broad shouldered. Blond hair."

"Hmmm," Packard said. That didn't describe the old man in Otto's mug-shot at all. For one, Otto was bald. For two, he looked every bit his seventy-one years. Not middle-aged unless Julia thought people lived to be 140 years old.

It did sound like Thielen's description of her attacker.

Why was someone impersonating Otto Fredricksen? And where was Otto?

"And you haven't seen your landlord since?"

"No. I call his cell if there's a problem. I thought the septic was backed up earlier in the spring 'cause the smell outside was so bad. I left him a message and a few days later a truck came out and pumped it. The smell didn't go away. I figured out later it was coming from the shed."

"What kind of smell?"

"Just…ugh. I can't even explain. The shed has a padlock on it. So does one of the bedrooms in the house. Otto told me it would violate the lease if I tried to enter the places he's got locked off so I've stayed away."

"What's in the shed?"

"No idea. The windows are covered in newspaper. Maybe an animal got inside and died."

"Maybe," Packard said.

There was something dead in that shed. Packard didn't think it was an animal.

He thanked Julia and called Deputy Harker again. “I might be way off base here, but I’m wondering if you or someone else can go out to Otto Fredricksen’s and take a look at the shed on the property. Get consent to search from the renter. She says there’s been a really bad smell coming from the area.”

“What are you thinking?”

“I think there’s a body in there. It might be Otto.”

He described the man who claimed to be Otto and rented the house to Julia and how her description of him didn’t match Otto’s mug shot at all. He told her about the man using a dead person’s identity to rent motel rooms in Sandy Lake.

“Let me get on the phone. I’ll send a deputy over and call you back.”

“Do me one more favor and show the renter Otto’s mug shot and ask her if that’s her landlord.”

“Got it. Anything else?”

“Tell your deputy to bring bolt cutters. And a mask. It’s gonna stink.”

CHAPTER THIRTY-FOUR

In Shepard's office, Packard sat on the edge of his chair with his legal pad on Shepard's desk in front of him and went through the notes and the conclusions he was coming to.

"Is that how you solve a case? By doodling?" Shepard asked.

Packard froze his face. "This is exactly how I solve a case, Sheriff," he said. "Everything is entered into the system, but pages and pages of reports can't help you visualize things. This helps me see everything at once. The act of writing and drawing helps me get things out of my head and make connections."

Shepard rolled his eyes. In his perfect world, cases were solved by confessions and everyone got to go home at 5:00 p.m., and if it didn't happen that way, well, you couldn't win them all. Sorry about your unsolved murder and all that.

"I want a deputy across the street from the motel in that place that used to sell carpet remnants," Packard said. "It's empty now. I'll find the building owner and get permission. I want to know how many people are staying at the motel and who's in what room. I'm trying to write an arrest warrant but I don't know who to arrest. I don't think Otto Fredricksen is at the motel. I think someone is impersonating him. Might be this Charlie guy. Might be someone else we haven't identified."

Shepard was starting to look bored. Packard wondered why he even bothered when Reynolds stuck his head in the door.

"I just talked to Tabard again. I showed him Otto's mug shot. He said that was not the guy who rented the rooms for all the roofers. I also talked to Tabard's daughter who does the room cleaning and she told me who was in each room. Kind of."

He looked over Packard's shoulder at the drawing of the motel he'd made. Each door had a number on it. Starting at one, Reynolds said, "Her words, mind you—white guys, empty, empty, white guy—room is now vacant, Mexicans, Mexicans, white guy, white guy. She also said tonight is the last night the Matthias Fredricksen rooms are paid for. Whoever's still there might be getting ready to leave town."

Packard swore. He was unsure what step to take next. He could go to the motel and question everyone about Francisco Ayala, the man who got his head cut off. What did they know about him? Where was he from? When did they last see him? Who was he with? In all honesty, he was less interested in who killed Francisco, and not just because it was Reynolds's case. He was almost as certain that Francisco's killer was not at the motel as he was that Ashley's and Gerald's was. Having law enforcement stomp around and make noise about Francisco would tip off the killer that they were watching them. Packard didn't want to ask questions. He wanted to make an arrest.

He looked at Shepard, who was staring at his computer screen. Packard could see Facebook in the reflection from a framed photo behind him. There was no help there.

If there was a dead body in the shed on Otto's property, he'd have enough for a warrant for his suspect, even though all he had was a description, no name. Everything depended on what he heard back from Wisconsin.

Behind him he heard Kelly's voice. "Packard, there's someone here who wants to talk to you."

"Who is it?"

"Blake Cooper. He's a high school kid. Plays football."

"What does he want?"

"He says he wants to make a confession."

Packard sent Reynolds up to reception to get the kid and bring him back to his office. He detoured down another hall to dispatch. "Get a deputy at the carpet place across the street from the motel. If it looks like anyone is packing up to leave, I want to know about it immediately."

Back to his office. The kid sitting across from his desk was tanned and had sun-bleached hair. He was wearing a button-down shirt and a tie like he had dressed for court.

"Mr. Cooper. What can I do for you?"

The kid looked nervous. Reynolds was standing against the wall with his hands on his duty belt. He might have been intimidating if he didn't have such a baby face.

"I need to tell you guys about something that happened."

"Is this something you did?" Packard asked.

"No. Well…kind of. Maybe."

"Okay. There's a lot of answers there. Start at the beginning."

Blake took a deep breath and let it out. "I have to tell you about the last stupid thing I did before I tell you about the most recent stupid thing. This spring I was at a party with a bunch of other kids. There was a bonfire at someone's house. Everyone was partying pretty hard, right? Anyway, this one gay kid was there and his car was parked there, and at some point these guys started messing with it. His car got effed up pretty bad by these dudes."

"I'm aware of the incident. So is Reynolds." Packard was trying to remember if he'd seen this kid in the video of Noah's car getting vandalized.

"I was there and I was drunk and showing off. I didn't touch the kid's car but I climbed in a tree and was egging those guys on. When I saw the video the next day, all I could hear was my voice…chanting…."

"What were you chanting?" Packard remembered but he didn't mind watching the kid squirm.

Blake couldn't look at him. "I was yelling…'Faggot, faggot.'" He looked up. "Sorry. I know you're a gay dude. I was being an asshole."

"You don't have to apologize to me for being an asshole. You should apologize to Noah and then try harder not to be an asshole up a tree."

"I know. I've been sick about it all summer. Mostly for selfish reasons. I got a scholarship for college and there's a clause that says if my behavior reflects poorly on the school, they could take it away. I've been waiting since that party for my name to come up or the police to come around. When I heard Noah's mom got killed…I was worried the car thing was going to come up again."

"Noah and his family have been through a lot. The guys who vandalized the car are the ones who have to worry about the fallout. Your role in whipping up the crowd, while not admirable, probably isn't a chargeable offense."

"I guess that's good news," Blake said. He didn't look relieved at all. "This whole thing has made me realize how awful it is to wait for a knock on the door and someone to ask you about a terrible thing you did. Then something worse happened and I didn't say anything and now I can't…I can't live with this."

"What did you see?"

"I've been working on a roofing crew the last month."

Packard and Reynolds both shifted positions so suddenly the kid looked frightened. "What?"

"What crew?"

"With some guys staying at the motel. I've been staying there with them."

Packard looked confused. "You go to high school here but you're staying at the motel?"

"Because we had a tree fall on our house during the storm," Blake said. "There's a contractor working on rebuilding the back half of our house. My parents went to South Dakota to stay with my grandparents. They said I could stay here if I found a job and a place to stay. I saw these guys working on a house and I drove up and asked if they'd hire me. The foreman guy said yes. Said I could stay at the motel with them but had to pay for my own room."

Packard got out his legal pad. "What room were you in?"

"Number 4."

"Who's the foreman?"

"Guy named Charlie."

"Who else is on the crew?"

"Me, Charlie. Two Mexican guys named Juan and Luis. Another Mexican guy named Francisco. And then there was this kid from El Salvador. His name was Miguel."

"Is that everyone?"

"There's another guy who does sales. Matthias."

"Last name Fredricksen?"

"Yeah. You know him?"

"Bigger guy? Blond hair. Broad chest."

"That's him."

Packard asked Blake which room everyone was staying in and wrote names above his drawing.

"How come you have all those notes already?"

"Tell me this," Packard said, ignoring the question. "Are you the guy who got kicked in the balls by the prostitute?"

For a kid who'd spent the summer outdoors, Blake was suddenly pale. "How do you know about that?"

"Darla's a friend of mine."

"I wasn't trying to hurt her. I swear to god. There were two other guys watching us go at it. One of them said, 'Choke that bitch. That's what whores like.' I put my hands on her throat and she kneed me so hard my balls still hurt."

Packard was unsympathetic. "You probably should see a doctor about that," he suggested.

Blake was near tears. "I just wanted a summer job. I didn't expect all this other shit to go down. Do I need to tell you about the kid dying or do you know about that, too?"

Packard looked up from this drawing and put his pen down. The simple act made Blake look terrified. Packard leaned back so as not to give the impression he was about to come over the top of the desk. "What happened to the kid?" he asked.

Blake took another deep breath and put his head in his hands. "There was an accident at a job site. The roof was rotten and the kid fell through and died. I helped Charlie bury him and agreed not to say anything."

"Where did this happen?"

"At that big red barn out on Highway 12 where people have weddings."

"Where's the kid buried?"

"Under a compost pile behind a shed on the property."

"Who else was there when it happened?"

"Me, Charlie, Juan, and Luis. I thought I was sick waiting for someone to ask me about the party." He started sobbing. "I'm sorry for what I did to Noah. I'm sorry I tried to choke your friend. I'm sorry about everything. I think I'm going to puke."

Packard handed the garbage can from under his desk to Reynolds, who passed it to the kid. "Blake, don't throw up in my office. You did the right thing by coming to us. I appreciate the honesty. I'm going to need you to hang out for a while—"

Packard's desk phone rang. He held up a finger and answered the phone. "This is Ben Packard."

"This is Sheriff Griffith in Stevens Point. You stirred up a real hornet's nest over here, Deputy."

"How so?"

"We found a body in that shed."

"Any idea who it is?"

"It's a mess from what I've been told. Male, bald, wearing a wedding ring.

He's wearing a pair of boots and we found a photo of the homeowner in the house wearing the same boots so I'm pretty sure it's Otto Fredricksen."

In his head, Packard heard engines revving. He saw lights flashing. It took him a minute to realize he was getting a call on another line.

"Hang on, Sheriff." He switched calls.

It was Patty in dispatch. "You said you wanted to know about activity at the motel."

"I did. Is someone leaving?"

"No, it's on fire. Trucks are en route."

CHAPTER THIRTY-FIVE

Charlie came back to the motel with two one-liter bottles of whiskey. He'd debated whether a 1.75 would be enough and decided it would not. He wasn't planning on being in any condition to drive anytime soon and he didn't want to run out.

The good news was that he was temporarily flush again. Turned out he and Matthias (or whoever the hell he was) had more in common than they thought. Neither one of them was keen on answering questions from police.

Charlie couldn't remember the last time he'd been as proud of himself as he was when he turned things on Matthias by telling him he'd seen his real ID. Right when he was about to lose everything, he saved himself from the fire. Again. So what if he couldn't remember the name or the address on the ID he had seen. Matthias didn't need to know that.

"You don't tell the cops about me, I don't tell 'em about you," Charlie said. "I want my wages for the week and the same bonus you gave Juan and Luis. It's only fair."

"As fair as you trying to steal the whole payment for this job from me?" Matthias asked.

Charlie shrugged. "I want you to replace the wages that whore stole, too."

"Fuck all the way off, Charlie."

"Okay, fine. All the rest though."

Matthias put a bunch of hundred-dollar bills in his hand.

"Are you still going to Arkansas?" Charlie asked.

"You don't need to know where I'm going. And I couldn't care less where you go after this. You're a real piece of shit, Charlie."

"What about your vehicles?"

"Juan and Luis will bring them to me when I figure out my next move."

As soon as Matthias left, Charlie considered himself officially unemployed. Luis reluctantly handed over the keys to the pickup after Charlie promised it would be at the motel later.

He stopped at the liquor store, drove around for a while with a bottle between his thighs, surprised how quickly half a liter of whiskey went down.

Back at the motel, he carried one bottle in the bag, one by the neck. Tried his key card a half dozen times on his room until he remembered he'd switched with Matthias. Key worked in the last room.

Inside, he took off his shoes, dropped his pants. Finished the first bottle standing in his underwear and fell into bed with the second one under his arm.

I should write about these adventures, he thought as he lit a cigarette. *Call it My Year on the Run. Or The Roofer Who Was Afraid of Heights. It'll be about late-stage capitalism at the end of the world. Living and drinking on the fringes of society. I'll dedicate it to Miguel. The boy with the iron feet. The boy who fell from the sky.* El ruferito.

He held the whiskey bottle to his chest, unscrewed the new lid, and felt liquid glug into the hollow of his neck. He laughed like he'd been tickled and righted the bottle. Noticed how its sides came in like a waist.

My dream girl does exist

She's made of glass

And likes to kiss

He put his mouth on the bottle, drank, put it on the nightstand.

He thought he had a cigarette going. Felt around himself. Nothing. Lit another one.

If I'm smart, this will be the last bottle, he thought as he smoked and stared at the ceiling. *I'm going to get serious and write. I've finally got a story to tell.*

He thought about going home and facing the charges against him. He probably wouldn't have to do that much time. Jail would be a good way to dry out and get some writing done. He remembered his idea about writing poems about all the jail cells he'd slept in. What if he wrote them while he was in jail? Brilliant. He also wanted to write about the orange sky, the sound a wall of laundromat dryers made, and the judgment of turkeys.

Everything seemed so easy and obvious when he was this drunk.

Charlie closed his eyes. His body twitched with tiny spasms as his consciousness gave up control of his limbs. His hand tilted, tilted until the burning end of his cigarette touched the polyester comforter and burned through to the cotton batting inside. The cigarette he'd dropped earlier had already started the frayed edge of the bedsheet burning where it touched the floor. The dirty dry webbing holding the thin carpet together smoked and caught fire like hay. More smoke came from the bed. Orange and green flames.

By the time Charlie came to with a gasping cough, the bedspread had melted to his skin. He hacked and reached for the bottle, knocked it off the table. When he tried to stand, the bedding stuck to him and came with him as his knees gave out and he fell face-first onto the bed Matthias had slept in. He felt heat on his back. Wetness as his skin cracked and split. Through one open eye, he watched flames eat at the blanket beneath him.

Somewhere an alarm was going off and someone was screaming.

It was him.

He was the one screaming.

CHAPTER THIRTY-SIX

By the time Packard arrived at the motel, black smoke was pouring from the end unit. Two firefighters moved toward the broken window with a hose putting out a wide bell of water. The smoke slowly turned from black to white as the fire was doused and gave off steam.

Two men who tried to leave the hotel in a van were stopped by deputies and put in the back of a patrol car. Packard knew they were Juan and Luis, according to Blake. They would figure out who was who later.

"Get our Spanish translator on the phone and tell her we could use her help this evening," Packard said to a deputy. "Try to help these guys relax and understand we just want to ask some questions."

Grant Tabard showed up in a rusted Dodge minivan and raised hell, screaming at anyone who was standing around and watching his motel burn.

Packard ignored him and went to the far end of the parking lot where the tree guys had moved their trucks and were sitting and smoking on the end of their trailer.

"I need you guys to come in and answer some questions about Matthias Fredricksen."

“We don’t really know the guy,” Pete said, picking something off his tongue.

“I need you to come in anyway. Tonight. Head to the sheriff’s office when you see us leave. If I have to arrest you for operating a tree business without the proper Minnesota licensing and permits, I will. If I have to arrest you for solicitation, I will. I don’t want to but I will. Understand me?”

They did.

It was another hour before the firefighters confirmed the fire was out and the structure wasn’t in danger of collapsing. Packard put on blue plastic gloves and ducked through the doorway. Reynolds was right behind him.

The ceiling was low and blackened and dripping, the floor soft with water. A dead man was half-folded onto the bed closest to the door. Charred. Covered in blistered, black skin. Chunks of synthetic fibers melted to him. Underneath the smell of burning chemicals was another odor, too close to the smell of BBQ for Packard’s liking.

“This is Matthias’s room, according to Blake,” Packard said to Reynolds.

“Is this him?”

“Hell if I know.” There was no hair left on the head. The burned skin on the face was pulled tight, showing a terrible amount of teeth.

A bottle of whiskey that had cracked from the heat was on the floor between the body and the nightstand between the beds. Packard pulled open the drawer and found a soggy notebook and two inexpensive phones, one with a shattered screen, sitting in a little bit of water. The phones lit up when he touched buttons on each. Packard used his phone to call the number that had been deleted from Ashley’s phone the day she was killed. The phone with the unbroken screen vibrated and showed Packard’s incoming call on it. He let it ring until he heard the voicemail from Red telling him to leave a message.

The real Matthias Fredricksen had died in a car crash as a teenager. His father, Otto Fredricksen, who went by the nickname Red, was dead in a shed in Wisconsin. Was this blackened corpse the guy pretending to be Matthias? It was his room. It was his phone that had the voicemail for "Red" on it.

The only other person on the crew, according to Blake, was Charlie, who wasn't accounted for. No last name. He wasn't next door in his room. SLFD had made sure the building was clear while they were fighting the fire.

"Look at this," Reynolds said.

In one hand he held a dripping-wet pair of charred pants by a belt loop. In his other hand was a leather wallet.

Packard looked at the body again. No pants on him.

Packard took the wallet. Pulled out a driver's license.

"This isn't Matthias," Packard said. "This is Charles Richardson. The foreman."

"There's a wad of cash in the pocket too," Reynolds said.

Packard had been certain on the way over that he was about to put his hands on the guy who killed Ashley Turner and Gerald Hall, the guy who also tried to kill Thielen. What he got was everyone but. Even worse, they didn't know the guy's real name. They didn't have a photo of him. No permanent address. No known associates beyond this crew.

The killer was in the wind and they had no way of tracking him down.

CHAPTER THIRTY-SEVEN

Packard questioned people back at the sheriff's department until eleven that night. Juan and Luis from Matthias's crew. Pete and Dustin, the tree guys. Blake, the college kid, surprised Packard by hanging around as asked when he and Reynolds ran out after getting the call about the fire.

A deputy babysat the group in the department's press conference room. Packard ordered in pizza and bottled water to show goodwill and keep everyone complacent. No one was under arrest. He needed them to be willing to stay put for as long as it took to get the answers he needed.

It took Reynolds less than two minutes to find Charles Richardson's outstanding warrant. He came into Packard's office carrying a laptop while they were waiting for the Spanish language translator to arrive.

"He was working as a bartender in a beachside dive near Wilmington, North Carolina. There's hours of security footage from inside the bar showing him matching a customer drink for drink while he was working. That customer got into her vehicle and crashed into a young nurse on her way home from her shift at the hospital. Killed her. The drunk customer had a blood alcohol of .19. She survived. Charles is being charged as an accessory. Manslaughter."

"That's harsh for a dram charge." Dram shop laws allowed businesses that sold alcohol unlawfully to someone to be held liable in the event of that person causing an accident.

"He's got a list of alcohol-related charges going back almost two decades. Guy like that shouldn't have been working as a bartender. The nurse's family will end up owning that bar for hiring a guy like that."

From separate interviews with Juan and Luis, Packard learned that Matthias recruited his crew using ads on craigslist. Juan was in Florida at the time and said Matthias offered fifty cents a square foot more than the crew he was currently working on. Matthias wanted to chase storms and needed people who were willing to travel. At the time, Juan was living with eight other roofers in a squalid apartment. Getting far away from there sounded pretty great. His cousin, Luis, was already on his way to Florida from Mexico. Matthias agreed to hire them both.

The crew came together over about a week. Francisco Ayala, the beheaded gang member, was part of the original crew that also included a guy named Alberto and another guy named Eduardo who stayed behind when the crew made its first move to Texas to clean up after a hurricane that made landfall between Houston and Corpus Christi.

Charlie saw Matthias's craigslist ad when the crew reached North Carolina. From there they went to a midsized town in Oklahoma hit by a tornado, then the site of a hailstorm/derecho that wiped out the July corn crop in central Iowa, which was where they picked up Miguel.

They didn't know much about Matthias after eight months of working together. Matthias told them he had a father in a nursing home. They didn't know where. He was kind to them and didn't try to steal their wages. They were happy working for him.

When Packard asked about Miguel, their answers got shorter. He watched both men shrink in front of him. It was Charlie's idea not to call the police, Juan said, and they weren't in a position to argue. Luis broke down in tears at the end, mumbling something over and over into his chest that Packard couldn't understand.

"He wants to go home to be with his family. He has a son he hasn't met," the translator said.

Pete and Dustin checked into the Tabard Motel about a week before Matthias and about two weeks before his crew showed up. They didn't know anything about Matthias other than what was on his business card, a copy of which Pete gave to Packard.

FREDRICKSEN CONSTRUCTION
MATTHIAS FREDRICKSEN
WWW.FREDRICKSENCONSTRUCTION.COM
RUSTLER, WI

If Matthias got a job where there was a bunch of tree damage, he recommended Pete to the homeowners. Pete did the same if he was up in a tree and saw the house needed a new roof.

Packard hadn't found a card for Matthias in Ashley's house but he hadn't looked hard either. Dustin said sometimes they didn't hand out cards; they just gave Matthias the address and told him to check it out.

Neither Pete nor Dustin wanted to talk about Darla. When Packard asked if she offered them drugs, both said no comment. Pete said they ate at the Silver Dollar once when they first got to town but never went back. Food was too expensive.

A lot of this information was good to know but it wasn't helping Packard figure out who was impersonating Matthias Fredricksen or figure out where he might have gone.

Packard asked Juan and Luis what was the last thing Matthias said to them.

"He thanked us for our hard work," Juan said. "He paid us our money and gave us extra. He asked us to keep the vehicles for him and said he would pay us more to deliver them when he got to the next place."

"What were you supposed to do until then?"

Juan shrugged.

"Did he say where he was going?"

"He said he wasn't sure. Maybe Arkansas because of a storm there. Maybe somewhere else."

"Where will you go from here?"

Another shrug.

They talked to Blake again last. He had taken off his tie and jacket and looked like a tired high school kid. They went over the details of his time with the crew one more time. Blake didn't know Charlie had died in the fire at the motel. He didn't know about the murders. Packard could see the confusion on his face when all the questions kept coming back to Matthias and weren't about Miguel.

Packard was running out of things to ask when he realized something. "You didn't work today, did you?"

Blake shook his head. "I quit this morning. I couldn't go back to the barn. I also wanted nothing to do with what else Charlie was planning."

"What was that?"

Blake told them about the original plan for Matthias to leave town and head for Arkansas and for the rest of the crew to meet him there in two weeks. Charlie didn't want to go to Arkansas. He wanted to steal the payment for the barn job, split it with the crew, and take off in Matthias's van.

"What made Charlie turn on Matthias?"

Blake ran a hand over his tired face. "I think he was turning on Matthias before Matthias turned on him. His drinking was out of control. They were fighting about the size of the crew and wages. If Charlie made it to Arkansas, Matthias probably would have fired him right after."

"And you said Matthias didn't know about what happened to Miguel."

"He didn't. Charlie lied to him and said he put the kid on a bus."

"What happened when you told Matthias you were quitting?"

"I told Charlie first. I went to his room. The door was open and he wasn't there. I wanted a drink after what we'd done and thought he'd have a bottle by the bed. There was no bottle but I saw two wallets sitting there. I knew Charlie and Matthias had switched rooms and I thought maybe I would take Matthias his wallet and tell him I was done. I checked the license to make sure it was his. It was his photo but it didn't say Matthias on it."

Packard's ears perked up. He felt like Frank anytime he heard the fridge open.

"Do you remember the name?"

"No," Blake said.

Packard dropped his head. Of course. Nothing about this case could be easy. The progress felt circular, going nowhere.

"Did you tell Charlie about the ID?"

"He came back to the room while I was looking at it. I asked him what kind of scam he and Matthias were running. He said he didn't know anything about who Matthias really was. That was the last straw for me. I had a bad feeling all of sudden, thinking about this guy pretending to be someone he's not. What else did he lie to us about? The next morning I told Matthias I had to go. Charlie told me not to say anything about the ID or his big rip-off plan so I didn't. Matthias paid me my wages, didn't ask any questions. He seemed like he had other things on his mind."

He was planning to drive by Thielen's house and kill her on his way out of town, Packard thought.

"You don't remember the name? Maybe just a first name? Or what state the license was from?"

"I don't remember any of that," Blake said, reaching into his pocket for his phone. "But when I looked at his ID, I thought about him coming after me after Charlie stole all the barn money. I thought I might need something to protect myself or at least be able to identify this guy if everything blew back on me as the only one who lives around here." He thumbed the screen and turned the phone in Packard's direction. "So I took a photo of the ID."

Packard laughed as he reached for Blake's phone and stared at a picture of the man he'd been chasing. "Nice work, Blake. Next time, lead with the photo."

CHAPTER THIRTY-EIGHT

THURSDAY

AIR QUALITY INDEX: YELLOW (MODERATE)

"His name is Travis Kimball," Packard said the next morning.

He handed Shepard and Reynolds a printout of Kimball's driver's license photo and data. Blond hair, blue eyes, 5'11", 49 years old, 245 pounds. Already that morning, Packard had shown the photo to Kristie, the bartender at the Silver Dollar, who felt fairly certain he was the man at the bar with Gerald Hall. The renter of Otto Fredricksen's house ID'd him as her landlord. Packard hadn't had a chance yet to confirm with Thielen, but he was certain on her behalf this was the man who'd attacked her at home.

"Kimball had asked Charlie to trade rooms with him when his air conditioner went out. Kimball got locked out of his old room after they traded keys and left his wallet on the nightstand. Charlie and Blake went through it. Kimball was carrying his own ID, which identified him as someone other than Matthias Fredricksen, as well as Otto Fredricksen's ID."

"The sheriff's department in Stevens Point ID'd him as a person of interest almost the same time we did. They found a filing cabinet of old job orders and receipts for Fredricksen Construction in the locked room in Otto's house that the renter was told to stay out of. A lot of them have Travis's name on them."

"So, who is this guy?" Shepard asked.

"We're still putting the pieces together. He's got former addresses in Denver and Minneapolis. His driver's license has an apartment address in Stevens Point. We're still gathering bank info and employment history. It looks like at some point he worked for Otto Fredricksen. Maybe he was the young blood the old man needed to keep his business running after doing roofs for forty years. The invoices they found in that locked room covered several years."

"What went wrong between them?" Reynolds asked.

"I don't know that we'll know unless we get Kimball in custody and he decides to talk. One thing that's interesting is that I shared his name with my contact at the Stevens Point Police Department. Kimball came back in a search of their RAND data. Turns out Kimball was in the truck with Otto Fredricksen the night he was arrested for shining and poaching deer. Kimball didn't get charged with anything. Maybe they had a falling-out after that and Otto wanted to push him out of the business."

"So, Kimball kills Otto and decides what? Take the show on the road?" Reynolds asked.

"The prosecuting attorney can put together the timeline of all this. I can't imagine I'd stay around long after I murdered someone. If Kimball was deeply involved in Otto's business, he likely had access to all of Otto's personal information, his bank accounts. Fredricksen Construction has an online presence, it's on the business cards. Otto's photo is on the website. Kimball couldn't refer customers to that and pretend to be Otto. Easier to claim to be his son. He knew Otto well enough to know he had a son named Matthias he could impersonate. But he couldn't stay in Stevens Point and pretend to be Matthias, and no one in Stevens Point could know he was using Matthias's identity, which is why he had to pretend to be Otto to his out-of-state renter. It would have been risky for her to tell anyone local that she rented Otto's house from his son. The locals know that Otto's kids died in a car accident years ago.

"We learned from interviewing the motel residents that Kimball recruited most of his crew in Florida. From there they went to Texas, then cleaned up after an Eastern Seaboard hurricane hit North Carolina, where they picked up Charlie. Then Oklahoma, then Iowa, then Minnesota. Chasing bad weather to rural areas without a lot of competition or regulators."

"Do you think this Kimball is a serial killer? Did he kill people in all those places?" Shepard asked.

"It's a good question. He's killed several people, but I don't think he does it for fun. I feel like he's a reactionary killer. He killed Otto over some kind of grievance and stole his business. He killed Ashley Turner because he had the very bad luck of meeting a woman who knew the actual Matthias Fredricksen and knew he died in a car accident when they were in high school. I imagine she saw his business card, pressed him on his identity, and he stabbed her to protect himself."

"And Gerald Hall?" Reynolds asked.

"Gerald Hall loved to rant about illegal immigrants and aliens and lizard people. He probably got into it with Kimball about who his workers were and where they were from. Maybe he threatened to call ICE or the sheriff's department. Kimball felt threatened again and took care of the problem. Thielen happened to drive by right as he was standing over Gerald's car and he recognized her from the birth announcement in the paper. On his way out of town, he tried to clean up one last loose end. Luckily, Thielen doesn't go down easy."

"How are you going to prove any of this?" Shepard asked.

"We've got the killer's blood at Ashley's house. I've already collected DNA samples from everyone else at the motel. We've got the phone the killer used to contact Ashley. We can talk to other people contacted by that number and ask them to identify the person they met with. If he still has the knife, we can match the broken tip to the piece of the blade left in Gerald Hall."

"You have to catch him first," Shepard said, sitting up and pulling on the front of his shirt. He looked pleased with himself for his astute observation.

"Yes, that is the important final step. Luckily, we have his name, his ID, we're getting all of Otto's bank accounts and credit cards, we're getting all of Kimball's. If he tries to charge something or use an ATM or open a new account, we'll know exactly where he is. He can't stay off the grid forever."

CHAPTER THIRTY-NINE

Packard stopped in Suresh's office. "What have you got for me?"

"I have downloaded the call log and the data from this phone. You will have all the numbers called from this phone in a spreadsheet. I have highlighted that Ashley Turner's number is on the list. This phone was also getting forwarded calls from another number in Wisconsin."

"I bet it was Otto's phone. That's why his voicemail said 'Red' on it. In case anyone called looking for Otto."

Suresh nodded. "In the photo app there are many pictures of roofs and shingles. I have flagged the photos that are time-stamped as the same day as the killing."

"Thank you, Suresh. We're still waiting for the information from the provider but now we have the phone in evidence. That's actually better."

"Yes. This other phone with the broken screen has a number associated with it but no service. He was only using it on the Wi-Fi network at the hotel. WhatsApp, TikTok, Snapchat. I am learning a lot about something I did not know."

"What is that?"

"On TikTok there is a whole subculture of young people who work on roofing crews. They use the hashtag #ruferitos on their videos."

He pointed to a screen where he'd searched for the hashtag and the resulting videos had come up. Videos of kids on roofs smiling into a camera high above the ground, roofers racing to see who could rip up shingles the fastest, people hauling rolls of underlayment up ladders. Nail guns and utility knives. The language and music all in Spanish.

"The boy who owned this phone was recording and posting his own videos." Suresh switched to another tab that showed the videos posted by elruferito_miguel. The videos had no captions other than rows of El Salvadoran and American flags. His videos were short. They showed the crew cleaning a roof surface with leaf blowers, stacks of shingles laid over the ridge line of a roof, Francisco gathering up a pile of old shingles and tossing them down into a trailer on the ground. A video of Juan with his heels off the edge of a roof while he nailed down the first row of shingles. Short videos of his room and the guys sitting at a picnic table outside the motel. Packard caught his first glimpse of Travis Kimball. He was wearing a blue baseball cap with no logo. He bent down to grab a beer out of a cooler and popped the top. He didn't seem to be aware he was being recorded. No one did.

"He also made a video of each crew member," Suresh said. They watched thirty-second videos with quick cuts of Juan and Luis doing just about every task imaginable on a roof job. Short clips of Juan and Luis clapping along to a pop song. There was a video of Charlie smoking a cigarette with his back against a truck tire, grilling chicken, sitting at a picnic table with a beer, and a last shot of him from behind—trying to walk across the motel parking lot, leaning farther and farther to the left with every step until he overcorrects and leans backward. Lots of laughing emojis and comments on that one: *brio, borracho, el beodo.*

"There is no specific video of Travis Kimball. This one of Francisco is probably what attracted his trouble."

Francisco on a roof, Francisco reading a Bible at the foot of his bed, Francisco shaving in the wide motel mirror outside the bathroom. His broad tattooed back, the large XIX on his chest visible in the reflection.

"This is his most viewed video. You can see how many times it was viewed and shared. There are many comments and hashtags related to a Mexican gang called the 19 Knights. People warning Miguel to be careful."

"Francisco probably had no idea any of this was online."

"Agreed. In the comments, someone asked '*De donde*?' Miguel replied with 'Sandy Lake Minnesota.'"

"Five days later, Francisco gets into a van and comes out missing his head," Packard said.

"Right."

"Okay, that solves the mystery of how the cartel hit men knew where to find Francisco," Packard said. "I'm sure Miguel had no idea the potential trouble he was causing. To him, he's just making videos about his life."

"He has several conversations going on WhatsApp. I believe some of them are family. They are sending messages and asking why he is not responding."

"I'll work on family notifications and if there's any international process for returning the boy's body or ashes to them. This is a first for me. Get me any clear screen grabs of Travis Kimball from these videos. See if you can see the vehicles and their plates in any of these videos. Two of them are sitting in the motel parking lot. Let's see if we can get a visual confirmation on the third. It's gotta be what Travis is driving now."

"I will look. I will also compare to all the video collected on the days of the two killings. The AI has been useful up to a point. I can go through all the data quicker now that I am looking for something specific."

Back in his office, Packard and Reynolds debated next steps.

"Unless we get a hit on the BOLO or he uses his cards somewhere, we have no idea where Travis Kimball is."

"Do you think he went to Arkansas?" Reynolds asked. "We could get one of those heat maps that shows where the winds and hail were the strongest and use that to narrow down where he might be."

"I don't think he went to Arkansas. That might have been the plan before he tried to kill Thielen and was unsuccessful. He left town without his crew, his vehicles, his equipment. If he went to Arkansas, he'd have nothing he needed to set up shop again unless he planned to start from scratch."

"Is it possible he hasn't left the area. He's in hiding?"

"Hiding from who or what? As far as we know, he doesn't know we're on to him. He doesn't know we know his real name. But he's got to be thinking it's time to dump the Matthias identity. Things got out of hand here. There're too many dead bodies. We know Charlie and Blake found out his real name. Blake said he didn't say anything to Matthias about it. We don't know if Charlie confronted Matthias before he died in the fire. If he didn't, Travis could be relatively comfortable with the idea of going back to who he used to be."

"Does he do that in a brand-new location or someplace familiar?" Reynolds asked.

Packard flipped through his notes. "He's got former addresses in Minneapolis and Denver. What do you like?"

"Denver's a lot longer drive."

"I was thinking the same thing. Maybe we can draw him out based on what we've learned about him so far."

"You got an idea?"

"I do."

CHAPTER FORTY

craigslist

MINNEAPOLIS > HENNEPIN CO > FOR SALE BY OWNER > HEAVY EQUIPMENT

Roofing equipment and vehicles ($30,000 OBO)

Time to get out of the business. For sale is

- 2010 Ford E Series cargo van
- 2013 Ford F250 Super Duty pickup truck

Miscellaneous roofing equipment including ladders, generator, air compressor, shovels, forks, saws, nail guns, staplers. Everything but the crew. See attached photos.

Selling as a lot only. I have the vehicle titles. You have cash. Call or text Charlie at 641-448-0135

CHAPTER FORTY-ONE

SATURDAY

AIR QUALITY INDEX: GREEN (NORMAL)

It took two days to confirm their hunch that Travis Kimball was in the Twin Cities. Otto Fredricksen's social security check was deposited on a Wednesday. On Thursday, the entire amount was withdrawn from an ATM in south Minneapolis. Packard called Detective Easton and with a little help from the Minneapolis PD was able to secure video from the ATM that showed Travis Kimball making the withdraw. Video from a nearby security camera showed him getting out of and into a white pickup truck.

Packard called Easton and told him how they were trying to smoke out Kimball with a craigslist ad showing all his shit for sale.

"Does this mean you might be headed this way?" Easton asked.

"If Kimball bites, I think the face-to-face will be down there. Can I stay with you? I could use a jumping-off place."

"I'll give you something to jump on."

"I said 'jump off.'"

"And I said what I said."

Kimball still wasn't using his own cards. They didn't know where he was staying or where he was shopping. Packard interviewed the owner of the wedding barn and found out that he'd paid Kimball for the work in cash the same day as the motel fire. If Kimball got the money, then Charlie's plan to steal it and the van had fallen apart. The cash they found in Charlie's pocket wasn't anywhere near what the barn owner claimed to have paid Kimball.

Packard and Reynolds photographed the two vehicles Kimball left behind and all the equipment in the parking lot at the Tabard Motel. They made sure the motel was clearly visible in the background except for the room on the end that burned. Suresh made them a new SIM card with the number of the cell phone Kimball had been using.

Kimball was a heavy craigslist user, according to the men on his crew. Packard was counting on Kimball recognizing the name, the number, and all the gear he'd left behind. Could he let it all go? Could he stand to see Charlie make $30K selling off his things?

Three hours after the ad went up, the first text came in. An hour later, a voicemail. Scam messages came through using anonymous emails.

They waited.

A day went by.

More messages that they ignored.

Then.

Midnight.

Packard was in bed, still awake. Frank slept beside him, snoring, dreaming his best dog dreams. Packard had picked him up at Gary's two days earlier and suffered a lot of baleful looks since. Whether they were for leaving him for so long or not serving sausage for breakfast, he didn't know.

Packard's mind wandered from wondering how he was ever going to get his house put back together to listing all the ways Travis Kimball might slip through their fingers again. Best-case scenario was Minneapolis PD snagged him on the BOLO. Packard selfishly wanted to be there when it happened. For Ashley and Gerald and Thielen. For everyone in Sandy Lake who lost sleep worrying about a killer in their midst.

The phone Suresh set up with the new SIM beeped by his bed.

I know you don't have the titles to those trucks, Charlie.

Packard sat up in bed and stared at the phone. He fought the urge to respond right away. What would Charlie do? They'd used Shepard's relationship with the publisher of the *Sandy Lake Gazette* to keep the motel fire and Charlie's death out of the local news. Kimball knew Charlie as the guy who drank himself to sleep every night. Charlie wouldn't jump right on this. He'd be passed out now or too drunk to text. It would take him a while to respond.

The next morning Packard and Reynolds crowded into Suresh's office with all its monitors and glowing power indicators.

"You should keep your responses brief. No capital letters. No punctuation," Suresh said.

"Right," Packard said. He typed.

I do too

"Are you sure Charlie knows the difference between 'to' and 'too'?" Reynolds asked.

"We found his notebook in the motel room," Packard said. "He was some kind of a poet. I think he knows his grammar."

"You could just type number 2," Suresh suggested.

"Enough," Packard said. "This is fine." He kept typing.

I do too

can bring them if you want to meet

He hit Send.

They stared at the phone like it was an egg about to hatch. Nothing happened. Suresh sipped his tea. Packard set the phone on the table. They waited.

"Well, I've got better things to do than stand here all day," Reynolds said.

"Me too," Suresh said. "Please go away."

Packard grabbed the phone and went to his office. An hour went by before he got a response.

How can you have them when I have them?

A second later a photo came through of a Wisconsin Certificate of Title with Otto Fredricksen's name on it and the vehicle information for the van.

I'd offer to sell them to you but I know
you don't have any money.

Packard considered his response.

will find a buyer who doesn't care about title
are you in arkansas

No. You?

minneapolis
drove vehicles here with help from Juan and Luis

Where are J & L?

gone

Where are you staying?

Kimball had picked up Charlie in North Carolina and left him in Minnesota. It was unlikely Charlie had any friends in Minneapolis. They'd found just under $2,000 in cash in his pants in the motel room which wouldn't last long.

in the van

The afternoon went by without a response. Packard tried to focus on other work. The county attorney wanted to appear tough on immigration and thought Juan and Luis should be charged for mishandling Miguel's remains.

"I'm not arresting those two," Packard said. "It was Charlie Richardson's decision not to involve authorities after the accident. If you want to go after Juan and Luis, you also need to charge Blake Cooper, a white eighteen-year-old, college-bound local kid who was also on the crew and went along with the decision."

"Come on, Packard. You know those two are in the country illegally."

"I don't know that because I didn't ask."

Juan and Luis had their wages. Packard put them in touch with a local Hispanic organization that would help them get home. He cut the tree guys—Pete and Dustin—loose, making sure they knew it was time to leave town and take their business elsewhere.

Kimball's next response came in the evening as Packard was eating a burger he'd grilled with some asparagus.

Where are you parked?

Packard chewed thoughtfully. Kimball was bumping his bait but hadn't bitten yet. It was close. Now it was his turn to let Kimball wait for a response.

Later that night another message from Kimball.

Let's meet

Packard looked at the time on his phone. It was a three-and-a-half-hour drive to Minneapolis. If they were going to meet tomorrow, he wanted to be there. He needed time to come up with a plan with MPD. He called Easton.

"I'm heading your way."

"Right now?"

"Leaving here in thirty minutes. Can you arrange a meeting tomorrow morning so we can coordinate taking this guy down?"

"I'll give my sergeant a heads-up now."

"I also need to bring Frank," Packard said. "He's been boarding with others for too long. I feel sick about it."

"Bring him. I love Frank," Easton said.

"Thank you. See you in a few hours."

CHAPTER FORTY-TWO

Let's meet

why

That's my stuff

you left it

finders keepers

Let's make a deal

i need cash

not a deal

have others interested

I have cash

Tell me where you are

CHAPTER FORTY-THREE

Minneapolis Police wanted to arrange a meeting somewhere remote, in the open, away from crowds.

"He'll be looking for the van in that scenario. He'll be looking for Charlie. We don't have either," Packard said. "I'm envisioning a public place where he doesn't see me coming until I'm right there with the cuffs. What about along the river? By the Stone Arch Bridge, where all the coffee shops and restaurants are."

Easton's sergeant was an old white guy, heavy through the middle, short white hair. "It's summertime. That place will be crawling with runners and bikers. We can't have a shoot-out around that many people."

"I'm not planning on having a shoot-out," Packard said. "He stabbed two people in Sandy Lake. The early word on the dead body in Wisconsin is that he had a fractured skull. This guy isn't known to carry a gun."

"He hasn't been known to use a gun. Doesn't mean he doesn't have a gun or hasn't procured one since you last saw him," the sergeant said.

Packard had no authority here. He had to go along with their plan or he had to convince them his plan was safe. He asked an officer sharing his computer to pull up a map of the area.

"Let's not overthink this. We've got a natural funnel along the river there. Once he's inside our perimeter, we block off access at Merriam and at Third Avenue. Central is a high bridge. If he parks above the river, we can block him off on Second Street or University."

"Here's your biggest problem," the sergeant said. "And you should know this being former MPD. The downtown side of the river is the First Precinct. Other side where you want to be is Second Precinct. In this room, we're the Sixth Precinct. Maybe we could chase him up through north and get the Fourth involved, too."

Packard knew he was right. The sergeant repeated his suggestion that they work with Bloomington police and arrange a rendezvous near an empty warehouse. He wanted three days to plan everything out. He wanted BCA involved or at least on alert.

Packard stopped listening. Maybe he should let them do what they wanted. He was grateful this was going down in Minneapolis. It wouldn't involve the already stretched resources at home. It wouldn't be another swarm of lights and sirens to alarm his already exhausted community.

The meeting droned on. Everyone had an opinion. Packard looked at Easton, who dropped his head to hide a smile. This was the bureaucracy Packard remembered. The self-sustaining parasite that fed on the good work of any large organization. He wanted to catch a killer and these guys wanted to have meetings.

The sergeant said he needed to run the plan up the chain of command. Packard nodded and thanked him and shook hands with everyone. He and Easton left the room and walked out of the building. It had been raining in the Cities for the last three days. The parking lot was full of puddles shimmering with rainbows of oil.

They stood under the awning. "I'm not waiting for MPD to organize a parade," Packard said. "We've got a small window to grab this guy. I think the only reason he's biting is because he's seen the news about Otto and needs the money to disappear."

They'd managed to keep Charlie's name out of the *Sandy Lake Gazette*. They hadn't been as lucky with suppressing news of the discovery of Otto Fredricksen's body on his property in Wisconsin. "I think Kimball's plan is to kill Charlie, get his stuff back, and sell it himself. He's going to need a lot of cash to lay low once cops start looking for him in relation to Otto's death."

"What do you want to do?"

"I'll grab this guy myself. Follow my own plan. You want to help me?"

"I could be in huge trouble if this goes south," Easton said.

"You don't have to if you don't want to."

"Fuck it. Let's do it."

CHAPTER FORTY-FOUR

I have cash

Tell me where you are

Minneapolis at St. Anthony Main

in front of coffee shop by movie theater

10 am

Ok

CHAPTER FORTY-FIVE

The first mistake they made was not having enough guys.

Easton reached out to a friend who'd retired from the MPD recently and was now selling real estate. His name was Tony Zigman. The first thing he did was give Packard his card in case he ever changed his mind about moving back to the Cities and needed to buy a place.

The sun was out after three days of rain. Blue skies. No haze, no smell of smoke. It was almost enough to make Packard forget that this was the second summer in a row with prolonged air-quality issues, that there was still plenty of Canadian wilderness left to burn. He turned his face to the sun and took a deep, grateful breath.

They came in three separate vehicles. Zigman parked on Second Street where he could see anyone pulling into the nearby parking ramp or the surface lot. There were stairs that went down to the river level where Packard had taken a spot on a bench under the trees nearest to the coffee shop. Easton was on the far end of the Stone Arch Bridge in case Travis Kimball decided to park on the other side of the river.

They should have had a fourth guy who could have floated somewhere between all three of their positions.

The second mistake they made was expecting Kimball to arrive in a white pickup. That's what they were all looking for. They had Kimball's picture on their phones—his driver's license photo and a fairly clear screen grab from one of Miguel's TikToks. They expected to see the truck first and then identify the man who got out.

They took their positions ninety minutes before the agreed meet time and kept in touch via text. No police radios. Packard had his gun in an interior waistband holder on his back under a loose short-sleeved shirt. Zigman and Easton were unarmed. They checked in every five minutes.

A tour group on Segways went by on the bike path, reminding Packard of ducklings following their mother. Two women in tight running gear ran by in one direction. An old man in baggy shorts and over-the-ear headphones went the other way. Packard missed city scenes like this. The dedicated runners and bikers. The outdoor patios packed with diners. This beautiful river that cut through the asphalt and high-rises.

He was about to send another *No sign* message when he spotted Travis Kimball fifty yards away, walking his direction on the other side of the narrow cobblestone road between them. He was wearing jeans and a gray T-shirt that was a size too small on him. His blond hair was tucked on the sides behind his ears.

Packard put in a white earbud and called Easton. "He's here. Never saw the truck. He must have taken an Uber or parked way south on this side and walked in."

Kimball was swinging his head both directions. Not nervous but taking everything in. Probably looking for the van. He was twenty minutes early. Packard noted the vinyl knife holder on his belt. Travis Kimball came here with a purpose. Convince Charlie they could restart the business with a new crew, bygones and all that. Get Charlie in the van and then slip that knife between his ribs like he'd done with the others.

Packard looked away, trying to appear engaged in his phone conversation. A UPS van banged down the cobblestone road in Packard's direction. A delivery truck going the other way slowed and tried to move farther to the right just as a car pulled away from a parking meter, blocking its path. The truck honked. Packard stood up. By the time his line of sight was clear, Kimball was gone.

"Shit. He clocked me," he said to Easton. "He's running. Text Zigman. Stay on your side. We're heading south."

Kimball was a hundred yards ahead of him. He'd crossed the road to Packard's side and was on the bike path. He looked back over his shoulder. Packard watched him barrel into an older woman dressed in a full cycling kit as she came off the Stone Arch Bridge, walking her bicycle. Kimball picked up the bike and threw his leg over it. Packard ran after him but the distance between them got bigger.

"Tell Zigman to get on East River Parkway. Kimball is on a bike on the bike path," Packard said to Easton.

Packard knew this road. Marcus had been a runner and for a while Packard had tried valiantly to keep up with him on long runs beside the river until they decided running would just be Marcus's thing. The trail went along the parkway, dropping steeply behind the University of Minnesota, followed by a long climb up as it approached the intersection at Franklin Avenue.

Kimball was out of sight. Packard kept running. He felt the damage to his lungs from the house fire last winter and the last ten days of breathing unhealthy air with every step. If Thielen, a marathon runner, was here, she would have left him in the dust.

The road started climbing, slowing him even further.

He hadn't seen Zigman go by, didn't know if he was in front of him or still catching up. He kept running.

He heard a truck coming up behind him, heavy on the gas. It shot by as Packard reached the top of the hill. His thighs were burning. He had sweat in his eyes. In his ear, Easton said, "Zigman crossed Franklin. He doesn't see Kimball on a bike anywhere ahead of him."

Packard stopped and tried to catch his breath, hands on his waist. "I don't have eyes on him." He looked behind him. "Shit. There's a road behind me that goes down to the U of M boathouse. He probably took that. There's a trail right along the river. Tell Zigman to pull over, make his way down to the pedestrian path, and start coming back my way."

Packard ran down the hill and made a left into the boathouse parking lot. At the other end was a narrow path. A middle-aged couple coming his way already looked pissed.

"Is there a guy on a bike that way?"

"Yes," one of them said. "This is not a bike path!"

"Thank you," Packard yelled over his shoulder.

The path went from asphalt to dirt to a narrow, raised deck with a railing on either side. Packard was directly above the brown churning water of the Mississippi River. There were more people than he expected. Ahead of him, walkers were stopped and looking the direction he was heading. He heard someone yell and tried to run faster. His shins were on fire.

"Heads up! Heads up!" Packard yelled as he dodged around slow walkers. The bridge straightened ahead of him and he saw Kimball, who had been stopped by a big guy in a tank top and short shorts. He was facing Kimball with his hands on the handlebars. "You need to walk your bike on this path," he insisted.

Kimball saw Packard coming behind him. He wrenched the bike away from the gym rat, ran with it, then threw his leg over it again when the walkway ended. He missed a left turn to stay on the asphalt and plowed straight ahead onto a sandy beach. The bike lost traction and tipped over. Kimball went down hard on his side.

Packard was right behind him, closing fast. Kimball scrambled to his feet. Looking for something. He grabbed a length of driftwood from the remnants of a beach campfire and faced Packard.

"It's over, Kimball," Packard said, trying not to sound breathless. "We've got you on both murders in Sandy Lake. We've got you on Otto Fredricksen. Drop the log."

Kimball swung at him. Packard ducked and put his hand up, meaning to grab the club. Instead, he took a blow to the forearm. The immediate pain made him think something was broken. Kimball raised the log again and Packard charged, going low, hit him squarely in the midsection, and they went down, kicking up a fan of sand that rained on top them. Kimball rolled Packard to the side, got up, and dropped an elbow into his midsection that very nearly knocked the wind out of him.

Packard pushed himself up with one hand. Kimball was looking for a way out. Blood was soaking through his pants near his upper thigh.

"Is that where Ashley got you with the knife, Kimball? Did I open that up for you again?"

Packard heard Zigman yelling and running toward them. Kimball saw him coming and went back the way they came, onto the raised footpath. Packard got up, holding his left arm close with his right hand.

On the bridge, Kimball barreled through walkers, creating a path for Packard to get closer. Ahead of both of them, the muscle guy in the short shorts had stopped again and stood with his arms across his chest blocking the whole path. Kimball slowed enough for Packard to trip him from behind. Kimball went down on his belly, rolled, and kicked Packard in the knee.

On his feet again, Kimball was trapped on the narrow walkway. Packard in front of him. Muscle man behind him.

Kimball climbed the railing.

The river was wide and swift, a leviathan emerging from some deep source, a strong brown god with thousands of eddies swirling like eyes.

"You'll drown if you jump," Packard said.

Kimball jumped anyway.

He splashed in the water on his belly and was immediately swept away by the rain-swollen current. He swam farther from the shore while the water carried him downstream. Packard ran alongside. Last winter he'd dropped through a hole in the ice to try to rescue someone who'd fallen into a lake. There was risky and there was stupid. There was no way he was going after this guy.

Zigman ran up and asked if he was okay.

"I'm fine," Packard said. People were gathering, filming them with their phones. Filming the man in the river.

Packard pulled out his phone. He'd lost the earbud in the fight. "Call in a water rescue," he said to Easton. "He's in the river. I'm with Zigman. We'll follow him on this side until he goes under or gets away from us. I don't know if he'll make it across or not."

Kimball was still close enough that Packard saw the moment when he realized he was not in control, that the river was a wild animal and he was riding its back. Kimball stopped swimming. He looked frantically at the shore he came from, then where he thought he was going. Both were far away now. He paddled weakly.

The river swept him away.

CHAPTER FORTY-SIX

Later that evening, Packard sat in Easton's bed in just his underwear. He had a cast on his left forearm and his knee was the color of an old apple.

"I need to refresh my defensive training. I took a beating from that guy."

"He had adrenaline and fear on his side," Easton said.

"And fifty pounds. And a club."

"You got him. That's all that matters."

Travis Kimball managed a minor miracle and actually made it across the river. He tried to navigate the water to the pylons for the Interstate 94 bridge (missed) and the Franklin Avenue bridge (missed). He hit something underwater that gashed his inner thigh. Farther downstream he crashed into a pylon for the Short Line Bridge hard enough to break a rib. From there he was able to make it to White Sands Beach. People had heard about the man in the river. They helped him ashore. A helicopter overhead beat a steady rhythm. Before Kimball could catch his breath, a tall Minneapolis police officer with big biceps and sweat popping through his crew cut put him in cuffs.

"He was compliant by the time you got to him because I softened him up for you," Packard said.

"I think the river softened him up. He wasn't running anywhere with that broken rib."

"Fine. I'm just glad he didn't drown. He's got years of misery ahead of him and he deserves every minute of it," Packard said. He was coming off the Vicodin they'd given him at the hospital for his arm. The pill had made him tired and his head feel like it was packed with sand. At least the pain was down to a dull throb.

He'd called Tom Turner from the hospital while waiting to get his arm bandaged.

"We got the guy who killed Ashley. More details will come out after he's formally charged. You might get harassed by the media for a few days. Give the boys a heads-up."

Tom was weepy and grateful. "Thank you. A million times thank you. I'll call Ashley's sister and everyone else. Let them know you got him."

"All right then. I'm sure we'll be touch. Tell Noah if the LGBT group at his new school ever needs a speaker, I know a Minneapolis cop who would be happy to do it."

"I'll tell him," Tom said.

All evening his phone kept ringing. Thielen wanting every detail about how they'd taken down the guy who tried to kill her. Kelly telling him the interpreter had been in touch with Miguel's family and had informed them of his accident. Reynolds saying he'd informed sheriffs in North Carolina of the death of Charles Richardson for the purposes of their warrant. His mom already wanting to know about Christmas plans.

Now another call from a number he didn't recognize.

"This is Packard."

"I saw you on the news. I said to Ruby, why is that man fishing fools out of the river in Minneapolis? He said he moved away."

Packard struggled to place the voice. Ruby? Then it came to him.

"Ms. Simmons. It's nice to hear your voice." Ruby's grandmother. They'd visited when he brought Symphony back to Minneapolis. Felt like a lifetime ago.

"Well, you gave me your number so I thought I'd be nosy."

"I'm glad you called. That man killed two people up where I am. I chased him down here. He tried to get away by jumping in the river but we got him."

"Good for you."

"How's Ruby?"

"Mad at me 'cause I won't let her sleep her summer away. She's gotta learn to get up now 'cause I'm not about to have battles about waking up when school starts."

"That bus comes early."

"Yes, it does."

"Any word from Symphony?" Packard asked.

"She's doing as well as can be expected. The chemo got her wore out."

"The what?" Packard sat up in bed, more alert, more pain in his arm.

"The chemo. She didn't tell you?"

"She didn't tell me."

"She got breast cancer. She gonna beat it but it's gonna be a journey."

Packard felt the word *cancer* as a heaviness in his limbs. A weight that made it hard to hold his head up. "I can't believe it. She starts getting her life back on track and now this."

"Mm-hmm."

"What kind of support does she have down there?"

"I don't know too much about that."

"Will you find out? Find out where she's getting her treatment? Let her know I have some things for her that I'd like to bring down." He was thinking of the box with Marcus's badge and family photo album that was still in his truck.

"She's kind of private. I'll call her and let you know."

CHAPTER FORTY-SEVEN

Packard got up at five the next morning and started driving to St. Louis. Easton said he was fine taking care of Frank. Packard felt bad for leaving his dog with so many uncles. He needed to do better.

Every tiny bump in the road rattled his broken his arm. In Apple Valley he stopped at a HomeGoods store and bought a small pillow with ridiculous tassels that fit in his lap so he could rest his arm. If Thielen or Reynolds ever saw him with his precious pillow, he'd never hear the end of it.

He had a late breakfast/early lunch of a giant omelet and hash browns in Cedar Rapids. He got coffee to go and kept driving, eight hours total to St. Louis. Symphony told Ms. Simmons it was fine if he came. He wished he could have talked to her himself. Heard her tone. Last time he saw her, she'd left him a phony address and slammed a door in his face. There had to be reluctance on her part to seeing him again.

He parked on a ramp beside a hospital and followed the directory signs to the infusion center. The space was organized into open cubicles that all faced a curved wall of windows that looked out onto a garden of blooming flowers and manicured bushes.

He found Symphony reclined in a big chair. She had a scarf wrapped around her head and a weighted blanket in her lap. A plastic tube went from a dangling bag of clear liquid into a pump on a stand and then into a port on her chest. Her eyes were closed. She was listening to something on her phone through headphones.

Packard had a seat in the guest chair beside her. There were six other people getting treatment that he could see. He sat quietly in case she was sleeping and looked at the garden. Fat bumblebees crawled over coneflowers and black-eyed Susans. Two hummingbirds chased each other around a red feeder.

"What happened to your arm?" Symphony said. She pulled out her headphones.

"I got my ass beat trying to catch a bad guy."

She chuckled and reached for a mug beside her with a straw.

"What did he do?"

"Killed a man in Wisconsin. Killed two people in Sandy Lake. Tried to kill one of our deputies in her home."

"But you got him?"

"We got him."

"Good for you," Symphony said.

"What are you drinking?"

"Tart cherry juice. Supposed to help with the neuropathy pain."

"Does it?"

"I don't know. It might help a little."

"Where are you at in your treatment?"

"This is cycle three of six. I was between cycles when I came to Minnesota."

Packard looked at the bag of clear liquid hanging above her. "How long does it take to get all the medicine in you?"

"These appointments take about five to six hours total."

"A whole day."

"Pretty much."

"How do you pass the time?"

"Read a book. Watch things on my phone. I got Hulu on there."

"Does someone pick you up or do you drive yourself?"

"I don't have a car. Sometimes a lady from church can drive me. I get here on the bus, too. It's only twenty minutes. Brings me right to the door."

Symphony unscrewed a lid from a container of peanut butter pretzels and offered it to him. He reached in and took some.

"I'm surprised you came all this way," she said.

"I said I would."

"People say a lot of things they don't mean. Me included."

"I meant it. I'm here. If Marcus was alive, he'd be here instead of me. I brought you this."

He handed her the USPS box with the family photo album and Marcus's badge in it. On the front was the phony address she'd given him.

"I'm sorry for this," she said, looking at him and tapping the box with her finger. "And for the things I said. I imagined a whole life in my head for my brother, and when things weren't how I expected, I acted poorly."

"You don't have to apologize to me for anything," Packard said. "I'm glad I could you bring you these things."

Symphony looked at her brother's badge, rubbed her thumb across its surface, then put it in her lap and opened the photo album. She turned the pages silently. Her lips moved as she quietly named the dead. She turned another page and laughed.

"Looks at that little fool with his baby Afro and Star Wars underwear. I think he's about five years old here."

"That's one of my favorite pictures of Marcus," Packard said.

Symphony stared at the photo for a long time. "I like to think we would have reconciled once I got back into a healthier place. In my head."

"I know you would have. Marcus didn't hold a grudge. I'm the type to stew about things. If he got mad at me, fifteen minutes later he was over it. It was like nothing had happened."

On the next page she stopped on a school photo of teenage Marcus from the nineties. No smile, pimples, flat-top fade. "What else was he like?" she asked.

"You want me to tell you some stories?"

"What else we gonna do? I got two more hours here."

"I could sing a little bit of 'In Those Jeans.'"

"Oh Lord."

"The underwear picture is proof that he was a nerd from an early age," Packard said.

"Yes. Star Trek. Star Wars. I thought it was so dumb."

"He never outgrew it. We went out for Halloween one time. He dressed up as Worf in the tightest gold Star Trek tunic you've ever seen. Shaved his head and glued a Klingon ridge on top. He had a wig stand in the closet where he kept the Klingon headpiece when he wasn't wearing it."

"No."

"Yes, he did."

"What did you go as?"

"Um…a cop. I just wore aviator sunglasses and a T-shirt that said POLICE on the back."

Symphony looked at him sideways. "My brother was a dork but you going as a cop… That's lame as hell."

"I know. I hate Halloween."

"Marcus loved sushi. If we went out for sushi, it was a $200 meal. Easy. He wanted to go to Japan and visit the fish markets. He could eat nigiri and never get full."

"What did you call me?"

Packard laughed. "He made that same stupid joke."

"He learned it from our uncle who introduced us to sushi as kids and liked to make white waiters squirm."

"He had a golden retriever named Jarret when we met. His perfect Sunday was to walk the dog to the coffee shop with the paper, then walk to the used record store to see what had come in that week, then buy groceries for dinner."

"I'm imagining him wearing that Star Trek forehead doing all that," Symphony said.

"Oh. Now *that* would have been his perfect Sunday."

"His whole purpose in life was to try to keep kids from getting in trouble. He was active in the Big Brothers/Big Sisters program. He'd already seen one kid all the way into college. The organization loved him. Some of the families said no when they found out he was a cop. Even more said no when they found out he was gay. He was still waiting to get matched with a new Little when he got killed."

Symphony had taken the bus to her treatment. Packard gave her a ride home to an apartment complex with four three-story buildings in a row like dominoes.

"What do you need, Symphony? You should be comfortable and not worried about anything while you're going through this. I told you about Marcus's money. What can it buy you?"

She sighed and looked out the window on her side. "A bed," she said reluctantly. "I bought my mattress used. It's killing my back."

"What kind of bed do you like? Hard or soft?"

"Hard as a rock."

"You want me to get you a sheet of plywood and put a blanket over it?"

"Not that hard."

"Okay. I'll be back in an hour with a new mattress. We'll need help to carry it. You're tired. I have a broken arm. Do you know any of your neighbors? If not, I can just knock on doors."

"You start banging on doors around here, you'll get your other arm broken. I'll find someone."

He bought a solid latex mattress that was firm on one side and extra firm on the other. He went to another store and bought four pillows and sheets and a comforter, and at the checkout he purchased Uber gift cards and DoorDash gift cards and grocery delivery gift cards.

When he got back, two men were standing outside her building with the old mattress leaned against a light pole. They carried the new mattress inside and put the old one in the back of his truck.

Symphony came outside and he gave her the gift cards.

"Come on now," she said.

"None of this is coming out of my pocket. It's all from Marcus's life insurance. When I get home, I'll figure out how to transfer the rest to you. Maybe create a trust. It might help with taxes."

"I didn't ask you to do that."

"Symphony, it's a lot of money—a few hundred grand. Not enough to live on for the rest of your life but enough to do whatever you want."

"I don't get to do whatever I want." She looked like she wanted to jab a finger between his eyes. "I'm a felon with a mental illness. That money won't get me off parole. It won't erase what I did to my baby or cure my cancer. I'm rebuilding my life my way. I don't want that money."

Packard nodded, embarrassed that he'd been so blind to the limits of what his help could do. "I hear you. I'm sorry for not listening."

"You need that money more than I do," she said. "I've seen your house. It's a mess. Worry about yourself and accept the reasons why Marcus put your name on that paper. He left you that money because he wanted to take care of you if something happened. If that makes you uncomfortable because your feelings weren't on the same level as his, too bad. Giving the money away doesn't change the intention or rewrite your history together."

Packard looked up at the streetlight, at the moon. His arm ached. "You're right. You can't buy absolution or a time machine. The money is part of his legacy. I'll figure out something to do with it that would make him proud."

"Thank you for the bed and the gift cards. And for bringing his things."

"You're welcome."

"What are you going to do now?" Symphony asked.

"I'll probably start back tonight."

"Don't fall asleep behind the wheel."

"I'll pull over when I get tired."

"All right then," she said and turned toward her building. She moved slowly. He wanted so many things for her but it wasn't about what he wanted. It wasn't about what Marcus wanted or what Marcus might have done if he were alive. Symphony decided for Symphony. The freedom to make her own decisions after years of having them made for her was nonnegotiable.

Packard watched her until she was inside the building, until the lobby door closed behind her and he couldn't see her anymore.

Symphony would decide if they crossed paths again.

He hoped they would.

CHAPTER FORTY-EIGHT

He made it two hours down the road before his arm started hurting and even his dainty lap pillow wasn't helping. He got a room at a hotel, ate dinner at the Golden Skillet next door, took half a Vicodin and slept hard.

He drove back to the Cities and was napping in Easton's bed with Frank when the Minneapolis detective got off duty. He took off his clothes and slid under the blankets.

"That was four on for me. Now I got three off. Want to stay a few days?"

"I should get home and get some work done on the house. Want to follow me back?"

"You just want more nursing."

"I want more than that."

Packard herded Frank off the bed as Easton moved closer. His hand found Packard's chest, his nipple, up to his chin, turning his mouth in his direction. They moved under the covers.

"Wait. My knee," Packard said. "Ow. My arm."

Two days later, Easton was slicing into baked potatoes and pushing their soft insides out. Frank was begging. Packard was setting the table on the back deck and finishing the steaks. Cooler temperatures had moved into the area. The only smell of smoke came from the charcoal grill.

Yesterday, Thielen's husband, Tim, had come over and the three of them got new drywall in place for the living room ceiling. It still needed to be taped and mudded but at least now the attic heat and insulation stayed where it was supposed to. He and Easton had added bracing to the side of the house and used it to connect straps that pulled the chimney snuggly back into place. Tomorrow Easton was going to rebuild the top part that had fallen off and touch up the tuck-pointing all the way down. The house still needed new floors, a new roof. Packard was going to make sure his roofer was local and not wanted for murder.

A lot of work remained but already it felt more manageable. The way to get through this disaster and the one after that and the one after that was to ask for help and share resources and grieve what had been lost. A bridge, a riverbank, so many trees. A long time from now, when the people of Sandy Lake told stories about the summer of the storm, he hoped it was with a sense of awe at their strength and resilience, and he hoped the stories came from a place of comfort, and not some dark, unimaginable future that made them long for the past.

His phone rang. Packard moved the steaks to the cool side of the grill and answered.

"Deputy Packard. This is Chief Steve Ridley with the Dodge City Police Department."

"Where's Dodge City?"

"It's in Kansas."

"Got it. What can I do for you?"

"I got three men in custody down here. No IDs. No English. They were in a cargo van with a perforated oil line. Lost all their oil and the engine seized up. They walked to a gas station at the next exit, carjacked a driver, and made it about a hundred miles before one of my officers spotted them on a back road not far from our city."

Over the lake, Packard watched a bald eagle drop down and scoop a fish out of the water and flap hard to bring it back up to a branch in a tree. "I see. I think I know where this is going."

"We found something interesting in their van."

"Was it a cooler full of ice?" Packard asked. The doorbell rang and he walked through the sliding patio door to answer it. *Bring the steaks in*, he mouthed to Easton.

"It was," Chief Ridley said. "And do you know what was in the cooler?"

"I'm going to guess a human head," Packard said.

"Bingo. Took us a few days to put all the pieces together—so to speak. I found your recent reports about Francisco Ayala in the database. I'm pretty sure this head belongs to the body you guys got up there."

Packard opened the door. It was Kyle.

"Hang on one second, Chief." Packard lowered the phone. "Hi," he said smiling.

Kyle grabbed him by the front of the shirt and kissed him on the mouth. Fresh breath. Rough beard. He smelled like sandalwood.

Packard was too stunned to blink. He touched his bottom lip and remembered a time when this was what he'd wanted—before he leaned in and Kyle pulled away, before Easton made himself indispensable.

"I've been waiting to do that since the last time I saw you. I need you to know that," Kyle said.

Packard slowly turned and looked behind him at Easton holding a platter of steaks in one hand, tongs in the other. "Well, this night took an unexpected turn," he said. "I'm Garrett, by the way." He waved the tongs.

On the phone, the chief said, "Hello? You still there?"

Packard stared at the phone in his hand. He looked at Easton. Looked at Kyle. He had the sudden urge to drive to Kansas and pick up the head himself. Let these two eat steaks. They might have a lot in common.

"Chief, I gotta call you back."

HAVE YOU READ *AND THERE HE KEPT HER*?
DON'T MISS THE UNPUTDOWNABLE
BEGINNING OF THE BESTSELLING
BEN PACKARD SERIES!

CHAPTER ONE

4:30 A.M.

Rain lashed the boy as he ran from his car back to the old man's house. It was cold enough that he could see his breath. Water dripped from the ends of his shaggy hair, ran down his scalp and under his shirt. At least the clouds had hidden the moon. The news had called it a *supermoon*. All night it had followed everywhere he went, an ivory face watching him, reading his mind.

The road was gravel and getting muddier by the minute. Jesse tried running along the edge, but the ground was soft and soon his feet were as wet as his hooded sweatshirt.

On his left, houses faced the lake. He ran by a mailbox that said MILLER in faded letters and then by another mailbox that said MADIS N, this one pitched forward with its door hanging open like it was about to be sick. He stopped in front of the small gray house set back from the road and realized he was looking right through a hole where the door should have been and out the other side at the water beyond. He looked back at the MILLER house and noticed it was missing most of its roof and all of its windows.

Jesse ran on, already wet to the skin. He turned off the road and followed two muddy ruts past a stand-alone garage. The house ahead of him was a dark-brown rectangle without a straight line or a sharp corner. A wooden staircase went up the front to a sliding glass door and small windows with the blinds drawn.

Jesse stopped to catch his breath. In the dark, the house looked like it had climbed out of the mud or was sinking back into it. No part of him wanted to be here, to have to pay back his debt like this.

"In and out. Get it over with," he muttered.

He bypassed the staircase, pulling up his hood as he skidded down a muddy set of uneven steps alongside the house.

The lower level of the house was cement block. A narrow yard widened in the direction of rusty metal chairs overturned around a fire pit before gradually descending to the lake. The house had another deck on the back. Underneath were the remnants of a depleted woodpile and a battered storm door with access to the basement.

Jesse pulled open the storm door and set the clip that propped it open. The back door had individual glass panes set in a crosshatch pattern. Jesse hit the window closest to the dead bolt with his elbow. The sound of breaking glass made his breath catch in his throat. He counted to ten, waiting for lights to come on. Nothing happened. He reached inside, undid the bolt and the twist lock on the doorknob. Thunder rolled overhead as he pushed the door open and stepped over the broken glass.

It was pitch-dark inside. A clock radio on a shelf flashed red numbers 12:00…12:00…12:00. It smelled like cigarettes and garbage and wet, rotten things. Jesse took a penlight from his back pocket and used it to sweep over a workbench on his left littered with scattered tools and boxes of nails and spools of wire and plastic grocery bags. A telephone with a tortured, twisted cord hung on the wall. On his right an old refrigerator droned. He pulled open the door hard enough to make the beer cans inside dance on their wire racks. The light reached all but the basement's darkest corners. He left the door open.

Shelves made from concrete blocks and long sagging planks split the room in half lengthwise. In front of the shelves he saw a rocking chair with cracked leather on the seat and on the back. A sawed-off section of tree trunk was being used as a side table. He saw an enormous ceramic ashtray filled with cigarette butts and a garbage can overflowing with beer cans and crushed cigarette packs and boxes from microwave meals. On the floor behind the chair, a damp cardboard box had split its seams and let slide an avalanche of magazines. Nearly nude women stared up from the covers. Jesse picked up one closest to his foot—a moldy *Penthouse* from August 1981. More than twenty years before he was born.

He circled behind the shelves, past a wall-mounted sink and an open toilet in one corner. The other corner of the basement was built out into a small room with a metal door. It could have been for storage, but his gut told him it was something else. Jesse shivered at the threshold, his skin clammy and prickling with a million hairs. He made a sideways fist around the door's sliding bolt and pulled it backward, stepping out of the way as the heavy door swung open on silent hinges.

He thumbed the penlight again. He wasn't sure but he thought the walls were painted…pink. The color had peeled away in places, leaving discolored spots that looked like scabs. He saw a thin mattress covered in dark stains on a metal frame. A heavy chain hung limply through a steel ring bolted on the wall at the head of the bed.

Nothing about the scene in front of him made sense. He wasn't sure what he was looking at, but he knew the last thing he'd ever want was to be left alone in this room, in the dark, with the door shut. He blindly reached for the inside door handle to pull it shut again and found there wasn't one. He shined the penlight on it just to make sure.

This was a prison cell of some kind. A cage. How else to explain a door with no handle, no way to get out from the inside?

He shined the weak penlight across the blistered pink walls again. He felt like he was staring into the mouth of something that wanted to swallow him. When he killed the light, the darkness inside seemed to go down and down to a place that had never known the sun.

Behind him, the furnace made a loud ticking sound, then *whoomp*ed to life. Jesse turned away and shook off the bad thoughts. He stuck the light in his pocket and headed for the stairs that went up to the main floor. At the bottom, he stared at the closed door above him. He'd been told the old man would be drunk, at least. Passed out, if Jesse was lucky.

He labored up the first three steps, pausing on each one to talk himself out of turning around and making a run for it.

He turned one last time toward the dark room in the corner and thought about the stained mattress and the door with no handle.

Someone stepped on the broken glass by the basement door.

Jesse crouched and froze like a rabbit with no cover. The refrigerator door was still open, spilling light into the room. Behind it he saw a dark silhouette through the window in the basement door. The shape paused with one foot on the broken glass, then took another step into the room.

Jenny.

"What the fuck are you doing here?" Jesse hissed. He took out the penlight and flashed it at her so she could see where he was standing against the wall on the stairs.

"I got worried," she whispered.

Jenny was much less wet than Jesse was, thanks to the oversize letter jacket with sleeves that went down past her fingertips and made her look like she had no shoulders. In the dark he couldn't see her freckles, or her green eyes, or the eye tooth with the twist to it, the imperfection that made every one of her smiles perfect.

"Where's the car?"

"I moved it a little closer. I have the keys."

She came over and stood by his side at the bottom of the stairs. They both looked up at the door overhead. "We shouldn't be here," she said.

"I don't have any choice. He's threatening my family."

"We can figure out something else."

"No," we can't. He doesn't want money. It's this or something bad happens to my sister."

"Jesse, come on. He's messing with you. If you go back and say—"

The floor creaked over their heads.

They stared at each other, wide-eyed, frozen. One second passed. Another. There was only the sound of the furnace blower and the drum of the rain, coming down hard again at the open basement door.

Jenny put a hand on Jesse's arm and eased him a step backward.

The door at the top of the stairs crashed inward with enough force that it hit the wall and tried to bang shut again. The double-barreled shotgun leveled down at them kept it from closing all the way.

Jenny screamed and ducked behind Jesse. Jesse raised his hands in a pleading gesture. He waved the penlight at the fat, naked man standing above them with the shotgun and an oxygen mask over his mouth.

"Hold on, hold on! We made a mistake. We were just leaving," Jesse pleaded. He felt Jenny's body small and hard against his back, her hand tight around his arm.

The shotgun boomed like the end of the world. The light went out and fell from Jesse's hand. Jenny screamed again when Jesse crumpled without a sound, all his weight falling back against her. They went backward down the steps, Jesse on top of her. Jenny hit her head on the concrete with the bright crack of a glass jar breaking.

The fat, naked man stepped down through the cloud of burning gunpowder and fired the second barrel.

READING GROUP GUIDE

1. Discuss the tension in Sandy Lake post-storm disaster. Who was affected and how? What does the storm reveal about the town?

2. Some of the chapters include an air quality index at the beginning. Why do you think that is? Does it tell you anything about what is about to happen next?

3. Describe Packard's relationship with Symphony. How does the lingering death of Marcus affect them getting to know each other? How does their relationship change by the end of the novel?

4. If you were Packard (and without knowing the end of the novel) who would your main suspect be and why? Were you right?

5. Many of the characters in the roof crew are hiding something. What are their secrets? What is it about being on the crew that allows for secrecy?

6. What did you make of Charlie's relationship with Miguel? Do you consider Charlie responsible for what happened to Miguel?

7. Charlie, Symphony, and Travis are all involved in another person's death. Compare and contrast their crimes and consequences. Do you consider them equally guilty? Why or why not?

8. Compare and contrast Packard's relationships with Easton and Kyle. What sides do they each bring out of Packard?

A CONVERSATION WITH THE AUTHOR

This is now the fourth book in the Ben Packard universe. Was your process writing this one different from the rest?

I wouldn't say the process was any different. I knew the story was going to center on the aftermath of a storm. I knew there was going to be a crummy motel filled with people from out of town, all of whom had a secret. I wanted Packard to be hot, exhausted, always on the back foot. Then it was a matter of writing the worst first draft imaginable and continually refining everything with helpful feedback from my writing partner and editors.

What inspired you to introduce Symphony's character? Did you always know she would make an appearance?

I thought after solving the mystery of what happened to Packard's brother in the last book that this book would represent a clean start. Everything from the past resolved. Then I had this vision of a Black woman showing up on Packard's front step, and I knew she was related to Marcus. I think she showed up to remind me that there are no clean starts, that some things from the past can't be resolved. It was interesting to imagine some of the good times Marcus and Packard had together, the stresses in their relationship, and how the passage of time impacted Packard's memory of things. I wanted to make sure Symphony wasn't there to offer Packard easy absolution. He hasn't always done the right thing, and he needs to face that if he's ever going to move forward.

Charlie is a complicated, tortured character. Why end his story in the fire?

Figuring out Charlie was the hardest part of writing this book. Who he was, what he was haunted by, what he wanted, his relationship with the crew all kept changing as I wrote and rewrote and rewrote. In the first draft, he didn't die in a fire, and Packard got all the answers he was looking for from Charlie. That didn't feel very satisfying. There are so many tragic aspects to Charlie's story that it lent itself to a tragic ending.

Packard basically ends up in a love triangle at the end of the novel. What made you make that the final scene?

If you've read the other books, you know I don't mind a bit of unresolved business. The goal is to answer all the questions related to the central crime, but Packard's life outside of that extends beyond the borders of each novel. Things bleed across. Kyle and Garrett have been developing as characters for multiple books now, but the time covered by those books is short. By the end of *Beneath a Broken Sky* (book 4), it hasn't even been a year since Packard lost the election at the end of *Where the Dead Sleep* (book 2). Things have been slowly building to where he now has two guys vying for his attention. This isn't a romance novel where the reader expects an HEA by the end. It's going to take time to resolve this. Let's enjoy the ride and see where it goes.

Is there anything you hope readers take away from *Beneath a Broken Sky*?

All my books, save for the first one, have been written under the shadow cast by the murder of George Floyd by Minneapolis police. It continues to be a trying time to write about a sheriff's deputy (from Minnesota no less) when the term *law enforcement* is being used to tear apart families and violently attack people based on the color of their skin or the language they speak, when masked federal agents wearing POLICE badges are killing U.S. citizens on the street.

Sometimes I struggle to answer for myself whether I'm writing about a gay man who works in law enforcement or if I'm writing about a small-town cop who's gay or if I'm writing about life in rural Minnesota through the eyes of a gay cop. All those things feel different to me. Am I writing for entertainment, or I do have something to say about policing and public safety and does it matter and does anyone care?

On a good day, the answer to all the above is yes.

Ben Packard as a character may be idealistic. He may be unrealistic. My hope is that he represents the best of us. A flawed human being with a strong moral core. Someone who tries and fails, admits when he's wrong, and learns from his mistakes. Someone who shows up for his community, stands up for the little guy, and calls out bullshit when he sees it.

ACKNOWLEDGMENTS

This book is for the people of Minnesota who were meant to be made an example of and instead set the example for the rest of the country. My writing partner, Gretchen Anthony, reminded me the Minnesota state motto is "L'etoile du Nord" (translation: "Star of the North"). Like a north star, Minnesota is showing the way. Thank you to everyone on the front lines battling for our shared humanity, protecting our neighbors, and standing up against the actions of this disgraceful administration. Thirty-two people died while in ICE custody in 2025. In 2026, ICE killed two U.S. citizens on the streets of Minneapolis. Renee Good was a mother and a poet. Alex Pretti was a VA nurse and a cyclist. They should both still be with us.

I'm incredibly grateful to the people who keep showing up for Ben Packard's adventures. Your time and attention are invaluable. I appreciate all the reviews, the posts, the DMs, the emails, the word of mouth. I've witnessed again and again the amazing community of thoughtful, caring readers growing around these books. I am thankful for every one of you.

My thanks to everyone at Sourcebooks. The words inside are mine, but the book in your hands is their work, and it is beautiful. Thank you to Jared Oriel for this incredible cover. Thank you to my editors, Jenna Jankowski and

Anna Michels, for finding the gold in the huge mess I make. Thank you to Mandy Chahal for making sure the whole world knows when I have a new book coming out. Thank you to my agent, Barbara Poelle, for bringing us all together.

Our country needs artists and readers more than ever. Thank you to the booksellers and librarians who feed our love of stories. Thank you to the festival organizers and book clubs and bookstagrammers who lift up authors and their work.

My grandmother died at 101 and a half years old just as I was doing my final review of these pages. When my brother and I were little, she brought us big bags of M&Ms in her makeup case, put lipstick on us, and bought a lot of Stars Wars figures. I told Grandma not to read *And There He Kept Her* because it had too many bad words in it. She didn't need to read the books to be proud of me and tell everyone in her senior living community (we called it Shady Oaks) about her grandson, the published author. She was a great lady.

As usual, the final word is for Chris. In a world gone mad, all I need to be at peace is to be close to you. Thank you for always being there. I love you.

ABOUT THE AUTHOR

Joshua Moehling is the *USA Today* bestselling author of the Ben Packard series and a two-time Lammy Award nominee for Best LGBTQ+ Mystery Thriller. He lives in Minneapolis with his husband.